Pengui

# MEDEA'S CHILDREN

Con Anemogiannis is a writer, producer and director with fifteen years' experience in the Australian film and television industry. He has worked on a variety of documentaries and dramas, and in 1996 he received an Australian Human Rights Award for one of his films. This is his debut novel, with a second novel, on the life of the poet Cavafy, currently in progress.

# medea's children

con anemogiannis

PENGUIN BOOKS

Penguin Books Australia Ltd
487 Maroondah Highway, PO Box 257
Ringwood, Victoria 3134, Australia
Penguin Books Ltd
Harmondsworth, Middlesex, England
Penguin Putnam Inc.
375 Hudson Street, New York, New York 10014, USA
Penguin Books Canada Limited
10 Alcorn Avenue, Toronto, Ontario, Canada M4V 3B2
Penguin Books (NZ) Ltd
Cnr Rosedale and Airborne Roads, Albany, Auckland, New Zealand
Penguin Books (South Africa) (Pty) Ltd
4 Pallinghurst Road, Parktown 2193, South Africa

First published by Penguin Books Australia Ltd 1999

1 3 5 7 9 10 8 6 4 2

Copyright © Con Anemogiannis 1999

All rights reserved. Without limiting the rights under copyright reserved above, no part of this publication may be reproduced, stored in or introduced into a retrieval system, or transmitted, in any form or by any means (electronic, mechanical, photocopying, recording or otherwise), without the prior written permission of both the copyright owner and the above publisher of this book.

Design by Ellie Exarchos, Penguin Design Studio
Typeset in 11/14 Joanna by Post Pre-press Group, Brisbane, Queensland
Printed in Australia by Australian Print Group, Maryborough, Victoria

National Library of Australia
Cataloguing-in-Publication data:

Anemogiannis, Con.
Medea's children.

ISBN 0 14 027012 4.

I. Title

A823.3

To Peter Blazey,
What is given is returned . . .

To family who know the difference between fiction and reality,
and to Alan, without whom I wouldn't have bothered.

## acknowledgements

I would like to thank John Bridges for his gimlet eye on the things that escaped me; Judy Menczel and Tim Herbert for their encouragement; Ian MacNeil and Tony Ayres for reading some parts of the original; Lisa Mills – the gentlest, most encouraging editor anyone could have – and especially Clare Forster, both at Penguin, who took the plunge.

book one **peephole**

**1**   I was both born and brought up in a male brothel. Well actually a boarding house, but it felt more like a brothel because my mother only rented rooms to spectacularly beautiful men between the ages of eighteen and thirty. No younger and definitely not older. Although seventeen and thirty year olds who came cap in hand to the door got sympathetic hearings, if they were especially cute.

Even today when I think back on that period during my formative years, I swear I can't recall one of them I would describe as unattractive. Each was handsome in his own way, handsomer than the run-down pink and green house with the ten bedrooms we had in Newtown, which we let to these youths during the 1960s.

Maybe, by only letting rooms to gorgeous young men, my mother was consciously or subconsciously training me in how to be a homosexual. Maybe she was fulfilling some unrewarded sexual wish my ageing father couldn't provide. Maybe she wanted to run a male model agency.

I can't be exactly sure of the reason. And I was happy with the sexism and taste that governed her principles of accommodation, not being the sort of eleven-year-old gay boy who would complain about having his own harem. After all, she was the one who ran the show – a powerful concierge, like Barbara Stanwyck in *The Big Valley*, whom no one would dare cross, unless they wanted a life of shelterless peril.

Sometimes, even though she was the decision-maker, she used to ask my opinion of the applicants. I would reply compassionately, 'Nah, the last one was cuter' – a view with which she normally concurred. A view she still concurs with in her old age. Her view of handsomeness and mine are still closely aligned.

When our boarders first moved in, I'd look at them through the peephole of the communal bathroom on each landing, and watch them undress. Watch them disrobe, taking off Y-front underwear – the industrial standard of the sixties – original ones, not the regulation fashion items of today. Watch them fondle themselves, thinking they couldn't be seen, pretending they were alone in their passions. Spy on them as they waited for their coins to heat up the gas boiler. Transfixed as they ejaculated into fists which were held under a warm shower spout to clean off that sensual glue.

Until things changed, when they began to notice the young eye in the keyhole, jealously seeking an invitation, beyond the peephole, away from voyeurism, to enjoy their shower – and savour their flesh.

Nothing was ever said. What could be said to an eleven year old? Silence somehow made the whole thing less seedy, less pederastic on their part. And I didn't need chatter. Just the touch of their much more developed bodies and chests was sufficient poetry. And rarely did I get a knock-back. But when I did I made sure they did it nicely, not tolerating back chat, or sneers, otherwise I would act determinedly as the agent for their eviction.

## peephole

I still maintain that a boy's first orgasms, before he can produce any juice, are the most intense – those blinding orgasms of vision and light where the whole body spasms as if shot from a shell. As if the prick being pulled is a fleshy pin attached to an imploding grenade. And the first time one of these male lodgers ejaculated over me, under a shower that grew cold because his coins were expended, I thought he was bleeding. That somehow he, or we, had done something wrong, something terminal. I thought his spunk was blood bleached white.

Until the second guy (or was it the third?) I got off with allayed my fears – again, not with conversation but by putting this sauce up to my lips and his lips before we kissed, sealing desire with this youthful Perkin's paste.

Most of these young men were Greek. Like me, my father, mother and brother. Young Greek émigrés, apprentices of Ulysses, who had heard the siren of the economic miracle that was Australia, now wanting to make their fortune away from the poverty and beauty of the homeland. Away from their inherited village or any opportunity of finding a local girl to marry.

Some were sailors gone AWOL. Others, happy peasant youths ready to use their brawn and tightened muscle in the steel works of Port Kembla. In the glass factories of Dowling Street or the jam factories of Darlington and Enmore they were called to.

They had two desires it seemed to me: the desire for frequent sex and the desire to make enough money to go home. I made sure they achieved the first objective, but most never achieved the second. Except as retirees on holiday – twenty years on – seeing, too late, relatives and a country that had matured and aged even more than themselves. I like to think (and I know my mother did) that we got them, and held on to them, in their prime.

Let me describe their beauty. There was the handsome lad from Salonika with jet-black hair that fell across his face, crew-cut on the sides. A modern look even for then. His foreman's clothes made love to him with suffocating tightness. Then there was the Corfu lad who could spurt three or four times without prompting. There was George, the thick-set Greek/Macedonian boy whose blond pubes and ginger hair interested me (a rarity among the lodgers) as much as the yellow hair on his balls, hair finer than the beaten gold Alexander the Great had in Vergina, his capital.

There was Demos, from Sparta, whom I imagined to be a warrior. He did have a military gruffness to him and his prick looked like a spear, with its long brutality tapering to a point.

And then there was my favourite, Antony, a sailor from the Piraeus port city of Athens. He was one of the few that spoke disparagingly about Greece. Antony, who said he never wanted to go home. Antony, who looked like all the naked statues in my picture books: the *Belvedere*, the *Hermes of Praxiteles*, the *Wounded Gaul*.

I'm not sure if these boys (young men really) chatted among themselves, or if they compared notes about what it was like to get off with the landlady's son. Or what it felt like to fuck with an eleven year old.

They never gave any sign that they did. It wasn't one of those topics you could joke about, certainly not in 1968, and I watched their expressions carefully, their brown, olive or green eyes, for flashes of shared knowledge, for betrayal. Maybe my suspicion could have been averted if I'd combined them in an orgy. But I preferred each separately, believing each coupling indivisible, not capable of sharing forbidden trysts.

Sometimes they bought toys for me as tributes. Adolescent toys like bubblegum cards, comics, or milky, semi-translucent glass marbles. The cleverer ones bought me books, making me feel a courtesan, someone important enough to bribe, like the Trojan, Paris, who had to constantly choose. They didn't understand that there was no need for supplication. Because I loved them all. Each and every one of them.

Now I sometimes dream that maybe they loved me. And that they missed me the way I missed them, as intensely as I did then. When they left. Because whenever they did leave, I would be broken hearted, feeling abandoned, rejected, until a new youth moved in, whom mother had uncannily made sure was prettier than the last. To cheer me and herself up. To dispel the gloom that arose from me losing a lover and her, a vicarious husband. Perhaps another adopted son.

**2**     Maybe I should explain what it was about our boarding house that made it so sought after. What it was that brought so many people pounding with that great Victorian mallet, the iron knocker as big as a prick. It always startled us from our peace, annoying my father and brother. But not me, for whom it was the single high note of a nightingale.

I can't say the beauty of the house attracted these young moths. And no one in their right mind could say it was an architectural pearl beyond price.

Maybe it was all these young men could afford. But then again, ours wasn't the sole bright torch visible during the protracted eclipse of their homelessness. The other hostels in the street were cheap as well.

I think it was word of mouth. Most of our lodgers had heard of us before they came to our fateful street, Edwina Street, full of so many similar crumbling terraces. Tumble-down shacks where the deprived and the emigrant could doss down in blissful relief. Maybe they had heard of my mother. Maybe, just maybe, they had heard of me through rumour.

Does it matter? The fact is, and was, that they came. And there was no reason to be upset about such good fortune, particularly now, when so many of my friends tell me that all they enjoyed was an unhappy sexless pre-adolescence.

## peephole

The best local rumour though, was that our street had once been visited by none other than Charles Dickens. And that the biggest house, the one we occupied, was the house that had given him the inspiration for Miss Havisham's in *Great Expectations*. In the local library, I read this rumour courtesy of some decayed parochial history group's newsletter, as well as the novel.

I liked that rumour, I liked it very much. Because if by accident of birth, poverty, fate or design I was the new Miss Havisham, or Master, I had certainly rejected the notion of admiring stale and festering cakes. As well as the coy idea of only holding out a shy hand masked by a glove. I was too busy for that – with my young hot cross buns, my lodgers, marrying each of them in my mind as we did the deed. To my satisfaction.

Sometimes when these boy boarders caught me staring at them through the peephole (the signal that I was available) I wouldn't enter. To tease them, to show them that I couldn't be had on every occasion. Only when I wished. When I was in the mood. Which was often. My occasional coquettish refusal was a show of power, proof that, despite my youth, I was the gay piper playing. Leading my lodger rats into my private and steamy sewer. But I refused them only when I was being nasty, capricious. Hardly ever.

Sometimes I would do the opposite. I would be altruistic. I would let them masturbate me, or suck me, because I could tell they were desperately lonely, or because I had heard that they had been fired. Or because mother told me of a telegram announcing one of their relatives . . . back home . . . in Greece, where they had been sending money (the place of my picture books and nude heroes) . . . had ceased to exist.

I remember blowing one whose father had just died. My blow job, though beguiling and expert, insufficient to prevent a new wave of despair and self-recrimination welling up in him like spoof, due to his inability to attend the funeral.

If we were having a particularly good time, I would often open the coin-catcher at the bottom of the shower with my keys, reusing the coins to prolong our time together. Amphibious pleasure our poor boarders could never usually afford. But that was a special treat, if what we were doing was particularly fun or dazzlingly new.

Maybe in a way they were my prostitutes and me much like my mother, both client and madam. Governing them, buying them. Five cents a piece, the way in those days other kids bought pyramid-shape ice blocks to lick and suck.

**3**   In those days Newtown was not an area gifted with restaurants, gay bars, fashionable boutiques, dykes or students. Nor was it the extension of the University, of Darlinghurst and the city of Sydney, that it is today. It was more like the outer-western suburbs, despite its proximity to the CBD. A place for failures, for broken families, drunks, and the immigrants who depended for their livelihood on the nearby factories, a place where life was cheap in terms of mortality and finance.

It was a long way to go up the street in those days. You had to wonder if you would come back alive, unscathed and unintimidated by the gangs which roamed the streets, known affectionately as 'sharpies'. A moniker that had nothing to do with their wits.

It was a place for the railway workers who worked in that vast iron empire which stretched from the Eveleigh Street goods yards to the Newtown we lived in – really a sub prefecture of Newtown called Macdonaldtown. A sorting and charnel house of people from other lands trapped in the architecture of unrenovated Victorian shambles. It was a place you would dream of escaping from if you had any sense or ambition because at eleven years of age it told you that your life was over. Even though you hadn't reached the age of the young male boarders who made life so tolerable.

Hadn't progressed to the level where, like them, you could produce white wads that would shoot into your fist. Against your chest. Towards the roof and the sky.

In my street there was the antique Russian man next door who said he grew peach trees in the garden because he had dreamed of them when he was in Mr Stalin's frozen holiday camp. Unlike us, he rented out rooms to old men in singlets who leant out of windows and looked at the housing commission flats across the road, while listening to transistors announcing breathlessly, that their horse, much like them, had come last.

There was the black house a few doors up occupied by Aborigines who lived in some great communal splendour. At which, practising my childhood skills at persecution, I'd throw a paddle-pop stick. A courtesy the occupants usually returned with a rock.

Besides them, other Australian-born families were rare. At that stage of my life I only ever saw them, the way I first saw the new boarders, through a peephole, except this was through that other peephole, TV. In programs such as *Homicide* and *Matlock*. They looked a bit like Americans I saw in a program called *Charades*, where people used fingers for syllables.

But despite the then seediness of Newtown, I didn't hate it, I loved it. I imagined all of Australia was like this – an ignoble place full of boarding houses, radios with breathless horse races, and people passing out drunk, except in the bathroom where I kept my boys. My real toy soldiers. My strategic command. My happiness. And there were nice things about Newtown no one noticed then. Like the Moreton Bay fig trees in the park, whose tall dark shady branches splattered small ripe figs that got crushed under foot. Tall sombre and beautiful trees which must have been planted before we immigrants came. Earlier than Federation. Maybe even by Captain Cook.

And I enjoyed primary school where we were made to stand stiff and upright at attention once a week in the playground assembly. I enjoyed school the way most bright kids enjoy it. Because their egos are constantly stroked. And fondled. Caressed by teachers and principals, who recognised possible future replacements.

I enjoyed school, despite the fact that it looked like a cemetery, with its long granite lists chiselled on an obelisk, the roll call of heroes who had saved Australia from menace. Convincing me the reason why there were so many Greek and Italian kids at this school was because all the Anglo-Australians had been killed in fields and deserts whose relevance was only to collectors of exotic place names. El Alamein, Tobruk, Gallipoli, Gaza, Antioch . . . Featuring names like Smith, Jones, Carpenter, Rayfield, Forbes, all etched on our suburban Cleopatra's needle.

Even then I felt these poor deceased but once youthful Australians would've been better off in my bathroom. Or someone else's. Rather than at war. But I knew they would never have been let into mine, because although they would've passed the young and handsome test, and the male test, they would've failed the other one set by my mother. They would've infringed the exacting rule that said all our boarders had to be non-Anglo, non-Australian. Their applications for tenancy (admittedly few and far between), strictly forbidden.

**4**     I can't remember the exact date fisting was invented. Gay lore has it that it was around the end of the 1970s or 1980s in San Francisco. But I'm here to tell you that as an eleven-year-old I discovered it in February 1968, with my favourite boarder, the gorgeous one I described, my eighteen-year-old sailor Antony. The coins he had put into the gas meter had long run out and I didn't bother opening the catch to reuse them. We were too busy, too darkly wet, having fun during an excruciatingly hot summer, the water going from hot to warm to cool then cold – delicious. I don't know how long we were under that shower. Maybe for the length of three ejaculations. Lustrous thick creamy ones from him (I still couldn't produce any), great dollops of it coming out as some sort of final largesse or compensation for the fact that he, my favourite, was deserting me by leaving me in the morning.

Even though Antony had been the one who always spoke disparagingly of Greece, apparently six months in Australia had been enough. He had booked his passage, like so many of the others, aboard one of the ships named after dead Mediterranean heroes: the *Achilles*, the *Marconi*, the *Galileo*. I guess like me, he wanted this last forbidden copulation to last or be at least remembered. I remember him lying in the half-filled bathtub, drawing me down with him. Guiding my lathered hand through his open legs and inside him. Into that mysterious place that felt so warm, so wet and tight, so close to the source of his soul and sex. So much the ultimate glove of form-fitting happiness. Guiding the first four fingers of my small fist in and out, a practice I didn't find odd or repugnant, but soft and beautiful like him. Until with his free hand he climaxed in a way that made me think he was going to pass out, evicting a greater amount of that creamy paste than I would have thought possible.

Like the others, he was sensible about pederastic sex – he never tried to fuck me and would not have considered returning his human gauntlet as a favour. There was the silent assumption his hands were too big and rough from manual labour whereas mine were perfect for the task, the small white fingernail-chewed hands of an undeveloped but eager pupil.

'Well that's the last of them,' mother said, shutting the door on Antony the following day. I didn't say anything, I was too upset.

'Oh, come on, darling,' she said. 'Don't be so glum. You'll see him again one day.' She used to say that about all the boarders. I don't know why. I was old enough and wise enough even then to know I would never see them again.

'And there'll be others, dear,' she said. 'Lots of them. Soon.' She stroked my hair, but it wasn't the same way Antony and the others used to stroke it, heavy as they were with admiration and envy. She stroked it for a short time, the way you buff and polish a shoe.

'I know he was your favourite, honey,' she said. 'And I know that he also liked you. Very much. They all seem to.

I'm just glad you're a little boy and not a girl because if you were, I think they would all fall in love with you. They might even steal you.' My mother could be prophetic. But I refused to be strayed from the point.

'Why did you say there goes the last of them?'

'Well, the rooms are sort of empty now,' she said.

'But others are coming?' I asked, frightened they might not. 'They always come. You promised.'

'Yes, they always come, honey,' she said. 'You'll have more friends in future,' giving my head of hair another spit and polish. 'It's just that your father and I have decided to close down the house and renovate. Upgrade. Make the place posh.'

I felt as if I'd been assassinated. 'Why?' I asked, my heart pounding at this widowhood come too early.

'Well, we're going to put bathrooms in each of the rooms so that the boarders don't have to use the ones on the landings.'

'That's a waste of money,' I said.

'Not at all,' she replied. 'It'll make the place more modern and we'll be able to charge more.'

'How long is this going to take?' I asked.

'Oh, I don't know,' she said. 'Six months, maybe a year.'

'But, mum . . .' I protested.

'But mum nothing,' she said. 'I thought you'd like the idea of a little privacy. Now go wash your hands for dinner and scrub your fingernails, they look filthy.'

**5**     That was the end of my innocence. My golden age now turned to bronze. It collapsed or was violated under a welter of work benches, drilling and plumbing. The workmen were far too old and fat to be considered cute, making me go into depression. Deep, dark and foreboding depression, hiding myself in my room, immersing myself in books rather than bathtubs, no longer drawn to the peephole through which could only be seen industry, hammers and saws. Ugliness, where once could be seen masterpieces and splendours more beautiful than those hung in the Tate.

And the worst of it was that now at twelve, when I was beginning to produce my own white or yellowy wads in great thick streams, there was no one to share them with. Only my fantasies could watch the new profusion of growing squeaky pubes; because while work clanged on interminably around me I was their only unhappy and silent witness.

The noise and the work seemed to go on forever. Which made me wonder what on earth they were building, bathrooms or Sistine Chapels. Every time I asked when it would be completed, my mother would say, 'Oh, when the workmen find time. They also have other jobs you know.' Or if she got tired of my inquiries, 'when your father and I have enough money to pay them, dear. I don't know why you're so concerned. Most of the noise goes on when you're at school.' Or if she was really annoyed by my resistance to modernisation – that hideous closeting of desire – 'Shouldn't you have a bath? I haven't seen you go near it for two days now. Use the one near the laundry.' Then more suspiciously, 'Or are you saving your little boy dirt until the bathrooms are finished?'

It was heartbreaking watching mother turn away so many of the beauties that still came to the door – beauties unaware that we (or me rather) were closed without a reopen date. Heartbreaking and frustrating for all of us as I saw them turn on their heel with their suitcases, rejected.

Except once, when mother had gone shopping with her plastic floral bag, and I was the only one at home to answer the door that opened up on to Apollo.

That's the only name I can give him as I never got to find out his real name. I had to tell him we couldn't help him, that I couldn't help him. Not for a long time. A confession that made me cruelly, but reluctantly, slam the door on his blinding beauty. On the shirt that hung open from his day's hot work in the factory. On his dirt-stained steel-cap boots, that I would have gladly licked. Bursting into tears as I watched his disappointed shadow departing through the lead-light glass, crying more passionately than a kid told he couldn't go to the movies.

I did many other things while those infernally smug private bathrooms were being built. I played a little football, finding the moment of collision with the other boys in tackles the only thing worthwhile about this herd-like endeavour. I went swimming, finding glimpses of nude men in the rag bag that was the chlorinated change-room

peephole

of our public baths insufficiently selective. Not enough of a reward for the coldness and wetness of crowded lanes, fogged goggles and fudged strokes.

More than anything I became sullen. Resentful. Unable to appreciate my friends at school and their simple pastimes, finding them inane, lacking in the full-bodied naked contact, that explosive male charge I was so accustomed to. Hopscotch compared to fisting – a poor substitute.

I also found my peers curiously dull in their ignorance of pleasure, childish in their naïvety about delights that were torn away from me by the intervention of architects and builders. Ignorant of what could be had between their legs, inside their jeans, packed away in college greys like cling-wrapped sandwiches. But I forgave them, knowing they had never been accorded the privileges of life in our home.

Some kiddish things though I did enjoy during this unplanned and uncalled for sexual hiatus. Like occasional visits to the fish shop to buy greasy potato scallops wrapped in newspaper. The hot bland taste of which was sharper to me then than anything I have tried since including Beluga and truffles. And occasionally playing in the backyard with the local alley cats I liked to feed, until mother said they carried disease and got rid of them.

Maybe like many fags I escaped out of the public library of the world and its disappointments into the private world of books. Into the folds of their more forgiving pages, reading everything from *Jane Eyre*, to *Wuthering Heights*, among other literary neophyte classics like *1984*, *The Fox*, and *A Tale of Two Cities*. And of course *Catcher in the Rye*. Although in that book I couldn't understand why Holden

Caulfield turned down the advances of that nice homosexual man. It baffled me, making me put that otherwise interesting volume to one side. Under magazines.

During free moments, when I wanted to show off at school, I read *War and Peace*, impressing teachers and students alike, enjoying their admiration more than the confusing Russian names. Wisely not confessing to my intellectual admirers that my twelve-year-old literary tastes judged this book in need of serious editing, although I must say reading it was quicker than our renovations.

I continued this process of sublimation by becoming, at the age of thirteen, a famous writer. A poet better known than T. S. Eliot, writing pieces of poetry that I considered far too exquisite to be aired in public. Most having to do with some half-remembered lodger who had vanished down time's drain. Using a pen given to me by my father whose barrel featured the cable car in Katoomba riding past the Three Sisters. Up and down in time to my brilliance.

I also became a film director. A much more important, precocious and successful one than Cecil B. De Mille, who had to wait till middle age for success. Projecting grand slides I'd purchased at the toy shop in my own Hollywood of torn sheets raised in the basement laundry. Showing transparencies featuring the great cities of the world — which is why, to this day, I can tell you the name of the main square in Caracas. And the name of the man on a horse in the central plaza of Montevideo. Even New York and London, cities that didn't look so different to Newtown, just taller, wider, more distorted. Mother insisting I also keep slides of Athens. I don't know why, that city looked so broken down and ugly. But I charged the local kids the way I had charged my boarders — a five-cent piece for this still life, still-born cinematography whose only advantage over television was the frozen use of colour.

This was in the days before colour television. When colour TV only existed in glossy picture ads displaying coffin-like American TV sets for sale in the pages of *National Geographic*. A magazine where, some unclad Amazon tribes, occasionally allowed me to observe with salacious and comparative interest what I once had often held in my hands. Grown men's large and dangling penises.

'My little director,' my mother would say, after each of my screenings was complete. After the local kids went home satisfied with my international commentary learnt out of atlases, that added spice to this new but less entertaining peep show.

Or if she caught me yet again immersed in a book, or writing a poem, the Katoomba cable car active, 'My little writer,' and I'd get another hair tousle of approval.

'Good to see my kid not wasting his time with football,' Dad would say, a sport whose aggressiveness and ultimately whose Australianness he hated. 'Don't want him growing up to wield the jackhammer,' the perpetual threat he held against me and my brother. A threat that said if we failed our studies we could only ever hope for a life as lackeys like him, in the Department of Main Roads. Vibrating with unprotected eardrums to the doomed pre-ordained rhythms of class.

But I began to worry about this praise, began to worry that my newfound interest in books and films and projectors and television had been pre-planned by my mother. Like my homosexuality. Maybe closing down our boarding house was a new plot of hers to censoriously persuade me of the merits of quiet, nurtured study, of untried heterosexuality.

Maybe the building of these interminable bathrooms was a *cordon sanitaire* around my now full-steam-ahead adolescence.

Whenever I allowed this conspiracy theory full vent, I wanted to defenestrate my books. It made me want to burn my slides of the great cities of the world. Like pig fat over a Bunsen burner.

Then one day, two years later as I approached my fourteenth birthday, just after my voice lost its Joan Sutherland appeal, the bathrooms were finished. It was an event so momentous in my life that when I peered through the peephole at the workmen clearing up the last of the debris, taking down their workbenches and saws, I had to rub my eyes. Disbelieving the evidence.

'They're not coming back?' I said to my mother.

'No, dear, they're not,' she said.

'Can I have a look?' I asked her, impatient to see this architectural wonder, these hanging gardens of Fabulon that had caused me much *coitus interruptus*. So much early pre-teen distress, which later in life would never be unravelled by either architects or psychiatrists.

'Well of course you can have a look, dear, but first go hang this outside,' she said, giving me the *To Let* sign to dangle in its former place. Something I did with the pride and anticipation of a young doctor expecting his first patient.

**6**     'Isn't it beautiful?' she said, switching on the light and revealing the first completed bathroom in all its glory.

'There's no gas boiler. Or meter,' I said, noticing an oversight which signalled that, depressingly, they weren't finished.

'Oh, these are electric, darling, they won't need to use those old coin things any more. And over here is the kitchenette. We thought we'd install them at the same time so that they could cook snacks for themselves. That way, they need never bother us again. In fact we'll hardly see them,' she said, making my heart sink like a cat drowned in a weighted-down stocking.

So Rome had been built, but the sexual civilisation I hungered for had been destroyed in the process. And they were ugly, tiny little cabinets. Like telephone booths, so out of place in their surroundings. They looked as if they'd been dropped by crane from outer space, having neither the spaciousness of the old communal bathrooms, nor a window from which you could stare at the cityscape while you masturbated, melding with Sydney's towers and its factories. Melding with Australia and its culture. With vistas. With beautiful imported young men getting sudsy.

Just ugly exhaust fans whose gleaming blades lay ready to expel into unappreciative air all the steam that could've clung and cleansed their unclean bodies.

'Well, what do you think?' she said.

'Of what?' I answered.

'Of the renovations, dear, you asked often enough.'

'They're all right,' I said.

'Only all right?' she said. 'They're gorgeous. Now we won't have to do another thing to this house until you're twenty-one at least.'

But they weren't all right at all, and she knew it. They were ghastly little cells, fumigation chambers where stick insects should get sprayed not places fit for my lovers. My gentlemen callers. My beaux.

'Soon that knocker will be going nonstop,' she said, looking forward to reclaiming her past role as the arbiter of beauty.

'All those requests for rooms, bang, bang, bang, will drive your father and brother nuts. Just like the old days,' she said.

'Just like the old days,' I said, knowing it was nothing of the sort.

But no one came, in the first week of the house's opening. And no one came in the second week, or the third. Not even in the fourth, which was perplexing for my mother and even more unsettling for me. It was like throwing a party and forgetting to invite the guests, or worse, as Dad used to say, the ouzo, by which he meant the booze.

Curiously though, I was pleased, feeling a *Schadenfreude* about it because I'd been vindicated. I knew that the communal bathrooms should never have been removed, that tampering with them had brought a curse down upon our house.

'I can't figure it out,' said mother. 'I just can't figure it out at all. No one. Not even in a month,' unaware that now, for her, I had no sympathy. She was genuinely upset, going through all the reasons why they avoided our establishment in quiet conversations with my father, snatches of which I sometimes overheard.

'Well, most of the immigrants have settled down now,' my father said. 'They're no longer coming in great invasion waves. And there's been an awful lot of guest houses that have opened up while we've been closed.'

'But theirs aren't as good as ours,' mother said, defending the quality of our establishment.

'That's not the point,' father said. 'They don't know that. And I suppose, theirs are cheaper. They haven't gone to as much fuss as we have.'

At one point it must've got critical, because I remember mother saying to me before I set out for school, 'I can't give you any lunch money today dear, your father forgot his wallet somewhere.' Handing me two pieces of fruit for lunch, offerings I knew spelt poverty. At the very least financial hardship, which we on the top rung of the working class had never had to face. It was the first time I had ever been denied my fee for school attendance.

I tried to turn it into a game, when I got home with a heavy suitcase full of textbooks such as *Europe Since Napoleon*, *Trigonometry: An Introduction*, and the paradoxical *History Today*. As well as whatever novel I was reading and my slightly pornographic copy of *Films and Filming*, borrowed from the library purely for the study of cinema and its mysteries.

Not for what the editors discovered, the bare-breasted boys in each and every major Hollywood production. Asking, 'Anyone come today?'

'No, no one today. Or yesterday. Maybe we'll have to take whoever comes along,' she said sadly, her exacting standards of beauty collapsing. Like our neighbour the Russian man, maybe we would have to let to people over thirty. An event so dreadful I knew my mother must be desperate to give it a second thought.

Then one day towards the end of term when I came home and saw her crying I stopped asking, ceasing my vindictive though silent, 'I told you so' game of vengeance. Even my *Schadenfreude* was wearing off, or getting warm. And both for her and myself, I was sorry.

'What are you going to do?' I asked, playing with her hair a bit longer than she played with mine.

'I don't know,' she said, wiping away a tear. 'We might have to sell, or advertise . . .'

Then the awful truth came out. 'In the English papers.' She hesitated before proceeding. 'For . . .' she couldn't bring herself to say it, '. . . Australians . . .' she blurted out, like a nun ordered by the Abbess to swear, and at this she sobbed even more profoundly. But she composed herself. Blowing her nose, obliterating the sound of the word, of the people, who had been up to now invisible, unmentionable. Untouchable.

'You're going to have to write the ad, dear,' she said, something I was aware I would have to do as they didn't speak English.

'What should it say?' I asked.

'Oh, anything you like,' she said. 'You know how to phrase it,' and she went out to tend to the cooking as if she'd handed me a shameful assignment on which our lives depended.

I guess it was a little bit of a diminution in status to go from being a famous writer/poet and director to that of a mere copy writer. Even with a cable car pen. But I got over this slap in the face to my pride. And the ad I was going to write would be a doozy. I knew that with the powers of my pen there must be a way to subtly spell out what it was mother and I both wanted.

First, I toyed with the idea of ads that read:

EXTREMELY BEAUTIFUL YOUNG MEN CONSIDERED FOR POSSIBLE ACCOMMODATION, MANY EXTRAS,
or
BLEAK HOUSE FULLY RENOVATED WITH GREAT EXPECTATIONS SEEKS MUTUAL FRIENDS.

But these early puerile efforts went straight into the garbage bin of self-censorship.

I was stuck, unable to convey what it was we wanted without attracting undesirable elements, such as the vice squad.

Then I hit on it. My talent for copy, not to mention the practise in writing this ad keeping me in good stead later in life when I started seeking attention through the Personals. The ad I came up with said:

ARE YOU UNDER THIRTY? SINGLE? MALE? PRESENTABLE? SEEKING SOMEWHERE TO LIVE? IN GLORIOUS HOUSE WITH PEOPLE WHO UNDERSTAND YOU? THEN APPLY IN THE FIRST INSTANCE TO 69 EDWINA STREET, NEWTOWN, AND YOUR DEEPEST FELT PRAYERS AND LODGER LONGINGS WILL BE ANSWERED.

I thought that said it all. Really. For all of us. And if they turned out to be unattractive I'm sure either my mother or I would have sufficient tact or skill to say, 'No Vacancy.'

'Can I read it to you, mum?' I said proudly. But she didn't answer.

'Mum, shouldn't I read it to you?' I said, but she just smiled wanly in my direction. I began to think that with all the clatter of the renovations tacked on to her advancing years, perhaps mother was going a little deaf. But then again maybe she was just distracted, so I read it aloud to her. In translation.

'That's nice, dear,' she said, but I still wasn't sure she had heard correctly, as she had the tone in her voice normally reserved for praise when I was showing off some completed piece of homework. It wasn't the tone of elation she reserved for conversations about our boarders. And their merits.

'Now you run along.'

**7**     The Herald in those days was not a glamorous building that scrapes the sky on the shores of Darling Harbour as it is now, but an ugly chequebook-grey building situated on Broadway. There, trucks and men screamed abuse at each other while great bundles of newspaper got tossed into vans urgently wanting to deliver news that could usually wait. I could see conveyor belts thumping out print ceaselessly in a big dipper of information that left a fourteen year old like me in awe of the enormity of apparatus required for publishing.

Which left me somewhat scared of even entering the building to place our ad, as The Herald's large portals were so forbidding. But I steeled myself because I knew that behind mother's polite request was emergency.

'This your ad?' the man at the ad desk said, looking at it dubiously, looking at me as if I were a harlot advertising her services.

'It's my mother's,' I said.

'Why doesn't she place the ad, then?' he said.

'She doesn't speak English,' I explained.

'Cat got her tongue?' he joked, shocking me with his insensitivity. I wasn't even sure of this feline expression's meaning.

'Just kidding,' he said. 'How many weeks?'

'Depends,' I replied, 'On how many come.'

But at that point I thought he lost interest in Little Orphan Annie doing her errands. I was wrong.

'We'll run Wednesday and Saturday for a month,' he said. 'I'll only charge you for a week though.'

'Thanks,' I said, thinking he might be trying to atone for his initial slight towards my monolingual family. He looked so much like the detectives in *Homicide*, I wondered if he'd ever investigated any murders personally. In his capacity as a newspaperman. That's what they called them then. At least they did in my *Superman* comics. Probably because they eventually looked and thought like the tied-up bundles.

'He said he'd give us a run for a month,' I said to my mother when I returned.

'Did you take that ad down like I told you or haven't you written it yet?' She answered, convincing me that unless she was teasing, there was indeed something wrong with her hearing.

And so we waited anxiously for results. Mother and father for some easing of our financial difficulties, my brother 'for things to get back to normal', as he put it innocently, while I waited for more. To find out what Australians looked like underneath their clothes, hoping I could resume my (what would soon hopefully be) multi-cultural activities.

Then a few days after that, when the ad first appeared, we got our first visitor. Poor thing I figured, he didn't even have time to get to the front door because I could see from the window he was already deep in conversation, trapped by my too-eager father. He was a tall, thin, blond man in a suit, carrying an attaché case. He looked far too well-kept and successful to be a boarder, but then Australians, according to my imagination, were capable of anything.

'This is Mr Maxwell,' father said, bringing him in.

'He's representing his father's company, Maxwell & Sons Real Estate,' he continued, probably pleased there were family companies even in the antipodes.

'Young Mr Maxwell wishes to make us a little proposition,' my father explained in Greek, obviously understanding more of Mr Maxwell's purpose than I would have thought his limited English permitted.

My father was always a very fair and equitable man, never making a decision on his own without consulting the entire family. Mother said it was because he was a coward, but I think it was because he was decent.

So we all sat at the dining table, in the grand but decayed Victorian dining room of the house, under the round fluorescent lights, our feet on the lino that we'd similarly installed, while we listened to his proposition. It came out with two clicks, like bullets fired from a pearl-handled pistol. Straight out of his attaché case. In a neatly bound folder.

He said a lot of things about this 'proposition' most of which had to do with how well off we would be if we sold our house to his father, Mr Maxwell. He pointed out that they were eagerly seeking our house in particular, because of its position, because of its size, and then, looking at me, its potential.

He himself had heard we had installed private bathrooms in all the rooms on each of the levels. He said his father would be glad to compensate us for our efforts. To take it off our hands so that they could run it more efficiently. A proposition I listened to and interpreted with resentment for my parents. My mother also listened, but whatever little she understood or heard must've troubled her also, because she scowled with anger. And junior Mr Maxwell talked for what seemed like a very long time, saying the same thing again and again. Making me wonder which part of my translation, or my brother's even poorer paraphrasing, he thought we had avoided.

'On behalf of my parents . . .' (I heard myself say) '. . . we will think about it.' Allowing them to show him the exit.

So, things were bad. Apparently much worse than I had anticipated. But I didn't realise we had reached crisis stage. Having to sell off our first-generation inheritance, the bricks and mortar my parents, along with Mr Dickens, had struggled so long to refine, to find inspiration from. In which years earlier, I'd first become lustfully aware of literature's value.

'Well what do you think of them apples?' father said, returning to the table where we sat motionless as in a seance. Actually he said 'lettuce' – lettuce being the idiomatic equivalent in Greek.

There was silence. 'It's a pretty good deal,' he said. 'And it would free us up to do other things.'

'Like what?' my brother asked. Even then my brother was conservative, a Tory politician who feared the slightest element of change. One day, despite his working class origins, I could see him getting preselection as a Liberal.

'We could travel a bit,' father said. 'Show you boys a bit of the world. Where you come from.'

My brother blew a raspberry, unable to swallow the spoof of our origins. Our ancestors.

## peephole

'There is no reason for us to sell,' mother said. 'Things have been slow that's all. And what would that hideous young turtle know anyway,' she said, referring to junior Mr Maxwell's appearance.

'What's his looks got to do with it?' my father replied. 'He's a businessman, not a bridegroom . . . Making an offer. A good offer. That we should probably take.' Then he said, 'All those in favour . . . ,' raising his own hand, which stayed for a few seconds in the air unescorted and lonely. 'Well, at least we've made a decision,' he said. 'Let's hope we're right, that there'll be better times ahead. I'd hate to think we missed out on an opportunity by hoping our house's golden days aren't over.' And with that warning, he left. To go out for groceries, which our non-drinking household knew meant the pub.

**8**     But he didn't have time to leave, or to allow his words to resonate with their doom-laden prophecy, because just then, like a stage device I had seen in melodramas we'd acted out at school, the doorknocker banged.

It banged loud and long, continuously, not giving anyone a chance to answer, shaking the windows and making us all a little scared. No one had ever banged that loudly, with such insensitivity, before. Only once in my memory and that was when the police came looking for an escapee rumoured to be holed-up in some Edwina Street boarding house. No one said a thing.

My father was just about to get the other arm into the sleeve of his pub jacket when mother, always the bravest, somehow heard the noise through the veil of her impaired hearing.

'Don't any of you move,' she said. 'I'll sort this one out.' A statement that meant she would send packing whoever the incessant caller was. For his obstreperousness and rudeness – despite our need to fill the vacancy. Then, to check as if uncertain, 'That was the door, wasn't it?' Convincing me of what the others didn't already know. She was only months or moments away from deafness.

'What's left of it,' my brother replied sardonically.

She seemed gone an inordinately long time. Even father

was getting cross because, mother at the door with whoever was disturbing our harmony was now a barrier to his excursion.

But mother returned soon enough, although not soon enough for our anxiety, padding down the long hallway whose Victorian tiles echoed her steps like a boarding school corridor. But she wasn't alone. Next to her was someone we hadn't seen before.

A young man so blindingly beautiful, I had to shield my eyes as if from too much sunlight. A young man she introduced as, 'Mr Australia', pointing at him proudly with the palm of her hand the way the referees introduced new combatants each Saturday afternoon on TV in *World Championship Wrestling*. Combatants like Killer Kowalski, Mario Milano and Larry O'Day. But unlike those combatants, normally hooded, masked or fat and unattractive because of the weight they had to put on so as not to get used as projectiles, this Mr Australia was different.

When I was finally able to look up at him, once my eyes got accustomed to his dazzle, I saw clearly Balder the Bright and Beautiful. A Norse God I had read about who was so handsome that when he died the whole world, including stones and rocks, wept bitterly at the loss of his beauty.

He had short blond hair that shone with its own special lustre, not quite as yellow as the hair of the Macedonian youth described earlier. With eyes that were neither blue nor green, but more aquamarine, shining like the lagoons I had seen in *National Geographic*. A colour so astonishing I thought at first that his eyes must be made of glass, or precious stones that should be locked up in a museum. Maybe the Tower of London.

He had a mouth on him that opened in an easy smile, showing teeth whiter than sand. His complexion was masculine, wrapped around a square jaw flawless in its smoothness and enhanced by a tan he must've acquired by accident, either stripped to the waist on a hot building site or on Bondi Beach. In near nakedness. He was like the two-dimensional Australian men I saw and envied. The only full-colour ones I'd seen outside of television and magazines. The ones in posters behind glass, smiling, holding beer cans and a towel to wipe themselves down, in pictures attached to the walls of toilet pubs.

But it was his body that was the most amazing thing of all, so perfect, so muscular he looked carved out of air. I guess he was wearing what I would now recognise as moleskins. Cream coloured moleskins that seemed not so much worn, as an integral part of his body. His legs and skin undulating down to where his cock must be, in a manner that suggested (to an expert such as myself) that what he had beneath there must be awe-inspiring. Capable of ejaculating from where he stood in our dining room doorway past me. Even as far as *The Herald*. Maybe higher than the school's Cleopatra needle.

'Mr Australia,' my mother repeated with glee, perhaps thinking that we too in the family were partially afflicted with the creeping deafness taking hold of her.

'Not Mr Australia,' the vision said, 'Wayne, Wayne Hogan, from way past Wagga.'

As a multicultural person, I've always thought that Wagga is an unfortunate name for a township. In fact I was often called by that township's name myself. In the street. By children who knew quite well that the insulting mantra did hurt. Using it at school so that if anyone complained to the teacher they could deny it, saying that they were only talking about where they spent their holidays.

'It's down near Victoria,' Wayne said. And he held out his hand, first to my father, then my brother and then (a little bit too casually I thought) to me.

'Pleased to meet youse,' he said. Then, 'Great old house you've got here,' looking around. 'Must've been built with the ark.'

My father made a motion to my mother with a nod of his head, for her to show him the room.

'Please,' my mother said. This time her outstretched palm pointed up the staircase leading to the spruce new chambers. And he offered his arm to her as if he, not junior Mr Maxwell, were the bridegroom father had been speaking about. She taking it chivalrously, delighted by his charm and innocence.

I think that was the first time in my life, that I remember at any rate, when I flushed from my natural olive to forest green, or was it more créme de menthe? That monstrous and luminous shade of envy.

True, I had experienced other deadly sins: lust of course, and certainly gluttony, in my desire for more lust. Malice I'd already witnessed in my smugness towards the folly of renovations. Leaving only one final arrow in the quiver of damnation – sloth, or what teachers call laziness.

'Do you want to bring in *Wayin's* bag from the front?' my father asked, pronouncing 'Wayne' like an entrance. 'I think he's here for good.'

'No!' I said. 'He can get it himself.' Placing the last tile of sin on my road to perdition.

I don't know why I responded in this manner. Wayne's startling beauty was the thing I wanted. So startling that just a touch of his body, just a look at his face again would have atoned for the years of indignity suffered in having to wait for the infernal completion of the rooms.

Maybe I responded in this manner because mother seemed so suddenly interested in him, suggesting to my childish mind that all the boarders, all the boys I had before were now nothing and of no interest. Consigned to the scrap-heap of a personal lurid history. And it seemed to me she had discarded too easily those racist Greek feelings against Australians that I had respected and cherished.

Maybe something told me he wasn't going to be the usually pliant type of boarder I was accustomed to. Regardless of whatever success I had in finding a suitable time or location for us to have sex. And not being Greek, I reasoned Wayne might not like my adulation. My peering. My fingers. Which made me strongly believe such a refusal would herald with swift wings a bitter tragedy.

Worse, there was also something in the way mother took him by the hand that first time, to show him our house's splendour, that said he would now be her primary interest. Clearly she, the powerful concierge, the sorceress, was going to sacrifice my father, my brother and even me for this young man. Very much like that woman in Ancient Greek tales called Medea who experimented with her sons for the love of Jason, in a primitive demonstration of The Blender.

Perhaps I was scared not so much of segmentation but of a contest against her for his affections. Or of his foreignness.

'I'll get the bags then,' my brother said, forever the peace-maker of the family, almost as if he understood the jealousy I felt, understanding that my refusal to play porter was the cry of a petulant Achilles, to his tent withdrawing.

## peephole

You may think these are all exaggerated emotions and allusions, that mother was only being solicitous towards someone whose money we needed. But I don't think so. And as it turned out, I the noiseless and silent Cassandra, was vindicated. My reward for prescience was similar to hers, being shame and derision.

**9**     We didn't see Wayne for the first few days, few weeks even. He was always up early and out the door. And he would come in late at night after everyone went to bed. He had said that for a few weeks, to get some cash under his belt (in that lotus land of pubes and flesh) he had asked to do double shifts. In his job as a bus conductor. Probably magnificent in a short-sleeve grey shirt, undone at the front. Exceptional in blue shorts that I knew would be too short for what I had immediately appraised as fine, long, strong legs. I'd seen such a uniform on others. And I knew his occupation meant he possessed a leather ticket holder and leather shoulder bag that swung at hip level. His tools of trade. His arsenal.

Those first few days and weeks, when he went in and out unsighted, I spent imagining what it would be like to brush against him on a hot afternoon. On a bus so crowded that as he turned, my face would already be in his chest, his cock hard against me. Weeks went by with me fantasising how I would then slither down and undo his shorts, like a fireman descending. Heedless of the commuters' horror, I would wind myself around the twin poles of his legs. To do his bidding. Anything.

But deprived of direct sightings of Wayne because of his overwork, I filled in his image by staring at his shirts and shorts which were occasionally hung in the biggest theatre in the world. In the theatre that's bigger than Sydney's State, New York's Radio City Music Hall and where my epics were often showing, admiring his shirt dripping near the screen that often gave itself over to major retrospectives of my talent in our laundry. Where mother washed for him (it was part of the service) using a giant witch's cauldron, first boiling them, then whitening them with the Tyrian Imperial Purple of the Caesars. It came as a bleach, an ultramarine substance called Reckitt's Blue, now sadly unavailable.

Unfortunately I was never quick enough to get to the smalls of this grandly beautiful young man before they were washed. They were always smelling already of detergent, immersed, preventing me from cheerfully engaging in a practice I knew to be more dangerous and enthralling than carbon monoxide sniffing. The almost lethal (if discovered) craft of *inhalation*, done by using young lungs with underwear across your face imitating the mask of a bandit.

But clothes whether wet or dry are only a very small consolation, insufficient apology for the absence of their occupant. So I resolved to make sure I saw Wayne again, painfully aware that this was hypocrisy when measured against the stagy disdain I initially exhibited.

I also knew that seeking his re-acquaintance was going to be difficult. Though only fourteen I wasn't an early riser. And sharing the bedroom with my brother meant it would be impossible to set the alarm just to glimpse Wayne, prepared for work in his grey and blue armour. And only having the status of a schoolboy meant staying up past midnight, when he was liable to return, was a forbidden dissipation.

So I comforted myself with other signs of his presence. Waiting for a plan to hatch or for his double shifts to end, once his belt loops had become as he wanted, jammed full of dollars. Seeing signs that announced him, little tokens I would have once thought impossible in our household.

For instance some five weeks after his arrival, I saw mother making sweets, not the *kourambiedes* I liked, nor the *galaktobouriko* I adored. Not even her renowned *baklava*. I saw her using pieces of sponge cake whose staleness she disguised with melted chocolate and coconut. Of all things, she was making those bricks I'd seen in the school canteen but never dared touch. Lamingtons.

'Who are they for?' I asked, reaching out to take one, thinking since she made them they must be all right. My hand got smacked politely.

'They're for Wayne,' she said, not so much in answer to my question, but almost predicting it, because I'm sure she hadn't heard it, the slap a startled response just to my presence.

'Nora gave me the recipe,' she explained and pre-empted my next question, referring to a Greek friend of hers who lived up the road. Whose powers of sorcery were greater in that she could consult books of spells where recipes were written in that old Celtic-Germanic language so mysterious to my mother called English.

'Nora says Australians like these,' she said, putting the black coconut-dusted bricks on a serving tray. Ascending the stairs to where Wayne lived like a god in the clouds using the best bathroom of all alone, in our now to me hateful terrace.

She ascended like a serving girl rather than his superior or equal – no longer the powerful goddess she had been.

As if entranced. Embarrassing me, recreating in my soul that curious hemlock of anger and envy. And the next day it got worse when I saw her repeating this process. Not with lamingtons, but with rice bubbles mixed with a sweet black gravy made into what I had only tried at school fetes: chocolate crackles.

**10**   So I did the only thing appropriate in the circumstances, for the frustrated and uninspired. Late one night before Wayne got home when I was sure my brother was asleep, I broke into his room and waited.

I sniffed his sheets to occupy the time. Running my fingers over the bathroom tiles on whose clean surface I knew he must've ejaculated, tracing the shower spout and its droplets of water with my fingers. Going through his drawers where there was nothing but clean clothes which were useless for inhalation, a lurid murder mystery, and snapshots of a place called home, (written in biro on the back). The photo showed people smiling against a background pinker and more empty than the Gobi desert. Noticing, while I waited, that next to his bed was a jar of another substance popular at the time called Brylcreem. Uncapped. Most of it expended. Finding it curious because from my one brief sighting, Wayne didn't strike me as the sort who would grease the gold of his hair which swayed so naturally back from his forehead with abandon. So I did what any youth would do when faced with boredom, dull snapshots and an uncapped lubricant.

Undoing my pants, pyjamas really, I lay back on his bed, dipping my hand into this Brylcreem, feeling its oiliness. Masturbating.

peephole

Taking long smooth strokes, during which surprisingly, though a powerful warlock in my own right, I decided not to conjure up Wayne's image, but the Greek boys I missed. The ones who had boarded their boats and departed from the Troy of Newtown.

I conjured up the images of all those lads and our shared vices. Antony who had abandoned me featured strongly. I saw him, them, and our adventures, unfurl in front of me against the fake walnut wardrobe, in both seventy-millimetre and Panavision.

I wasn't scared while doing this. I wasn't even worried. It seemed to me the natural culmination of my desire to see Wayne. A filler, a trailer. Then, just as I was about to blow but fortunately before the point of no return, Wayne entered.

He looked at me, taking in at once what I was up to and smiled before getting on with his business. Unburdening himself of his ticket holder and his money pouch, flinging both straight on to the floor like a gun slinger. But he didn't go any further. He ignored me, going to have a look at himself in the wardrobe mirror, checking his image quickly, almost as if he wanted reassurance that he existed.

'Good to get it out,' he said, still not looking at me. 'Keep it stored up too long and it drives you nuts. Don't mind me mate. Just pull it.' And with that endorsement, I ejaculated.

He didn't even see me do it. Or want to. He went over to the window to look out past midnight at the Victorian square that faced our house. Almost as if he were listening to the fruit bats invading the darkness. And the pips and sweetness of the fig trees they fed upon each night, lighting a cigarette that he blew angrily straight out the window as if it were mustard gas. The same gas used on other Australians in the trenches.

'You'd better get to bed,' he said very quietly in the dark. 'Have a shower. Then I might have one myself. I'm pretty buggered. I've got to hit the sack.'

An instruction I silently executed. Thrilled by his casualness. Bewildered by his indifference and worried by what seemed to have come over him. A midnight depression. As he washed and dried himself alone in his bathroom, I hoped he would join me. Knowing he wouldn't, exiting when it became clear he wasn't going to, leaving backwards like a beggar who'd faced a king. Trying to keep the drawstring of my pyjamas together, now partially soggy and matted, agreeing with my estimation of him as a creature beyond loveliness.

**11**     I probably forgot to tell you that throughout this time with the strange tenant who so attracted me, no one else came to our door. Not one other lodger in response to the ad I had crafted. Wayne was our sole mainstay. Arriving as he did out of thin air, unasked for, uninvited. But this low occupancy far from causing continual problems in our family – anxiety for my mother or concern for my father – seemed to do the opposite. It had a stabilising effect on them. Our house, though shared with only one lodger, now had a purpose again. Wayne's sole presence being sufficient ballast against the Black Sea of despair felt by all when faced with its former emptiness. Maybe we attributed to Wayne the powers of a magician, investing in him an authority he did not have, a feeling that while he stayed there all would be well for us.

A couple of days after my bold break and enter, I came home from school, weighted down with a Globite case in which juvenile knowledge rested. A novel by Henry Treece, another by Robert Louis Stevenson, a book about gum trees by Judith Wright that could not have been written in Newtown. When I saw my mother at the stove finishing off not ever more surprising Australian delicacies, but a moussaka, a dish we hadn't had for a long time.

'Is that for tonight?' I asked.

'Here darling,' she said, ignoring the question, 'Wayne bought you this.' Giving me not a slice of it but a small box tied with a ribbon. Which I looked at cautiously before untying its crude bow to reveal a brand new unopened bottle of Brylcream that rested in my hands like a murder weapon.

'Isn't that sweet of him?' she said. 'I'm so glad you two have made friends. Although I'm not sure where you would have seen each other. He's always away so early and back so late. But he did say he's going to keep more regular hours after Friday,' returning to her more pressing chore of getting the consistency of the béchamel neither too thick nor too thin. But correct. She was humming. Perhaps both dish and humming exasperated signs that in this war for his beauty, I'd won with subterfuge the first and most important battle.

Saturdays were always very exciting in our house because regardless of the weather, the heat, the cold, the rain, the hail, we always got to watch TV. And the programming was genius. There was *World Championship Wrestling*, and *The Roller Game* where American lesbians tried to knock each other off their skates, while pretending to go around in a harmless circular fashion. And there was *Joe the Gadget Man*. His inspired products and appliances made us all feel we were part of a revolution bigger than the industrial one, a major scientific and domestic revolution peculiar to the late twentieth century. There was also *Divorce Court*, where a man in a wig, sitting on a higher level than a man with short hair, would listen to why a divorce should not be granted to the wife, whose hair was a beehive.

More importantly, sandwiched between these shows,

was the weekly afternoon broadcast from Australia's President, Bob Santamaria, named after Columbus's ship though he was neither Portuguese, Spanish nor Irish. We watched him religiously because he had an uncanny sense of knowing exactly when the country was liable to be invaded. By both the Chinese and the Russians. A date we always craned an ear for but which he, week after week, ran out of time to announce. Probably because of cutbacks to airtime afforded him by the Parliament or Congress he ran called the National Civic Council. Sometimes he was more frightening than the violent lesbians, the medium-length hair judge, and even the wrestling.

But that day when President Santamaria began his broadcast I couldn't concentrate on what he was saying. Nor on the date of the imminent invasion, because I heard the door go, the knocker. Knowing since we were all in the TV room that it could only be Wayne, finally here in our house, at a civilised hour. Maybe even with time on his hands. For recreation.

I could hear him padding down the hallway which made such a distinctive echo. Fearing that in another minute unless somehow I accosted him he would vanish into his room, eliminating any hope of us effecting a reconciliation. So I did the only thing I could do in the circumstances. Deciding to avoid any other deadly sin, I resorted to the device for which no one gets sent to damnation, borrowing wisely from our President. I resorted to fabrication.

'That's Wayne,' I said, jumping up off the floor where I normally watched TV on my stomach, my chin in my hands and my legs crossed behind me Gidget-fashion. 'He promised to take me to the movies.' My family startled by my new enthusiasm for this boarder and the suddenness of this appointment. Running out of the living room, past the dining room, to the kitchen that connected with the staircase on which he was about to ascend to his level of safety. I was breathless.

I said: 'I just told them you promised to take me to the movies. Don't make a liar out of me. I'll get in trouble.'

He paused, hand on the bannister, astonished at the effrontery, the boldness of one so young. Then turning to me he said, his aquamarine eyes flashing, 'Yeah, rightio, but let me change first . . . As long as you don't pick a western.'

Which I didn't. I already had the right movie in mind. And a few minutes later Wayne and I sailed out of the terrace watched by my parents and my brother, as if seeing the exit of what they always expected I was. A hero. Or Cinderella.

'Don't be late,' mother yelled out after us, 'I'll have dinner ready for you,' immediately returning to the kitchen to whip up a feast. Now it was clear to her that I had won the initial contest for his affections and there was value in not objecting to, but cultivating, our union.

**1 2**　　Wayne and I walked up Edwina Street in silence for a while, me in the shorts and long socks of early teen de riguer, Wayne in his moleskins freshly pressed by my mother. Only a tight T-shirt guarding him and his chest from rape by the whole population of Australia. Then halfway up he said, 'You really like me don't ya?'

I smiled in answer. He appreciated the smile, but more than that I think he appreciated the fact that I didn't spoil things by over-articulating. By saying something corny that would embarrass us out of love, that could've embarrassed us to death and alienation.

'Now what movie have you picked out?' he asked.

'It's a surprise,' I said.

'Okay,' he said. 'I like surprises. You're full of them anyway so let's hope it's gonna be a beauty.'

And it was. I took him to see a gladiator movie. It was playing in a Newtown cinema acknowledged as the centre of the world called The Hub. A cinema which in all honesty I didn't think equal to the baroque rococo Gothic splendour of the cement-decorated theatrette of my laundry.

The picture we saw was about a Greek or Italian man from long ago, maybe Hercules, who had to fight many monsters before winning the hand of the girl he hadn't recognised as his disguised assistant. But the toy boats floating in a large swimming pool or bathtub as a supposed harbour set were spectacular.

These days such diversions are called sword and sandal films. But if someone had suggested it to me then I would have been mystified by such a label. My attention was never drawn to what was on either the protagonist's feet or in his hands but to his bare chest and the briefness of his tunic. Anyway, the film was unimportant. What mattered was being with Wayne. Sitting next to me in the dark he shone more luminously than the achievements of Hercules or Jason. As well as whoever else had to suffer in the Colosseum that the end credits said still stands in that marvellous Italian city called *Cine Citta*. And during the bright exterior scenes when the hero, Jason or Hercules, was in the sun, the beauty of Wayne's face compared to their Italian swarthiness was lustrous. Receiving all available light from the screen as if it was radioactive. As if he was the real star who should have lit up the screen, if Australia had then a film industry.

Wayne seemed to eat a lot of popcorn as well as Jaffas, crunching in his mouth their perfect chocolate roundness, their balls. Their orange colour giving his lips a slight effeminate vermilion, and he too seemed to enjoy the movie immensely, even though this gladiator film was a bit like a western, the emperor as evil sheriff. Similar because though the baddie didn't have a gun he did have a net with which to snare the hero. So as to puncture him with a trident, the way earlier the lion tried to do with its teeth but failed dismally.

Boldly I held Wayne's hand through these tribulations, taking his non-Jaffa, non-popcorn holding hand in mine. He casually accepted this, not caring that he was holding the hand of a boy, not a girl with whom this practice would have been more appropriate. Not wincing at all or feeling uncomfortable or pulling away, convincing me that he thought what I thought. That what we were doing was the most natural thing in the world. As natural and as fair as the evil gladiator caught up in his own net, forced by the hero to sit on his own trident.

Then the lights were up, the worst of it being not that the film was over but that we would now have to stop holding hands. So we wouldn't get lynched, which I'd read and heard was likely if people were confronted with our male disgrace and obscenity in public.

But Wayne didn't let go of me, he went one step further and put his arm around me, cuddling me, holding me, in a friendlier gesture when we left the cinema.

'That certainly was something,' he said as we walked up King Street, his arm draped over my shoulder, pausing under three pendulous balls to look in the pawnbroker's window that said *Money Lent*. A window that featured behind it tennis rackets, cameras, golf clubs, jewellery, private items people had hocked in some vain belief that this act of sentimental sacrifice would get them out of debt. I had seen some of our own lodgers walking out with such items on rent day, coming back after a successful transaction empty handed.

'Well what do you want to do now?' he said, again pausing in front of another shop, a framer's where a print of Turner was on display, *Slavers Throwing out the Dead and Dying*, or was it *The Fighting Téméraire*? Featuring a sea and sunset whose blues, pinks, yellows and cyan taken from my watercolour paintbox were better, I thought, than the real thing. Nature's originals.

'I don't know,' I said. Because other than make love with him, I truly didn't.

'You want to go into town, to the beach? Your choice.' Maybe the Turner print suggested something.

'Both,' I said, thinking that if I picked both somehow the time we had together would be prolonged – that this day, where he and I were wed in unconsummated friendship, would last forever.

'Well, why don't we?' He said. And we boarded a bus marked Circular Quay, the 422, the 423, maybe the 426, on which neither he nor I had to pay, because Wayne recognised the driver as a colleague, and flashed a gold pass at him. A pass that allowed us to go past that fearful place called the University where gargoyles and griffins on the roof ate young boys for breakfast. Ugly creatures but sort of intellectually beautiful, since they knew everything, having read all the books in the place.

A gold pass that allowed us to go past Grace Bros and its roof that held two crystal balls rotating on bayonets. Ushering us past the church belonging to Saint Barnabas', protecting us from the scary news always pasted on its billboard.

Until we wound up in a place I'd never been to before called the Botanic Gardens but which was in fact the Garden of Eden. Maybe even the lost city of Atlantis, if that city was ever governed by happiness. We strolled down by the water's edge looking at ferries that today are the same as they were then in the seventies, the sixties, even as they were in the fifties. The timelessness of whose green and yellow livery would have absorbed like a sponge the stares of other youths in the throes of love or of homosexual discovery, blooming bigger than any blossoms contained in this park, whose balls and pricks must also have been full, thicker than those fat, inflated trees Wayne said were 'bottles'. And then he pointed out to me a flower which to this day is still my favourite, called *Yesterday, Today and Tomorrow*. It was as white and as purple as the bleaching agent mother used on the sheets. All the while never letting me go, protecting me from everything evil in Australia, not the slightest bit fussed about what other people thought of us. In fact, much like in the movie house, the way he held on to me was so natural, so masculine, so unashamed, that somehow his very grip forbade like an order what I'd heard many people feel towards homosexuals. Revulsion.

**13**   I remember him holding me in this fashion while he pointed out suburbs I never knew existed that gleamed with a low afternoon light. Kirribilli, Balmoral, Mosman, as well as what I knew were Scylla and Charybdis, though he called them the Heads of Sydney. I felt as if he and I were like those idyllic lovers you see on anniversary cards from Hallmark, framed by sunsets, even though I'd never seen that company feature homosexuals.

'Don't you ever come down here with your olds?' he asked.

'We never go out of Newtown, unless it's important. I thought all of Sydney was the same.'

'No,' he said, 'it isn't. Although maybe it should be.' Leaning over to accommodate my height, giving me a faint kiss on the neck as if he wanted to smell perfume, my youth, my young maleness, giving me the slightest and quickest kiss to show that from now on he would adore me.

'We don't have much of this back home,' he said, recovering himself and looking out again at the Bridge and Sydney.

'Much of what?' I asked, hoping he meant me.

'Harbour. Water. Just lots of sand, red earth. You know, the colour of beer.'

And he started to tell me stories about where he came from. About his homestead, his grandparents, with me instantly recognising that he described the place I saw in his snapshots that reminded me of the Gobi, except he kept calling it 'the Bush' as if it had a capital letter attached to it, or the Gibson, which I knew was different. Telling me his family were once drovers, people who were a bit like migrants except they never went overseas, though they kept moving about and instead of suitcases used cattle.

He talked for a long time, telling me about sheep as well. About droughts and floods, about shearing, about the dogs he loved that his father disgustingly and melodramatically forced him one day to shoot, to make him unafraid and masculine. Then he asked me if I liked these stories about, 'the Bush', or if I'd heard similar ones before. Asking me whether he should shut up, saying I should tell him when to stop if I got bored. Perhaps not realising that would be never. Casting a spell over me with his beauty, with his voice, his eyes, much like that gladiator's net, making me long for him to either kiss my throat again or to let me feel his sword.

Then he went quiet as if out of steam. As if he knew he had all too quickly seduced me, not just with his looks but with stories that had enslaved a kid imperceptibly, making whatever future humiliation I might suffer in his hands not only desirable, but necessary.

'Come on,' he said, noticing my beguilement. 'I get sick of gardens, let's go to the beach. There's still some light. Do you like the beach?'

'I've never been,' I said, which was true, I hadn't. Only to swimming pools.

'Where were you brought up,' he said, 'in a cave?' I

## medea's children

wanted to answer 'yes', if he meant by 'cave', a bathroom, a laundry, an old house, a crumbling suburb. Alone.

And so we went to Bondi Beach where I said I didn't have my cossies on. Where he said it didn't matter, no one would know the difference between underwear and cossies on a kid, while they wouldn't care what a bushie like he wore. Taking off all his clothes except his underwear, putting them down on the sand as a towel and mattress for us to lie on. Stripping off quickly to catch what was left of the sun, a process I imitated, placing my clothes like his on the silica between the flags. In front of what's still there, the Pavilion, the beat I was many years later to visit, and *Mr Guido's Gelato*. With me cuddling up to his chest, with its largish erect nipples. He still with his protective arm around me as waves smashed and crashed on the shore unable to come up to Wayne any closer. Unable to abduct him, to steal him from me, their sound just fury and jealousy.

It was so warm there on his chest, which unlike the chest of my previous boys was hairless. But though I loved being there, I regretted how the hot sun and the blueness of the sky took energy away from him, sapped his desire to tell me any more stories about his background. The blueness of sea and sky sufficient silent entertainment, instilling in us, in me, that calm, quite elation you feel when you realise you and the universe are neither separate, nor equals. But identical. One body.

And though I did want to put my hand down his jocks it didn't seem appropriate. What we were doing was sexual enough. As if again, this would have spoiled the mood, would have been another one of those 'over-articulations'. So I enjoyed it for exactly what it was which I can tell you was perfect homosexual love and attraction. I mention these words without shame because this happened before they were bastardised. Before they went out of fashion.

True, lying there on his chest I could see many other handsome men and boys. Most of whom were like him – Australian. Beautiful young Australians I hadn't seen before, with bodies that made them look as if they should be starring as slaves or as protagonists in their own gladitorials. But all of them combined were ugly as lepers compared to he on whom my head rested. What they had in their Speedos, that clung to them so tightly and wetly, was of only academic interest which I filed away for some future time's reflection.

Maybe, just maybe, after all this time of searching among my boys I hadn't realised the truth of who I was and who he was. Perhaps I'd been wrong in thinking that my previous boys had been Ulysses. Maybe I was this person, because I felt intoxicated by Wayne with his unworried freedom, feeling in my ecstasy that he was Calypso in Bondi.

But the sun did start to go after a while. A small wind like a siren announced the cool of a southerly blowing away our idyll, its low whistling sound, though obtrusive, like music. Wayne heard it too, saying to me, 'I'd better get you home. Your parents must be waiting.' Getting up and putting on his clothes, covering up his magnificence. Making me wonder why he and I couldn't be forever entwined together, either on a beach or at home like those figures on Attic vases, destined to be resplendent in nudity. Eternally.

**14**   There was silence when we got home, when Wayne and I entered the dining room. My father, mother and brother were all seated, not having eaten, as if they decided not to take a forkful until Wayne and I returned, as if they knew the exact hour. As if it was expected. They did look up from the table as we walked in, sullenly noticing that I had a bit of a blush, the beginnings of a tan from my exposure to the sun. A colour that looked odd, strikingly gold amid the long yellow shadows of our Newtown terrace. Then they bowed their heads again, embarrassed, as if they knew that our entrance from our excursion to the movies, from the gardens and the beach was not an excursion at all. But the first act of what was inevitable. Our betrothal.

'Please,' my mother said, using one of the few words in English she knew. Indicating telepathically to Wayne that though our betrothal was a depressing thought because I might soon be lost to the family forever, she would not stand in the way of true romance.

'Please, Mr Australia,' she said indicating a place at the head of the table the way she had once indicated to him to accompany her up the staircase. A place my father now vacated, choosing a seat next to Wayne on his right, a position that was less illustrious.

## peephole

'Great picture,' Wayne said to break some of the ice.

'You like?' my mother asked generously and incautiously and touchingly, using the last two words, the last two bullets in the clip of her English vocabulary. But she wasn't referring to the movie. Even if she had understood English she wouldn't have responded. Because mother now seemed irrevocably deaf.

She meant did he like moussaka, which she piled on to his plate as if there were no tomorrow, as if the others were not going to eat any, as if it had been made only for him. Making me think that she really didn't care if the rest of us starved, became bones and marrow, as long as Wayne was surfeit.

'No, that's too much for me. Thanks anyway,' Wayne said, having the decency not to take all the food away from my family's mouths.

'It's delicious, I'm sure,' selecting with his country politeness a portion from the server everyone thought was appropriate. But then while we ate in silence, he said the oddest thing. A thing that convinced everyone at the table we were no longer in the company of just another boarder, another of my lovers, but with an emissary who promised fearful change. Upheaval.

'Mighty fine son, you have here,' he said, referring to me, slapping me on the back. 'Do anyone proud to have him.' Forcing me to blush red, not with shame or embarrassment, but with pride. A statement that made my father and brother nearly choke but which my mother may have understood from the context because she began to cry, almost inconsolably.

'You okay?' Wayne said to her, getting up from his place at the table and putting his arm around her. Something no one else would have dared do regardless of whatever was distressing her.

'I didn't mean anything.'

'Okay, okay,' she said, appreciating his gesture but pushing his arm away from her. Rising, clearing away the plates from which we hadn't even finished eating, leaving the room, leaving us there where the fluorescence burned the room white, in some ugly, modern, last supper canvas. Perhaps feeling betrayal.

'Gee, I didn't mean to upset her,' Wayne said to my father.

'No worry, mate,' my father said as if it was not Wayne's problem, assuring him it was not of his creation but a private grief in our family, a problem better left undisturbed. An emotional Gordian knot incapable of being cut by strangers.

'She just gets carried away,' my brother said, then, changing the subject away from mother's outburst. 'Hey, do you like football or cricket?'

'Both!' Wayne answered. And to everyone's relief they rambled on about scores and heroes, in an idiotic conversation that I was glad took the limelight away from my sobbing mother and from what they all knew. What they all feared. That soon, Wayne and I, if not granted the status of betrothed, would consider the thing that would shame and make outcasts in perpetuity any Greek family. Elopement.

**15**     But I misjudged my family because they got over their initial astonishment easily, treating my friendship with Wayne over the following weeks adequately, neither complaining about it nor encouraging it. Seeing it for exactly what it was. An asset. And I wondered what it was that made me think they would react so negatively to our association in the first place, perhaps just fear built up over so many years of containment. And Wayne was fair to all of them too. Sometimes when I was busy reading, he would even play with my brother although it was never anything more than cricket, or football, hardly the real ball games I knew he reserved for me.

We went to a lot of pictures then, in the city in cinemas that are not there any more. To see films no one can remember, in the days when they handed you picture books like theatre programs to explain the complexity of what you were about to see (which was always simple).

Sometimes we would stroll through the Haymarket and look at all the shops shut tight like fortresses valiantly defending Australia's laws against Saturday and Sunday trading. Shops that pulled and locked birdcage bars against their plate-glass windows. Maybe this was because on weekends, they, like our President, were also scared of some Hun or Vandal invasion. It gave the city an unhappy feel particularly if it was overcast. But this too I treasured, as it provided the perfect black and white backdrop for the colour of my happiness, accentuating it and amplifying it. Sometimes Wayne and I returned to our first magical meeting place in the Botanic Gardens.

Sometimes, if we were feeling particularly brave, we would take a ferry to Manly. A suburb named after him and his beauty. Always holding hands or with his arms around me, something they only did in Asia and Northern Italy as I found out ten years later.

I confess I did begin to ignore my parents a little. Finding whatever it was they wished to say to me insufficiently interesting compared to whatever Wayne said, even if it was only, 'G'day', or 'How ya goin'?' Something I'm sure they noticed but which they successfully ascribed to common parent-child teenage resentment. Boxes of sweets mother placed in my room, of Turkish delight or anything else she made to give me a Greek sugar hit during my study, I sent back to her confectionery shop. Her *zaharoplasteion*, the kitchen. Untouched and unopened. Even the picture books about Greece and its heroes and Gods who were forever hiding, raping, arguing or abducting each other in high mountains which she purchased because of my interest in such things, I now found staggeringly dull. Inept, compared with what Wayne told me, during our walks and excursions, about Mount Kosciusko and the early explorers. Most of whom I was certain would have looked like him or could have at least passed as his brothers.

And school, now that it was high school, was more interesting, because some of the other boys in the change rooms on PE days got stiff in the process of disrobing. I could tell, from the way they saw me notice them tumescent, that they

peephole

must have had vaguely similar experiences in their own bathrooms. Maybe not in terraces, but in semis, made of weatherboard or fibro. Perhaps in flats or bungalows.

My high school was different from the elementary school I had attended, being all boys and selective, thus taking in boys from a wide catchment area. Ostensibly because they were clever. But I think because, like me, the education authorities had a way of knowing who were homosexual or at least likely to develop this way given the right amount of exposure. And nourishment. A selection process that was essential if, in the best of British tradition, Australia was to remain a country as corrupt and as much of a male gaol as originally intended. Like the British House of Lords, all the kids at this school called each other by their surname as if that represented an estate passed down the generations. Or a dukedom.

And throughout all this time, I didn't sleep with Wayne although I wanted to, something which drove me to distraction but which in a way I appreciated. Because it showed that he respected me, that he wouldn't be just someone else using me as a filler whose bags were packed for departure. Although there were times when he led me or teased me close to the act. Sometimes kissing me on the neck, making me feel as if I would explode with frustration, in a great ejaculated white puddle that would splat wherever we were. In the cinema. In the park. On the pavement. But, I knew from the wisdom of women's magazines I sometimes read in barbers' shops or at the milk bar, such as The Weekly, that this process of denial was essential. Particularly if you had found he with whom you would share your life forever. Such sexual thrift meant that when you finally did it, then all the other orgasms you had previously, all the other experiences compacted together, would be nothing. Cheap flashes compared to the two-day orgasm you would have as a reward for this virginity and patience.

Like a tiger denied food but knowing up ahead would be a T-bone, I waited.

**16**   If I am to be completely honest, I must admit that there were things about Wayne that I didn't like. For instance sometimes when he kissed me on the neck I could smell a very sweet and acrid aroma of beer and cigarettes. Things I knew were essential for his private entertainment, to relieve 'the pressure' as he put it, but which (like occasionally when I smelt it on my father) I detested.

And because we were only in the early throes of courtship and hadn't signed copyright documents granting each other exclusive access and rights to each other's body and company, sometimes he went out with other Australians. 'Mates' he had from the 'buses'. Going down The Rocks he had pointed out to me, where he would do a lot of this 'drinking'. If it preceded one of our outings to the beach or a movie it sometimes left him short with me. And irritable.

Once, when I complained, he lashed out saying, 'What would a wog kid know about drinking anyway?' Tearing himself gruffly away from me, calling me that which from anyone else's lips would be unforgiven, but calming down, coming back into my arms contrite, almost teary with apology. Making me feel sorry for him, making me promise to myself to never level such criticism at him again, no matter how much his beautiful mouth smelt. I convinced myself of the power of the truly incorrigibly smitten of one thing. That this occasional breath of Dionysus when emitted by him from now on would be nothing less to me than the vapour of one who had tasted not beer but ambrosia.

But there was something else about these little arguments I liked which puzzled me, because when he became contrite and came back into my arms it made our affair so much more tender and loving. Making me wonder what it would be like, how much sweeter making up would be, if he did the thing which in my imagination curiously turned me on. The thing my Greek parents would never do to their children. The thing that my teachers at school would rather die than exact on me. Their soft pet and protegé. If he hit me. Violently across the face. In a rage. In an ungovernable temper.

So on future walks I began to goad him, to tell him things that were untrue. Telling him that I wasn't especially interested in his stories about 'the Bush', wherever that was. Telling him how all Australians like him should really be in prison, where they belonged. That the place he called 'Home', was nothing. Just an empty desert filled with kangaroos, most of which were better looking. Lying. Telling him that for me the only real place with great people was in a country peopled by Gods and heroes and stories that stretched back several thousand years. A country that had places called Parnassus, Arcadia and the vale of Tempe. Not stupid sounding places like Dubbo. That Greece was paradise – rich and fertile with more in its mists and gardens than gum trees, flies and stockmen, until enraged, he did the thing I wanted.

He slapped me with a backhander so hard it echoed

round the harbour. As if all of Sydney had heard it, making a sound louder than the shriek the Ionian Sea gave off when a passing sailor told it that the great God Pan was dead. Forcing me to sink to my knees in pain more exquisite than honey, drunk with the tears that I emitted deliberately for this humiliation. Until he stopped, breathing hard and regaining some of his senses, picked me up, swearing that he would never do it again. Telling me that it was my fault for baiting him, for telling him he was inferior – something he had heard all his life and one of the reasons he had abandoned his rural selection. He was almost on the verge of tears himself, but he held me tighter, saying that he would never ever do it again and how sorry he was, asking me to forgive him. Saying that, maybe the problem lay in the fact that he and I had both held out for too long against what we wanted, desired and needed. Saying to me close to my hair and throat, in my ear, asking really, if I still had any of the gift he had given me. The Brylcreem. With me saying, 'Yes, I think so,' with him saying, 'Bewdie!' He had hoped so.

**1 7**   He took me home and undressed me in his room, something I let him do motionless. Instructing me to lie down on the bed where he spread my legs and dropped his shorts to the floor. Grabbing a fistful of Brylcreem, oiling my bum, the cream an ointment to salve our argument, to put an end to it forever.

So we tried this most delicious of all things that he called 'fucking' but which I with precision called penetration. Although before we began I did turn over and say 'no', wanting to look at him first entirely naked. Which I did, marvelling at my powers of control which for so long had resisted this easy consummation, sucking on his dick before he applied more Brylcreem on the biggest one I had ever seen. Certainly the first I'd met that was circumcised, cut at the tip as if some greedy and envious doctor had wanted to keep a bit of it for himself. As a scalp or a trophy.

Sucking on his nipples that were as stiff as his erection, tracing the lines in his stomach made by muscles more knotted and sculpted than a maths diagram. Until, unable to contain himself, he entered me, not slowly and softly, but with one thrust, violently. Making me scream in pain that subsided with a strangulated pleasure. In, out. In out, with me preferring the ins, wishing that I had more space, less tightness to give him. He said things to me that though angrily breathed and dirty, were finer and more lyric at that moment than any school poetry.

Saying how he liked fucking my tight wog arse, my little Greek bum with his roo meat, perhaps lacking some originality in his passion. I say this because I had read similar exhortations about 'roo meat' and condemnations about 'wog bums' on toilet doors, but which coming from his mouth, as our bodies kept up their combination, turned into a sonnet. A stanza of sex and splendour.

Until my mother came in unexpectedly, holding aloft some sweet or other she had concocted, seeing me on my stomach, while Wayne inside me coincidentally ejaculated. As I did on his Reckitt's Blue starched sheets, the moment my mother's pupils and mine met for their last engagement.

They clanged together, in amazement and anger. Like the swords of Arthur and Mordred, in the death throes of battle before they impale each other. The final conflict. But she spared me her blow for the moment, not saying a word, leaving the room disgusted, just setting down her tray and shutting the door on my slatternliness, my virtue forgotten.

'She sure timed that right,' Wayne said withdrawing and laughing.

'I guess so,' I said, exhausted by our passion and cuddling up to him, both of us wet with sweat and the culmination of what we had, from the moment she introduced him that afternoon, wanted.

**18**   I didn't see mother the next day. It was as if she was hiding from me, from the embarrassment and anger of what she saw. She seemed to always be in every room of the house I wasn't in.

If I were in the living room, she would be in the dining room. If I were in the kitchen, she would be in the laundry, almost as if she didn't want our paths to cross, a small and pathetic attempt at ostracism. Until late one afternoon I thought the only thing that I could do would be to confront her, to confess that she did indeed see what she saw, to tell her that's the way it would have to be now. Out in the open for all of us. Not hidden in bathrooms, whether private or communal, regardless of their quality. No longer would it be in the distance through peepholes, or as slides against a sheet in the laundry.

But that afternoon she went further. She seemed to have locked herself away in her bedroom, I mean my parents' bedroom that sometimes operated as her study. She often went there if she wanted to be alone, pursuing what she hated doing on the side for a quid, seamstress and sewing repairs. For neighbours whose worn-out clothes required her skills as couturier.

I could hear her sewing machine going, the machine obviously working overtime. It made more noise than the helicopters Australia had in Vietnam which the defence forces used to show off in the evening news bulletins, courtesy of that much more important Gadget Man, Roger Climpson. It sounded like thousands of them whirring.

'Mum,' I said, knocking on the door. But no answer. There couldn't be. She wouldn't have been able to hear either the knocking or the sound of the sewing machine despite its satanic engine, so I looked through the peephole to see what it was she was doing. And I saw that she had taken out her wedding dress and was making stitches and adjustments to it. Desperately. As if it was something she had to do for a deadline. As if the future of our house, her mind, her sanity and our safety depended on it.

She was pushing it with her hands through the bridge of the machine as if it were a tree being wood-chipped, sewing up a seam that she had opened. Her hands moving backwards and forwards like a speedy masseuse. She seemed to have a wild look about her, her head bobbing up and down with this activity, with the exactitude she exerted in getting this dress just right. I don't think I'd ever seen her wedding dress before. It had probably lain in one of the blue steamer trunks that we kept in the basement and dining room covered with lace doilies. There, precious clothes shipped from Greece lay, with their pungent aroma of naphthalene. And I couldn't figure out what she wanted it for, and why it was so imperative that the garment be restyled now.

Until she saw me peering at her through the peephole, when she switched off the machine, daring me not to look away from her, holding my line of vision. Dragging the dress with her, coming and opening the door on to my voyeurism.

'Well, come on,' she said rudely, pulling me in. 'It's ready.' Dragging me by the arm with the force I'd seen her only use once, many years ago when she evicted a minor, pretty, but completely unpaying tenant.

'Come on,' she said, 'get your clothes off. It's finished.'

'Mum, what are you talking about?' I said, fearful of the rage that was in her eyes, at the tightness of her lips and teeth that announced she had lost her reason.

'You want to act like a girl,' she said, 'then you will be a girl. But no child of mine is going to be an Australian *poutana*. A slut.' First slapping my face with disgust then putting the wedding dress over my head, pulling it down to the floor until it covered me completely. While I just took it. Standing there too amazed by this idiocy.

'Mum,' I said. 'Calm down,' but she didn't or couldn't. She was too busy fitting the veil over my head and pulling on the white silk gloves over my arms and up to my elbows. Fussing and primping with the frock as if the church had already been booked, as if the photographer and priest were already waiting.

Then she stood back to admire her handiwork, relaxing for the first time, her face composing itself, assuming more of a human stature, and for the first time smiling.

'There,' she said. 'Now you can look at yourself in the mirror,' turning me around to show me off in the fake rosewood dresser. In which, despite my heart's pounding, I could see that I was beautiful.

True, the dress was a little antique, not modern, being a heavy lace affair, flouncy rather than streamlined. But I suppose it had to do with the fact that she had worn it, and her mother before her, and before her. Possibly farther back in Greece than Miss Havisham.

'What do you think?' she said.

'I like it,' I said, but she just looked at me as if seeing herself, still not hearing, bending down to my level, putting her head close to my neck the way Wayne did. Not to kiss me, but so that in the mirror shaped like a chocolate heart ice-cream, both she and I were framed – mother and daughter. In a Valentine.

I *was* beautiful. Honestly. Although the tension of the situation, the oddness of it made it difficult for me to breathe. She had over-altered it, made it too tight, in the rush of her enthusiasm. Maybe it had additionally shrunk in the wash because I couldn't smell any naphthalene and parts of it were still cold and damp. In its bodice where my boy's chest rested against the bra, a certain wetness.

'Now, go show your young man,' she said. 'Your husband-to-be. And tell him to get ready,' leading me by the hand out of that bedroom, to the staircase, to make sure, I ascended its tall length. With me taking looks back, stopping every few steps, but knowing I would have to go forward, because she would not leave the base of the stairs. Guarding it until I had complied, until I'd vanished, out of her sight, all the while giving me encouraging nods, to dispel any trepidation or cowardice I felt in the process.

**19**   'Wayne,' I said softly, knocking on his door, holding the train of the dress as far off the floor as possible feeling ridiculous.

'Wayne,' I said knocking again, saying his name the second time louder. Knowing he must be inside, because I could hear the shower running. Knowing that despite the absurdity of all this I would have to explain it somehow, hoping he with his common sense and casualness might have an answer, a solution no one had thought of.

A third knock was unnecessary because he opened the door wearing only a towel. He looked at me, with astonishment, with bewilderment, before shaking some of the water out of his hair, like a Labrador at the beach. Then he burst into unrelenting laughter.

'What's all this?' he said. 'You going to a fancy dress ball, or something?' Holding his side lest it split with more laughter.

I did look funny I have to admit. And I liked being able to entertain him even though now it was very hideously at my expense. So I smiled and laughed a little as well, saying, 'Do you like it?' waiting for him to flatter me, to say he adored it.

'Like it?' he said. 'I love it. You look beautiful. What are they going to call you, Maria?'

Then he paused and recovered a little before asking. 'When's the party?'

'There has to be a wedding, before the party,' I answered.

'That's right,' he said. 'I forgot.' And with that he went into more howls of laughter which this time I found somewhat less endearing. Less pleased with myself that I'd entertained him. Probably because not only had he not paused to ask me the real reason for my get up, but he had gone one step too far, treating me as a figure for mockery.

'It's not that funny,' I said.

'It is where I'm standing, mate,' he said, noticing my irritation. But he took his arm away from the side of the door and stepped back into his room allowing me to enter, which I did carefully, picking up my train and bringing it inside with me. Arranging it in a loop fashion on his bed where we had done the deed, before sitting on the bed, my voice like my throat, thick and heavy, with the burden of explanation.

'They think we should get married,' I said. 'In fact, they're arranging it.' A statement that perhaps was the over-articulation he had feared for a long time, a statement that he now found not in the least bit amusing.

'They're out of their minds,' he said. 'Blokes don't get married in Australia. Something's wrong with you wogs,' again using that word whose syllables were like scalpels. 'And even if they did, we'd be a laughing stock.'

'They want you to get ready,' I said, almost on the point of tears.

'Ready for what?'

'Church,' I said, immediately imagining how even more handsome than his now near-nudity he would look in a tuxedo.

'You're as mad as your deaf-post mother,' he said. 'You're all nuts. What's brought all this on anyway?' Then a pause before he answered his own question. 'Don't tell me . . . Because we were fucking.'

He could be so cruel at times, making me issue a few unsuppressible sobs beneath the veil.

'Well, let me tell you son,' he said, making matters worse 'and you can tell your crazy wog parents I said so. There ain't goin' to be any wedding. No engagement. No betrothal. Nothin'. Get that? I've fucked lots before. Don't go thinkin' you were the first. And they weren't all wogs, dagos and spics. Some were boongs, and chinks and some . . . even real Australians like myself. But none of 'em were stupid enough to think for a moment we'd marry.' He kept pointing at his chest as he said this. Particularly when he said 'real Australians', and he looked at me with the same enraged look mother had when I first saw her sewing.

I said, 'I think they'll kill you if you don't,' causing him to look at me astonished.

'Now, hang on, mate,' he said with great seriousness, 'we've had a lot fun but don't get me involved in some peasant brawl. I never made any promises I never . . .' Trailing off before he had a chance to say . . . that he never loved me, which I knew is what he wanted to say. Sparing me the enunciation, the pain, the flight of these last two javelins.

'What am I talking about,' he said talking to himself, 'this is screwy. I'm gettin' out of here.' And he took his suitcase down off the dresser and started throwing the few possessions he had inside it. Putting on his shorts and shirt quickly, as if they were chainmail he now needed as protection against the wave that had finally come. What our President had feared. The invasion.

'Please don't go, Wayne,' I said, clutching at him and trying to pull him from his suitcase, while he pulled more strongly back.

'We won't have to get married,' I said, 'I promise. Please don't leave. It was a joke.' Tearing away my veil and realising that indeed this had all gone too far if it was forcing him to leave, to abandon me forever.

'No mate,' he said, turning around and giving me one last look. 'It's too late for that and it's no joke.' And then without sensitivity, 'Take care of yourself.' Flying down the stairs, leaving me there in the room with the dress I was now trying so hard to remove, devastated.

**20**     Between the sobs and the hysteria of the situation I couldn't get the dress off. It stuck to me. The zipper in the back too far away from my fingers to allow me an exit. So I had to struggle like a snake trying to slough off its skin to remove it, breathing too hard, desperate now to get it off. Hearing, between the rustle of the dress and my sobs, Wayne's heavy footsteps down the tiled corridor, then the door opening and closing. The wind releasing with his departure the death knell sound, just once, of that large Victorian doorknocker mallet.

I was on the floor at this stage, thinking that somehow I could wriggle out of it from this position when I realised there was something else going wrong with me this day. Something quite serious that possibly had nothing to do with the dress, my mother, or with Wayne's frightened and ugly exit. I was feeling unwell, sick to the stomach, as if I were about to throw up because I had eaten something that was disgusting. My stomach, my heart and chest were slashed with pain cut by a million razors.

'Mum,' I yelled out. 'Help!'

By now unable to get off the floor, let alone out of the dress. Feeling dizzy, feeling myself about to pass out not into unconsciousness but to an early grave. Managing to get one glove off my arm, making me feel a little bit better, then another, which slowly delayed my transit into painful coma. Getting one shoulder out, calling for help again as I slithered down the hall, realising as I yelled that she wouldn't be able to help. Never. Because she was the one who had caused this. Realising too late what I should've known from my picture books, from her power and sorcery, from the films that I saw and the culture I came from, from the wetness of the bodice. This wedding dress she had given me was never meant to be used. It hadn't been washed. In fact for revenge, to kill me, she had it poisoned.

She had dipped it in her witch's cauldron, but not in the imperial purple. In snake venom and hemlock that I could now feel seeping into every inch of my skin as if etched and chiselled into a rock by acid.

'Mum,' I yelled out again, but I knew she wouldn't be able to hear, the poisoning, like her deafness, preplanned. A way to shut out the truth. A matter of fate and predestination.

'Mum,' I yelled one last time, more faintly, but it was pointless, she knew what I was going through upstairs. How Wayne had deserted. She knew, because I could hear through the echo chamber of our house her laughing, shrilly in a wild animal cackle. At how her feminine wiles, and her wisdom gleaned from antiquity, had finally undone and reduced her son, the way millennia earlier a poisoned shirt had undone invincible Hercules and the Centaur. The dress was a net that any moment would kill me, without the necessity of a *coup de grace* from a trident.

Her voice echoing in my ear, a mockery, as loud as all the other mockeries I had suffered at school, in the street, from Wayne, and at *The Herald*. So I did the only thing I could do, I stumbled and slithered back into Wayne's room, into his bathroom.

Turning on the water, I lay on the floor of the shower, hoping the cold water could leach out some of the poison from this garment. Could cleanse me the way waves and foam restored the modesty of Aphrodite near the shores of Cyprus. I lay there under that spout for what seemed a long time. Perhaps eternity. A sodden mess, but I think I was right to do so. The water having a calming effect on me as I correctly predicted. Neutralising some of the poison, taking it out of the dress and into the drain, to the sewer and Hades, easily. As if the water had been a handsome young man leading out a spinster at a charity ball. In a dance.

And after what seemed about half an hour, but in fact could have been two years, I began to regain some consciousness. Some sense of purpose and action. Rising, holding on to the soap ledge as if it was a vine in this quicksand of infanticide and humiliation.

Finally, I was able to unzip the dress. I cast it off as if it hadn't been just a clinging poison vest but a wild animal, a beast whose neck I'd finally broken. Standing wet and pruned in that lonely room, weak, unescorted and naked. But alive. Ready for the next task or battle. In my life's assignment.

It had been close I grant that. Very close. And as I looked at the dress still under the shower spout, I saw it was just as much a matted mess, as the toilet paper and tissues I used to scrunch up and discard after I'd masturbated. I must admit, seeing it like that, like an afterbirth, it looked rather harmless, pretty, not to be thrown away. Worth being dried, and altered. For preservation.

I dressed slowly and casually. I put on long trousers for once, arming myself with a T-shirt Wayne had forgotten in his haste And though I felt weak, I knew downstairs all the powers of my mother would now vanish, because, older with the protection of my own Gods, I would now confront her.

So I went downstairs, not angry. Not even seeking redress or vengeance, almost with a sense of dignity, knowing it was she who would now have to collapse on her knees, to beg for forgiveness. Going past the temple of her kitchen, arriving at the inner sanctum, the propylaeum of her bedroom door. Which was open, taking away any reason for me to stare through the peephole to see what she was up to.

Only to see her unashamedly naked, on the bed, delirious, not with Wayne, but with young Mr Maxwell.

He too was nude, his attaché case wide open like a chasm next to the bed, the *To Let* sign stuffed rudely and vertically like a licence plate in its mouth. The way his dick was in her, as they, in the midst of passion, oblivious to my needs, kept laughing, making insincere promises to each other. While they planned to make good their escape, after they had betrayed Sydney, the good people of Newtown and Australia, that they said didn't interest them. As they kept doing exactly what I'd been blamed for, and for which in future I would be cursed and spat upon. Not peeping, but fucking.

**2 1**     I had to escape, I had to get away from that house, from her and whatever she was doing. Otherwise she would kill me. Worse she would let me live – a form of death – by taking me with her. Away from Newtown and everything I'd loved. Away from Australia, the land of my dreams and sorrows. Away from any chance of ever meeting someone who could look like Wayne. Who could teach me to be like him – long and beautiful, swaggering and proud.

So I tiptoed away as if she and Mr Maxwell were thieves no one should confront, breaking into a canter down our Victorian hallway, knowing its echoing tiles betrayed my exit. Until I was out.

In the light, cascading swiftly past the Moreton Bay figs whose pitying leaves reached down from their unassailable loftiness to whisper, 'Run. For every God's sake. Run,' exactly what I was doing, hoping I wasn't pursued, because though younger and faster, her anger was an arrow.

I ran past the other boarding houses that immaturely I once despised, thankful they'd forgiven me, thankful they'd forgotten the insults I cast at them, my hurled paddle-pop sticks.

Now the houses were sentries, their presence marking posts of the increasing distance I put between her and me.

peephole

Until I was on King Street, the greatest boulevard in the world, built to accommodate the carriage of all emperors and victors. Leaving behind me in my flight my original temple, The Hub, and the milk bars, and the public bars that had affixed to their yellow tiles stained glass icons and posters of Wayne at the beach. Wayne surfing. Wayne wiping himself down. Wayne with a towel. Wayne horribly drinking. Smiling. No, laughing. Mocking me and my passage. As I flew past the hidden Laminex coffee shops where aged Greek and Italian men who sired similar women to my mother sat exhausted by that long ago effort. Playing sterile games of backgammon over tiny phials of a Turkish brew they prayed would bring restitution to their balls.

Until I was back at my primary school. Not so much to seek a safe haven, in a school I did not cherish, but because here lived the one thing, the one object that could save me from kidnap. From extinction.

The obelisk. The obelisk of the dead – Cleopatra's needle, smaller but in reality greater than the pyramids of Giza. The obelisk that had the names of those young men cut down as I was about to be, in graveyards, in foreign caves, on islands, in the place my mother wanted to take me. Anywhere. Across the harbour. To Chalkis. To Greece. The reason she had sold herself and our house to the enemy.

Breathless, I stared at the monument. And though only made of stone, its extremities blunt and polished granite, it seemed to recognise me. To regard me as suppliant to its power, knowing like the Sphinx, its sister, everything. Knowing I was humbled by its peculiar brass engraved magic. Bowed by the many Waynes it had ingested. And I'm sure despite its heart of stone, at that moment, in that instant, touched by my terror, it loved me. I stepped up to its perimeter, stepping over the tiny square iron fence spikes that guarded its rock-hard magnificence, and knelt in front of it. In front of all the names, which for just such an occasion in the last few months I had learnt by rote.

But it neither waited for me to speak nor did it move, being exactly what it was and what the lives embossed on it were – hieroglyphs of silent and deathly enduring Australian patience.

No matter. I knew what I had to say. It had been taught to me, to us in class, but with such fearful provisos that this chant never be used except in complete danger, *in extremis* as one of our teachers put it. Because to use it on any other occasion was blasphemy. At least that's what the Friday morning Baptist scripture teacher said, as he shouted.

Wrongly used, this chant would provoke fire from the skies that would burn not only the blasphemer but everything around him including the innocent – the very world he stood on. Worse, it would incinerate everyone, like a giant version of the flame throwers the Germans used, in the First World War, the weapon that burnished the names of Australians on the obelisk's side. A flame applied to them while they were still alive and beautiful. Lonely. Caressed in the trenches only by thin military wool.

Finally my heart regained its pace. Neither startled nor racing, it was calm, almost as if begging my mouth to begin the invocation that no one should ever vainly utter. The only spell that my teachers and my years had taught me to value.

I began when the street was quiet. So no one could see me worshipping what they would have mistakenly perceived as an idol. I began, the words at first soft and

## peephole

inaudible since I was sobbing with fear and trepidation at what I might unleash.

'Core of my heart my country,' I said. 'Her pitiless blue sky ...' Then, certain I had the next line correct, 'With sickened heart around us we watch us cattle die,' but I was unable to finish the stanza due to not knowing what came next, realising too late I'd rushed it and something was seriously wrong.

Perhaps I hadn't learnt it properly, with the intonation required. Perhaps some of the words were misplaced. Sickened, I began to fear that instead of summoning up help I'd summoned up the uncontainable powers of the damned.

A great wind blew up as I stared at the tip of the obelisk, apologising to its silence, 'I'm sorry, I ...' I said, just as it conjured up a great storm for my mistake. For my ignorance. For my having dared to defile the nobility of this chant and its sentiments.

Lightning rent the sky, veins whiter than the iced almonds I'd been given at christenings, which I too could've dispensed with my own hands, if I'd been given what I'd hoped for. A wedding.

Frantic to appease the heavens and the obelisk's indifference, I began again, 'Core of my heart, my ...' but this time the stanza grew even shorter. The words were lost in my throat, the way words and even syllables were lost by so many martyrs when forced on pain of the stake, that stick shaped like a cricket stump, to tell lies about Popes they should've worshipped and prayers they should never have revised.

'Core of ...' my sentence whispered shorter still. With me ever more fearfully uncertain, as the wind, now gale force, wrapped the suburb tighter than a strangler's stocking, in a pincer movement from the north, the south, the

## medea's children

west and the east. Rain flooded down like bullets from a Gatling gun. In this my own Gallipoli.

It was a wind and rain so strong I thought buses would be overturned, vehicles flung upwards like the cars I once called Matchbox, against the grey brick wall of heaven.

I even feared the obelisk itself would be uprooted, that it would fly first around in a whirlwind like a dervish then straight as a spear against all enemies, wherever they may be found. Even in Europe.

But nothing flew up into the storm. Nothing. Despite its force.

I remember the coldness of the rain and the wind's intensity as I left the obelisk. As I retreated from the school. Away from the obelisk's shininess. Its flat, oily sides in the wet, equally tearful and crying. Going back down King Street, a street which now neither victor nor captive could presently negotiate, a street barely visible through the unbleached sheets soaking it.

Retracing my steps slowly, as the wind pushed me back, the only sound besides the tempest's howl that same mocking voice of Wayne in the posters. His male and hearty loudness was in direct competition to the elements. Maybe it was the voice of the most feared man in Australia coming from transistor radios kept on the counters by shopkeepers. A talkback radio host, I believed was master of the courts and of justice.

'Hello, world,' he said, laughing. But I think he meant goodbye. Forcing me to retreat to the only place I knew, my home, even though down Edwina Street the other boarding houses, their sentry duty of encouragement abandoned, and egged on by Wayne's cackle, similarly mocked me for failure.

They made me walk a gauntlet, my court martial done, in agreement with my mother as to my doom.

**22**   Wet as a soldier's sock, I entered the hallway, listening for moaning sounds, any sound that would tell me what she was up to or whether she and he had finished. But I heard nothing, other than what the tempest provided outside. Nothing that could be construed as signs of life. Of death. Of sex. Not even the sighs I was used to. Of melancholy.

I could say she then sprang upon me, from a hidden door or corner, snakes and flames coiling from her hair. Or with a sword and a shield with which to crush me, like a lemon.

I could say she assumed the might and mantle of what was rightfully hers and what she had for so many years been denied. But no such terrible apparition came, and when with the last bit of courage I managed to go to her room, there was no one there. The sheets seemed undisturbed. No sign of father, brother, or even her lustful suitor, Mr Maxwell.

It was all as it had always been, pristine and untouched. The metal chests, the steamer trunks she had once brought with her, still covered with doilies and still proclaiming in white war paint on their side *Piraeus-Sydney*.

Until I got to the living room, where my mother, father and brother, even Mr Maxwell, all of them were listening attentively to President Santamaria. Mr Maxwell stroking a five-year-old girl who was next to him, maybe his daughter or his youngest sister, who blew bubble-gum in my face. Wrigley's Spearmint. Letting me know who she really was, not Mr Maxwell's daughter or young sister, but what my Baptist scripture teachers called the Handmaiden of Nebuchadnezzar. No, the Whore of Babylon. In common day modern parlance, a slag. Just itching to replace me.

President Santamaria was speaking directly to all of them from the screen, saying it was time for people like us to leave. At once and forever. Even though our skin wasn't yellow, nor our clothes red, the colours he most feared.

'There, you see, even he says it,' said Mr Maxwell to my parents, supported by the highest voice in the land. The blue light of the TV illuminating him like a saint as he took out money bundled up like bricks, the same as those once used to build our house. Our bathrooms.

'It's all there, you can count it,' he said, lighting a cigarette the way they did in movies to celebrate a drug deal. But she didn't count it, nor did anyone else.

They just smiled at Mr Maxwell with trust, with devotion, as if he were a friend. Being more experienced, though, in the craft of deceit scientists call deduction, I could see a shape in his trousers which showed he still had an erection. A big one that he lightly touched and stroked with his free hand, pretending his outfit was too tight, too badly made and constricting. Perhaps wanting to come again. Quite literally. But none of them could see this, only me as they turned and stared and smiled to convince me that though wet, I was not abhorred. And never forgotten.

'Come,' my mother said, extending her hand to me kindly, beckoning me. '*Ella*,' in Greek, making me go over to where she was sitting, making me sit next to her where she stroked my hair with a dry cloth. With compassion. Asking me after she had done this, after they had all bid Mr Maxwell '*Adio*,' to take out one of the valises, *valitses* in Greek. They lay in a neat row as if they were museum pieces, artefacts depicting the relics of refugees, lit up in an exhibition window. She asked me to take the lightest one and place it on the street like the others. Handing me, once I had finished this chore, two small pieces of wood, a nail and a hammer.

She said to me, 'Now nail up the door,' which I did according to her instructions. Making with the two planks and the nail that intersected them the sign of the Cross. To forbid trespassers. Or people like us until Mr Maxwell or his designates took up residency. Or perhaps to ward off those vampires which came to feed in the fig trees that had become my companions so briefly.

But she was more her old self during this carpentry ritual. Neither scary nor threatening. She was like anybody's mother, as we stood outside, in Edwina Street waiting for the rain to cease, waiting for a car to take us to the airport.

Then, just as the rain and wind I'd caused eased off, I made another error. The worst so far. I said unbidden, not even asked my opinion, five words tainted by what my teachers in school said was the greatest crime against their person. A crime chatterboxes committed when there was silence in the class. The teacher's silent drumroll of wisdom that preceded a recitation about a sheep dog with dynamite in its mouth. I committed the crime of *impertinence*. And worse, the felony of *insolence*.

I said, 'I don't want to go.' A statement at which even my father and brother cringed. A statement to which my mother replied, 'Repeat that.'

## medea's children

Foolishly I did.

'I don't want to go to Greece, I love this house,' goading her now that I'd gone too far. Needling her the way I'd needled so many of my boys to reveal what they were really made of. Forcing her in a fury to grow five times her original height, ascending like a cloud into the heavens, the way the God of war, Ares, did when slashed at by Diomedes. Dragging us after her, laughing like a madwoman. Dragging us across the freezing sky, the way Elijah once did to find happiness, the wheels of her chariot propelled by Bunsen burners I had seen in science class.

Dragging us past clouds and above rain, to lands I'd never seen, fringed by palms and rice fields in all the shapes we learnt in geometry. Until all but exhausted by her will and determination we arrived, descending to Greece. In whose air and by whose waters we would not meekly or with self-hatred sit down and weep. But a place where we or I would grow. Like Mr Maxwell's blood-engorged erection.

Where I swore I would return to that house, to Newtown, to Wayne. If he was lucky. Swearing by all the Gods in the clouds we'd passed, all the Gods of Olympus. Even if it took a lifetime. Knowing if I didn't that the house would come back and haunt me. Calling on witnesses to my oath and promise, witnesses disguised as passengers milling around the airport.

book two **body remember**

**2 3**   In Athens, which looked every bit as bad as it did in my slide collection, there were processions and parades in the streets on our arrival. Conches and trumpets were blown to drown out my protests. And there were escorts with festoons and fanfares to greet us. Pennants, banners, ships unfurling red sails of welcome, more decoration than I had ever seen. Surpassing even the bunting of used car lots on our Parramatta Road. All around me, millions of shrines disguised as 1960s apartment blocks from whose terraces and balconies hung bright pelts deceitfully shaped like underwear and bras.

'What are we doing here?' I asked in the cab. 'This place is weird.' Seeing on both sides of the road funnelling us in carriages and chariots strewn with garlands and olive branches as well as naked young men on colts taking us speedily to the centre of town. Where all of Athens waited anxiously to see if the prophecies were true. To see whether, despite her crimes, she to whom they had promised sanctuary had returned.

That's the way I saw it, but my brother said the parade was just heavy traffic and that the colts I was staring at were Lambrettas and Vespas, motorcycles owned by Greece's leather-clad young men. Maybe he also said that the Athenians were actually relatives – aunts and uncles who'd rented chambers for us, what he called a flat. A series of rooms all on one floor lacking what our Newtown home had – different levels, staircases and passages.

These relatives, horrible flatterers really, were showing mother the many rooms of the flat. Its marble hall. Its long terrace overlooking the temple of her rival Athena, as well as the city and Mount Imitto's. A mountain covered, like the rest of the city, by incense that fools mistake as smog. Seen from a balcony that was nothing like the one in our Newtown terrace, a balcony that had corner drains, so burning oil could be poured on people trying to scale its battlements.

'It's beautiful here, just beautiful,' Mother said. Which it wasn't. No one daring to say anything different. Everyone scared of mother, because now she was in Greece, her powers had grown immense. As if replenished and renewed just before touchdown. Maybe by the refresher towel the stewardess handed out. Maybe by the money Mr Maxwell had given her. Making all of us, including my aunts and uncles, immediately defer to whatever it was she needed. All of them advising her hastily when she opened her mouth as to where she could get her magic ingredients. A stove, a fridge, a washing machine. Her infernal tools of trade.

They were just lucky that on this first day mother kept her dark plan, whatever it was she really wanted, in check. Pretending that the flight from Australia had weakened her. Saying she was grateful to Athens and her people for the welcome, the refuge, but that she was tired, and needed to rest.

'I'm worn out, worn out,' she lied, staring at me who disbelieved her. I knew she was lying because it was obvious that with acclimatisation and confidence she would soon break jet lag's adamantine chains. And then, not the dress rehearsal we'd been through, but the real show would commence. Maybe father was aware of this too, because he enrolled my brother and I in a Lyceum, to keep us away from her. For safety. Saying, 'You'll get to like it here.'

Me, saying, 'I'll never like it here, I want to go back,' and already plotting this.

Father saying, 'If your mother doesn't like it, we will. We'll give up this flat and go. Now cheer up. Give it a chance.' Just to give me hope.

Sending us off to the Lyceum which was very much like a private American school, a place where the spawn of equally fearful mothers studied. More a fortress than a school. Moated, no . . . protected by the fact that real Greek kids weren't allowed to attend. By the fact that Greek, the local language of spells, wasn't used in class for instruction. Or correction. Only English. A Lyceum defended by armed guards who stood at the entrance.

'Here at this school young man,' the principal who enrolled us said, 'we have the highest standards,' looking at me askance. As if someone had sent him my sexual report card. 'Our motto is, ever onwards and upwards.' As if talking about an erection he didn't seem capable of.

An American-British school, full of kids in regulation Levis, instead of the Australian college greys I preferred. A school housed in a free-standing old mansion nothing like our terrace house. Its garden dense with plane trees and cypress trees.

A large driveway built for parents who drove limousines rather than for immigrants trudging around Newtown on foot. In the grounds, there were also willow trees that hadn't been chopped down to make cricket bats. The actual house having a vestibule with sweeping stairs leading to tall rooms whose ceilings clung on to chandeliers, rather than to round fluorescents, rooms that had parquet rather than beautiful lino. The walls pasted with pictures of assassinated American presidents and Greek revolutionary heroes instead of pub tiles and posters of people like Wayne. And antiques for hallway furniture, junk from a bygone era completely unrelated to the laminex wardrobes I loved.

The teachers, unfortunately not Australian but American, kept saying, 'Move it, move it. Move your ass.' As if this school were a military camp. Worse, I could tell they were renegades whose rebellion in the USA was viciously put down by a secret weapon called The Draft, both the reason why they taught here, and the reason why they'd emigrated. And Englishmen, philhellenes from Oxbridge who wore sandals with socks, men who made tea more often than geishas.

'I'll make you a nice cup of tea,' they kept saying to each other like mad hatters.

There were only two Australian teachers, both of whom disappointed me. A hairy ginger teacher called Terry and a bald one called Bruce.

'G'day mate,' they said to me, but I knew they were kidding. It was so obvious they were rootless, like me, homeless, travelling the world, taking great clumps out of their lives that neither tonics nor toupées could restore or conceal. But I didn't like Terry and Bruce much. Probably because in class they said disparaging things about Australia, calling it barren and remote. Forcing me to speak out and say, 'I don't agree with that.' Compelling them to reveal to the students what I already knew – that they were talking about themselves.

Teachers who taught us in this fortress, in its drawing rooms and conservatory, in its attic that reverberated much less than the Jenolan Caves. A school where kids, mainly from the diplomatic corps, chatted about obscure countries and even more obscure facts.

'In Burma, they have these really great teak bungalows . . .' Big deal.

'In Paraguay, there used to be these amazing houses whose roof slid . . .' So what? I knew the places they talked about could never replace my boys, let alone Wayne and our house.

Then the senior class I was in got marched out, told to fan out under the willow tree at the front because it was too hot inside, over near a fountain lacking water. Which we did, while I tried to think through what father said about how if mother didn't like it here we might go back. The class splayed out, like a bunch of Southern Belles and Northern Beaux, listening to one of the rebels, I mean one of the teachers, talk.

'Now, the American Civil War wasn't just about black versus white. About slaves and abolitionists. We know now it was complex,' the history teacher said, holding in his palm the cob of a pipe he used when not allowed to fondle his manliness. He looked like the swimmer Mark Spitz.

'Tara,' someone said.

'They all wanted to live in Tara.'

'No,' he said. 'Tara doesn't exist. That was in the movie.' God they were dumb. 'Who can tell me what it really had to do with?' he asked, but I would have learnt a lot more if he just stood there and took off his clothes. To show me what Americans were made of. Whether their substitution for Wayne, like this school and flat for our house, was enough.

'Okay,' the history teacher said. 'Let me give you a personal example,' becoming more interesting by digressing to stories about his childhood. About what it was like to grow up in Kentucky. Which I understood to be like Newtown but with more trees, except its parks had blue grass rather than green, to match the blood racing through its thoroughbreds. This teacher talking about how he and his family grew up in a trailer park which sounded cramped and dull. Insufficient space for lodgers. But I guess he was trying hard to make some parallel between his life and the conditions of blacks.

Which made me like him, as the day wore on. Deciding to, because he had a strange accent like mine, a voice that seemed to whisper that an imperial edict had also banished him, the way I'd been banished from Wayne and our house.

'You, fresh face over there,' he said to me. 'You will have to work hard to catch up to the rest of the kids,' not knowing I was advanced.

At times a shadow covered his grey eyes, hiding a secret like divorce. Maybe lost love. Sometimes his eyes doing the opposite, shining, showing you they were on a quest for that elusive opal no one has yet found in either Coober Pedy or Lightning Ridge – the philosopher's stone. A quest begun by ancient Greeks when their bodies became useless for sex. A quest less specific and more foggy than the one I'd already embarked on – to get back to Newtown, if not to the man I loved.

A quest – I mean a caper (in today's terms a *scam*) – that

required what my *Superman* comic books used to call *henchmen*, or cronies, what boring people call friends, careful who I selected for this honour. Choosing them at school by avoiding jocks playing basketball who might put me through the hoops.

'Hey, new kid, wanna do a bit of dribbling?'

'No, thanks,' I said. 'Not right now.' But I meant not his kind. At least not with him. Selecting kids like me – simple and powerful whom I could spot as descended from gods. Kids who might have an equally lurid personal history. As well as the same interests – men and literature, men and cinema. Boys who might have lived or still live in a similar house. Maybe I just mean other gays.

And I saw some. Yes I did, in that killing field called the playground, recognising them because they disdained cockerel wrestling and bear-baiting, what the Phys. Ed teachers called 'games'. Deciding to win their friendship with my greatest weapon, the two syllabled word 'hell-o', which when I was young in that Newtown terrace, I had used to excellent purpose.

'Hi, yourself, what brings you to Athens handsome?' A lanky boy with bad skin called Mark said, standing next to a pair of twins who looked like emaciated, bleached cherubs. Other than bad skin, Mark had fair windswept curls that made him look ravished. And a duffle bag, that I later found out was only full of vaseline and cigarettes.

'Usual stuff,' I said. 'Treachery, betrayal.' While the other two, the bleached twins who introduced themselves as Don and Tom said together in unison, 'You mean your parents,' and then just laughed. Mocking me for being held hostage.

'Take no notice of them,' Mark said. 'They're English

assholes. Think they're better than us. I'm from Ohio myself.' Mark as proud of this as I was about the limbo world I wanted to return to. Actually, Ohio sounded from his description like the outback. The place my primary school teachers talked about, where they said the Spirit of Australia lived. A spirit I imagined to be a lonely spook that wore a white sheet with slits for eyes, like Casper, the friendly ghost.

'Cheerio, Mark, and you, precious, whoever you are,' Don, one of the twins said to me. Then to Mark, 'Don't keep him to yourself. He's part cute. We rather like his homesick hangdog looks, don't we Tom?'

Tom saying, 'Rather,' as he left with Don.

'Wise guys,' Mark said. 'Don't let them get you down. Ever since they got told they looked like Michael York in *Cabaret*, they've been insufferable.' Mark lighting a Winston he took out from his duffle bag, because in our American school you could smoke. It was really relaxed that way, they didn't even have school assembly. Me seeing in his bag its companion, the vaseline. I think he noticed me staring as he ruffled through it.

'You the new school stray?' he said, exhaling.

'Could say that.'

'Could say lots of things. Like you are gay, right?'

'Guess so,' I said, even though this was definite.

'Hell, great. Come over my place tonight and hang out. Knew you would be. You have that far away look.'

The invitation thrilled me, figuring he might have a similar house of his own. A den. A lair. But when I got there I saw no such thing. Only an apartment like we had, a small one though. *A-part-ment*, a word I now bitterly understood.

Forgiving Mark, first because he was being friendly and second because I hoped hanging out meant we were going to compare size. A contest I graciously wanted him to win. But all Mark wanted to do was lie on his bed and talk, which was boring.

'About what?'

'Books, what else do fags talk about? And sex,' much to my relief, 'but first I wanna hear about you. Shoot.'

'Okay,' I said, telling him my sexual history straight out, figuring there was no point keeping it secret from my peers. Maybe just showing off.

'Well I'll be,' he said, through my tirade. And other things like, 'No kidding. Woweee. Don't blame you for wanting to go back.' Lying on his double bed smoking dreamily the thing Americans invented years ago that they now despise, cigarettes, whose blue wafting smoke couldn't fool me, because I knew what they really were. Burnt laurel leaves. The type incinerated at oracles by women called Sybil before they tell the truth. The plumes of which Wayne used to expel like mustard gas over the rail of our balcony. Me, stopping the story before Wayne's departure and the sale of our house, so as to give it a happy end. I think I said, 'Wayne had to go away on holiday, so we left the house with family friends.'

'Well, if that don't beat all,' he said. Jumping up off the bed. 'To think I missed out coz I was brought up on a farm.'

'So, what do you reckon?'

'Reckon?' he said. Not understanding.

'What do you think?' I simplified. 'How should I go about getting back?'

'Hell, I don't know. Why don't you just enjoy this and

medea's children

live in the present?' Which was depressing. 'Ask Don and Tom, they might have some stuffed shirt English asshole way of getting there. Come on, I said we'd meet down the square,' meaning Syntagma, the centre of town.

There, lit by neons from the nearby airline offices and the *son et lumière* reflection of night time Athens, Don and Tom sat alfresco, on deep vinyl armchairs, at the café nearest the toilet. Tom using a make-up compact to both admire himself and check on men entering and exiting. Maybe more on himself than them.

'Who's a pretty boy then?' Don said. And, 'How good of you to come. Been for a constitutional have we? Needing a little *boomsen* perhaps?'

'Don't be an asshole,' Mark said to him again. 'Let up will you Don.' Then to me, 'Well go ahead, ask them.'

'Ask what, my pretty?' Don asked.

'Nothing,' I said.

I don't know why I didn't want to tell them about my past, about mother – who she really was and what she was capable of – since I'd sort of just told Mark. At least a rose-coloured version. I mean in their own stilted English way, Don and Tom were trying to be nice. Nor do I know why I didn't mention Wayne to them, or Newtown and the bathrooms that no longer exist. I honestly don't know. It was definitely the sort of thing they would've liked to hear, and as Mark said, they may have had valuable English information about how to return. And realistically that was the whole point of me acquiring henchmen.

Maybe I just didn't want to give away any more, in case it got back to mother simply by being aired. Certainly, I didn't want to tell them about my previous successes. About me being a film director already, as well as the world's greatest poet, figuring they'd think I was lying or worse, boasting. And having tried all these things I suppose deep down I knew already what I was – a mythmaker. A maker of my own gods. A teller of tales, a fabricator, more accurately or simply, as vulgar people put it, a liar.

Maybe I'd learnt a bit of what ruins so many spinsters' lives – discretion. Not wanting to make myself sad again by raking over the personal loss of our house, my harem that had been so cruelly disbanded.

Also I didn't feel like asking them anything, since they were more obsessed with their looks. It was them doing the asking. Behind each other's back after each went to the toilet, who was the more beautiful, as if Mark and I were named Paris.

'You are, of course,' I said to each of them at different times. Just to win their trust. 'No, really Don has very good reasons to be jealous of you,' then to Don, '. . . Tom has very good reasons. I'd watch him if I were you.' Which made them contented. Made them relax. Maybe they weren't vain. Like all of us they wanted the elixir that made life sweet. Potions called Endorsement and Uniqueness, brews capable of dissolving asphyxiating bonds.

But they were friendly enough and there was a feeling in the summer night air that Mark and I, begrudgingly maybe even Don and Tom, my new cronies, were destined for greatness. Since we mainly spoke about careers that would see us living not in terraces, but castles and palaces.

**24**   'I have real talent,' Mark said. 'The type that doesn't grow on trees,' ordering a beer called Fix. He was telling us how eventually he was going to live on a ranch or in Malibu with an enormous swimming pool. After he became an actor.

'A star,' he said, 'to be accurate.'

'Absolutely. A star,' I confirmed, just to give him encouragement. Mark doing an impromptu rehearsal of an Oscar acceptance speech, thanking everyone who had ever occurred in his life, thanking me for my juvenile perception, for knowing he'd achieve this. Mark dismissing my criticism that his speech was too long, saying it was only courteous to include everyone who ever existed.

'If you don't, in Hollywood they'll just run you out of town.' A horrible fate with which I was familiar.

Don and Tom (naturally both) were going to be 'Artists actually. Don's going to paint and I'm going to sculpt,' Tom said, explaining between ever closer examinations of his compact, how when they graduated and returned to London they'd need to find studios large enough to fit their canvases. Maybe they meant their mirrors. Or male models, who would always be naked and inferior to them. London studios I imagined that would have to be bigger than my house and the studios of Warner Brothers.

'And what will you practise?' Don asked.

'I don't really know,' I said.

'Well where are you going to live?' they asked.

'That, I do know,' I said. 'But I'm not sure how to get there.'

Finally, after a third ouzo, melodramatically breaking down, uncharacteristically sobbing, telling them, adding a few lavish details I'd left out of my story to Mark.

'Dear oh dear, brilliant. No small wonder you want to go back,' Don said. 'That's a career in itself. Although if you don't mind me saying so, you do sound a bit common.' Which I wasn't. But I guess he just meant that in terms of class. The snob.

'Just a tad though. I'd be in tears too. No small wonder,' Tom echoed.

'But I'll be stuffed if I know what to suggest old china,' Don added, Tom saying, 'Ditto.'

'Perhaps,' Don said, 'you're approaching it the wrong way. Perhaps you should forget about this Wayne and your house for a while. Find a new man. I mean to say, there's an awful lot here.'

'Really think there's a right guy?' I asked.

'There is no right one,' they all said in chorus, like the Fates, laughing. Don saying, 'Darling, get on with it. Forget about the house, fab as it is. If you don't, the sweet bird of youth will just fly out the window,' a statement that filled me with dread. The sweet bird of youth sounding like a vulture.

'You'll be eighteen soon,' Mark emphasised. 'By twenty you're finished. Besides why wait to get back to Australia just to fuck?' Trying to horrify me, to shock me, which was unlikely. 'Anyway don't look so appalled, we just say stuff like that to be literary because we love old Tennessee, as you may have gathered.'

'Okay,' I said, 'you've convinced me. Show me what's so great about being here.' Thinking, 'well there might be something.' Being overly optimistic.

But all they did was take me cruising with them around the Plaka, going to louche bars frequented by extremely effeminate old Greek gigolos, and the millionaire ship builders of Greece, more commonly called tourists. Where Don said, 'This is much better than any old house.' Which wasn't true. Louche bars called The Mykonos, but more appropriately, The Why Not? The name of the bar already suggesting a line of legal defence if the cops busted it. Another called The Zodiac, possibly because our sexuality was governed by constellations affixed by the Gods. Bars run by fat men with half-smiles and winks, who made cryptic comments about our youth suitable to gangsters and extortionists. Merchants of real estate.

'*Ti mou kanoun ta pethia?*' How's the kids?

Shooting off to places I didn't enjoy, in the nooks and crannies, in the streets of Athens' cruel heart – nooks and crannies more constricted than the alleys of Macdonaldtown, where each man we met told us he was a gigolo.

'*Ime zigolo, mono yia hatziliki to kano,*' they said. 'I'm a gigolo, just for the pocket money.' Believing penury the licence you needed for sex. Finding more gigolos beneath the Temple that mother first gazed at with hatred on arrival, remembering how I once gazed admiringly at green and yellow ferries.

Boring me by taking me to their favourite bench in the King's Gardens, near the statue of Eros and his bent bow, under a pink street lamp I knew 'sputtered', because of my early successful dabbling in poetry. Deep in the heart of the Gardens where after midnight only the most valorous dared enter. Maybe the not-so-brave, because in those days there was hardly any crime, no teenagers with flick knives of whom to be afraid.

'This is the neatest place,' Mark said. 'Here you can pick up whoever you like.' Referring to young recruits from the armed forces hiding in the bushes, the bushes some sort of sexual camouflage. All I knew was that in my Newtown terrace there hadn't been such a need for furtiveness. Not until the end anyway.

Sitting on this bench like a bunch of crows on a telegraph wire waiting for a change in weather. Quiet when a shadowy male figure passed by our lamplight, astounded that youths like us were all in a row, happy to be easy pickings.

'Best behaviour now, he's about to come past. For God's sake, smile.' My cronies competing for the attention of such shadowy men, each of them vying for preference. Naturally Don and Tom thinking it'd be them. As did Mark. Me, utterly bored, too modest because of experience to offer an opinion until it was clear I was that night's temporary Helen.

'Well, go on, he wants you,' Don said, maybe to cheer me up. Oddly not wanting to disappoint a stranger. 'God knows why.'

Me complying, just to be agreeable, going with them and this man to his apartment in Kolonaki. It's a suburb that clings like a strangler vine to Syntagma's heart, unlike the way Newtown and Macdonaldtown spread around Sydney their golden rust. There, my cronies spun discs or smoked dope while I went to the bedroom.

'Hurry up in there, will you? Haven't got all night. Don't be so slow.' I could hear them through the thin walls.

When once I'd never been hurried. Perhaps they were admiring my escort's artwork, or his statuary pinched from an ancestral home. Statuary the guy I picked up claimed was real, classical, given to him by his family, perhaps by his own admirers, when he too could elicit trophies for being young. Me, finding both the sex and the apartment unsatisfactory.

So much so, that as the night came to a close, I was grateful to go home, promising to meet my cronies the following day, which was Saturday, just out of politeness and to see if there was anything else they could show me, because so far everything I'd done with them I thought dull.

A Saturday afternoon where we sailed into the toilet block near the Zappeion having to hide there because of a summer hailstorm, the heavens throwing down ice the size of Polyphemus's boulders. Trapped inside we fended off twenty men groping at us, holding us, trying to disrobe us to bugger us. Old fools who thought we were innocent. Slapping at overly impertinent hands, to show we still had discernment. Dignity.

'*Ase me,*' leave me alone, I said, what I should've said to mother. Me, relenting, allowing them to fondle me only because running out in the hail meant I would have been stoned by the heavens, the way Arabs stone adulterers. The way, no doubt, mother would've wanted me humiliated. Until the hail stopped and from this pit we could emerge knowing that we'd prevailed in this battle of young gods against Titans. A cinch for people with experience.

My cronies, though noticing they weren't convincing me about anything here, getting more desperate to beguile me.

'You're in quite a state. Come on. Need a bit of shock

therapy.' Taking me for more cruising around Ommonia Square, the square of Harmony, the poorer end of town where The Britannia Coffee Shop and The Kafeneon are. Coffee shops that still serve coffee and sweets to every new generation of homosexuals, but not the way they did in King Street coffee shops with its lino floors behind beaded curtains.

'Now don't tell me you don't like this, because I won't believe it.' Me, thinking, 'Well, don't believe it.' Because I didn't. There was no comparison, although I must say Ommonia at times did appear to me a bit like Sydney's Haymarket, which was better, older and more dilapidated. In Ommonia our group gliding past added 'attractions', where Mark, Don and Tom showed me the real ropes. Not the yo-yo strings that so far had been my cautious and unsatisfying introduction.

Mainly more soldiers, sailors and village boys looking for work among the crippled lottery sellers, the pretzel sellers, and the kiosk vendors in their telephone booth-size shops, that housed more books and periodicals than the British Museum. But I didn't feel as if I knew them. I felt estranged from them. Curiously seeing them as foreigners.

My cronies getting desperate to convince me of the superiority of their Athens over my Wayne, my Newtown house.

'Wait till you see this,' they said. 'You, in particular, will love it.' Taking me down some of the side lanes of Ommonia near Odos Athinas, strangely, to visit its heterosexual brothels, to look at proud boys glaring at doorways guarded by prostitutes. The scene rather than entertaining me, bringing back bitter memories.

'You don't know what it was like,' I said.

'Shut up about that house and look.' Boys who stared

silently at girls, smoking cigarettes in a dense semi-circle, a young halo of sex. Boys to whom we couldn't get any closer because of the invisible demarcation line drawn in the ink of pre-cum leaking from their penises.

My henchmen longing to trade places with the women. Purely to give the prostitutes guarding the doorways a rest. To shrink that circle. To erase it. A consolation for them, but not for me.

Each weekend the same routine.

'Ready?'

'Ready.'

The legs that supported my cronies, against the wall where they waited, leaving it, returning to earth as I collected them from the street corners near their homes. I don't know why I bothered. There was nothing they could advise. Most of what I did with them I found sleep-inducing. But I persisted.

First Mark. Favourites first.

Then Don and Tom. Picking them up, the way old ladies collect unfed cats. Our group like Xenophon's *Anabasis*.

Maybe just a fag gang. Supposedly vulnerable but in reality, wolfish, predatory, moneyed, of whom the quarry, Athenian youth, should have been afraid.

But it wasn't all bars they tried to beguile me with. They used other devices to teach me to forget. Like the movies.

'Now if you tell me you don't like films,' Don said, 'I'll get violent.'

'No, I do,' I said, 'but it depends on the picture,' thinking of gladiators I'd seen with Wayne.

But being sixteen and high-minded, they didn't go in for tasteless Hollywood films, opting for the supposed European masters. Nothing to do with the toy boats, tridents or nets made in *Cine Citta*. All of us going to retro houses and art houses, to see the old chestnuts that have titillated critics, *Satiricon*, *La Strada*. And an Italo-German biographical film about us called *The Damned*, in which we were portrayed, I thought, accurately.

'Why is Helmut Berger wearing a suspender belt?' I asked. Or was it Charlotte Rampling? But they just said, 'Wait till the picture's over.' But I liked *The Damned* very much, particularly the end scene where the matron dies, when their house gets abandoned. The scene where she is lying back in an armchair – ghostly, looking at white dust sheets covering the furniture.

Occasionally at the climax of a movie, or at some orotund point, allowing ourselves to be pulled off, by strangers kind enough to warm our loins with their jackets. In respectable cinemas such as the Danaos or the Ilisia, that were surprisingly bigger than The Hub. Glamour parlours filled with the middle class who keened with respect at directors' names ending in *ini* and *onti*.

'*Thavma*,' women after the film kept saying. Miracle. '*Thavma*,' when in fact compared to what I had seen in films to do with Sinbad and Hercules, these were perfectly ordinary.

The cinemas were full of middle-class women, who would have liked to have Luchino and Federico over for an afternoon *Nerantzi* – the bitter green oranges Greek matrons shrink in sugar syrup, the way heads are shrunk by cannibals.

'Have one of these, darling,' Mother said, offering me one whenever I took a break from my friends and went home. 'Just eat a bit. You look a bit under the weather. You sure are

## medea's children

busy. Night after night. Must be enjoying it here.' Which was a lie.

Me refusing, not wanting to be poisoned again.

Keeping contact with mother to a minimum.

Going back out to see other films, the ones less favoured by acclaim, the ones that had entirely dispensed with sword and sandal. I mean pornography that we saw at the Kotopouli Cinema on Odos Athinas, where my cronies were the prize of its boisterous, boysy symposium. Films my henchmen liked but which bored me shitless.

'Wait till you get a load of what goes on in here,' Mark said. 'And I really mean a load. It'll make what went on in your house look like a picnic.' They loved that cinema because in it, the butch sat on the right with open legs, and the bitch on the left, or in the Priam's Tower of the Gallery, waiting for peasant-boy Hectors to pin them with thrusts to dishonour them in the unlit aisles and on the staircase where they collided. Their masturbating comrades cheering, since they also wanted their masculinity to be beautifully degraded, on uncleaned spoof-crusted carpets.

Me, watching the butch caressing, pummelling, tearing away at tight shirts already unbuttoned, refusing all the while to kiss, as if in their mouth and in their teeth lay their own home, the cave. The secret of their several thousand years-old passion.

It was as if our Athens by night was like a glass bottle emptied of wine, where aboard a toy boat we sailed beyond the safe and unsafe reaches of family. Across the beer froth and semen wave-crested Lethe. But I felt in these forgetful waters, no matter what they showed me, my Newtown house was incapable of bathing.

**25**   But I've talked enough about Athens and my friends, the cronies who tried and failed so miserably to beguile me with replacements. Enough. It's only to give a flavour and taste of what life was like in a city-state I'd been removed to, so far from Wayne and our Newtown house. A city-state that had seen, or rather invented, so many people like me. Like us. They were just school kids. What would they know? They'd been unable to suggest a single thing that would get me back. And as for what they enjoyed, all those places of sexual frenzy they took me to, I considered rubbish.

No, I decided to give them a rest. Decided I needed more senior servants to assist me. Maybe a teacher, an adult. Or both.

'Need to talk to you about the Civil War,' I said to the history teacher. 'A couple of points I don't fully understand.'

'That a fact?' he said, playing with his moustache, looking at me suspiciously. 'Okay.'

'I'll see you after class,' I said. When it should've been him giving the orders.

Deciding to have an affair with him. Perhaps not as dramatic as the one in the Newtown terrace, but equally scandalous since he was a married man. Scandalously appropriate for me, the outcast. A married man who dug up the souls of the dead that comprised so much of my life and that of my parents. A married man who went by the name of Archaeologist.

He was exactly that. An archaeologist, as well as an authority on the Civil War, teaching at the school while he planned a dig on the island of Paros. Apparently, like a child in a sand pit, he opened his dig, played in it and then closed it at the end of each summer. Putting his toys away for next season. Perhaps hiding whatever was unearthed of value so that grave robbers wouldn't destroy his handiwork.

I was sure he'd be able to help me, he'd know how I could get back to Newtown, either by plane, diplomacy or secret passages. After all, he wasn't a schoolkid like my cronies, but a grown-up. And I already liked the way he taught, his personal examples that were so sad.

'What did you want to see me about?' he said.

'Lots,' I said. 'Got a couple of questions to do with geography.'

'Anything I can do to help?'

'Remains to be seen,' I said. 'But you might have some suggestions.'

'Have you asked the kids in class to help you out?'

'Yes,' I said, 'but they drew a blank.' For the purposes of this story I will call him Archie for short, because of his career and because he was American. A man I finally seduced at Thermopylae where he took us on a school excursion. There I allowed him, much like Ephialtes, to betray the rest of the class by leaving them near a picnic ground, to take only me to the final steps of the Pass, to grab me (as befitted the spot) from behind. To wrestle me to the ground, to tell me that of all the statuary he had so far unearthed I was the finest.

Perhaps this happened at Marathon, on a different excursion, although I can't remember running away from him. But I do remember rolling about buried in the surf and sand, an archaeologist and a *kouros*, in a mock imitation of *From Here to Eternity*.

'You're really something,' he said.

'No,' I said. 'Everything,' just to excite him. Going back later to the class we'd left behind at the picnic ground who eyed us with suspicion. Shaming me for going off with him. Shaming me the way I'd been shamed before, me, the Greek-Australian hussy.

**2 6**   Like everyone else, Archie didn't live in a house, but in an apartment, but his block was one of the strangest in Athens. It was a low two-storey job, tattooed with bullet holes, situated on an unpaved street away from the prying eyes of pedestrians. The holes riddling the apartment block hidden from civilised society so people wouldn't know it was the result of the Second World War, more likely the guerrilla war between left and right that Greeks murderously fought and continue to do so. Even in their own families.

The yellow plaster-walled apartment block and the children who played around it giving the place the look of Newtown after a blitz. The street much like the painting *The Mystery and Melancholy of a Street*, by the other Greek master, of alienated fervour, the futurist, Giorgio De Chirico.

'Come on in,' Archie said, opening his creaky door. 'I want to play for you.' But I think he meant with me. As a prelude, playing music that was beautiful. On the piano. Music composed by Austrians called after werewolves, or by Germans named Ludwig.

'Sometimes,' he said, 'I feel as if I should've been born in Strasburg, rather than Kentucky. I've told you about Kentucky haven't I?'

'Yeah.'

'Sounds a bit like your Newtown.'

'You're catching on.' God I could be impertinent.

Anyway Archie liked playing because as well as being a teacher and a connoisseur of the souls of the dead, once upon a time he'd been a concert pianist. Had, that is, until the American government told him what I already knew about the other renegades, the other teachers, that like them, his knowledge of sonatas and fugues, the deftness of his touch might be best applied to a trigger. To be pulled in their greatest Opera House, Vietnam. A place where they had sent plane-load after plane-load of symphony orchestras, air-dropped with cellos and violas for one long but massive performance.

'Like that?' he asked. 'Got plenty more.' As if he were a comedian.

'Sure you have,' I said. Cheeky.

And while I listened to his tunes that I got to know so well, he talked about how much he had admired me from afar, in class. More recently and quite physically on the school excursion to Marathon. Telling me the very sight of me was what inspired him in the perfection of his renditions and his need for excavations.

'You're perfect,' he said. As if I were a piano piece by Beethoven.

Telling me he knew of my friends, my fellow gay voluptuaries, but, 'You're nothing like them – you're made of finer bone, and mettle, even bronze, compared to their iron.' Maybe he didn't like them.

'I know you're homesick and there's problems with your mother. Mighty powerful woman, from all reports. God knows you've told me often enough. But I really don't know what to suggest.' Agreeing with me, saying that he too was fearful because of her weapons, particularly the one he called public exposure.

'I've seen her, boy she's amazing.' Saying that for me he felt sorry. Explaining he was also powerless against her, and that the most I could do was wait for her decision to leave. 'Or maybe,' he said, 'just tell her you want out, confront her.'

'Confront her?' I echoed.

'Yeah, if you can't win her round. Confront her,' he said. Telling me he recently confronted his wife with his male infidelities. His wife saying she would divorce him, using words surprisingly modern for the time, words dug up by an Australian judge some twenty years later – words ending in *phile* and *esty*.

The way I confronted or rather submitted to him was usually at the end of a number of passionata, as he sucked me off, careful no juice should discolour his ivories. Those Orphean moments of sex, recalling me from the dead land of family, from Newtown and memory – recalling me for a season that barely lasted an hour. Teaching me the folds and creases of his body that, too, required pedaling. Piano. And forte. Before I sipped on him not greedily, but politely, since I didn't really like him. Was trying to use him. Unsuccessfully. Doesn't matter, he didn't know anyway.

Archie giving me the school prize if I recall correctly, saying when I protested that everyone would know why.

'Well who else am I going to give it to?' The prize? A book of *kouroi* I was surprisingly grateful for – at least it wasn't a book to do with ruins – even though I would've preferred an atlas.

'Yeah, okay. Have it your way. Thanks.' A book in whose leaves his own fancy had already pressed me like a dried Narcissus.

'But is that all I get, a book?' I said, spoilt since infancy.

'We can take a trip if you like.'

'I would like,' I said, as usual subtle but demanding.

'Don't get too carried away, now,' he said. 'I can't take you back to Sydney. They'll nab me for kidnap.'

'Yeah okay, fair enough,' I said, for the time being letting him off the hook. 'Where then?'

'Meteora,' he said. 'The monasteries there.'

So he took me to Meteora, to the monasteries perched high on rocks that the ignorant say are the apex of orthodox faith, but I know to be more than that, the pinnacles of male sequestration.

I say this because all I could see on these cliffs were corridors and cells, isolated and remote Byzantine versions of my terrace, structures where women were similarly forbidden. Anyway at night there, accommodated only by others with a penis, we listened to the sound of wolves baying below, maybe for me they sounded like dingos. The ghosts of Turks wishing to conquer and rape, demanding sexual favours.

'I love you,' Archie said by moonlight, that tired phrase that means so little if you've heard it too early in life and too often. Besides, I wanted him and the baying dogs replaced not just by Wayne, nor by strangers to the park, but frankly, by my house in Newtown.

'I love you,' Archie said again, as he and I, the morning after, watched basketloads of tourists ascend to this particular part of Heaven, not possibly knowing the importance of these rocks.

Me not responding, because really, like my cronies, ultimately he was useless. Any advice he'd given me so far had been a dead end.

His 'digs' though, I did enjoy, using a brush and whisk to find seal stones, merds and broken crockery probably rent asunder in domestic fights by ancient boyfriends. Showing me in his trenches, layer upon layer dug into the side of the earth where time – a creature more powerful than shame – had annihilated all the homes and houses that were beautiful and precious.

'See here,' he said. Was it on Paros? Or Naxos where poor Ariadne got so unceremoniously jilted, where he pointed to another layer, an embedded set of stairs, deeper and more soot-infested than the first.

'You can tell a fire has taken place because of the ash. Maybe even an earthquake.' Delightful information for anyone who has an interest in history rather than just a fascination like mine with young ancient Greek men. My preferred belief was that time had conjoined them in their houses, rather than buried with the noisy dirges of war, flood, fire, famine.

But I raised the appropriate amount of enthusiasm, which delighted Archie.

'Maybe I will steal you away, I can't bear it.' As if he were some sort of art thief (which he was) and I a forbidden export object of Greece's Department of Antiquities. A department that should've existed in the Antipodes.

Good flattery really. Enough to keep me and him amused. In bed, propped up on a pillow, usually after some feverish penile expulsion, he told me how when he was young he briefly became a prostitute after his parents threw him out.

'I kinda think they did me a favour.'

'Maybe,' I said. 'And maybe not.' Archie going on to say how he then went to live with one of my rivals, a famous poet. 'Not in a terrace mind you, we only have those in New Orleans, but a houseboat, near Alcatraz. This guy took care of me the way I'm taking care of you.'

'Yeah,' I thought, 'with verses. Stanzas. And lyrics. What I'm not really seeking.'

A poet who'd written, 'Howl'.

Maybe not him, but someone equally famous. Anyway, Archie liked reading 'Howl', to me, rustling the pages, clearing his throat, he would begin.

'*I have seen the finest minds of my generation* . . .' Something like that. I don't really remember. Didn't really care. Also for Archie's confession about having been a whore I had no sympathy. No more than I have for an old man at an Australian railway station whose skin drink and rage have reddened like a bottle brush.

To tell you the truth his confession about being a whore sort of revolted me. 'I find it sort of creepy,' I said, as if his life had been a horror show.

'What's creepy about it?' Archie said, defending why he had been so mercenary, charging for something I gave away gladly, out of desire and charity. As I did with him, to while away the time, to fritter the few remaining shards of innocence in exchange for advice that wasn't forthcoming. Advice that stumped him.

But occasionally Archie could be interesting, I'll grant him that, like when he took me to the island of Delos, to show me how the Athenian Empire was founded on threats and coercion, practices I'd suffered. I say this because Delos's temples were full of pricks made of stone, huge ones, like cannons. Some circumcised by time, others non-jewish, proud and erect. Looking at them in the Temple of the Phallus, I almost goaded them to release what this completely dry island didn't have; rivers. Surely they'd do that at the sight of me – the young satyr with his mentor, who flattered himself, like so many others, that he'd taught me.

And could help me return to innocence.

**27**     Back in Athens:

'One ticket for you, and one ticket for me,' he said, picking me up after school at some discreet corner near our apartment. But the ticket wasn't for Sydney.

Taking me to hear a lesbian singer, a remnant of the expulsion of Smyrna called Sotiria Bellou, whose manly voice, boozy Rembetiko singing and reputation are very much legend. A woman reputed to have done time in gaol for killing a girlfriend who threatened to leave her – an act Greeks view not with loathing, but admiration. I have to admit that for this ticket I was grateful, because I heard her sing.

'*San pethano sto karavi, pes tous pethane to pethi*.' (If I should die upon the ship tell them the kid is dead.) Which I thought she sang for me specially.

'And also, here,' giving me a Byzantine ring, one of a pair that he unearthed on a dig. A ring of agate and tin, trapezoid, a shape in which some sort of tiny scroll had become embedded. My first tribute in ages.

Don and Tom were a little bit jealous of this ring. And of Archie, as fitted their personality. Mark was wiser, viewing my affair with greater equanimity, even though he eventually came down against him.

'Personally I wouldn't fuck him even if you do think he

medea's children

can help you. He looks like that boring swimmer,' he said, but they were all curious, asking me to describe Archie's gonads, the hair on his legs (ours were still unshadowed), and what he liked doing after bouts on the piano, but when I did, they really lost interest.

'Is that all?' they said. 'Oh, brother.' They were so jaded. And try as I might I was at a loss how to make our fucking sound less catalogued and perfunctory, since it was. But enough of Archie, let me cover him with sand, to await someone else's exhumation. He was just another byroad. A pair of grown-up arms where I sought the solace of replacement. Maybe a copy. And anything he advised me to do was purely academic.

No, I just had to face it, the only one who could take me back to Newtown was mother. It was entirely dependent on her whims and will. Which were considerable. Mother the woman I'd been successfully avoiding by going out most nights. As well as most of her special food, like *Nerantzi*.

But one night I remember creeping home only to find mother waiting up for me.

'Where have you been all these late nights?' she said, accusing me of consorting with another woman in preference to her, saying that she could smell their sweet perfume on my clothes. What she called the cheap scent of hookers. Actually, it was aftershave.

'I have a good mind to ship us all back to Australia, where men, both young and old, are decent,' obviously forgetting what had happened in Newtown. But I didn't believe her, even though I was sort of thrilled to hear it.

In the meantime, telling me, 'Don't be late tomorrow night because we have to visit a family acquaintance,' someone she'd met while wearing her mortal mask. No, I'm wrong it was to a black tie Charity Ball the American School was giving. I reasoned, 'Well, she's the only one who can effect our departure, I'd better be nice to her,' showing up on cue the following evening, mother adjusting my bow tie, brushing lint off my tuxedo's shoulders, plucking at imaginary loose threads, making sure of the freshness of the gardenia in my buttonhole. I mean I had to put up with this, the way she manhandled me, treating me like a child, since I'd tried and failed miserably to find people who could help me.

'Now don't make a fool of yourself when we get there by drinking too much.'

'Have I ever let you down?' I said, refining my irony.

'Well, no,' she lied, ignorant of satire and other literary devices. 'But remember it's Mr Stavropoulos, not Mr Savouropolis. *Savoura* means rubbish,' considering her advice funny.

A Charity Ball where I was her lone escort, held at the American Club, in Kifisia. A country club like the sort found in Pasadena. Dining rooms, billiard rooms, saunas and gyms accommodating American accents that always made the past sound like 'pest'.

The ball ostensibly held to raise money for the school was in effect a corroboree celebrating American social superiority where a guest of honour spoke. A spy disguised as an ambassador, his stuffy dinner jacket no doubt hiding his bombs, and walkie talkie wristwatch.

Mother leaving me by the buffet table with strict instructions not to eat too much.

'Don't make a pig of yourself,' with more truth than she knew.

Just before she snuck over to the other ladies dressed like her, but in different colours, she was careful to replace on the waiter's tray any stray champagne flute or Martini glass I may have taken. I just wanted to ease the suffocating formality and ennui at this macabre gathering of deracinated Rotarians. Maybe Archie, Don and Tom, if nothing else, had helped me become sophisticated. I mean I wasn't going to talk like a kid forever.

Returning after she'd gossiped enough with the American women. To stand by me. Her man. As the spy, made some unctuous speech, about living in interesting times, talking about the necessity for us to dig deep into our pockets for the upkeep of the old mansion that housed our school, which he said was crumbling.

'We wouldn't want it falling on our children's heads.'

'No, we wouldn't,' I thought. 'Not much we wouldn't.' Bored by his speech which was about as original as 'a chicken in every pot', I guess essential though to this PTA/New Deal of self-interest.

'And now the band will play, *Begin the Beguine*,' the spy said. 'Or as my Australian mates say, I should be going.' A parting joke. With a parting glance towards me and mother. As if he knew us. To guffaws and heehaws of matrons and their escorts.

Mother smiling back at him, looking in her get up very much like some out-of-date Mata Hari. Taking my hand in her gloved palm, to lead me in the first waltz of scholastic philanthropy. Sometimes holding me close. A little too close. Dancing. Dream-like. Trance-like. With happiness. As if we were on our first unescorted date. Which we were. As if there were someone else she'd replaced. Saying in my ear, 'You don't like it do you?' Meaning both the ball and Greece. 'You think it's my fault for bringing you here. I'm only trying to save you from that horrid man.'

'What horrid man?'

'That vagabond.' Actually she said *Aliti* in Greek, referring to Wayne for the first time, being both archaic and insulting. Then more angry as if remembering, 'From those *alites*,' she added, using the plural, meaning our boarders, forgetting though how much she and I once adored them.

'You're the one who's turned us into vagabonds, *alites*,' I said.

'Nonsense, at least we no longer live in a *saravolo*,' a *saravolo* meaning a dump, damning our Newtown terrace. As usual lying.

'You don't mean that and you know it,' I said. 'Anyway, I hate it here.'

'And why do you hate it here young man?' *Neare mou?* she demanded.

'Just do,' I said, looking at the dance floor, the obvious betrayed, now that she'd brought up the subject. 'Look at these people,' I said, meaning the patrons of the ball. 'Corpses the lot of them. The dead are dancing with the dead.'

'I think it's beautiful,' she said.

Me answering, probably referring to us, with another fistful from my bag of poetry, 'The dust is whirling with the dust.' Then the couples separated and we stood side by side. Clapping, acclaiming the school band despite its false notes and tonal errors, her mood changing because I'd revealed myself.

'Do I always have to lead in everything? Can't you just enjoy this?' Maybe she too was regretting that during the dance she'd interposed third parties between us. Our house, a man – the trance broken, as she smiled royally at couples she obviously envied.

'Excuse me a moment,' I said. 'I need air,' escaping through the still applauding or gavotting crowd. Through the French windows of the American Club. Was it the Hawthorne room? I can't remember. To the colonnaded portico overlooking the garden where in the twilight I smoked a cigarette. Remotely. Without my crazy Zelda. In an exact replication of F. Scott Fitzgerald. Her old fashioned word vagabonds, *alites*, that defiled my old lovers; and *saravolo*, our house, ringing in my ears, as I looked at one or two boys my age huddled at the other end of the portico.

'How ya doing?' they yelled. Me, wanting to yell back, 'Badly.' I imagined them to be similar escapees from similar mothers, boys I wanted to literally divest, not from drill shorts and grey shirts, but from their tuxedos. From their starched white shirts and even tighter underwear. In fact from any garment that kept us from sexual jubilation. Feeling dizzy because of what mother said, fearing she'd keep me here in Greece, forever captive.

Don, Tom and Mark weren't at this ball. They hadn't been press-ganged into playing escort. And they didn't have to fear a goddess who hated *alites*. Probably because they'd never lived in a *saravolo*.

No, the other boys on the portico were ordinary kids from school, some familiar, others less. Although, there was one at the farthest end of the terrace whom I didn't know at all. A boy who wore dark glasses. He snapped a white stick into pieces as if it were a toothpick, not because he was angry as I initially thought but because he was blind, folding and unfolding his stick for amusement.

As I looked at him, I wondered what it would be like to have sex with him, with someone who'd basically have to fuck with you on trust. Deciding it'd be great.

'Enjoying the ball?' I asked, having wandered over to his side with a great deal of aplomb, putting my hand on his crutch in the pornography of double entendre.

'Jesus, am now,' he said.

'Let's enjoy it further,' I said, taking him by the elbow leading him down the marble stairs of the club into the garden near a group of cypress trees, those unfortunate phallic trees usually associated with funeral parlours. Pushing him rather gently up against the tree, saying, 'I can help you,' as he stumbled in taking off his jacket, denuding him in no time. Like a fig. The perfection of his now naked body making up for the flaw in his vision.

'Know who I am?' I asked.

'Yeah, I do actually,' he said. 'You're the Australian kid in Ancient History who's always talking about going back.'

'By my voice?'

'It's kind of sexy.'

As I nobbled his Porgy amid jazz groans of elation I gave as Bess.

And calls from mother on the portico, who screamed into the dark just as the blind boy came juicily, my mouth and throat absorbing spunk like Aegean sponges.

'Where are you? Come back this instant. They're cutting the cake. I know what you're doing you swine,' as I swallowed to prove I too was an *aliti*.

'You never change do you? Swine.' She screamed again into the dark suspecting what I was up to, probably galled that bringing me ten thousand miles had been a Pyrrhic victory. The exact response I wanted.

'I'm sorry,' I said to the blind boy as he pulled up his pants. 'I have to go. She'll kill me.'

'My mom's like that,' he said, buckling his black dinner trousers over his white wet underpants. 'She's a real shrew, but she lets me get away with more. On account of this.' Taking the snapped rod out of his back pocket. Asking politely, 'Put it together for me?'

Which I did, almost reluctant to give it back though, since I quite liked it, but doing so any way, allowing him to stumble away like a prophet who had tasted of all the sexes. Tapping into the tufts of the American Club's lawn a silent melody. Making me think that perhaps, like Oedipus in the classics, his blindness was caused by maternal demands and insistence. But I hoped he'd enjoyed what we did as much as me, since from what he said, he too needed a break from being exploited.

As my Zelda screamed into the dark, 'Where the hell are you? If you don't come back this instant, I'll make such a scene you'll wish you'd never . . .' I knew what she was going to say, '. . . left Newtown,' where she'd first caught me being illicit. Foolish really because that was a time and a place I considered perfect.

Compelling me to race back to the terrace. There she lurched drunkenly, slovenly, in her Mata Hari evening dress, still holding a cocktail, the strap of her gown slipping over one shoulder. Her shoes in the other hand like some flapper from the twenties, a starlet from *La Dolce Vita* drunk on the dregs of life's absinthe.

'Really should take you home,' I said, referring to our flat, but really meaning our house, trying to adjust the strap of her dress, trying to relieve her of the drink.

'Get your cotton-picking hands off of me,' she said, perhaps imitating some American hostess she'd overheard. 'You're not a man yet. You hear that? Just a boy. And I've warned you before.' But she meant this purely as an insult. Still not having realised what I was up to, what I wanted, possessing no insight.

Taking her home by cab, kicking and screaming. Handing her over to father who was there watching television. Giving me admonishing looks. As if it had been my fault, first for always taking solitary walks, and then for this, winding up in Greece and leading her astray, in this night's – like so many other nights – lack of tenderness. When in fact it was the opposite.

**2 8**   But the blind boy inspired me, his condition giving me an idea.

I thought, one more date, along with a little reality therapy (a really strong dose) might help, might be the thing that would make my return assured. Would make her snap back to her senses. Make her realise what we'd lost and needed to regain. So the next night when she and I were alone, when my brother and father had gone to visit some relative with whom she was currently feuding, I sprang it on her. The way the previous night she sprang the ball on me.

'We vagabonds are going out,' I said. Which shocked her. I don't think she ever expected me to take the initiative. I don't think she ever expected me to take the lead, as she said, let alone use words like *alites*.

'Where?' she asked, hung over but pleasantly perplexed, thinking I might be teasing to see how she'd react.

'To the theatre, to another *saravolo*,' I said. 'My treat.'

'But I don't like the theatre,' she said. 'I never understand what they go on about. I prefer what we used to watch.' Meaning *Divorce Court*. Maybe *World Championship Wrestling*, or what she and I were caught up in, *The Roller Game*. Maybe I was winning.

'Go on. Get dressed,' I said. 'This one I guarantee you'll

like.' Which thrilled her. I could see this from her flashing eyes, not caring where we went as long as it was on another date.

'Hurry up, we'll be late. Starts in half an hour.'

'Doesn't matter if we're late,' she said. 'In the theatre, the beginning's always much like the end.' And she went to the bedroom, taking out dress after dress that she loathed. I know this because I could hear her muttering, despite the rustle of so much fabric, that she had nothing to wear. I just hoped it wasn't a wedding dress.

'Wear anything,' I said. 'You're not the one on stage.' A statement lacking truthfulness.

'Well?' she said, coming out wearing a sombre black dress and pearls, twirling around. 'How do I look?' Clearly wishing to look more respectable than the mutton dressed as lamb Mata Hari-look she'd sported the previous night.

'Like a princess,' But I think I meant a Mycenaean queen.

And I did take her out, to the Herodius Atticus theatre built in the Hellenistic age by an eponymous merchant who was richer than Rupert Murdoch and the Aga Khan. An amphitheatre, built like all of them in a semi-circle, an onion cut in half, so people could cry at the climax. A theatre exposed to the elements, allowing whatever emotion and truth was portrayed on stage to climb rapidly to its patrons and instigators in the stars.

There were hundreds of people in the audience as if they feared this tired old classic we were about to see would never be performed again. As if they feared this ancient stone theatre itself was about to be pulled down, like my previous home and life.

'Do you know the name of the play?' Mother asked, settling down on a cushion placed on the stone seat.

'I know more than the name of it,' I said. 'In fact, I think I know it line by line. You do too.' But she found this suspicious. Maybe I offended her.

'No need to be rude,' she said. 'Don't expect me to know everything.' Which, itself, was also a lie. The lights went down and the spotlights came on to reveal a chorus with heavy make-up in the play *Oedipus Rex*, a play she, like me, knew word-perfect.

It was fascinating to watch this production, to hear it in almost the original language, and the passion with which the actors threw themselves into every gesture and word. But it was much more fascinating watching mother's reactions. She seemed to be in a trance, her lips moving, this time not to music but to the words, like a backstage prompter to a cast that has forgotten the text. As if the movement of her mouth gave them the power to go ahead. She bent forward in her seat with her hands held under her legs, craning, listening in rapt attention in case anyone left out a line. Maybe because of her incipient deafness.

Finally when Oedipus came out blinded, she burst into laughter, forcing him to look up towards her, towards us where we sat in the gods.

'Oh,' she said, oblivious to the irritation of those in proximity and Oedipus, just as the lights went up. 'I do like a good comedy. Don't you? Remind me tomorrow to take you to an optometrist. Have your eyes checked.'

Taking me by the elbow. Walking with me out into the street below the Acropolis, along Theseus Street, as blind as Oedipus to people who thought her a heckler and me someone who put her up to it for a bet. Then still puzzled.

'Please tell me,' she said. '*Pes mou, sas parakalo*,' using the plural and strangely, the polite form, as if I were an adult.

'Why did you pick that one? I prefer tragedies myself.' As well as something about Oedipus's poor mother and the indignities she had to go through. And how if she had a son like that she'd have him whipped. Convincing me more than ever why it is always important every waking hour even in our entertainments for us to reinterpret our myths, frightening me that my plan to make her come to her senses had backfired when she said, 'You know, if you and I went out more often, I would never want to leave Greece. That's a promise.'

**29**   Yes, my entire plan had misfired. To be vulgar, I'd really ballsed it. I'd thrown a net over myself from which there was no extrication. I say this because rather than showing her what was going on between us, that I needed my own life, my own love, things I could only have by going back, it confirmed my imprisonment. The play didn't cure her at all. Worse she started to treat me like a lover. In fact she started to think I was my father.

Honestly, it was as if she could no longer tell us apart, although in looks, age and temperament we were complete opposites. But she only did this when father wasn't around, when he'd gone to visit friends, his absence being the very thing that changed her. If my brother wasn't home this also made the situation and her confusion much worse.

It first happened one Friday after school, nearly a week after our outing to the theatre, when on softly opening the door I almost knew something was amiss. Not having time to brood on this preternatural sense because mother flew at me, throwing her arms around me. Giving me a big kiss and saying, 'I'm so glad you're back, darling. Come see what's for dinner.' As if she feared that on my own bat I'd escaped to Newtown for good.

Taking me into the kitchen where there was a roast, some *pasticcio* and *makaranoda*, my favourite. There, taking off her apron and serving only me food, since I was the only one around, she sat and discussed her day. Telling me how expensive she found Athens, and how if we'd made a lot more sensible investment decisions over the years, like buying more boarding houses, now we wouldn't have to count each drachma, or ever consider going back. Scary stuff. Saying,

'I wonder how the boys are, I wonder if they really enjoy it here. Maybe they'd be better off back in Australia, in boarding school.'

'Maybe,' I said, finding the thought of being sent back to Australia ahead of time, even if it was to boarding school, sexy. The word boarding eliciting this thought.

'We might've been too hasty coming here,' she added. But I knew what she was doing, trying to shift the blame for the decision, to share it with Dad. Or teasing. Then she said to me as if I were really father that she was worried about the youngest one, meaning me. And the hours I kept, not to mention my relatively few but oddly theatrical-looking school acquaintances.

'Very strange gang he hangs around with,' she said. 'Very slight youths. Almost wolfish. I wonder what he hopes to get out of them. And that teacher, that gravedigger, I find odd.' Referring to Archie.

Saying these things to me as if I wasn't there, as if the hearing loss she had ages ago had now been replaced by a loss to do with sight. Maybe even cataracts, since she couldn't distinguish me from Dad.

Then, 'Come,' taking me inside to the master bedroom where she put me to bed in Dad's pyjamas for a nap. Putting out my, or rather his, slippers under the bed for when I woke up with the rest of the city, once the heat and humidity abated after six.

But this didn't worry me too much since mother and father hardly ever fucked, and she and I had played dress-ups years earlier. And compared to how we'd clashed then, this was child's play. Much less deadly than poison.

But the second time she put me to bed for a nap my father caught me, coming into the room, finding me the way Papa Bear once upon a time found creases in his bed that represented decay and usurpation.

'What's wrong with your bed?' Father said. 'You've got your own room. You've always had your own room.' Waking me, forcing me to take off his pyjamas, to go barefoot without his slippers, to my own room, the room I preferred. But I don't think he caught us out often enough for it to be a real problem. And mostly, mother's husband/son confusion I found to be like me. Pretty and harmless. Something I had to put up with if I were to gain her confidence. If I were ever to be able to persuade her to leave. Which I have to admit now was looking a bit unlikely.

The third time this happened though she really got personal and nasty. We were sitting on the balcony overlooking the Acropolis on a day carbon monoxide smudged it, giving it a mother-of-pearl translucence. Here, in a stage whisper, she said about the Acropolis, 'Ugly isn't it? Why don't they tear it down?' Probably thinking it'd look better if they did a concrete pour on the whole hill, like the backyards and porches in Newtown. Something I didn't agree with, first because I liked it and second because it belonged to her rival, showing my disagreement with vehemence.

'No,' I said. 'Never.'

'Don't be silly,' she said. 'Look at it, it doesn't even have a roof.' Laughing. 'You know,' she continued, disappointed

I didn't take the bait and becoming overly intimate, 'you and I should have gotten a divorce a long time ago, don't you think?' But I didn't answer, embarrassed by how little they loved each other. Embarrassed also by their displacement, their hate.

'When the boys start university, we might. We weren't suited anyway. If you'd used contraception, instead of those condoms left over from the war . . .'

The fourth time this happened she really got nasty. 'I hate you. I hate everything about you and what you stand for. Which is nothing. If you'd been more of a man with your son, we wouldn't even be here.' Was she now blind? Couldn't she see I was her son, not my father or her lover? At which point I have to admit, I intervened, cautious not to give myself away though, since I needed her to help me if I was to ever go back, whispering so as to appease her, the way I had heard father do on many occasions.

'Keep your voice down, will you,' but not going so far as to say, 'you're going to wake the kids', fearing in this fantasy of mistaken identity of hers I might get accused of collusion. Fearing worse, that if she got used to this routine, became mollified by our pact, she might abandon any thought of returning. I mean her notions about what to do with the Acropolis were frightening.

Fortunately I was saved by one of my friends (was it Mark? or Don and Tom?) who rang, even though she hung up on them abruptly, saying 'No, I'm sorry, he can't. He has family you know. Children. What sort of depraved country is this?' Slamming down the receiver, coming back to the balcony angry. 'Your boozy vile friends,' *remalia*, 'wanting you to go out, but I said you no longer drink and not to call again.' As if I were really my father, back in Newtown, receiving a phone request to go to the pub. Maybe Wayne being asked out by his mates on the buses.

All this was ludicrous really because I had yet to develop a passion for alcohol and Greece had no pubs that I could readily identify. Only tavernas. And the bars I'd been taken to that I didn't like. Pubs only existed over the hill where Don and Tom came from, in England.

But this confusion of hers, this substitution of me for my father, became so frequent it got silly. Laughable. Once she raced out to the street in the morning shouting after me to come back.

'Why?' I said. 'I'm going to be late for school.'

'Forgotten something?' she said with her teasing eyes.

'Like?'

'Something important,' giving me hardly a clue. 'I don't know.'

'You do.'

Making me give her a peck on the cheek thinking that's what she wanted. But no. Curtly drawing away, saying, 'Don't butter me up. You know perfectly well what I want.'

'I don't ma.'

'I don't ma.' She mimicked. 'You sound like the children. What are we supposed to live on? Answer! What am I to buy groceries with?' But I ignored her. Then pleading, 'Aren't you going to give me anything?'

'No.'

'Well obviously, we can't afford to live here any more so we'll have to go back,' she said. Exciting me. This bit getting sexy.

At which point, just to make it look good, just to look sad, I took out of my lint-filled pockets the allowance she or my father had given me half an hour ago. Handing it to her like Oliver Twist. Money she greedily snatched, saying, 'Anyone would think I wanted a new dress. As if they have anything decent here you could call a dress.' Me, hoping this meant she missed the elegant stores we had in Newtown like Coles and Brennan's.

Later in the evening when I got home it became worse. Her confusion that is, her slipping in and out of roles and incipient madness, although my hopes for our return improved.

I say this because she walked around the living room dusting, softly singing songs no one had ever heard. Beautiful songs from far away places. In a dialect that was neither English nor Greek. In a dialect I couldn't understand.

Songs whose beauty could have shipwrecked sailors, unless their tight chests like Wayne's and the ones I liked to stroke, were bound. Affixed firmly to masts. The songs sounding vaguely Australian. Songs convicts might have sung at the sight of Moreton Bay. Almost as if she was wishing us there, singing us there with the melody as she lightly touched her slightly greying hair waiting for me to comment, for me to say something that from the moment I'd entered, I should have divined.

'Notice?'

'Notice what?' Playing dumb, not wanting to say that for me, what she sang was the music of the spheres, lest the inevitable decision to which I was pushing her got postponed. At the same time I was hoping we could get this game of sexual confusion over with as soon as possible so I could grab a sandwich from the fridge, a ration pack to sustain me on my pilgrimage to Mark's shrine, his apartment, or maybe it was to Don and Tom's current more modest studio. Or the King's Gardens, where peacocks and soldiers may be waiting, sitting, smoking, preening by the garden's lake. Maybe just to give another whirl to what my cronies had shown me: an inadequate substitute.

'You notice nothing?'

'Nothing except you've dusted. More dust here than in Newtown,' I said, wanting to inflame her nostalgia.

'Unromantic deadshit,' she said. Uncharacteristically swearing. With an Australianism to boot. 'My hair, you fool. *Vlaka.*' Then hot with rage, 'A little was left from the groceries so I thought I'd treat myself. I'm a woman. Rather than the drudge you and the kids treat me as, the way everyone treated me in *that* house.'

Knocking over a vase in her flight of tears to the bedroom. Tears that said her feelings were hurt. Pulling at her beehive hair, wanting to destroy the creation the beautician had taken all afternoon to make. To topple a tower that had to fall, put on her head just for humiliation.

Compelling me to go to the bedroom after her. Where she sobbed. Compelling me to kneel by her and apologise, whispering softly like she often did. Again becoming stagy.

'I'm sorry, I had a really hard day,' careful though not to say, 'at school', but by the same token not silly or foolhardy enough to say 'at the office', or 'the factory', as if I were the husband she wished me to be in this pretence. Stroking her by now matted hair. Saying over and over, 'I didn't mean it. I did notice. You look beautiful. Younger. I wasn't sure what to put it down to.'

'You're just saying that. You hate me because I brought you here.' For a moment coming to her senses, realising I was her son.

This was the signal for me to lean over her hot and heaving neck and kiss it softly, to try and make it better. To do anything to conceal the fact I knew she was close to breaking point, and me close to winning. At the same time I was gracious enough to try and raise her sobbing face from where it had sunk into the pillow of sorrow and despair. Using my index finger to run down her back, extended and at a distance, in case she was electric like her tools of trade, my finger like that large naked man, Adam, in the Sistine Chapel.

Touching her and saying, 'We used to do this. Remember?' Which was true, we did, when I was a kid, she guided my finger over wax paper used for tracing. But I left the period ambiguous, so she'd believe this a game of petting and seduction. Something she used to do with father, a game I resuscitated for this emergency.

'Remember where?'

'I remember,' she said. And it made her stop crying. 'And all those funny ads I used to make you write. And that dress,' she said, coming back to normal, her mood reviving.

'The one that didn't suit me,' I said, just to be agreeable.

'The one that didn't suit us,' she corrected. 'I was stupid.' Letting out a small giggle and turning to me. Raising herself up, throwing her arms around my neck. 'We can go back. It's only an air fare. We can get another house.' Looking crestfallen when I didn't answer, taking her arms away from my throat, wanting her to suffer a bit more now she was close to making the decision. Wanting to drink the milk of victory.

'Forgive me,' she said, shocked by my rebuff, 'I won't do it again. Never. I know you love me. I know it. I'll never hurt you again.' Wiping away the tears. Crocodile tears she shed while promising to keep all her powers in a box.

'Over there where the tissues are, get me one. My eyes are all puffy now.' Saying she 'wouldn't blame any man', who found her in this state. Repulsive. Getting up off the bed. 'Excuse me.' Slipping out of her dress into her petticoat and bare feet. Padding to the marble floor and tiled bathroom where she turned on the shower, shouting back, over the hot and steaming water, 'Come in if you want.' Almost as if she were Wayne, the man who once upon a time should've said this. As if she knew how much bathrooms and showers meant to me. Signalling it was time for me. To leave, to escape, at least from her.

That night in bed, looking through the filtered city lights permitted by the louvred shutters, I came up with a plan. Well, I had to. Time was of the essence. I mean if this went on for too much longer, it truly would become obscene and preposterous. It would go beyond myth and legend and become a matter for police files, investigation and imprisonment.

So I needed a plan to end the association with her that would damn us, as well as one that would get me back to Australia. I used the last vestiges of the brilliance I had in primary school that so astonished my teachers. In fact whatever remained in that brain space called my mind I now called to my assistance, coming up with a plan so perfect in its execution it would guarantee a ticket. A scheme so brilliant it kept me awake with the giggles.

I decided to give up the game I'd been playing so far of subtlety and understatement. Of what politicians call these days, 'engagement'. Borrowing wisely from mother, my enemy. I decided to go for hyperbole. Deciding to cause havoc, first in my family, and if that didn't work, internationally. Honestly I had to. It was the only way I would ever see my Newtown terrace again. And for that desire I make no apology.

**30**   'Is it all right . . . ,' I asked the next day, '. . . if I go with some of the guys to the islands? School's finished for the year.'

'But you went with that teacher friend of yours, the grave-digger, a couple of months ago,' she said, referring disparagingly again to Archie whom she didn't like. I don't think she wanted me to get close to anyone. 'And why go with them, that wolf pack? We can go together.'

'No,' I said. 'I mean, you wouldn't like it. We'll go later when it's less crowded.' Exaggerating the impact of tourism in July, and when that didn't work, exaggerating the damage done to my social life by exams, trying to elicit sympathy in the form of money.

'Then pay for it yourself,' she said viciously, the way she spoke to my father.

'All right, I will,' I said, extracting money out of her in a different way, the way the first part of my master plan intended. Money taken bravely like a Spartan from her purse when she wasn't looking. A feat so heroic Don, Tom, and even Mark were aghast. An act they were unwilling, perhaps unable because of cowardice, to copy. Saying stupid things, like, 'I don't know if that's wise,' referring to my plan. 'Maybe you should put the money back. Besides, we don't think this is going to help your cause at all.' As if

I were a terrorist. Thinking the procedure I used lacked honesty.

Mother was oblivious to the lightness in her purse, even helping me pack, saying, 'I don't know where you got the money but if you think a couple of days away will do you good, then go. I'm not the type who'd try and stop you.' Utter fabrication. 'But only a couple, otherwise I'll come after you,' more honest, handing me my back pack like a battle shield. 'Only a couple, otherwise I'll . . .' leaving her actions vague but threatening.

My theft was insufficient to buy a ticket to Australia but enough for a seat on a trireme full of tourists that I boarded at Piraeus, the port I first saw written in white letters on her steamer trunk. Deciding to go anywhere to get away from her. Anywhere. Needing a place of safety, a bolt-hole where I could safely launch my plan of attack.

I avoided the island of Delos though, since I'd been there, going to more flaccid islands, whipped by strong Cycladic winds. Alighting on Mykonos, the Provincetown, the Fire Island of the Mediterranean. An island of white cube houses, choosing this bunker to wait out the force of her explosion, for the devastation I hoped would send us packing.

**3 1**   Mykonos is a rich island whitewashed every year with brushes whose bristles might as well be dipped in cash. It's an island that has never suffered like its neighbours.

You won't meet Mykonisiates in New York, Chicago or Melbourne. Unlike other Greeks, they aren't fools who give up their homes to go into exile. They stick to their island's windmills and *pensions*. They're content to lease the island each summer to homosexuals, because in winter it is returned. The main beach called Paradise, is pawned to nude German tourists; the other, Super Paradise, is given to naked Frenchmen and the English, who love baking their white genitals in the red Cycladic sun.

'Lord if only England were sunny,' I heard one say on the boat. 'You wouldn't catch me going farther south than Putney. I just adore this solar fucking.'

The year-round inhabitants were those old Greek men with gold teeth and skin cured by sunlight and sea spray, wearing blue sailor's caps while clutching at the rudder sticks of small boats ferrying to Paradise younger men like me. Some, not so young, with capped teeth, and skins suppled by foreign moisturisers.

Some wearing caftans, others the briefest of monokinis, popular not in Australia or America but in the less butch parts of the world such as Antibes, Ibiza, Saint Tropez.

Monokinis and G-strings which I found gross compared to Speedos and Stubbies.

Wondering on the boat what the old captain thought of the man next to me whose toenails were pillar-box red, or the sixteen year old apprentice fag next to him about to cause havoc. I mean me. The captain saying,

'*Prosekse pethi mou*, careful kid,' because I was leaning too far over the side.

'*Entaxi*, okay.' Not caring, just happy I'd escaped. Anyway he probably explained my presence the way the ancients did, with the word *xeni* – foreigners – when once, the word 'barbarian' could condemn or forgive.

At night Mykonos town was more interesting. Glowing radioactive in front of loud louche bars, such as Pierro's and the Nine Muses, Germans and their perennial allies the French, rocked, jeered and drank, teetering with laughter, like something out of a 1950s illustrated Bible, showing Sodom's last day, a city my Bible suggested was destroyed for being hilarious. The picture showing the residents similarly throwing their heads back, charging their glasses and laughing. One drinker coming over to me, saying, 'Would you like to join us?' I forget whether he was French or German.

'Thanks, no,' I said. 'Maybe at some future point.' Which was prescient.

The first time in my life, I'd refused, feeling too young to join in. Probably guilty, that I needed to involve everyone in a nightmare if my plan were to succeed.

Preferring to sit at the cafe across the lane watching the action unfurl like a play seen through a proscenium arch, the way the local Newtown kids watched the shows I presented in that famous theatre I once had in my laundry.

At Pierro's they weren't singing the songs of my mother, or the lieder of Archie, but a disco tune called 'Don't Rock the Boat Baby', whose lyrics could have been a warning. I say this because neither the paradisiacal Germans, nor Archie, Mark, Tom or Don (wherever they were), knew I was planning for the whole nation to capsize. My plan was taking shape and form that very night, a hot one even by Greece's standards. A night so hot it made me refuse sleep's advances.

Against the whitewashed wall of my bedroom, lit silver by the moon, I was conjuring up jet planes, bombers, armies and tanks – all the weapons needed for slaughter. Conjuring them up the way I once did my boys in both Panavision and technicolour. Waves of them to crash and bomb Greece out of existence. Waves of destruction like the waves of flame that seared those names on the side of the obelisk. Maybe I was just dreaming of war and revolution.

**3 2**   And it worked. Well I'm not really sure I can take all the credit, some of it belonged to my mother, because Thor's hammer finally flew through the sky with a roar of military jets on a day as still and as blue as the sea, visible from my *pension's* terrace. Agitating and scaring the guests who were taking coffee with rusks.

'Just like Esther Williams,' one foolish young man said to his older companion, who read a stale copy of *Variety*, its copperplate banner bent at the tip and pointing to the planes.

'Busby Berkeley, darling, not Esther,' the older man corrected, looking at the sky.

'All right already, Busby, then,' his mate said, referring to the choreography of the planes in formation and getting it wrong, Busby never being my name. Only momentarily amused though by the dangerous aeronautics I'd called up. Because suddenly there was a huge double v shape of the jets forming the letter M, a warning from mother that her power was about to be released if I didn't cease this madness and return. The jets roaring past seemed to say that she knew what I was up to, a full throttle saying again she was ready to meet me head on.

Then true to her word, in the Heavens were more jets in grey waves. The younger man went running up to the

Greek widow who owned the *pension*, asking something out of earshot. The widow began wringing her hands then doing a charade about a candlestick telephone, crossing and uncrossing her arms in front of her. The *No Way* gesture of signalmen warding off Macdonaldtown's trains. 'Esther' coming back and shaking his head, more Humphrey Bogart now, pronouncing with masculine matinee dramatics first to Busby, the boyfriend, then to me and the other breakfast tables that 'all communications with the island have been cut'.

'What?' from Busby.

'All communications with the island have been cut. Hear that everybody?'

Maybe he thought us characters in some Agatha Christie mystery. Actually the way he said it reminded me of a Marx Brothers film, the scene when the house detective tells Margaret Dumont her jewels are gone.

'Didja hear? No boats or planes either.' He sobbed, 'Not even a cab,' just as Busby popped a panic pill.

'Oh my God, they've dropped the bomb.' Plausible really, except he shouldn't have said *they*, but *me* and *she*.

'Quick,' Esther said. 'To the dock everybody, our lives hang by a thread,' with more truth than he knew. 'You coming?' he asked me.

'Sure,' I said, but only out of courtesy.

Down by the dock thousands of monokinis and moisturisers were jostling for a view. But of what? There was only the empty Aegean. Pushing each other with the same restraint Abbott showed Costello in the Saturday afternoon movie. The more optimistic ones were singing, the way the Andrews Sisters used to, whenever Abbott and Costello went off-screen for counselling.

Fools they were, thinking there'd be one last boat to Athens before Mykonos, this Atlanta, was to burn. The throng were behaving like piglets and geese, threatening a travel agent on the dock with white-knuckled fists and the usual ultimatums available to powerless travellers – law suits, embassies, the wrath of important newspapers back home. I thought I heard someone mention *The Herald*. The travel agent replying, Delphically, 'Once you find out the name of the boat then we can sell you a ticket. If you don't know the ship's name, no ticket.' I was almost going to suggest the *Hesperes*.

Then another celestial roar of jets that made them cower, mother's anger scaring them but calming me, because it meant everything was going according to plan. So, blithely I went and sat at an empty cafe, knowing what all this was about and what waited for me back in Athens as both reward and punishment.

But I enjoyed listening to the crowd. Those denied my information were coming up with ludicrous stories to explain the island's isolation. Saying stupid things. My favourite, 'ICBM's and their opponents, anti-ICBM's have already destroyed London, and Paris.' So what. I thought those villages could never imitate the grandeur of Athens. I heard this from a Frenchman who briefly commanded my attention because he toyed with his G-string. A Frenchman who kept saying that now, in 1974, there was some strain in Sino-Soviet relations. He knew this because *Le Monde* said so, even though Esther said *Variety* said no such thing.

I knew it was rot. Maybe they spoke like this because they thought news of the end of the world should come through polite technological discourse rather than gossip.

From the things Mykonos didn't have yet, like telephones, radios, and TV. Certainly no one wanted to hear it from noisy planes sent by mother playing Circe.

Maybe they were as scared as I once was of leaving the place of my birth.

For a moment, flooded with charity and empathy, I almost got out of my seat to tell them, 'Mykonos is the last place I'd bother blasting off the map. That goes for mother too. Anyway while I'm here, you're safe. I'm the one who's caused this. Just so I can go back. Honest.' But the moment fortunately passed and I dissuaded myself from appeasement, plumping instead for containment, knowing they wouldn't believe me anyway.

The foghorn of a ship swelled the moisturised chorus, who now descended on the dock, obscuring my sea view. But I was in no rush to leave. In fact, I was the last to board knowing mother had sent the ship, also knowing that it was her foghorn that had turned the tourists back into humans with a belch of purifying smoke.

**3 3**   On board they heard the dull news that the world still existed. Their holiday had simply been spoilt by Greece invading Cyprus and Turkey retaliating. News I preferred to interpret as Greeks and Medes fighting once more over the fallen body of a lover. Everything was going exactly to plan, the ship bringing danger for me but a safe passage for them.

An old diesel bus took me back to Athens from Piraeus, belching a sweet perfumed fog. Past my American school with its heavily shut gates intact. Past the Polytechnic whose main entrance gaped, making the building look awe-struck, horrified that its students had recently been crushed by tanks in the recent uprising I caused. An old lady on the bus made the sign of the Cross at the sight of this, saying, '*Po, po, po, kita ti kanane*, Lord, look what they've done.' Poor old bag didn't know it was me.

Going to Mark's place, hoping to find him alone, to explain how I'd almost willed these events to happen so as to frighten my parents, mainly mother, into taking us back. Wanting to explain that the privately despairing believe all public tragedies are their fault.

Anyway Don and Tom were there so I didn't get a chance. I'm not sure Mark would've believed me anyway. All three quietly listened to the radio.

'Took your time,' Don and Tom said, but they didn't let me say a word, shooshing me because they wanted to hear what student radio had to say, a station reporting the results of mother's handiwork in between songs of Resistance. Ditties weaker than mother's, weaker than the conchs and gongs of the military on the television. So I didn't stay long. Anyway I wanted to get home and enjoy my victory, convinced this anarchy she and I had caused meant our stay in Greece would now be at an end.

A diesel bus took me home where I arrived with my jacket thrown over my shoulder, as if it were a golden fleece.

Mother was waiting alone in the living room, her legs bent over a chair she lent on, looking like Christine Keeler. No! Like Ingrid Thulin out of *The Damned*, a flapper band around her head, smoking. Then more threateningly she stood, crooking one leg at forty-five over the chair to adjust her suspender. The living room lights were covered in red or emerald shawls, anything to complement the mood of smoke and moonlight.

'Help me with this, you little thief, you little swine,' she said, pointing to her suspender, as if from her purifying smoke I'd been excluded. I didn't move lest this night's crystal pantomime broke. I didn't dare refer to how long I'd been away. It must've been weeks.

'You had no intention of returning, did you?' Silence.

'All you want is him. That *aliti*. You'd do anything to get him back. Anything to go back to that *saravalo*. That dump.'

'I'm tired,' I said, confessing nothing, reverting briefly to understatement.

'To hell with you then,' she said, snapping her garter loudly, then doing what I'd never have imagined, throwing her cigarette onto our parquet floor grinding it into the wood with her stilettoed heel.

'I'm tired,' I said, 'really, I . . .'

'Tired of what?' she teased and mocked, her voice and throat an angry slattern.

'Tired of women? Of honesty. Is that it? Go on, little boy, you can tell me. I know your type. You're only ever interested in yourself. Did you really think I'd let you get away? Or worse, that I'd take you back to be a slut?' She lit another cigarette and blew smoke into my face, laughing, goading me to do what I'd never done to anyone, but have had so fiercely done to me, to slap her.

Going over to the antiquated record player I took off the 78 of Rembetiko music whose bouzoukis extolled the virtues of exile, the pleasure of outsideness, of sex that had to have violence, to be good. Breaking the heaviness of the record like a potato crisp, I scattered it next to her, where sobbing, hair long over her face, mother traced the burn mark of the cigarette on the male chest of the flooring.

'Is that what all this is about?' she asked. 'All these coups and uprisings?'

'I have no idea what you're talking about,' I said, not wishing to betray myself, still refusing to be a pimp, though happy to be the cold Nazi of her imagination.

'Now clean it up,' I said. 'You've stolen enough from me.' This was my final helpful comment before retiring, sliding open the door to our balcony. I went up to its rail, my shaky hands resting on it as if I were on a cruise ship, like the one from which I'd recently disembarked, and looked at the Dead Sea of the city, at its shattered homes and flats. Thinking, maybe I shouldn't have been so rough with her, thinking it might have made her more determined not to return. It seemed now she and I had given up pretences of conciliation, the 'engagement' politicians so admire, completely at an end.

But then, as I stared at the city, gunfire began that I hadn't ordered. Gunfire that was sporadic and staccato, like Archie's arpeggios. Some of it muffled like pistachio shells shot out by toothless mouths in summer's alfresco cinemas.

Maybe mother, humiliated, had fired the starting gun with her threnody. Maybe that was the signal for the police to charge. I could see pink wisps behind hazy buildings lit like sunsets, as if Athens and its horizon were putting on a show for Turner to paint sinking ships. Gunfire that mother caused with her unsubsiding lamentation. Gunfire that only stopped when her tears dried as she fell asleep in front of a black and white TV, commanding the shots to be silent when her eyes fell into slumber.

**3 4**   I also had a short sleep, but when I awoke at dawn and walked through the flat like Persephone returned, I couldn't see any trace of the shawls or a cigarette burn. I felt as if I'd dreamed about mother causing the coup, certainly about mother acting like Ingrid Thulin in *The Damned*. All I could see was my parents watching TV, and a news reader saying that the 'elements' causing the disturbances had been removed. Military music, a brass band rather than lyres, followed – trumpets and drums I thought too un-melodic to entice boys out of their barracks.

Mother and father in slippers and robes, looking like *Divorce Court* judges. Maybe like out of that other show, *Consider Your Verdict*. Looking at smoke rising like burnt toast across the horizon, we ate cereal and jam that came from that other place from which we had been transplanted.

'*Kita ti halia*,' mother said to Dad. 'Look at this chaos.'

Me, thinking all this must be a nightmare brought on by sunstroke I got on Mykonos, or on the boat that brought me back. But then my dreams, like my mother's, always have a way of coming true.

'*Fasaries*, civil disturbances in these sort of countries are only the beginning. That's why your father and I have decided to take you boys back,' mother said, looking defeated and depressed, referring to the coup that had taken place, looking at me to see what I thought. The term, *these countries*, flattering another country by default.

'The people are barbaric here,' she said.

'Fine,' my brother said. Actually, *'entaxi.'* Maybe turning collaborator.

'Good. Then it's agreed,' she said. Then more gun shots backing her up, the radio going melodramatically dead, convincing me this wasn't a dream, but something perfectly calibrated and staged.

True, over the next weeks there were less staccato shots. The military drummer and his drumsticks must have got bored. Gossip that hundreds had died in the coup was nothing compared to the greatest crime of all, the curfew that began at six. It forbade visits to the gardens, cinemas and bars. I was entirely unable to see peacocks – young soldiers at the beat whose hands could be used for something better than gun placements.

But the streets eventually came back to life, the curfew lifting as if it had been a Victorian skirt hiding some sensuous left-wing disease, the moment mother, exhausted by the coups I liked to think we had caused when me made our dispute public, started to pack. Everything. Even her guises. Putting into the same marked steamer trunk, *Pireaus – Sydney*, whatever was left of her spells, ripped evening gowns and suspender belts. Truly, not much.

But looking at mother packing, I wasn't sure if I'd won, wasn't sure that with our imminent return to Australia, my home, my lover, hadn't been lost in the meantime. I thought this staring at a group photo of Don, Tom, Mark and me, taken a day before we left, showing us loutishly leaning against that other house she'd mocked, laughingly called the Parthenon.

# book three **gargoyle**

**35**   Unfortunately I was right. Australia had changed a lot in the time we'd been away. Maybe beyond recognition. For instance it no longer had a President but an Emperor who strangely called himself after Tiberius Gracchus. And we couldn't move back to Newtown, because the Newtown we'd known as well as Edwina Street didn't seem to exist. I couldn't find it on any map and the street directory's index simply said, 'see City'. As if the entire place had packed up and moved into the business district where professional people who drank very little, and who never bet on horses, could look after it.

'Anyway, I'd rather die than move back there,' said mother, just to be stubborn.

'You'll die if we *don't*,' I said, as if serpents had cleaned out my ears, giving me the gift of prophecy.

'I beg your pardon?' she said.

'Nothing,' I said. 'We'll all die,' I exaggerated just to be melodramatic. So she wouldn't think it was personal.

'Now you two stop bickering,' father said. But ignoring him and turning to me, glaring, mother said, 'When the Gods get tired of insects, they give them wings to fly.'

'And what's that supposed to mean? You're the one who's always putting us on planes.' That really got her mad.

'Go and live anywhere in the world you like . . .' she said, furious.

'I will,' I said, 'you watch me.' Because I've always been wilful.

'. . . when you're an adult,' she finished.

So for the time being we moved to the suburbs in Sydney's south, an area distinguished by nothing except bungalows and blocks of flats, constructed in auburn and blond brick to flatter the sun-bleached appearance of its residents. And I thought I'd left all flats behind me.

'This particular suburb, Como, is full of promise,' the real estate agent said, showing us around. I was glad he didn't say milk and honey. The agent looked younger than the Greek colonels on television, like a lieutenant, younger even than what I could remember of Mr Maxwell. An agent who said we couldn't afford a house, selling us instead a flat much smaller than the one we had in Athens, despite my opposition.

Worse, the suburb had neither Moreton Bay nor strangler figs, probably because Como didn't exist when Cook and his botanist, Banks, first planted them. Just jacarandas that wept purple tears each and every November, when they remembered Africa, their birth place, and recalled what forced them here – the oppressive tulips that ruled them.

There were gum trees though, suggesting that Como was much closer to where Judith Wright wrote her stanzas. Ghost gums and short squat paper barks.

'As well as being leafy, it's extremely quiet here,' said the agent, as if unlike Newtown, Como was made for meditation. It was certainly silent, as if peopled by librarians, maybe traitors who had their tongues cut out, or Helen

Keller's descendants. Peaceful. No jets in any pattern, and very little smog to disturb us.

The only brass bands I could hear belonged to American groups on vinyl disk, whose music fluttered through Venetian blinds from bedrooms hidden by diaphanous nylon curtains. Out-of-date bands called The Moody Blues, or Herb Alpert and the Tijuana Brass, whose trumpets sang about lonely bulls. Or Santana, singing about black magic women. Sometimes Sergio Mendez. More currently Skyhooks, a group singing about how they were good in bed, comparing themselves with me. The type of music depended entirely on the age of the inhabitants, on their K-tel and Music for Pleasure albums, featuring Kamahl.

But you could see a lot more of the sky than you could in Newtown or Athens, those lands of shadow. You could see the sky was often blue, not grey, with mauve spots like bruises.

That summer we moved in, the sky felt like the tip of a gas flame, ready to singe crows and kookaburras who flew too close to it for companionship. Me, saying to mother, 'You'll regret it here,' maybe getting repetitive but less dramatic, regretting my earlier bluntness, probably because I couldn't see the point of coming back from Athens, only to wind up here. It wasn't what I had in mind.

'We'll see,' she said, 'we'll see.' It was one of the last things she ever said to me other than, 'Now get me my pills, you've given me a headache.'

To which I responded, 'No, get them yourself,' the way I always do to people worthy of attention. Hoping this might be the beginning of her decline, that my vengeful prophecy was in some small way coming true, that more than headaches, fevers and plagues would ravage her.

**3 6**   There were interesting characters in Como though; it wasn't all bad. There was a paper boy with naked legs, who rode past on his bicycle, but he was too young for my passions.

'I like your bike,' I said, unsure what his bike represented. Maybe youth, or some sort of mobile freedom.

'Get your own,' he said, the punk.

Making me want to get a car to speed me to Newtown.

There was also an interesting old man who walked his corgi day and night, following it as if the dog had the power to lead him away from extinction. He was so lonely he spoke to everyone in the street, including the parked cars and the street lights, worried about their health, their view of the weather, their frailty. The old fellow saying, 'Mighty fine day, mighty fine day,' even if it was raining.

When I went down to the Georges River, he spoke to me, although not about possible rises or falls in the barometer. Mainly about his dog. 'I love him very, very much,' he said, bending down for it on arthritic knees, giving it a hug and a pat. Calling it, 'my one and only boy, my little darling', even though in dog years the corgi, like him, must've been eighty.

'Don't you love him? Don't you just love him?' True, he

gargoyle

was lovable, but I said, 'He's only a dog mister,' something I never repeated, noticing how much it upset him.

I have to admit though, Como's Georges River was lovely. Not a wide brown river, nor mighty like the Mississippi but holy none the less.

Like some of the rivers of Greece, it had its own collection of sea nymphs, spirits and nereids living comfortably in its eddies. I liked to think the stained sticks jutting out of the water were torches held up by them. Maybe they just identified oyster farms, the river's soft, slithery and somewhat sexual bounty.

When the old man left and I was alone down by the river I spoke to them. Calling on them to rise out of the waters. 'Come on, I know you can hear me. Don't act dumb 'cause it won't fool me.' Calling on them to join me on the sandbank, on the park bench, or by the swings so I could tell them about the Newtown I was torn out of, hoping they'd give me clues to its location. Maybe offer advice about mother's stubbornness. But they were big shots, too grand for that, seeing my request as an affront to their dignity. Perhaps viewing it in the same light as the old guy with the dog who in the distance scattered bread for pigeons.

'Well piss off then, if you don't want to talk.' Blasphemous and unnecessary.

It would be a lie if I said by the waters of this Lake Como, this Georges River, I sat down and wept, just because I was unable to find my way back to Edwina Street. Or forbidden to. Inept really. And quite untruthful. Besides, like living in Athens I preferred to think of living in Como as temporary. But it would be a complete fabrication if I said that elation saw me whirling like a dervish, since this wasn't the place where I wanted to be.

Looking at the speedboats owned by dentists and accountants that furled and creased the waters much more than their ironed and starched existence, I felt I had become more Roman than Greek. Stoic to be precise, adopting a steady as she goes indifference to the unescorted *passeggiata* of my years. Saying to myself, 'Give it time, give it time. You can't rush these things.' Knowing that all quests, all good things, really do take a long time. I wasn't going to beat myself up about it.

I guess I had also adopted those Australian traits of level headedness, strength in adversity, lack of assumption or pretension much admired by our poets. The stuff I'd missed. The pith and core of Australian stockmen's integrity. What the rest of the world abbreviates as apathy.

Not apathy about getting back to Newtown but certainly towards Dad and his enthusiasm for a labouring job he took on at a nearby factory. In the kitchen, packing his lunch into his worker's bag, he said, 'It's not that we're broke.' It made me lose a little bit of respect for him, thinking him different to me, overly sentimental and nostalgic.

'Well what is it then? Why do shit jobs like that?' But he didn't answer. Maybe work was his way of getting away from mother and her complaints about headaches caused by the air's freshness. Complaints that made me consider replacing her aspirins with poison to remove her obstruction.

Maybe he was taking the job because he missed the arduous work of Macdonaldtown, the smell of oil, the sound of lathes and metal. Missed it the way retired actors miss the limelight, the greasepaint, the roar of a spoilt and sycophantic audience.

Anyway, I also responded with complete and utter apathy to news just in, that the Senate had deposed or assassinated our Emperor, I forget which, despite the volatility of people on TV jumping up and down, crying like the jacarandas, lamenting the end of an era. The end of stillborn land reforms, which would've been completed if the knife hadn't been thrust into our leader.

**3 7**  I probably responded with apathy because I've always been apolitical, also because an even more spectacular thing happened in Australia that did not escape the newsreaders' notice. God they were canny.

'News has just come to hand that our country's greatest citadel, the most inviolate and best defended, whose stone buttresses and iron gates have repelled for centuries every attempt at invasion by the best armed phalanxes and legions – the University of Sydney – has fallen.'

Me, breathing a sigh of relief, because for a moment I thought he was going to say Newtown had been burnt to ashes, like the fire bombing of Dresden.

'Great,' I thought, 'it's been sacked. It's fallen to the Barbarians.'

And it had. Great hordes of them streaming through the gates the way the Turks ran through the gate of Byzantium, shrieking that their God was the only true God, taking no heed of who had gone there before, putting the library and all its contents to the torch in a massive conflagration, its viziers and lecturers to the stake, cut down against the sword of their ambitions.

By Turks and hordes I mean the sons and daughters of immigrants, since more and more of them were now allowed to attend. I guess it's also a long way of saying I got a letter.

## gargoyle

'Don't stare at it. Open it.' Dad said, handing it to me. 'Looks important.' Which it was, being a letter of surrender, from the Chancellor saying that my candidature to study arts had been accepted. Unconditionally. Well almost. As long as I stayed a minimum of three years, the keys to the city, in fact the country, would be mine. Forever. It was something I'd applied for casually but wasn't really considering, planning in my mind to get a job instead — money for that car, for that modern device that would steer me to Newtown at a hundred kilometres an hour.

'What's it say?' father asked. But I didn't answer straight away, distracted by the photo of the Chancellor who seemed a nice old man. Weak, tremulous, the chill of his years and poor circulation only guarded by ermine.

'It's just an invitation,' I said, 'to go to University. But I don't think I'll bother. I'm too busy.'

'What are you busy with? You haven't done a thing since we came back from Greece.'

'This and that,' I said, omitting to mention that I planned to leave them.

'You have to go,' father said, 'it's an opportunity.'

'Well, yes,' I thought. 'But for who?'

'Go, or be damned,' mother said from the bedroom, as if she had read my thoughts. But like most of her statements this could've been directed at anybody. Shouting this from the bedroom where at last her health was failing, her headaches worsening.

'Go yourself, if you think it's so terrific,' I shouted back. But I was just being rude. I had in fact decided to offer the Chancellor clemency, to forgive all the slights I endured in my youth that suggested this place was the forbidden city. A Reichstag best burnt, before being entered by those in the social vectors called immigrant, emigrant, worker. Vectors often intersecting. I accepted a little ungraciously, using Australia Post as my envoy, briefly replying that the Chancellor's humiliation had been sufficient.

'*Dear Chancellor,*' I wrote, '*Rest assured . . .*' Responding charmlessly, knowing that other immigrants, like me, had indeed sacked the city and been allowed through it, not with force but with letters of transit. Because we'd done well in exams, because we'd betrayed our way in with guile, art and wit, the things I'd learnt in my youth, the hallmarks of traitors. Anyway, from what I could remember the University was somewhere near Newtown, placed shyly on its outskirts. That's all I needed to know. Now, come hell or high water, I intended to make a beeline for it.

**3 8**  But I didn't go straight to Newtown, even though it was close to the campus. Having been away so long I was still fuzzy about exactly where it began or ended, or where the city started or expanded. Instead, I went straight to the University, where I was surprised to see, once the smoke had cleared and the rubble of tradition removed, how little carnage had been done. And how, despite the avalanche of Huns and Goths, Mongols and people like me – Dorians – how surprisingly intact the whole place looked. Strangely familiar. In some ways, all its grand buildings, even its zinc-coated Escorial, the library, were like the stockmen I emulated, unchanged, unaffected. Giving me hope that eventually when I found my Newtown, it too would be in a state of preservation.

The only sign of the war that had taken place on campus was a few tents and stalls on Orientation Day, the people manning them trying to persuade me to join various clubs, to sign certain treaties.

'Wanna join the scuba diving club?'

'What about mountain climbing?' All of which sounded boring. Pamphleteers at strategically placed corners prayed for and begged new people to endorse various ideological tumbrels, and an even more vague final revolution.

'All you have to do is sign here,' they said, pushing

membership to different political cliques. Maybe they just wanted me to have drinks with them in crowded bars, in buildings molested by ivy, to spend afternoons with them on the lawn, in *Déjeuner sur l'herbe* poses.

Anyway, to me University was a strange place, even for victors. Strange, because once inside the great quadrangle at the centre of the four paths that led to its arched exits, I could see that whatever it was that I had feared about this place had been a chimera, an illusion. As harmless and as unfrighteningly silly as the open mouthed gargoyles and griffins that looked lustfully at my body and my head. Faces turned to stone. Me saying, 'Fuck, you guys look terrible. You should get out more.' But they ignored this.

Anyway like everybody else I guess I was here in these holy acres to be borne aloft like Phaeton in a chariot. Borne aloft, not like last time, into dark clouds, when mother took us to Greece, but into the sunshine of understanding, stuffed with ideas and learning. To fly on wheels oiled by the ink of books, the neighing of steeds ringing out long and loud in discussion.

I wasn't so unhappy filling in time, promising myself to soon renew my search in earnest. Being eighteen and a bit more grown up, I was wiser, less stupid. No, I wasn't a complete idiot. I knew that my search for Newtown, our house, was partly psychological. Otherwise why was I so obsessed with it? So I enrolled in Psychology for a start, and History and English, in fact in any subject that could offer me clues or incentives. All right, maybe just for fun and a bit of knowledge.

**3 9**   I attended seminars about Thomas Hardy, listening to tutors who kept saying, 'The Wessex of Thomas Hardy didn't actually exist, it was a composite . . .' Such information was difficult to take in, because everything that came out of the tutors' mouths sounded ugly. Lecturers and tutors – babbling impotent men and barren women who were dispiriting me. Who kept saying, 'Next week we will continue with the imaginary Wessex of . . .'

'What the fuck for? What a waste of bloody time,' I thought, because time is always bloody.

Also finding it difficult to concentrate on the prayer we were taught, about stimulus leading to response, which in Psychology was sacred. Tutors saying, 'Once you've made the appropriate stimulus, then look for the appropriate response.' What a bunch of geniuses. A subject where for the purposes of statistics we studied infestations of rats, greater than in Hamlyn.

'Notice how many times the rat presses the pedal . . .' But I couldn't be bothered counting. Other professors talked about sons lusting after their mothers or mothers lusting after sons. Something I knew nothing about, a practice apparently popular not in Athens or Newtown, but in Vienna at the turn of the century.

In English tutorials because of D. H. Lawrence's first book, they said this took place near Nottingham.

In one particular English lecture my hand shot up where the poor lecturer, thinking I was going to embarrass him, said, 'Can we leave the questions till the end?' Then, after he switched off the lights that for close on fifty minutes illuminated storms of knowledge, he said, 'Now what *precisely* was it you wanted to ask?' But I was wasting my time. Academics like Archie had already failed me. And I sort of now knew there was no *precisely* about it.

**40**     There were some consolations though. While I waited for a lecturer or tutor to spill the beans and provide some clue as to where Newtown and ultimately that house was, I entertained myself by thinking that all the lecture halls were brothels. Which they sort of were. Truly.

Well, not brothels like my terrace, but brothels anyway, full of red velvet drapery, soft lamplight, distant piano tunes, and the sight of uncoiling flesh mixed with absinthe and splayed out on sofas. Sitting in the last seat down the back, I could see if not prostitutes at least gymnasts, discus throwers and shot putters resting before their next challenge. Boys who kept saying, 'I'm gonna thrash you,' to each other, meaning on the squash courts and hockey fields. Fields of contest. 'I'm gonna beat the shit out of you for beating me last time,' they'd say, referring to goals, runs and tries. Making it sound exciting.

I'm talking about the half-naked discus and javelin throwing youths who passed among us as swimmers, footballers and gymnasts. Students who were gorgeous.

Even the extravagant Heliogabulus, who searched all over the Roman Empire for young men with the biggest pricks, was nothing compared to what I could see from my position, in the last row of the lecture theatre.

I could see not what Archie had talked about – the *finest*

minds, but the *finest specimens* of my generation. Laid out like silks and cloths by a Samarkand merchant, to dazzle and beguile those unfamiliar with such materials.

Boys sitting on pews, on seats as hard as their penises, wearing neither damask nor satin. But finer clothes, a touch of which I thought would transport me to Indian palaces where Maharajas dressed for the battles required by the *Ramayana*.

Boys wearing suits of light called board shorts, track pants, and tank tops disguising nipples on chests more powerful than cannons. Garments that not even a Sultan would dare burn at the end of the day. Cloaks they wore day in, day out, so that the fibres would become suffused with their scent. Even body shirts. Exactly that. Flexible nylon casts made from their torsos, whose exquisite quality was surprisingly affordable. All were available in the souks and bazaars of Sydney, the malls. In shops named after each item, like Scarfs or Just Jeans and emporiums called Target.

I have to admit though, that they and their clothes, regardless of the effect they had on me, were as ugly as lepers compared to the most beautiful man in the world who had once occupied our house, our terrace. Now we were back I thought a lot about him. In fact, constantly. Even more about the house. I asked one of the handsomer guys, 'Where did you get that?' pointing to his T-shirt. Him saying, 'What? This? It's only a T-shirt.' But I meant the chest that was in it. I guess I was asking because it was the same colour as a T-shirt worn by Wayne, left back in the terrace still eluding me.

And although I said there were Huns and Goths, Etruscans and Dorians at the University, most of the young men were actually Celt, or the race that had always attended, the one that had so inspired St Augustine – Angels. I mean anglos. Young men who kept saying, 'Mate, breaks my heart to be here when the surf's up.' Boys who weren't from Newtown but the North Shore, a local version of Britain, on whose beaches they smeared themselves with zinc, a type of woad to scare off invaders. Saying their fathers were physicians or soothsayers trading in what they called Futures. Maybe they were just doctors and brokers.

Young men who seemed to know each other well, having gone to the same school, named simply Kings, after all the monarchs of England. Or after Saints that could have been St Augustine's brothers and sisters. Highly learned boys you heard speaking romantically about, regattas. Whose ancient families required their elder sons to avenge some unspecified past carnage every few years in a combat for a trophy made of ancestral bones called 'The Ashes'. A carnage quite different to the one I remembered emblazoned on the obelisk. These guys saying to me:-

'Can't understand anyone not liking the cricket.'

'Trust me,' I'd say. 'It's easy.' Not that I hated it, but I remembered Wayne preferred football and the races.

If I'm going to be critical I should mention that these boys weren't entirely perfect, they did have flaws. I mean no one's perfect. Their conversation for instance was a little dull.

'Howzat?' they yelled in response to a long description of cricket on the radio, a phrase they considered brilliant. Probably because in the schools they came from, rhetoric was considered effeminate. But I guess their physical beauty more than made up for it.

**41**     But I forgave the boys emptying out of the lecture halls because most of them, like our Newton house's magical occupant, Wayne, had similar short names like Mitch and Brett and Craig, often adding end vowels to lengthen them, so that Craig became *Craigo*. In case they needed to yodel to each other across campus. I wondered if they could be Wayne or my boarders' replacements, substitutes for my other substitutes in the King's Gardens. But then I remembered how that'd been inadequate.

'Hey Craigo, over here you mongrel,' they shouted through cupped hands, mongrels apparently a race, like Vandals. Shouted when assignments were due, when they needed to rush to that clandestine place in the library called 'Special Reserve', where the secrets that guaranteed good marks got distributed. Mysteries you had to either learn by heart, or transcribe by hand because they were too valuable to allow out to the public.

'You can only have the book for two hours,' the librarian said.

'Two hours,' I said, 'is plenty.' But I only kept the book for an hour though, so I could follow boys to the gym and the swimming pool, where they revived their health by lifting weights heavier than Atlas. I watched them swim free of constriction, wearing only tight chastity belts called Speedos.

Thankfully not the monokinis and G-strings that had appalled me on Mykonos. Some of them performed the most aggressive style of all – the butterfly stroke – cutting down the lane, bobbing violently like stump-jump ploughs.

After a while, the noxious smell of chlorine made me retreat to Manning Bar to seek out if not Dorians, at least Etruscans, I mean Italians who came from Leichhardt. I did this because Leichhardt gave me hope, since I'd heard it was near Newtown. False hope, as it turned out, because the Etruscans knew nothing about it.

'Hasn't anyone been there? Don't you know where it is?' I asked. But they hadn't and didn't. They weren't interested anyway, just sitting around, playing cards like prisoners waiting out a sentence.

'Shame,' I said.

'What's the matter with you mate?' said Sam, one of their aggressive leaders.

'You lost or something? Need a white stick?'

'Leave him alone, Sam,' a girl said, taking up my cause. 'You big ape.' True, he was big and hairy.

She was a kind Irish girl, shocked at his behaviour. 'Don't worry about it. I was just asking if . . .'

'But I do worry,' she said, being gallant. I remembered I'd briefly spoken to her the week before, on Orientation Day, when chatting to me in a queue she told me she was from Fairfield. Making me think that's why she was so fair-faced and fair-minded. Sam, the boofhead, saying about her, 'Dry as a nun's cunt,' under his breath, but loud enough for her to hear, obliging her to quit the table, calling him and his friends 'disgusting'. 'Come on, let's show them some manners,' she said.

I walked away with her in silence.

Her name was Kylie. 'In some Aboriginal languages it's *garli*. Like girl. My parents called me that so there wouldn't be any confusion. Because I was a bit of a Tom Boy. Sort of masculine.'

She was sort of masculine, but only in the sense that to me the world's most beautiful women have always been slightly masculine and the men slightly feminine.

'I like you,' I said to her.

'You're sweet.'

'I like you a lot.' I blushed at the fact that I'd said such a thing. So precious. For the first time to a female. At least to a female under sixty. To Kylie, who with her long red hair swept over one side of her face and her padded shoulders and tight long slit pencil skirt looked as if she'd escaped from Hollywood in the nick of time, before they made her a starlet.

'You're nice,' she said, flicking her long red hair. 'Different to them, even if you are originally from a roughies' place like Newtown.'

'You been there?' I asked.

'No,' she said. 'No reason to, but it's nearby isn't it?'

'Not really, well sort of, I guess . . .'

'What do you want to go there for anyway? People spend their life trying to get away from it. Something special there?'

'Hope so.'

'Want to tell me about it?'

'No.'

'When you're ready,' she said. 'Actually I remember going past it once. It was sort of shocking.' Kylie saying when she first arrived in Sydney she took the express train from Central. Going past ugly places she couldn't bring herself to mention, 'like Croydon, Strathfield . . . Macdonaldtown', she shuddered. The way she shuddered upset me. '. . . it was horrible, and the train was filled with boys wearing ugh boots, making fun of my make-up.' It was a bit heavy. Then before I could answer, she said 'Come on, let's take a walk.' She took my arm as we covered the grounds St Paul reserved as his oval. I told Kylie she was beautiful. 'Like an actress,' is how I put it, making her blush.

'Oh, I'm older than you think. I've experienced a lot.' Then, as the afternoon wore on she said, 'Don't look at me too closely. The light in Australia isn't like Europe's,' conveniently forgetting that I wasn't only from Europe. 'It's harsh you know. Ageing. I prefer twilight. The soft light on elm trees we have in Victoria.' Saying, when she saw me unsure how to respond, 'I'm originally from there. Marvellous Melbourne they used to call it. It's got boulevards and cafes like Athens and all the great cities of the world. There, we don't have . . .' She shuddered. '. . . suburbs. Only *arrondissements*. Places like Toorak and South Yarra.' She made Melbourne sound grander than London, full of big houses, much bigger than any in Newtown. Houses whose white columns supported, 'families that have been there for generations. In fact high society.' Maybe she meant the whole Australian fundament. Making my family and I sound very much like interlopers, both the first time and now, because again we'd become immigrants.

'Why don't we go have coffee? I know this great place. But it isn't near Newtown. It's really refined.' She took me in a Tuscan red gondola – the train – to Museum Station, then on to her favourite place, the Piazza San Marco, bordered one side by the Grand Canal called Liverpool Street and a smaller one called Castlereagh. It was situated on the shopping terrace of Mark Foys department store.

We became fast friends, the way the desperate do, who always need celerity. As the weeks went by, going to European movies, in pocket-handkerchief sized cinemas called The Roma and The Savoy, that screened films called *Les Biches*, art houses like the ones I used to go to in Athens with my cronies.

And to European plays, like *Equus*, which was about horses being blinded by a young boy's passion. And a really dreary play called *The Ride Across Lake Constance*. Lake? By the time it finished it felt like the Atlantic. As well as to concerts, where we listened to Archie's imitators. We danced to music Kylie put on juke boxes, music not played in years, whose lyrics said, *If that's all there is, then break out the booze and have a ball, if that's all* . . . Music so different to our neighbour's K-tel collections of Sergio Mendez and Herb Alpert.

Kylie took me to films she said were older than herself. There was one called *Funny Girl* – about a woman stranded on a New York ferry singing that rain had spoiled a parade she'd hoped to lead triumphantly. Afterwards, Kylie said, 'I love Barbra Streisand. Forget about Newtown, New York's my favourite place. I feel I know every building in it. They have terraces there too you know. Except they call them Brownstones.'

'Really?' I said, not wanting to show off about how much I already knew about New York from picture books and my childhood slide collection where New York featured strongly. Also because I didn't want her to feel naïve or silly since she was so pleasant.

'You bet,' she said. 'I know lots about its architecture.'

'Go on.' I said, which was better than, 'you don't say,' which would've been nasty.

## gargoyle

Kylie told me about the Flat Iron Building she assumed was built to honour the garment industry. About Central Park, whose cuttings and clippings must be coveted by every green house in the world from the way she talked. About Broadway, the narrow road to wide theatrical success. She described the subway smells the way Sylvia Plath described them in *The Bell Jar* – as fusty, musty, peanut smelling – being unoriginal. 'Anyway that's how Sylvia describes it,' she said, giving Sylvia credit. 'You should read her.'

But I had already read her and knew most of this from what the American kids had told me about New York at school. To me it was just a place to visit, another place lacking Wayne and my terrace.

'And I know all about its culture,' she said.

'Must be tons,' I said with more Socratic irony, knowing so much more than she did, at the same time, not wanting to appear the smart arse I always was.

'Is there ever!' she said. 'There's Andy Warhol for a start. You won't find people like that in Newtown.' She told me Andy didn't live in a Brownstone but a factory where they built prams, which sounded childish. About New York's Chelsea Hotel where behind yellow curtains Joni Mitchell had breakfast. About people who stayed at the Chelsea hoping to find themselves in its corridors and labyrinths. About New York's painters. About streets painted by Edward Hopper, a man sadder than Dobell. Stuff I knew already. Stuff that was mainly inaccurate.

Then she went on about all the novelists and short story writers who made the city much more than a city, an oasis, a literary pantheon. 'That's the only place fit for people like you and me. We should go, if not to New York, at least to London.'

'Maybe,' I said, wiser about these cities than Kylie with her childish enthusiasm. Probably because now I had friends in them, remembering Don and Tom. Maybe Mark. 'But I'm not sure I want to just yet.'

'Don't say *maybe*. Say *definitely*. Why hang back with the brutes. That's all Newtown's full of.' Then, seeing I was hurt, she said 'sorry, I didn't mean you.'

Finally she sang a song that started with lyrics of exile, and ended with lyrics of triumphant return. In fact, by the time she was finished I could hum it. Something about '... *being part of it, old* ...' A song celebrating New York much better than the way Tommy Leonnetti lauded Sydney on Channel 7 after the epilogue.

'I really will go one day. What about you?' she asked.

'Sure,' I said, just to be courteous.

'In between times,' she said, 'I'd be content to stay in Australia and become a school teacher. So I can change attitudes. High school, not primary. Hate kids. But I can't see the point if I'm going to wind up teaching people like *them*,' referring to Sam and the Etruscans, the Italian jocks.

'Hell no,' I said, for the hell of it, which shocked her. 'What's wrong Kylie? Did I say something wrong?'

She nodded yes.

'Shouldn't've said hell?'

'Don't say that word again.'

'Come on. I'm joking.'

'I know, but I'm a believer. Superstitious.'

I knew there were reasons why I liked her.

'In brimstone?'

'No, the eternal spirit.'

'I see,' I said. But I didn't.

'What I mean is I believe in the power of an individual

to make a difference, in magic. To find his or her own destiny,' she said. She was so high minded.

'Me too. But I don't believe in hell,' I said to be agreeable.

'Don't talk about hell,' she said. 'Hell is this place.' I didn't realise she was so conservative. It made me want to kiss her, a peck from which she withdrew.

'No, please. Little familiarities like that I feel obliged to discourage,' she said, showing me what she really was in this University she called 'a swamp filled with apes and tramps.' A lady. Before the term became unfashionable. She was playing more of a part than even me. Her lines directly from *A Streetcar Named Desire*, the play she was rehearsing for the Dramatic Society.

I apologised.

'I didn't mean anything sexual by it.' The peck, that is. This was true, I didn't. Bringing a smile to her face.

'You remind me of a young man I once went out with,' she answered, blowing her nose on a tissue, as if she wasn't young but a mature-age student.

'Who?' I asked, sensing that here was an opening, wanting to tell her when she finished about a young man I also once knew, and loved, as much as our house, when I was supposedly innocent. But I still wasn't sure if I could trust her. Kylie continued.

'A young man, who was the searchlight on the darkness of my life, who died because I accused him of . . .'

' "That thing?" ' I said, quoting from the play and the pose she'd adopted.

'Yes! You could put it that way. I was too immature. Now the only friends I have are people like you they make fun of. Candles.' (To be fair, I guess she and I could talk like that because we both did English.) She sobbed a little into a tissue, before composing herself, with the refinements of a Melburnian, a Southerner.

Then, when I felt I just had to explain my sexuality, had to trust her, she said she knew already, and that it was okay. Which I knew it was. But for her it was okay because she hated straight Australian men. The very sight of them.

'Their thongs, those meat pies they gobble, the fact they can't dance. Everything about them really.' Now meaning ockers. She continued criticising Australian men, having unearthed in herself a deep vein of hatred, particularly about what they wore. My praise for their suits of light, she dismissed, laughingly, as praise for straight jackets. She put down everything I liked about them – their rituals and articles I considered virtues. At one point she became angry, saying, 'It's because of them, Australia is dripping with mediocrity and conformity.'

I guess she believed Australians used hypnotic substances as ketchup, making me think she and I, despite our friendship, were in many ways opposite. She and I, moving in different directions.

'Are we still friends?' I asked when this conversation was over, because there was a little tension. Kylie shook her head.

'Actually no. Not the way we were, anyway. It won't work. I've tried it with your type.' She said this was because all my future friends would call her a 'fish' that didn't belong in their aquarium, or a 'fag hag' even though she wasn't that old and never touched cigarettes.

Kylie, my Kylie. Or was she, as I already knew, a latter day Blanche? Like so many people of the period, snootily hating the country they lived in, for all the wrong reasons. Kylie, foolishly preferring overseas vistas to childhood mansions.

Then one day, she tired of me completely. Or was it me who found her exhausting? Her style, her insistence on class, taste, money. Her insistence on culture that was either American or European. Perhaps the feeling was becoming mutual.

I say this because on the last occasion we walked through campus, I could feel what was opening up between us was a crevice, as wide as the tunnel that joined two parts of the campus, where she and I now stood.

'You know I'm leaving you.'

'I know,' I said.

'I'm only leaving because I think you're ready. What you're seeking is in there. That's the real Newtown. Remember even if it isn't. Believe, in magic. Don't put up with dickheads, even if once upon a time you loved one.'

Maybe she was telepathic. She kissed not me but what she had around her throat, a good Catholic girl's Cross and locket. Then, perhaps because of her own attachment to it and her for once realistic needs, when I held my hand up to touch it, she wouldn't allow me to stroke it.

She went to join a group of other like-minded girls, who called her in the distance. Other starlets she called the Pleiades. Maybe girls from the Dramatic Society she was starring with in *Streetcar*. Strangely appropriate since she was from the city of trams.

All of them now linked arms. All of them waved at me lovingly, pointing and encouraging me in the direction of this chasm.

**42**　　It was a long deep tunnel, darker than midnight, full of notices. On one wall was the picture of a phoenix, representing a much loved dead professor called May, recommended for resurrection. There were more posters. Also signs for shared houses, written by students wanting to share 'kitties', next to appeals to liberate people wrongly held in foreign detention. There were so many it was difficult to feel sympathy. But I couldn't see any sign pertaining to Newtown, making me think Kylie was a bit cryptic.

But then I saw the sign she must have meant. A sign that amused me, reminding me of an ad I once placed in *The Herald*. It said: *What are you going to do now that you've lost your looks? Gay lib discussion topic tonight. Holme Building.*

A seminar that sounded interesting but frightening, because I still had hopes of somehow recapturing the youth I experienced in our terrace with its magic occupant. If I ever found it. I hadn't given up yet. Anyway, I thought myself still pretty. So I wasn't really sure if I would go to this seminar, thinking this group would only be full of old dogs and faded hussies. But the sign did seem specifically written for me. It steeled my resolve to go to the Holme Building, one of Sydney University's oldest ivy-clad buildings, even though I hardly needed liberating, and couldn't imagine how on earth this would be useful to me.

**43**     I arrived late, hoping like in lectures I could just observe from the back and be impressed by every male present.

But the moment I went into the wood-panelled room, the group broke off its chatter and stared at me, as if at a faun. The oldest among them chairing the meeting got up from his seat as if receiving an honoured guest, saying, 'We've been waiting. What kept you?' Almost as if they knew me. Almost as if Kylie had rung ahead to tell them I was a person like the people she spoke of in Toorak, New York and London. Of substance. Maybe she touchingly told them that I needed to find my old place in Newtown. At least a semblance of it.

'Don't be shy,' this Elder said.

'I'm not,' I said, allowing him to take me through the room where on upholstered Chesterfields scattered through the wainscotted chamber sat about twenty people, smoking, planning revolution. More men than women.

The Elder was a nice man, thin, slightly balding, a bit like a kinder version of the Roman senator, Cicero. A man who said, 'I'm temporarily the leader, until a replacement shows up.' He explained he'd assumed this post because he had more experience than anyone else, having lived through the thirties, forties, and fifties when Australians considered people like him (and I guess me), as leprechauns. Fairies at the bottom of their quarter-acre garden. Cicero saying to everyone in the room, 'The only word they had for what we did then is the one they pin on the Himalayan snowman. Abomination. I mean abominable.' Cicero asking me, when the laughter subsided, 'What's your name?' A question so overpowering, I felt faint, giddy. A question no one in all my nineteen years had ever asked. Not even Wayne in the throes of our Newtown intimacy. Not even my cronies in Athens. A question I'd never thought closely about, making it look as if its answer I kept hidden. Making me stumble.

'I uh,' I said.

'Doesn't matter. Relax.' Cicero said, noticing I was a bit distressed. 'Tell us your name later. There's no rush. You're with friends now.' I tried again, 'My name is . . .' But before I could answer, he hastily introduced friends he called *Jodie* and *Paula* and *Mary*, even though they were men. Some of whom wore wild plumage – red clothes, vermilion and ochre, trimmed with bangles brighter than the dog star Sirius.

'That's so they don't get run over,' Cicero said, just as one man said, 'bullshit' and took the floor.

'Rubbish,' he said. 'You dress like that because you want to. In fact, I think it's because of the way the Birds of Paradise in this room dress . . . (maybe he said hippies) . . . that the media's view of us is unfavourable. Look at yourselves,' he said, pointing to guys whose multicoloured jeans were brighter than a toucan's feathers. 'You look ridiculous. What would your mums and dads say if they saw you on the news?'

But one of them, dressed in a rooster-red velvet jacket,

## gargoyle

velvet jeans and a feather belt plucked from a lyre bird, didn't let him get away with this.

'Sit down Geoffrey,' he said. 'We can dress exactly how we want. You're such a wardrobe.' Or did he say closet? His comment leading to a terrible clang of opinions, an uproar equal to the sophisticated rumblings in Australia's parliament and to a vicious debate, during which a man in glasses, who was the loudest of all, constantly yelled out the word, polymorphous. Saying all of us were 'polymorphous'. But he was so one-eyed about it, I thought he must've meant 'Polyphemus'. Then the debate got really heated. In fact I was afraid they were going to draw weapons, like Cretans avenging honour.

Until Cicero said, 'Okay, calm down girls, I mean boys. Behave yourselves. We have a new person here. Anyway its drinks time.' He unscrewed a couple of Methuselah of wine called flagons, now sadly only available in cardboard boxes. Then fortunately after the first drink everyone became charming, to each other and to me. They were pleased with themselves, the argument unimportant.

'I'm sorry we didn't get round to the topic of ageing as advertised,' said Cicero. 'But we're making progress with these meetings don't you think?'

'I guess so,' I said.

The others asking me scary questions, in that stuffy wood-panelled room whose joinery was beginning to split, like, 'How old are you?' Maybe they were returning to the advertised topic.

'How long have you been back in the country?'

'What are you studying?'

'When did you live in Newtown?'

'Why would anyone want to go back there?'

'How come you're living in Como?'

Questions I answered honestly as far as I could, saying things like, 'It's a long story.' The effect strangely alleviated my anxiety. But none of them could have possibly known where my Newtown was, in fact they weren't even interested. 'Who cares?' they said when I asked them again if any of them had lived there, returning to their own interests.

'Lits torque bout Gress (Greece). I jist love Gress,' one of them, a Kiwi, said, 'I hid the beast time there. The boys er juice gorgearse.' He looked wistful.

'You know,' he said, 'you and aye in encient Gress weren't consedered cremenul. Thit's why they hev so many statechews of us.' He made us sound revered, the way cats were in Theban Egypt. Unashamed flattery.

'You coming back next week?' someone asked. But before I could answer, Cicero took the floor to close proceedings.

'I just want to say a couple of words, guys,' he said.

'Oh, no, not again.' Groans.

Cicero, blinking with contempt at this, picked on one of them, making him an example.

'I don't care how many times you groan, Doris, I'm gonna say it anyway.'

'Well then hurry up,' said Doris.

So Cicero did, saying, 'I want everyone to hear this and hear it loud. All closets must be destroyed.' More like Cato than Cicero.

'A statement of doom he makes every week,' someone whispered to me.

'Suppose they're mahogany?' another shouted, but Cicero ignored him, and came over to my side, saying, 'Please come again. As you can see we're not as serious as we look. We'd like to have you. And don't feel you have to tell us your name until you're ready.' It was more flattery, making me feel they were serious, that he wasn't kidding.

'I'd love to,' I said, 'honestly.'

But this wasn't really true. In fact it was a lie. Because in that room it was clear no one had the faintest idea about my Newtown, nor were there, any of the boys I wanted, none of them remotely looking like Wayne. Worse, what they offered was something I'd never needed. And like Oscar Wilde, I thought this incremental quest for 'progress' would take up too many evenings.

**44**   Actually, most evenings when I got home, father would be sitting next to mother, who lay on an orange bouclé nylon couch, eyes closed, imitating the luxuriousness of the Queen of Sheba. She pretended she was in a coma. Or sleeping. Maybe dreaming about the power she had in our old house, or her failure to keep us or me, in Athens, even though she'd been pretty successful keeping me away from other places.

Father held her hand as if afraid to let go. As if the couch from where she contemplated her abstraction, in fact her sorrow, was a precipice. Which it was. Because while on it, despite her status as an immortal, she was barely clinging to existence. Her headaches, overpowering.

Unfortunately though, she'd given up on aspirin, and with it went my chance to poison her, to dispatch her once and for all to Olympus where she wouldn't be able to impede my search.

But just because she no longer took aspirin, didn't mean all was lost, because she started taking acid. Lots of it. She took more than Janis Joplin, The Jefferson Airplane and Timothy Leary put together. At one point she exceeded the amount Carlos Castaneda swallowed in Mexico, when he went searching for enlightenment among the coyotes and peyotes, maddened by sunstroke after the loss of his sombrero. More than even The Grateful Dead.

And in those days you didn't have to hang around Como street corners to get it. Nor did you have to go to San Francisco with flowers in your hair, with mimosa, or what we call wattle. It was readily available in Sydney, called by traditional Aboriginal names such as Tofranil and Largactil, as well as by two very camp and lispy sounding words, Lithium and Stellazine. The second was pronounced like magazine, as in the *Women's Weekly*. The acid was disguised as antidepressants.

Also, in a strong attempt to identify with every other woman in Australia, mother took Valium. But I thought this wasn't as classy and a lot less cool. Anyway, even though the acid and the Valium didn't help her headaches, her faith in modern medicine remained unshakeable. Maybe because I kept encouraging her to up the doses. Or she might've adopted this new chemical religion because her old Greek gods, now that we had returned, had proved themselves dead, museum pieces of stone, unable to move or emote, incapable of providing assistance. Also, since leaving Athens her legendary powers of sorcery seemed to have dried up, expended, as if she had to leave her phials and potions, her magic kit, in a locker at the airport. Perhaps it was forcibly removed by Customs. I don't know why she didn't put up a struggle, the way Mrs Petrov did in Darwin, on the tarmac, when one of her shoes was stolen by secret agents. It was more likely mother was malingering.

There, collapsed on the couch, which she now preferred to the bedroom, father told her stories, hoping, unlike me, she'd wake up. Stories to revive her, so she'd actually eat something other than tears. She was always crying and sobbing for God knows what. Father told her stories, the way I tell stories. Imperfectly. From the past. To fill in the sob-punctuated silence. Strangely, they were not of the Greece from which we had just come, nor about the Greece that had existed in their youth.

The stories were about that other magic land to which we were unable to return, where she didn't want to go, Newtown. He was careful though to omit our old house, and us, the children. Particularly me, her nemesis. Father just kept talking it up about the good old days, when they were courting, saying, 'The Roumeli, that was the best place in Newtown. Much better than those stupid clubs they have now. Those *vlakias*, idiocies, like the Cassie.' He was referring to a Greek nightspot in Kensington he'd heard of but never visited. The Roumeli being the opposite, one of the original Greek nightclubs of the 1950s where singers in high heels and beehives sang songs from the homeland. Women who tapped out the rhythm with red sling-back heels, clasping a microphone between the palms of two outstretched hands, rubbing it, saying, '*Oppa, sss*', hissing at it, as if it were a penis, secretly pleased with the substitution. Chanteuses who could skol shot glasses of ouzo, while taking the pound notes patrons eagerly thrust in their tits, with indifference.

'*Oppa, sss . . .*'

Greek women who looked like the young Diana Ross. The ShangriLas. No! Aretha Franklin!

Probably because they'd equally straightened their hair. Women admired and honoured in the 1950s because scarcities caused by the White Australia policy meant they had to be stand-ins for American blacks. Any blacks. Except Aborigines.

'Ladies and gentlemen, let's have a big hand for Martha

Reeves and the Vandellas,' the MC would say, the way I did as slide show host in our Newtown laundry. Maybe the MC just said, 'For The Three Marias. *Herokrotiste*,' applaud. Sexy women who also bellowed the songs of Sotiria Bellou, the one Archie had taken me to hear in Athens who had sung especially for me. My favourite –

*San pethano sto karavi pes tous pethane to pethi*. If I should die upon the ship, tell them the kid is dead.

It was a famous song from that other lost Newtown, the greatest of them all, Smyrna. Not a cue for sentimentality, but an option that would have guaranteed happiness. The Marias singing songs about 'teddy boys', *teddy boythez* in Greek, spivs and mods who had left their hearts, much like mine, in pieces. Finally they launched into their *piece de resistance*, the signature tune of that great Greek Jewess junkie from the 1920s, Roza Eskenazi,

*Apo to vrathi os to proi,*
*me preza steko sti zoi.*
From morning until night
Only junk keeps me alight

A woman who sang about the virtues of coke and smack, all the antivenenes of memory.

'There were also the dances,' father said to mother, still lying on the couch. 'Remember those?' Seeing her not stir encouraged him to other memories of dance halls, like the ones reserved for working-class revels at New York's Coney Island or England's Brighton where they have vast halls for the working class's summer entertainment.

In Newtown it was the Police Boys' Club of the 1960s. Such beautiful words – police and boys. But let me not get distracted. Clubs set up by the police, equipped with trampolines, boxing rings and punching bags to milk handsome but angry youths/lads of their insolence and spunk. In reality semen. Too much of which people said made them criminal. Working-class Irish boys, who could be violent. Clubs that were a last resort. An alternative to them being left up on the hill called Long Bay to die of exposure. As if such butch and fractious youths were nothing but disabled Spartans.

The lobbies of the Police Boys' Clubs, cleared of equipment by night, so that trestle tables covered with white butcher's paper could be set up in long dark rows, giving the place the look of a mess hall in Valhalla. Greeks drinking from the horn of plenty called Reschs while feasting on the inexhaustible flesh of Leviathan, succulent slivers that were cubed and skewered to look like souvlaki. Children crawling across the floor not abhorred as is the modern custom, but welcomed, recognised as the offspring of Giants.

'You try talking to her, I give up,' said father, when these descriptions of their life in a time and place equally immemorial raised barely a glimmer. But I didn't. Really I didn't. Or at least didn't want to. What was there to say? Why was it up to me? She was the one who made us leave Newtown in the first place, who loathed our house, its pink and green balconies and columns, who had come to despise Wayne, and the friends I'd made to replace him and advise me – the woman who said she'd rather die than return there.

Now she was fulfilling both her prophecy, and my own juvenile portent. And what was father implying? That like her I was also magical? Or that somehow she gave preference to me? I was no prince, only a student. And she was no sleeping beauty. Anyway I was pleased it had come to

gargoyle

this. It was her punishment for past sins, for making us move to Athens and then here to the suburbs.

'Mum,' I said, taking father's seat reluctantly, whispering in case undercover agents had bugged the place. 'Do you want me to get the doctor?' When I really wanted to say, 'I told you so.' Cassandra's satisfaction.

'Mmm,' she answered slowly, a signal she understood me. As I looked up at Dad, my expression not as sad as his, suggested, it was time to fetch her supplier.

A doctor. More like a magician who came with his black box of tricks. Card games, ping pong balls that vanished. Rabbits in a hat he called tricyclics. Better quality, he said, than the acid he had been giving her. Saying that it might help her 'tune in', because a woman like her should never just 'turn on' and 'drop out'.

The doctor took over from Dad, and from me. Sitting next to her in our living room, she briefly came to, crying about injustice in the world, and in her own life, mouthing slogans still in usage like 'it's not fair'. The doctor holding her arm while injecting her with truth serums, which honestly I thought were unnecessary. Sometimes when he was being really sympathetic, he wrote feverishly on a pad, jotting down mother's philosophic observations for posterity. Maybe just prescriptions.

But at least he took the criminality out of the proceedings, keeping her out of gaol. She didn't have to become a prostitute or hang about Kings Cross sleeping vertically waiting for the next revelation.

'Can you leave us for a moment?' he asked, probably because he wanted to talk to her privately, about the risks he was running, his need for protection or the costs that were spiralling.

Father graciously answered, 'Whatever you say, doctor,' and went to the master bedroom, which was only right. I went to my smaller bedroom, not wanting to hear a word, lifting the blinds made in the most Serene Empire in the spare moments of the Doges, I mean venetians, revealing what Como had in plenty. Not the Villa D'Este, with its balconies and buttresses, but another block of flats with tightly shut aluminium windows.

A red block, like the colour of Ayers Rock. Perhaps more burnt umber, the colour found in childhood paintboxes. Red flats, below which were rank and festering open sewers. Concrete driveways leading to garages. Above which hung one of my mother's sisters, Celine, the moon to whom I prayed for assistance, saying, 'Help her if you can. To live.' By which I meant, to die, escorted away by dragons. It was what I really wanted if I was ever to regain happiness.

This request that must've embarrassed Her. I know this because she immediately and callously hid, reaching for a fan-shaped cloud, plunging the river, Como, and its inhabitants into what my family and I already had, utter impenetrable darkness. Against which neither the boys in the lecture halls nor at the pool, nor Kylie, Cicero and his aviary, nor the undimmed memory of the house I knew and loved could strike a match, much less light the way with torches.

**45**　　So I did the next best thing. I lit cigarettes. Lots of them. Both at home and in the bars I drove to, to seek out information about our house's location, to see whether Wayne too had strayed out for an evening's refreshment. Bars situated beyond the Piazza San Marco on Oxford Strasse, meeting in bars whimsically named Capriccio's or The Cricketer's Arms, a pub I liked to think was named after a cricketer's legs, chest, or the long stump of his penis.

Other bars that were perhaps not so different to what father described or what I'd become used to in Ommonia and the Plaka. Where women who looked like sumo wrestlers in kabuki wigs said at the door, 'Kiss me first handsome if you want to come in.' Where other women who also looked like The Three Marias performed, Diana Ross with similar lipstick and make up.

Singing, *'Baby, baby, where did our love go . . .'* about the lost and found emotions picked up and discarded in train station toilets. Hearts like mine, as easily misplaced as umbrellas. Singing other songs by Shirley Bassey whose lyrics were even deeper, *I love you, hate you, love you hate you, but I want you till the world stops turning*. Songs that had nothing to do with lovers or houses but more with families and countries. Songs so magical they would not dare even breathe the lyrics, lest they commit sacrilege against the original recordings.

I guess they weren't really drag queens, but witch doctors, maybe shamans to the tribe. And the feather boas they shook above their heads in transported ecstasy and trance were like chooks dismembered at the song's crescendo, to protect the audience with voodoo.

But they also did revues and sketches. Some were like Australia itself – bizarre and funny. I remember one in particular about a woman in the desert whose vicious child kills and eats a dingo because it put holes in her matinee jacket, the mother then being forever hounded by the dog's ghosts, jackals called lawyers and journalists. Poor Lindy, everyone made her look ridiculous.

Another bar, called after what was used to repair the matinee jacket, Patchs. It was guarded, not by heavy women but by a male heavy who said, 'You don't look old enough to come in here.' I swept past, saying, 'Age has nothing to do with it,' referring to my experience.

In the main cocktail lounge was a mural bigger than the Bayeux tapestry. It showed a naked man the size of the Colossus of Rhodes straddling the Golden Gate Bridge, exhorting people like me, (much like Kylie had), to abandon Australia in favour of the land his behind pointed to – America. The gay guide book called *Spartacus* said gays had achieved great successes there, particularly in New York, Manhattan recently declared a gay theme park. There, contrary to the Sinai, Kylie believed Australia to be in the late 1970s and early 80s, a song celebrated an unrelenting downpour of boys and men.

Such men, the drag queens laughingly called *blokes*. In fact all their jokes began, 'This bloke came up to me and . . .' A joke that usually mocked a truck driver or a footballer for not recognising what they were in the low light of the boudoirs, actually bedsits where they had enticed them. Jokes cracked in pub parlours whose neons made our white shirts look ultraviolet.

My favourite drag was one who called herself after an ex-prime minister's wife, Sonia McMahon. She was immense, too big for her long slit frock. At *Capriccio's*, her torch songs were all to do with her own past functions and travels. Songs like 'LA International Airport. Where the big jet engines roar.' As she did, on a tiny stage, spinning her arms and girth like a jumbo jet. '. . . I'll never see you any more.' To claps, acclaim and whistles.

**4 6**   Later that night I drove to the 'temple' at Ramsgate, faintly aware that by using the expressway I'd bypassed Newtown.

There along the promenade that stretched for miles hung, bleeding rams' heads whose eye sockets dripped a bloody mercury vapoured fire. Maybe I mean the street lights.

They lit a temple honouring Cook and Banks, actually just a toilet.

I parked, dipping my headlights as a courtesy to the other fags who were already inside the temple worshipping in a sort of gay midnight mass of lost innocence.

Once I got inside I could see from the diminishing returns of a cigarette butt's embers, shadows and silhouettes of unzipped, unjeaned tumescence. Near the tripods and braziers – the washbasins, were marble altars shaped like cubicles, and the urinal's sacristy, where we didn't cut the throats of goats, but sucked and fucked, spilling, no, ejaculating in the dark, white seed as libation.

'Put that match out,' someone said, so I dropped it. Because there were no lights in this toilet. Nor should there have been. None besides our own incandescence, lips slavering over beer and whisky smeared mouths, connecting with

## gargoyle

the visions we conjured of each other, visions felt beneath our hands. Violently.

'Come outside,' one of them said, gripping me tightly where I gripped his long thickness.

'Come outside,' he repeated in my ear, as he tried to wrestle me away from the Gordian knot of men I'd become embedded in.

'Please,' he pleaded. And I did, coming into his hand as well as over whoever else's face was down there. On his knees. Needing to wet his features.

'Please,' again from the voice.

Outside I sat with him in my car, in the FJ Holden's humidicrib I'd forced father to buy for me as my fee for university attendance. I sat listening to a boy's confession.

'I'm sorry,' he said.

'What about?'

'About in there. It's so embarrassing.'

Making me feel embarrassed about his lack of devotion.

'I'm just a bit out of it,' he said. 'Took too many mandies.' The pills he showed me were inscribed mysteriously with the letter M, with a long tail like a serpent transforming and writhing into the letter X.

'Mandrax,' he said. 'Here have one.' Which I did, its orange bitterness slowing everything that reeled about my mind down to the thickness of a blur, limbs heavier than armour, as he and I slowly hugged at the chemical's insistence.

We woke up in each other's arms in a shaming burning sunlight that showed no temple. Only two smashed youths, in a fogged up car, in the car park of a toilet, watching peak-hour traffic surge towards the city, towards what we had just had, mindless occupation. It surged towards what I only now realised I'd bypassed – Newtown – on their way to North Sydney or the CBD.

'Come on, I'll take you home,' I said, a statement I've noticed always makes the person uttering it feel superior, momentarily caring.

'My name's James,' he said, 'Jimetha when I'm being camp.' Camp, being the time when he took R&R on the town, wearing a wig and lipstick. He said he once bravely challenged Sonia for supremacy in what he humbly called an amateur drag talent competition.

'Where do you live?' I asked. But even before he opened his mouth, I knew it wasn't Newtown. There was something about him.

'Across the road actually,' he said. 'But let's go for a drive. I love fast men in slow cars. I couldn't stand to go home now. They'll all be there listening to John Laws, yuk.' He grimaced, spitting out something more bitter than Mandrax, the noted radio evangelist.

'And then they'll say, "where have you been Jimmy? Where have you been? We've been worried sick." Sometimes I feel like saying, "Relax will you? I just spent the night across the road fucking in the bog." But I don't want them to think I'm a slut. Which I am of course,' Jimmy or Jimetha said, winking.

And so we went to Arcadia, actually to a waterfall in the Royal National Park. It was different to the ones I'd seen in the Botanic Gardens and the King's Gardens in Athens, the waterfall tumbling from a height taller than Everest, at whose base the Goddess Diana could've bathed uninterrupted by Actaeon. Jimetha said, 'Take your gear off, there's no one else around, how else are we gonna wake up?' We plunged like barrels over and into this icy Niagara, surfacing and flinging water from our hair, like long-haired dogs. We dunked and baptised each other again and again with friendship. And sex. Me fucking him a couple of times during the day, under water. He returning the favour, softly, a thankyou for my hospitality. Me allowing him, despite his nickname and chatter that suggested the not so attractive odour of effeminacy. He was pretty though, in a blond and carefree fashion.

'From a bottle,' he said. 'Get more roots that way.' Then, without pausing, 'Maybe more split ends than roots to be honest.' Laughing uproariously. It made me feel that being naked in this Royal National Park, if he wasn't quiet we would certainly get torn apart, mistaken as stags, or get shot as poachers.

We dressed and went for a walk through the Gymea lilies, red and purple, taller than any man's erection. Plucking flowers Jimmy said were proteas, flowers that Wayne had never pointed out to me in the Botanic Gardens, reeds and twigs from scrub thicker than pubic bushes, rougher and not as beautiful as bottle trees.

'So what are you studying?' he asked.

'English,' I said. 'And a bit of History. And a bit of Psychology. But none of it has been that useful.' Not wanting to tell him the truth that I was studying fairytales and lies, as well as their manufacturers. The deceitful mud pies and bricks of all obsessives and fanatics who want to rebuild their innocence.

'I was never good at English,' he said. 'You have to remember too many dates. No, hang on. That's History isn't it?' Laughing. 'You know what I mean.'

'And you?' I asked.

'Me? Call me *Jimetha*, Palease,' he repeated, wanting me to use his camp name.

'Jimetha then.' From my mouth it didn't sound so funny.

'Well,' he said. 'Sort of complicated.'

'Bet you're a hairdresser.'

'Excuse me,' he said. 'I look that trashy? I'm a businessman thank-you very much. Became one straight out of school.'

And with that he went into an explanation about how getting into business and staying in it was a difficult and ruthless process. How he had to network, write to people, constantly making appointments with authorities who generally didn't want to listen. And how he was scared they might throw him out of the exclusive Young Lions' Club he belonged to if he couldn't prove his credentials.

'Dole bludging,' he said, referring to his club and its members, 'is a real art. You should try it.'

'I guess I should,' I said.

'In Asia, where they have all the Asian people . . .' he said, waiting to see if I knew where Asia was.

'Yeah.' How come I knew where a whole continent was but not a house or a suburb?

'When kids turn eighteen or twenty, I forget which, they have to shave their head and run off and be a monk for a year. I think the dole is the same thing, don't you reckon?'

'Yeah,' I agreed, admiring his spirituality and simplicity. Taking his penis out there in the bushes, I stroked it to its full length, sucking him off skilfully, milking him the way he did the government. As he then did to me, showing true professionalism, making me think that perhaps my life

## gargoyle

from now on would only ever be a series of Jimethas, a series of pick ups. Ersatz encounters and replacements, unless I found our house and the young man who was my favourite occupant.

'Have another one of these,' he said as we headed back to the car, showing me again those mysterious pills marked Mx. Serpents. Exactly that. Snakes, transforming the Princes Highway into the crookedest street in the world, like the one in San Francisco, with me swaying at the wheel along with the car, over the median strip and back again and into half a dozen lanes of traffic.

'Don't worry,' Jimetha said. 'We're not gonna crash. The mandies will relax you.' He dozed off as I put my foot on the accelerator to avoid a big truck whose driver was too old for either of us to fancy. Dismissing the thought that if I drove fast enough this Princes Highway could actually lead to Newtown, knowing that was a delusion. A simple drug-induced fantasy.

**4 7**   'Call me if you like,' he said as he got out of the car, glancing at the Ramsgate temple, now empty of its lusty congregation. Perhaps planning tonight's sortie.

'Call me,' he said, through eyes that were still a beautiful Harpic blue, even though now at two o'clock in the afternoon, like his penis, they drooped badly.

He wrote his number down on the gold foil of my cigarette packet. The number was almost as valuable to me as the foil itself. I cherished it the way I have always cherished all numbers given to me after a night's fucking, by throwing it head first at the tornado that rushed through my side window. Scattering it to the wind. Wanting for one mad moment to go into reverse. To stop the car and crawl across the bitumen to find it.

But I put this moment of emotion down to the effect of drugs, burnt rubber, my final offering, as I flew past the factory where they made Stubbies, the shorts that are the loin cloths of bus conductors. Past wreckers' yards where tattooed youths tickled engines. Soared by sexless temples called churches. Some Orthodox, but mainly Catholic, Anglican, Uniting. Perhaps in their own way they reminded me of an event that should've taken place, where bells should've peeled in celebration, not mourning, where gold coins and confetti should've showered me rather than

## gargoyle

exile and insults. Where in our house and at our reception only photographers with flashbulbs would've blinded me.

I arrived home, if you could call the tiny flat we lived in a home, and put my car to rest in the dungeon, watering it, feeding it oil, taking up time so, unlike mother, the effect of the narcotics could wear off. Patting the hood of the car, I thanked it for its long overnight performance.

Maybe in some ways this dungeon in Como had replaced the fortress of solitude I had in my youth, except here there were no projectors or film festivals for locals' consumption. I had replaced these with canvases, bits of masonite and wood taken from discarded doorways into whose flesh I seared images that haunted me. Naked images of boys and men, in classical poses, God-like in black and red. The period – late geometric. Maybe they were images of Wayne standing nude in a room of our house, both he and the house, like memory, indistinct and blurry. Okay, maybe they were crude pornography, canvases done the way the Egyptians had illuminated tombs, except this was by the light of a shadeless sixty watt Osram dangling backwards and forwards in the wind. Like the scales of justice.

For a short while, I examined my masterworks the way Dorian Gray examined his reflection, not to see if I'd aged, but for signs of corruption, decay, more specifically madness. Then I hid them behind the dungeon's secret panels, up against the wall behind old mattresses, shutting the incarcerated images away from eyes that would have been baffled, pitying why they'd been segregated.

Feeling safe. I'd returned intact. Not in pieces.

**48**   But at home in the living room was a danger I hadn't counted on in the shape of a male stranger. He stood with my father and brother, as if at a funeral in front of a fake walnut-framed mirror hanging above the mantelpiece covering the fake log fireplace.

My father said, 'If you have any questions for the doctor, you'd better ask right away. Doctors are busy men,' referring to the stranger.

I turned around to look at mother's couch, which was empty, cleaned of sheets and bedding. Maybe ripped into bandages, needed for a new war in the Crimea.

'I don't get it, what happened?' I said, even though I already had a good notion.

The doctor, a new one I hadn't seen before, answered me very much like a paediatrician does an idiot child. Or perhaps more like Ben Casey, thankfully skipping the blackboard bit about birth, life, death and infinity.

'Okay,' he said, 'let me put it like this. Your mother . . .' is a very sick woman. You already know that.'

'Nothing wrong with her,' I said, lying. 'Tell the truth.' I looked through to the kitchen at a can of Pure and Simple we kept for emergencies, but it didn't inspire him.

Instead he went into some cock and bull story about how *home* was no longer a good place for her. How he'd

## gargoyle

found her a better place, filled with others like herself. Men and women who needed a very long rest. A place where she could get treatment. 'Medicine's come a long way since you were in shorts,' he said. But the treatments he spoke about sounded identical to her maladies since they, too, didn't exist a few years ago.

Then he went on to say there was even a slight chance she might return. And that I shouldn't complain, but be more of a man.

'Sit tight, son,' said the doctor, as if he, too, were my father, imagining I was upset.

'Can I have my stethoscope back?' he asked because I'd inadvertently wound it like a boxer's bandage tightly around my wrist. Taking its coils from me, he slammed the door on us so we wouldn't leave, or seek her. Something I had no intention of doing.

'I'll make you some tea,' said father after a minute or two of silence while we waited for the drop of information to sink in.

'Nice cup of tea,' my father said, already trying to fill her shoes, while I stared at spirals and whorls, the dots of an Aboriginal painting printed on our tea towel.

'Do you know where she is? Where he put her?' I asked, pretending to care. Father placed in front of me a cup with a slice of lemon by its side.

'Don't bother with that,' he said.

'What should I bother with?'

But he just fell back on that old cliché immigrants think solves everything.

'School. University. Your studies. What the hell do you think we came back for?' he said, briefly losing all trace of manners. Then, noticing this sounded too angry, he said,

'You never know, one day you might visit her, if she improves.'

'Is she going to die?' I asked, careful how I put this so I wouldn't sound pleased, superior or prophetic.

'No one knows,' father said. 'When they came for her, she didn't look well. They found her down by the river in her night gown.' Muttering something about an ambulance. Men in white. A motorcade without escorts. Mumbling some more about hospitals. The mentally ill. Therapies.

'They found her chatting to the river,' until the neighbours got alarmed.

'What was she talking about?' I asked, but he gave me a sharp look. 'I mean, did she know where she was?' I asked more seriously. Father answering pretentiously, saying the sort of thing only she or I should say.

'I don't know if any of us have ever known where we are. Ever.'

But he couldn't have been referring to Newtown, nor was he being philosophic referring to all human beings. Just us, burning comets, pieces unneeded, fallen and still falling from the home we left in the stars.

**49**   I guess though, now that the coast was clear, there was no need for me to hurry in my search for Newtown. I promised myself to take up my campaign in autumn when the weather became clear and crisp. Instead, during the summer I took father's advice about study, because study promised a future if you could regurgitate other people's indigestible past. Studies in Gothic literature I found quite tame, where doctors called Frankenstein created monsters who were poetic. Studies in the great tradition that applied only to writing from the places Kylie spoke of, America and England. Not Australia. Not by Australians or Greeks, or the mongrels of their union.

Social theory classes where sociologists wept bitter tears for the torments of the working class, paradoxically also weeping when research showed this class was numerically coming to an end. History classes that tried to persuade me the world was destroyed in 1914, because an archduke foolishly rode around in a convertible rather than a sedan.

Maybe in some ways all this study became more of a holiday than a hardship since I felt whatever happened to mother had nothing to do with me. Study absolved me from sin. Anyway, other authorities were now responsible for her, the way she was once responsible for everything, including how to make the perfect *kourambie*, as well as who

I was allowed to love and where I was allowed to live.

It'd been too hard fighting with her as a boy, and a heartbreak to leave both Newtown and my lover, as if there was a difference. Not to mention how downright criminal it was to be forced to the suburbs. But at least now it was peaceful without her policies of divide and rule. I reasoned to myself that I could find my lover and my old laundry in my own time, maybe as soon as I pleased.

The months passed, then a full year. The additional time not spent in study was spent in the smoke-filled aviary of Gay Liberation whose members no longer dressed like birds of paradise. In fact they were sporting moustaches and leather jackets, as well as unpressed jeans like rouseabouts.

'Has anyone else got an opinion on this?' Cicero asked. 'You with the moustache over there,' his gesture, inadvertently creating confusion in the whole group about who was next to speak.

'He meant me.'

'No, he meant me,' Everyone had identical moustaches; flannels and boots, looking like sets of quins the *Women's Weekly* always got into a lather about. They didn't look unique like the young man who I once loved.

But I didn't mind cowboy fashions, since gays now reminded me of *The Texas Rangers*, another television show I saw in my childhood. And I quite liked the horseshoe bars built to complement the prairie image, on the Ponderosa of Oxford Street, even if the bars no longer featured performers who imitated the Vandellas or Miss Ross who were considered too prissy for the new patrons. Too prissy for rooms full of peanut barrels, whose floors were strewn with sawdust in case there was bloodshed.

## gargoyle

I though, refused to grow a moustache and didn't wear flannel shirts. I was content with T-shirts and jeans, loosely worn so that I could slip them off later at night when I wanted to have sex in places I called the Signal, the Barracks and the Ox. The Signal was the largest of these establishments, capable of catering for any number of men blown in from the prairies of Caringbah and Beecroft. Big enough to accommodate all those who'd escaped Queensland by stowing away on the mail train.

All were welcomed. Some were tortured though, tied up with manacles to racks, to reveal the strategies of the sheriffs and posses they consorted with when they were straight. Whipped and flogged — that's the only way I can explain this new passion for bondage and corporal punishment.

Anyway, I felt these changes began the very moment mother got taken away. It was as if her removal had something to do with it. More importantly I felt I needed this time to myself, needed experiences under my belt before I could renew my search for our house and the man she had tried so vainly to keep me away from.

**5 0**     But as fate would have it, I didn't have to wait for autumn to launch my campaign. Didn't have to invest in a compass or a road map. Nor did I have to join the Royal Geographical Society or resort to raising money for a trek to the hinterland of the heart. The person I sought, the one person who would know exactly our house's location as well as the right time he and I could move in, just showed up. Just like that. As if my new cool-headedness about the whole matter had conjured him up.

It must've, because one day just outside Ancient History class, Wayne was there!

Well, I thought it was Wayne. I couldn't be sure, but it was a man so beautiful and so striking, it had to be him. The same gold hair, the same body and shape that seemed carved out of air, the same swagger that suggested authority and ownership, and that same country manner that said born to fuck and rule. It had to be him, older, but not decaying, rugged and intact. And as he turned in the corridor and looked at me, the very instant I saw his aquamarine eyes flash at me with recognition, I was certain.

My heart jumped, both with fear and apprehension because I knew he and I could only aim for some sort of grand reconciliation or a dreadful re-acquaintance. Seeing him at the door made me feel the small lamps and torches

## gargoyle

of hope I'd kept lit had been worth it. Also a curious unsettled feeling that this meeting between us could easily swing towards good or harm.

I wasn't really sure it *was* him. What would he be doing there? He was never the studious type. Looking back I was pretty foolish to believe that after all the years and incidents that had passed, his reappearance could be this simple. Maybe I just wanted to believe it, to avoid the hardships and disappointments of the search for our house that was ahead of me, projecting his image onto a stranger, projecting the man I considered its magic occupant. Maybe it was because I was desperate to believe Wayne didn't belong to yesterday, but to the here and now. That he was still a young man filled with form and light, with whom I could still catch buses and ferries, with whom I could still saunter to the Botanic Gardens, Circular Quay, down my old King Street.

'Mate,' I yelled from the class, embarrassing myself. I didn't care. I needed a response. All the students looked around the way theatre patrons had once looked at me and mother, considering us hecklers.

But he didn't seem to hear, vanishing down the corridor, despite the fact my voice was loud enough to wake the dead. Maybe in the late seventies he'd become so urbanised he didn't like people calling him 'mate'. When you're in love you tend to make excuses for a lover's deficiencies.

Fortunately the stultifying dullness of the Punic Wars gave me the urge to leave. I just had to check. So I said, 'Excuse me,' to the tutor. 'Stomach problems', pretending Hannibal's crossing of the Alps, the motion sickness of the elephants, made me sick. Carefully I packed up my prop, the foolscap folder I carried but never used for notes, also careful not to slam the door so I wouldn't look too crazed.

Chasing after this Wayne down a lino hallway, my footsteps sounded hollow but familiar, reminding me of the first time I had to run. The sound of the one-inch heels I was wearing, clicking like a dancer. Stopping, I heard other footsteps coming round a corner, their sound less flamenco, more like the heavy boots students buy at army surplus shops. Then nothing. A moment's silence – until there he was again. At least it looked like him. Really it did.

'Excuse me. Mind if I ask if you're from Newtown?' I said in a booming voice that carried down to where he was barely a speck. But he ignored it, as if he hadn't heard, or thought it addressed to someone else. He walked slowly the other way, like one is supposed to if confronted by a snake in the bush.

'Mate, I'm talking to you,' I shouted. I didn't feel comfortable calling out 'Wayne', just yet. Now, more than following him, I was urgently chasing him, hoping to catch up. Stopping. Turning every time he turned, heart beating fast, desperate to remind him about our street, our house, our past. To find out whether he, like me, wanted to return to that room, to our private and perfect location.

'Yeah, you mate, are you . . . ?' I shouted again, trying to catch up. My end words faded as he vanished down a side corridor, making me think this last chance to meet him was lost.

But I did see him again. Really I did. Not just outside Ancient History class but everywhere I went. Not actually doing anything, just being present. It didn't matter which part of the campus I favoured, he'd be on every lawn and every field. In the corridors, outside the lecture halls I called brothels, near the library, and the co-op bookshop. This Wayne lookalike was ubiquitous, but always at a distance, just far enough away for me to be uncertain.

Sometimes he was just leaning against a stone arch of the gothic main quadrangle, smoking, glaring at me beneath the rain-drooling gargoyles, as if he knew I was looking for him, knew I wanted information about Newtown, wanted him to both return and guide me there. But it was as if he had no intention of meeting me face to face. Almost as if he was making fun of me.

Maybe he had recognised me and just didn't want to know me any more. Maybe that's why this pursuit quickly descended into a kids' game of hide and seek. He seemed to deliberately give me the slip, going into the Wentworth Building that had a million rooms like a maze, where I'd never find him. And every time I yelled out, 'Hey mate,' my words were ignored by him as if addressed to someone else.

Worse, after about a dozen sightings, he no longer walked but ran. Honestly. Like a gazelle. Once I saw him running straight across the footbridge across Parramatta Road, the Bridge of Sighs, running towards the pub called The Student Prince the moment he realised I was behind him. Astoundingly, maybe he found me threatening and had developed a sixth sense that told him to avoid any meeting in case there'd be a confrontation.

The more desperate I got to catch up to him the more skilful he became at escaping. Once when I got off the train at Redfern, this Wayne who'd been in the next carriage, alighted just ahead of me, the closest I'd been in months. Then just as I reached out to grab him by the shoulder to say, 'Mate, slow down, can't we talk? I simply want to ask if you're from . . .' he vanished through the crowd at the ticket barrier.

I know this sounds ridiculous, I mean pursuing someone who simply has a strong resemblance to someone else. It wasn't as if his looks were entirely unique. I had seen others faintly like him in the various lecture halls where I desired them, where I described them, where anything they wore, even if it was corduroy, I considered a thing of majesty. But I can't say any of them were quite this close in appearance. Closer than a twin. That's why the more this particular guy avoided me, the more determined and preposterous I got, hoping to catch him off guard.

I resorted to disguises. I guess when you're obsessed you try anything. I put on sunglasses and a hat, but it had the reverse effect, making me stand out like a beacon. The detective trench coat was a serious but comic error. Maybe I was trying too hard to look like the detective in *Homicide*, remembering a show that belonged to him and me. And the look Wayne gave me said he knew who I was under these layers, an eccentric, to be pitied.

So I hid what was going on from everyone. From my brother. My father. Even Cicero and his group.

'You seem very quiet these days,' Cicero said at the end of yet another meeting in the same wainscotted room. 'Something wrong?'

'No,' I said, 'soon everything will be all right.' Perplexing him.

'An affair of the heart?' he ventured.

'Of the spirit.' I said, deflecting him, not wanting him to meddle.

I did come to the realisation, though, that being ignored

gargoyle

was not the fault of the Wayne lookalike I was chasing. Nor did it have to do with the fact that he didn't want to guide me to the Newtown where we'd been briefly happy. These are the complaints of those who blame their life on what happened in nursery school. It certainly had nothing to do with leaving Greece, or because my own mother's rage, power and antics were now such a palpable absence. I mean with her gone, finding him, catching up to him, should've been easy, since she all along had been the impediment, the granite block responsible for our separation. She was the one who had been responsible for everything in my life and that of my family's, the guardian of so many things, including time. Always deciding when we should eat, which entirely depended on the harvests of the local shop or the supermarkets she trawled. Also deciding when we should sleep, which she deduced according to the movements of her sister, Celine the moon. Calling in the seasons and our response, arming us with the clothes she said we must wear. Disarming us in the summer when the threat of cold had gone. That's how I saw it when I got sentimental or melodramatic.

But since I was thrilled she was gone and glad her tyranny was over, I couldn't understand why I didn't go down to the river any more to ask for the river's advice on how I could close in on Wayne. How I could once more possibly feel those arms, and the rest of him the way I felt him in the room of that house. Couldn't really understand why I now thought the river as a long thick stretch of quicksand, devoid of nereids. And it's a mystery to me why I completely stopped saying hello to the old man who had the corgi as his pet. Who still said, 'Don't you just love him, don't you?' almost as if he knew. And, 'Mighty fine day,' even when it rained.

**51**     I have to confess though that in a sick sort of way I began to enjoy my torment. There is nothing more exquisite than unrequited love, particularly if it concerns someone you only catch glimpses of, who may or may not know of your existence. I'll even say I became inured to it, finding the chase reliable and predictable. It was certainly calm, compared to the tempests and electrical storms I had lived through, shaped at times like hideous women, or the more fantastic lightning bolts of my imagination illuminating beautiful men. I even began to believe this daily ritual between us, of avoidance, was essential, that it protected me. But from what? Maybe emptiness.

I say this because if a single day passed and I hadn't seen the person I instinctively knew was Wayne, I felt it had been wasted. Feeling full only when I spotted him, only satisfied when I got close to him. And I was quite content with the occasional raised eyebrow or twitch from his mouth, which I translated for my own sanity as recognition, even as a compliment.

Gradually though, from afar, I began to piece together a pattern to his movements, writing down on my foolscap folder the times and places I spotted him, the way successful punters follow champions. On Fridays for instance, the day I dedicated solely to following him, he often walked

gargoyle

up Oxford Street, as far as Taylor Square, making me think he was still gay, or at least more comfortable in the company of men and boys. But if he was aware I was following him, he was careful not to go into any gay pub, choosing instead a straight one where it was always so crowded all I could see between shoulders were his eyes. Still aquamarine and emerald. Eyes that said, 'What are you doing here? Why are you following me?' At these times the angry look in his eyes more than the crowd preventing the meeting.

I have to confess though, whether I enjoyed it or not, this prolonged and unsuccessful stalking of him did make my work suffer. Essays went unwritten, books went unread, simply because I didn't have time to do them. I also knew time was really passing me by because people stopped speaking about Australia's Emperor, settling down with the new man in charge, who said on the TV that life wasn't meant to be easy.

Further, I felt humiliated and ashamed, that there was no direct evidence it was Wayne, since we still hadn't even had a simple conversation. Not that he'd ever been much of a talker.

Maybe the real problem was the fact that I didn't feel I could confide in anyone about this addiction, having abandoned my friends. Treating any new ones the way I treated Cicero and his group, without seriousness, the same way I treated Mark, Don, Tom, even Kylie and Jimetha, the boy with the ridiculous name, as freight trains, carriages I could shunt around and send to oblivion the way I remembered they were shunted around in Macdonaldtown.

Maybe, just maybe, now without mother's happiness or folly meant that I had none of her powers either. I mean I was not immortal. In fact I felt less than human, possessing none of the magic Kylie spoke about. About being an individual. Just a shadow chasing what he hoped wasn't the shadow of memory down dark streets.

'You don't seem to have many lectures on,' my father said.

'No, I don't.' I said to appease him. 'Don't think there's anything more they can teach me.' Which was true, they couldn't. Anyway I couldn't take any of it in. I was too confused trying to cast my mind back to a time lost in smoke and legend, trying to find the source as a way of curing my addiction. Doing crazy things. For instance in that most impregnable of all spaces guarded by titanium doors, my fortress of solitude, my dungeon and garage, I scribbled graffiti over my paintings, saying terrible things about Newtown and about him, turning them into billboards warning me to cease chasing. Things like STOP, the way it's fashionable now for artists to write statements over their canvases. And my favourite picture, the one that vaguely looked like some blurry recollection of the real Wayne I knew and loved, that was completed in my most romantic and impressionistic period, I deliberately smeared with black paint. Every inch of it, to get both him and our house out of my system.

Strangely, articulating the steps I needed to take with spray paint worked. I forgot about him and our house for over a week. In fact, when the calendar showed a second week had elapsed I thought I'd entirely succeeded. Until one infernal night when I woke out of a deep sleep and went to the bathroom.

I didn't bother to switch on the light, relying on illumination from the moonlit street, when suddenly, for a split second, I thought I saw him in the chiaroscuro of the vanity. Standing the way I first saw him stand and look at himself in the wardrobe mirror, seemingly ignorant of my presence.

But it was just me. When you're worried your mind plays paranoid tricks. The shock scaring me into action. I mean I decided then and there, if I ever saw him again, to walk as he had done, deliberately and speedily away. And to abandon the search for our house, our love. In fact as far as I was now concerned, they could both get fucked.

**52**   But like a cab in the rain, Wayne became unavailable the moment I decided not to follow him. He was absent from campus, neither in tutorials, nor in the library nor the pool, which infuriated me.

I questioned my sanity wondering if the person I was stalking was actually a series of people, whether I'd been the subject of unpleasant coincidences, or my own wish-fulfilling fantasies.

But on the third day of this absence, truancy really, I saw someone laughing at me from the clock tower. It was him, Wayne, standing next to one of the grand stone griffins, half lion half bird, I'd spoken to when I first enrolled. I could see him clearly, waving to me on the lawn, while he leant on the griffin as if it were his mate. Waving to me to come on, pointing to the direction of Newtown, doing charades, tracing the shape of a house, indicating with a finger on his palm the word only had one syllable. I know this sounds ridiculous but it's true. A few paces closer I saw he wasn't next to the griffin but a gargoyle, an ugly grey open-mouthed gargoyle, the biggest one that sat and wept and drooled forever and ever with no Amen. The gargoyle was not looking down on me lustfully, salaciously or with envy the way it once did. It was not even angry, but like Wayne, contemptuous. Wayne now pausing in his charade, hands first on his hips, then folded across his chest to show even he was tired of mocking me.

Perhaps it was the way they looked at me, or the way Wayne himself started waving to me again that made me abandon my resolve not to chase him. I'm not sure. But I knew I couldn't pass up this invitation. I couldn't miss this opportunity to corner him. To say, 'Mate, just tell me, is it you?' The timing was perfect, since the battlements leading to the clock tower only had one set of stairs, one entrance you could take. Finally I was about to see if he and I were capable of returning to that house of love, or if he was at least willing to point it out.

**5 3**     Luckily there didn't seem to be anyone else on the lawns. Just me. Alone. Staring at the man I thought was Wayne next to the gargoyle, thinking about what to say to him, also thinking about how many others like me over the generations the gargoyle had looked down on and mocked.

It was a strange sort of summer twilight. Strange because the more I looked, the more I couldn't discern which was the statue and which the man. The descending twilight heightening this confusion, its imperial purple aura almost vengefully plunging the campus, the city, and me, into the dark, the way mother once plunged white laundry sheets into a tub.

'You looking for me?' I yelled out, only to get an echo back.

'You looking for me?' The sound sprang around the University, clipping the buttresses, rebounding off stone carved by masons and prisoners.

'Looking for me, looking for me, looking for me.' And finally, '. . . me.' Once the echo finished.

I shouted again, this time louder than the cry Apollo gave when he saw that the west wind had deliberately deflected his discus to have Hyacinthus killed. 'Piss off then. Go on get lost.' I shouted thinking it might be one of the rugger buggers and that this was a humiliating set-up.

## gargoyle

But when I looked up, whoever was next to the gargoyle didn't echo back obscenity. Nor did he remain silent. More strange than anything I'd ever encountered, he began to sing a song different to all the other songs and tunes that had come in critical periods of my life. A song more beautiful than even those mother used to sing, lovelier than Kylie's musicals or Archie's lieders and arias. He sang in a voice not that of an individual, but from the self-pitying and suffering satanic choirs of hell, an exquisite tune he had mastered.

'I'm looking for someone . . .' then stopped as if expecting me to know the next bit, which I did, because I'd mastered it too.

'To change my life,' I answered, as if that banal statement was nothing more than a cheap lyric used to carry melodies better strangled at birth like so many things.

He continued.

'I'm looking for . . .'

'A miracle in my life,' I answered. The tune was familiar and ridiculously, I now sang along, knowing that what I looked at and heard must be if not Wayne, at least a friend. Someone who'd know the way back to our house.

'And if you could see.' Both of us together now.

'What it's done to me.' If I'd been less masculine, less ashamed of being seen by stray students I would've fallen to my knees and shed tears, knowing I was close to regaining if not the original love I wanted, then at least a vestige of the youth I'd lost.

But Wayne, or who ever was next to the gargoyle, unaware of my pathos, began the tune again. Slower this time, deeper, as if put through a reverberator, not a modern one but the great vaulted ceiling of the Cathedral at Chartres. Maybe the Caves of Lascaux.

The tune was becoming more compelling than sirens, making me climb the battlements like the hunchback to see who was there emitting this haunting truth, though still afraid that this might be some elaborate practical joke and that Wayne had placed a tape player and speakers up there.

So I went into the building, past the flapping exam results pinned on cork noticeboards and in glass cabinets, up spiral after spiral, landing after landing, at the end of which was always stained glass in dark reds and blues. Past false steps and deceiving passages, the sort found in Robert Louis Stevenson's *Kidnapped*. Actually, I felt stronger with each step, changed in appearance for the better, unburdened of a massive debt. I'll even say, almost cured.

Until I got there. On that Gothic building's mansard roof, next to where the flag of the University flapped. And I found nothing. Absolutely nothing but air.

I stared at the city before me. At the western suburbs to the left and to Newtown in the distance, heavily veiled in smoke like an industrial version of Camelot. Knowing it wasn't really my Newtown or Camelot, because English Lit had taught me that such places were only apparitions. Ignoring these smoke filled vistas. Seeing no one. Nothing on the corrugated roof. Only the gargoyle.

'Where is he?' I asked, as if it could speak. 'He was here wasn't he?' But it just stared impassively ahead.

'Well, where is it then?' I asked, referring to Newtown, our house. And when it didn't answer, I said 'What would you know anyway?'

When suddenly the gargoyle turned its hideous face to me, and in the rasping voice of death said, 'What it's done to me.'

gargoyle

Then, its voice becoming more satanic than that used in the song, it said, 'Go. Quickly. Leave. There is no place here for you.' As if it was the Wandering Jew.

'I'm going all right,' I said, making an on the spot decision, maybe a curse. 'But you'll be here until I return.' But it just laughed hoarsely at this blasphemy, rolling its stone red eyes. Fire coming from its nose and ears, blood from its mouth, in a scarlet cascade over the stone walls of the battlements, down the drains meant for rain, poisoning the lawns, the campus and the earth.

Okay. Maybe this didn't happen on the mansard roof. I know statues can't talk or emote. Maybe it happened one night at home, the result of listening to the neighbours' out-of-date Moody Blues album echoing in the distance. Maybe I thought of it as a result of staring one afternoon at a surfie and his panel van, decorated with griffins and naked warriors, scenes from the Apocalypse. Or maybe I thought of it because of my Lit course in Gothic Studies. I guess I have to say it was all these things and none of them that made me decide to go to the places where they had never heard of my mother, where there might be another Newtown, another house and another Wayne.

So I sold my car for a tidy profit, choosing New York and London, the places Kylie and the naked man in the mural at Patchs recommended. Cities immersed like me, in legends. I mean there was nothing here for me, no place in the entire country where I could experience my special love, feeling our house had probably been demolished. And who was to say Wayne too had not emigrated?

Grabbing a suitcase, I threw in socks and underwear like our evicted tenants, knowing that my mother would've neatly packed my suitcase if she'd been around.

'Now this is where I've put your jumpers and your ties,' she would've said, as if preparing another shield, for a different type of warrior. 'Return with it, or on it,' both repeating a threat and a process that had once caused us so much grievance, even a coup. Father would've looked on, cross-armed at the door.

'And I think it's important . . .' she would've added, '. . . you take extra woollens, extra clothes. You never know how cold it's going to get.'

But of course she didn't, or couldn't, still lost as she was in the dreamtime of some god-forsaken mental home.

Only father witnessed me packing, the mess I was making.

'Where you're going, you won't need any clothes,' he said, sarcastic, referring not to the New York summer I was going to arrive in, nor the London winter I planned to visit, but to the fact he believed I was only going there to sow wilder oats than he ever did.

'You know what they say, when the Gods get tired of insects, they give them wings to fly.'

'Come off it,' I said. 'Be original,' knowing where I'd heard this first. Besides I'd read some similar line in *King Lear*. Father's bitter view was echoed by my brother as he drove me to the plane.

'What do you want to go to New York for? To chuck a Ratzo?' Meaning the character Dustin Hoffman plays in *Midnight Cowboy* who is defeated by New York City while trying to escape, pissing his pants in ecstasy just before the Florida-bound bus driver pronounces the death sentence.

I suppose my brother's attitude strangely mixed anger and worry; angry I was deserting them the way mother

## gargoyle

had and worried because I didn't know anybody there and was what they called in that other Newtown, the Bronx, a klutz.

'Here,' my brother said, giving me an uncharacteristic hug, hearing the final call. 'We bought you this,' handing me a fountain pen, which I looked at astonished.

'What am I supposed to do with that?' Now, all I wanted was to find the place where Kylie said people were totally awake, where they refused to eat hypnotic substances.

'So you can write letters back home,' he said, wherever that was. 'It's got a gold tip and everything.'

But I didn't like it much. It looked like a bribe.

'You can always hock it if it's no good,' he said, a little hurt, seeing me hesitate in accepting it. Perhaps he and father, like me, had consulted the oracles. Maybe they'd augured this while going through mother's wardrobe the way priests once did with entrails, when they had decided to give away her dresses to a foundation for the homeless.

'There'll be something else for you here, when you return. Something small.' Father said.

I had no idea what he was talking about. It sounded portentous. And I was sick of all that. Besides, I wanted to go away and lighten up, maybe even to have a bit of fun. I didn't always want to live in a time of overheated emotions. I needed to search in the places where there was cool crisp air, where, as they say now, I could chill out.

# book four  **pinpricks and bayonets**

**54**   But I didn't go to New York first as I promised, I went to London. Call me mercurial, call me capricious, maybe just old-fashioned. I'm not sure why, whether it was because I feared my brother's forebodings, or the alabaster American financial capital itself. Maybe as an Australian I was just being traditional.

In London, penning a masterpiece about my search, writing,

*Dear Mum and Dad,*

from a bed and breakfast in Bayswater, that strangely had neither water nor a bay to look at. Feeling it perhaps unwise to start a letter whose first four words already incorporated a lie.

Amending it to,

*Dear Brother and Dad,*

which was more specific.

*The weather here in London is foggy*, also a lie, because only my emotions were. A mixture of loss and relief.

*And rainy*, I wrote. Equally untrue since London was in the middle of a drought. Continuing,

*Everybody in England is exceedingly polite and charming*, a curate's egg of honesty, written to put their minds at rest because the papers said the Yorkshire Ripper was on a rampage.

*I'm enjoying myself immensely*, not mentioning I briefly thought of throwing myself into the traffic while crossing a bridge appropriately called Waterloo. Probably because stagnant memories at times came towards me like red buses and at other times moved away like black cabs.

*I will write soon* . . . now that part was sort of true, if I didn't get too suicidal.

*Hope everything's well back home*, which meant I hoped the tectonic plates might sufficiently shift to drown the entire Australian continent.

*If you see mother or have any news* . . . the dots similar to dots I'd seen once before, dots I invested with the significance of Aboriginal paintings. Maybe hoping they'd show it to an art critic who'd understand it. Signing off melodramatically,

*Your beloved son and brother*, the way they did in the novels of Dickens, usually when they were far away or in gaol for a crime they hadn't committed.

London was an unreal city, unreal in the 'thrilling' Australian sense because I hoped this would be the original model for all Newtowns. And there were sufficient signs of encouragement. Although the street signs didn't say Edwina Street but The High Street, to cheer up people living low slung lives of desperation.

Some of the roads did look a little like King Street in Newtown though, having bits and pieces that could have been taken from it. I'm talking about lamp posts, shops also selling chips but with unrecognisable fish plucked from the cold Atlantic. Bits and pieces like unredeemed items at a pawnbroker's.

Spending most of my time down by the Thames that must've flowed very swiftly while singing sweetly and quietly because I didn't hear it. To tell you the truth it wasn't as beautiful as the Georges River. Far too icy for nereids and spirits to live in.

Also spending time in galleries to see if they were different to picture books. Thinking they might have clues as to where I could find my ultimate terrace, or at least something similar. Galleries like the Tate where I saw the first clue, the original of Turner's *Slavers Throwing out the Dead and Dying* clinging to a wall for two hundred years awaiting my approval. A painting I looked at closely. Identifying with its teeming passengers, lodgers, thrown overboard into rough seas no one predicted. The sea looking like the waters of that Italian harbour called *Cine Citta*. The raft possibly an early version of *The Marconi*.

Finding other clues in other paintings by Turner, such as *Rain, Steam and Speed*, whose colours were exactly how I imagined them from my balcony in Athens. Colours as violent as the coup I once thought I'd caused but instead merely witnessed. Clues in the form of oils on canvas almost as good as the prints in the Newtown framer's shop where I first saw them. With a brilliant flash, I thought there'd be more clues in the British Museum in Bloomsbury, much smaller and tinier than what I could remember of the telephone booth-size kiosks of Ommonia, which easily housed more manuscripts, magazines and first editions.

I was hopeful because the British Museum was basically a series of chambers devoted to what Archie had been good at. Theft and concealment. And I did find a clue in the Elgin Marbles, in their stark marble whiteness. I say this because almost supernaturally it seemed to me Phidias, in the friezes, like Turner, had captured all the scenes of my life. What I thought was its titanic agony. Its *Iliad* and *Odyssey*. Not to mention every single boarder I'd sipped and tasted.

Captured forever, a bit crudely I thought, but effectively in this, the ancient world's equivalent to Polaroids.

But the place in London I had the most faith in was Hyde Park, named not after the one in Sydney which I knew intimately, but after Dr Jekyll's violent but inseparable companion. That's how I liked to think of it. There, like other Londoners, I paraded around by the Serpentine, hoping the Lady of the Lake might care to stick her hand up, with or without sword. To point like a bobby the right direction, well at least to the mould on which Newtown had been copied.

Failing to get a response. In fact a complete flop with my inquiries. But I consoled myself it was early days, going back home to the bed and breakfast in Bayswater at night, which really felt like home because it was a terrace. Not as grand or as exquisite as our one, but a terrace nonetheless. Comforted not by the impending dark, nor by the thought of safety from ball-peen hammers, but by the penny gas heater in my room that I believed the proprietress borrowed from the Victoria and Albert Museum just for my visit, it was so old and decrepit.

It'd been a long time since I'd seen one, its bent lead pipes, dials and slots giving it a familiar face. And eyesight. A gas heater I often used. Holding out pennies as if offering oysters to a Persian cat. Brass molluscs it took willingly, giving me in return not purrs, but a heat softer than fur, lovelier than central heating. The laying on of hands. Also feeding another gas meter in the shower, but alone under its spout despite its heat I felt it only dispensed sterile water directly from the cold reception rooms of hell, compared to the warmth I'd experienced. Maybe its lukewarm water was from the Roman saunas of Bath.

## pinpricks and bayonets

A town I visited, thinking here, too, there might be clues because of its imperial associations. Walking around white colonnaded streets I adored, that people said were Georgian but I knew to be Greek, the usual representations of pricks made of stone, returning again that evening to my bed and breakfast in Bayswater and its three-storey gloom. Despite its shortcomings I think I was beginning to fall in love with it. Well, temporarily. Asking the landlady, 'Do you have any more pennies for the gas?' Handing her a ten-pound note. Which she changed, perplexed, saying,

'What do you want all them coins for? It ain't that cold. Cleaned me right out. Next time try the Bank of England.' Not knowing that the coins weren't really for the shower, but a cheap price paid for the recreation of memory. A bargain you only strike once, perhaps twice in your lifetime.

Finally posting my letter, my short literary epistle, on a rainy afternoon somewhere near Marble Arch, the rain smudging the address written by the gold tip of my fountain pen. The envelope held in my wet hands, romantically reminding me of similar scenes in movies. Jaffa crunching movies that compel the audience to reach for a handkerchief, because they know in their own lives, only a smudge, one small blunder, destroyed their happiness. The sort of smudge we used to do at school, tracing shapes scratched into paper with the ground-up lead of pencils. The smudge suggesting that it was entirely in the hands of the Gods whether my letter would arrive, let alone get me a reply, because I didn't include a return address. Also, like this chronicle, my letter contained so little truth, it reminded me of documents diplomats passed around at the Paris Peace Talks that always resolved the Vietnam War every time they had a meeting.

Visiting pubs, thinking they might be full of spies, informers willing for a bit of sex to sell me news about Newtown's location. Here they had peculiar hours, quite different from the pubs and shops I recalled in our Taylor Square and much longer ago in our Haymarket. Obviously the hours in England were more valuable than beer, being doled out like Red Cross parcels. Gay pubs whose soft lights and etched glass and velvet upholstered booths I felt were made for wimps. They didn't have the true and unbridled masculinity of Australia's pubs where men crook legs like dogs, giving space to the orbs that govern them. Pubs where returning late in the evening I got told, 'Time please.' Time for what? Another day's extinction.

**55**   'It certainly is time,' I thought, 'time to get a move on, if I'm to find what I'm looking for.' I thought this while splayed out over a copy of The Times, in the floral wallpapered sitting room the proprietress kept 'nice' as she put it, mainly by emptying ashtrays. The newspaper reporting a squabble in the Houses of Parliament Guy Fawkes tried to solve with explosives years ago. So I said to the landlady, purely for conversation, the way the English do, by avoiding eye contact, 'That new boy in room number thirteen is a good-looking young man.' Just for the hell of it. Even though I knew she could never be mother's replacement.

'Pardon?' she said. Her hand holding the kettle freezing.

'Young man in number thirteen,' I said. 'Girls would consider him a good looker,' referring to a Dutch boy I sighted moving his bags in that morning who in future I hoped to catch naked. I had to start somewhere.

'Pardon?' she said. 'Speak up child, I'm a little bit hard of hearing.' Giving me a reason for optimism.

'Number thirteen,' I said, loudly, reversing the order of information. 'Girls would think a good looker. Don't you think Mrs . . . ?' Me, looking up from The Times as if she and I were rehearsing Harold Pinter.

'Don't know if it's seemly for me to comment on

boarders,' she said, plugging in the kettle. 'What? An old woman like me? Anyway, I only like Prince Charles,' she added, showing beneath her curlers there was a spark of lust. And this was years before Camilla, who she looked like. But I ignored it, knowing it would take too much work for her and I to come to some sort of pact. To make that spark achieve what Guy Fawkes wished, detonation.

'Besides you should have an eye for the girls,' she said. 'London's full of pretty young things. If you had money they'd consider you a catch,' from her kettle, the age of steam was rising. I guess, telling me what I already knew, that most people consider money an excellent lubricant.

'Really, think so?' I said, putting *The Times* and the squabbles of the Houses of Parliament into the dustbin of history.

'London to a brick,' she said, referring to her small part of it. 'Get some quids under your belt, and you can have whoever you fancy.' Her comment about quids in the belt reminding me of someone who once said the same thing, about wanting to stuff quids down a place where he needed neither socks nor stuffing.

'Can you change another tenner?' I said.

'No, I can't change another tenner. Or a fiver,' she said. 'Now get about and make some friends. Won't have you sitting here all day with the heater on,' she said, 'like some old spinster,' a state of grace from which she, though unmarried, felt excluded.

'Go on, off with you child,' she said, holding a broom and pointing to the door. A witch needing privacy before she could mount it.

'And I want a full report in the evening. No more nonsense about boarders in room number thirteen, when out there are English roses for the plucking. Even if some do have thorns.' And just as I was going out the door, 'This is a respectable establishment,' deflating me. I thought I was being subtle.

Then on the spiral staircase of a London bus, a spiral staircase like so many other staircases, where I usually got inspired, I remembered I already had friends in London. The twins from school. Don and Tom who were going to be painters and sculptors. Figuring out they were bound to be living here, the way they promised, in studios the size of stadiums. They were bound to know if there were a town or a suburb, even a county that had a house like the one we had in Newtown. Somewhere that could be a home instead of what London was, merely an architectural reminder. They'd always been pioneers in everything they did, their knowledge encyclopaedic. Feeling warm at the thought of seeing them, knowing they already had a pencil sketch of my early lusts, my family. So I resolved to see them later in the afternoon. Definitely. Not now, because going to see them would require another search. A root about for their address, and quite frankly in terms of searches at that moment, I was overloaded.

Upping the stakes in my major quest, by going to Hampton Court Palace, going through its tired and scraggy labyrinth devoid of Minotaurs or any thread that could lead you back to the entrance. Looking from the outside of the palace at what were called, the Queen's Grace and Favour Apartments, where the island's greatest landlady, like mine, offered sanctuary. To be honest, I went there to fill in a morning, to at least contemplate what I'd say to Don and Tom, if I found them.

So much had happened in the lost years, so much that

on reflection it seemed like nothing. I guess the minutiae of life even though more interesting than its major events, is always quickly forgotten. I say this because Newtown now seemed as far away as Como, university, even Athens. A putrid shard of memory.

On the way back from Hampton Court, avoiding Saint Pancras station. Too many staring gargoyles. I'd had enough of them. Of Waynes that seem to vanish. Of people and objects that eluded me. Enjoying the fact that I could be so Victorian. Melodramatic. Like London.

Going to Belgravia, which I'd heard had the finest preserved terraces in London, finding that Belgravia was exactly that, a place of beautiful graves, where residents in style rehearsed how to behave at everyone's ultimate destination. Dismissing any thought that Don and Tom lived in such a marble wasteland. They had too much fire for that.

Giving up my private search for the time being, going to Scotland Yard, a place that keeps files not on houses but on every single criminal in England, thinking they'd surely know where Don and Tom were. Entering via a mock-up sign underneath big papier mâché letters that read British Council.

**5 6**　　'What they look like then?' the man at the desk asked.

'They're twins,' I said. 'They look the same.'

'Only need to describe one,' he said. So I did, going into detail about their appearance, their eyebrows, omitting sexual references to our shared passions.

'They look a bit like Michael York,' I said.

'Get off with ya. This ain't Actors Equity sir. I mean to say, wouldn't it be easier for all concerned,' he said rather bluntly, 'if you had their surnames?' Mistaking me the way the English do with everyone not English, as Irish, their version of plain stupid.

'Well, it would, but it was a while back and the names have gone out of my mind.'

'Easily done sir,' he said, disappointed. 'Sometimes I forget me own name,' trying to be funny. 'May I ask yours? For reference.'

'Well you can,' I said, 'but I'm not the one who's lost,' flagrantly dishonest. Neatly avoiding embarrassment.

'Lord help us,' he said like the Archbishop of Canterbury, glancing down at his desk.

'Well, the only two twins, we have on our books . . .' he said, desultorily flicking through a volume the size of the Domesday Book, in which all artists of whatever hue and persuasion were listed. Naturally by birth, and residence, but more interestingly, by profit and loss, with marks next to their name in red and black numbers.

'... Are Gilbert and George, two homosexual gentlemen. Mainly do pictures of rent boys, if you forgive me French. But they're old geezers.' Then, remembering wistfully, 'Sent them and their show to Russia a couple of years ago, or was it China?' His mood changing, 'Unfortunately the Reds wouldn't keep 'em.'

'Here,' I said. 'Maybe this can help,' taking out of my wallet a picture. A picture showing Don, Tom, Mark and I, taken in Athens where we leaned on each other's shoulders as if supporting the base of a French Empire clock. Four youths entwined as in a Victorian conversation piece. Maybe an Attic vase.

I suppose I could tell you sentimentally that the photo was leached of colour, its edges torn or even with some bathos that it represented youth caught in a golden age that's evaporated, but it's not true, because the picture looked as if it were taken yesterday. Today. Maybe even tomorrow.

'See here,' I said to the man at the desk as if I were showing him a picture of a recent holiday. Or angry. 'Over here, on this side, is me.'

'And a very good likeness too, sir,' he said, as if I weren't showing him a picture but an Italian cameo.

'Who's this one then?' he said, pointing to Mark.

'Forget him,' I said. 'he's American. We're in England. These two, leaning on each other, just in front of the second column of the Parthenon.'

'Oh,' he said. '*Them.*'

'You know *them* then?' I said.

'Course I know *them* then,' he said. 'That clapped out old

building in the background made my penny drop,' talking about the mouth that once housed the Elgin dentures reductively.

'Them, I don't mind telling you sir, are some of our most frequent applicants.' Turning the pages of his Domesday Book.

'... have them here, along with the others,' turning quite a few pages, '... filed under Young Turks. Don't know why they call them young Turks,' he said, 'Turkey I found cheap myself. Your twins and their mates are in fact our most expensive customers. Seem to want money from the public purse just for sneezing.'

Then ripping off a sheet of paper, which like everything in England (even toilet paper) had the Royal Crest on it the way at school I used to burn my initials on my pencil case so it wouldn't go missing, he began writing their address.

'Don't know if I should be doing this,' he said. 'Information is actually confidential. But if you're a terrorist, and would like to blow them up, you'd be doing the Old Dart a favour.'

Looking directly at me, handing the royal chit. 'Sort of funny looking though aren't ya? But I suppose it's because you're foreign.' Making me think he might be Australian.

'Thanks muchly,' I said, taking the chit, deciding not to look at it until I was on the street so I wouldn't appear eager. Maybe in a small way showing reserve, that though Greek or Australian I could also be English.

In the fallopian tubes of the underground, unfolding the chit whose address had the number twenty-two, (my age) next to the street, Old Chestnut Road, Hackney. Which isn't really true, but might as well have been from what I saw when I got there.

**57**     Twenty-two Old Chestnut Road was very much like Twenty Old Chestnut Road, which in turn was identical to Eighteen Old Chestnut Road, and so on until the last building in the street achieved the grand sum of zero. It was a warehouse like the others adjoining it, still retaining charm, like the ones I remembered in Macdonaldtown by which I mean it wasn't renovated. The cargo hook and rail high up on the outside, in the middle of the triangular lintel, probably being the same cargo hook the East India Company once used to hoist bales of Indian rubber and rattan. Anything that once made their fortune. Maybe their Indian suppliers. I mean it really did look like some of the warehouses of Macdonaldtown, the ones that accommodated trains at night when they went to sleep, so in a way I didn't mind it.

Its bricks were small and regular, sooted with age, from the coal and coke fires Londoners once used for heat and light, whose beauty Samuel Pepys described vividly. The warehouses' chimneys were also Georgian, as sensual as columns, flying pink smoke, a bit like the flag on Buckingham Palace raised to show that the Queen was in, and not just a figment of the public's imagination. Maybe the pink smoke a message to me to enter quietly in case Don or Tom were busy doing something thunderously artistic.

pinpricks and bayonets

Smoke and hook making me feel like a Gurkha heading for oblivion.

Inside the warehouse was a long hallway, and another sign, this one with an arrow marked *Studio*. And another sign next to it, a red one, saying *On Air*, probably lit during emergencies. And a smaller handwritten sign saying, *Don, three doors to the left*. Then on Don's door, *no knocking. Just enter*. But I didn't. Pausing, listening to what was going on inside, in case I caught Don fucking, which was likely, because it reminded me of having to wait for him the way he had waited for me outside so many bedroom doors during our schoolboy days in Athens.

I could hear Don's voice, loud as ever, saying, 'One, two, three, pull. Come on lovie you can do it.' Followed by grunting. This went on for nearly half a minute before being repeated.

'One, two, three, pull. Come on lovie harder.' So taking the original handwritten sign at its word I went in only to see Don on one side of the room, his face screwed up in pain, bracing himself against a wall, arms and hands one over the other. Like an Australian lifesaver, pulling someone in to safety. A tug o' war. Except it wasn't a reel he pulled at but a long shiny black ribbon. A small girl about twenty one, in a brown zip-up knitted jumpsuit, who could've been the daughter of Emma Peel, was pulling the same ribbon from the other end of the room. A girl who was no match for his brute strength and bulldog determination.

'Don?' I said from the door, question mark in my voice even though I knew it was him. He still looked like Michael York. But from which film? *Cabaret*? Or *England Made Me*? Startling Don into dropping the ribbon, Don saying, 'Thank Christ you're here, old man, could do with another hand. Haven't quite pulled this off yet.' Making me feel unsure whether he recognised me, because last time I looked I was still young.

'It's me, Don,' I said.

'Well of course it's you my lovely,' he said. 'Who else would you fucking be? Fucking super you're here. Celia, take five sweetheart. This is an old friend.' But as Celia dropped the ribbon on her side she angrily put her hands on her hips, a real Emma Peel now, saying, 'Cheek of you Don, telling me *when* and if I can take five. And *sweetheart* to boot. I thought we'd gone past the patriarchal bullshit.'

'Make it fucking six then,' Don said.

'Bloody hell,' she said. Obviously no minor disagreement.

'Want me to come later?' I said, ready to turn.

'No, stay,' he said. 'Don't worry. This'll take a jiffy. Please. Lots to tell old man.' And with that he went and tried to put his arm around Celia who brushed it aside, Don following her to a corner of the room where they had one of those loud whispering-type arguments you're not supposed to hear, even though you hear every syllable. Particularly the word 'fucking'.

Celia hissing that in their fucking 'project' their was no fucking hierarchy. That fucking hierarchies were best left to the fucking military and fucking clergy and how even fucking morons know hierarchy is the enemy of cooperative artists like them. Don saying, like a tired husband seeking divorce.

'Celia, you're absolutely right. Fucking hell. I'm a cad.' Also describing himself as a bounder for having even hinted she take a break, when both as an independent person in general, and as a woman in particular, 'You're perfectly capable of making such decisions.'

'Do I have to explain this each fucking time?' Celia asked.

'Celia, sweetie,' Don said. 'Right again. What can I say? Except I'm fucking sorry. Love.'

Celia saying, 'You patronising fucking bastard. You're only acting like this because *he's* at the fucking door,' pointing at me. The brief sight of us together convincing her we were co-conspirators, members of an exclusive group she called The Boys' Club, that had chapters not just in Belgravia, but all over London.

'Well, what do you want me to do then?' Don asked. For the first time losing patience. 'Ask *you* if *I* can take fucking five? Will it make you happy, love?' Sending Celia into another paroxysm of rage and tears, the sort you normally reserve for news of your only son's accidental drowning. Don guiltily raising her from her knees, apologising profusely. Saying he'd never do it again. Never.

'I'm fucking sorry. Okay? I was joking. I'll never again tell you when to take five, or call you love.' She, saying through sobs, that in a perfect world (apparently what they had in that room), 'no one needs *permission*'. Particularly for breaks. That way they could safeguard the sovereign rights of individuals, the thing John Stuart Mill and Kylie religiously believed in.

'Thank you for being so fucking understanding,' Celia said, her tears subsiding, then she exited, scowling at me. Making me glad I didn't arrive prior to their lunch break.

**58**   'It may seem silly,' Don said, once Celia was out of earshot, 'the way we go on. But she's very nice, and we do bloody good work together. Just a bit high strung. Her girlfriends left her recently in the lurch.'

'Girlfriends?'

'Plural, Celia doesn't hold much store for monogamy. Calls it *exclusionism*. I think you're supposed to fuck the whole human race. Should've been a gay boy. Now what brings you to London, old man? Still looking for something?' he asked, showing me a canvas seat next to a clothing basket where more ribbons, like pasta made by Italian women, hung to dry.

'Tell me all.'

'Really want to hear?'

'Fucking hell. Yes.'

So I did, telling him a bit about Australia, university, my life and tribulations, mentioning again first love, the importance of my old home. I forget how I put it. But not as bluntly as usual. I was more subtle and lyrical. A lot of which interested him because he was an artist. His attention totally focused. I could tell because all through my speech his eyelids kept drooping.

'How fucking sad,' he said when I'd finished, his eyes opening. 'All violins and no orchestra. All that looking and no finding.' Then brightening up, 'Tell you what I'm looking for and that's a place like Athens. I remember Athens distinctly. Now that's a place after my own heart. Surely there we were fucking happy.' But only one of his last two words was accurate. Then, tired of even the memory of Athens, getting his second wind he said, 'Say, why don't you help me out old man? We can knock this over in a tick.'

'Knock what over?'

'This. Help me pull it off.' Pointing to the ribbon.

'Celia won't mind?'

'No she won't,' Don said, jumping to his feet. 'I'll sweet talk her. Besides what she doesn't know won't hurt her.' Then more ruefully, '. . . An awful lot she doesn't know, come to think of it. Quite frightening really. Comprehensive school you know. A bit like your university from the sound of it, but not as sexy. Here,' he said, throwing me one end of the ribbon.

'I thought you'd be a painter,' I said.

'But I am a painter old man,' he said, joyfully. 'But I use film.'

Realising for the first time that the black, shiny oily looking ribbon he gave me to hold was exactly that, film, making me feel small, I won't say stupid. Probably seventy millimetre.

'On the count of three, now,' Don said, bracing himself again against the wall. 'One, two,' and with that we pulled with the force of Egyptian slaves dragging stones to a *mastaba*. Grunting and sweating. Pitted against each other, the way I remembered the hooded combatants in *World Championship Wrestling*. The stubborn long entrail, growing with our exertion, stretching out and twisting first by an inch, then several feet.

'That'll do old man. That'll do. By God, I think we've fucking done it.' Collapsing into the same canvas director's chair which squeaked, winded as if he and I had just hogtied the cattle of the Sun. I was breathless.

'What are *you* . . . I mean *we*, fucking doing?' I was beginning to sound like Celia.

'Film,' he said, as if it were self-explanatory. 'I make films. The way you make up fantasies about houses, I make fantasies to do with film. Except it's art.'

'Right,' I said, deciding to forgive the slight that said my search, my quest and passion was not artistic. 'Why the fucking muscle?'

'Shouldn't swear so much old boy. Doesn't suit you.'

'You swear all the time.'

'Bloody don't,' he said. 'Anyway I was saying, it takes too much bloody muscle if you ask me. I just dream of the day the process gets automated. I dream the dream of electric sheep.'

'That's from *Blade Runner*,' I said.

'Bloody right. I'm trying to say something about automation old boy . . . because when it does . . .' Don said, staring poetically into the distance, as if his eyes were field glasses, 'I will arise and go there, and by the lake shore wattle make . . .' moving from science fiction to Innisfree, and back. 'In the meantime it takes grunts, and grants . . .'

'Can I have the nursery version?'

'Nursery version?' he said. 'Oh dear, this is what happens when you get sent down without a degree. In your case I suppose, up,' Don said. 'It's bloody obvious.' Pointing to the dead snake on the floor. The anaconda throttled.

'Bloody is not.'

'No?'

'No.'

'Pushing the envelope, old man,' he said. 'What do you think we're doing? Pushing the envelope and trajectory of linear narrative. Avoiding closure. Why? I hear you say. I'll tell you bloody why. Because for too long we've been constrained by stories a bit like yours that move inexorably from the beginning to the end, like life was some fucking freight train. Some bloody Orient Express headed for collision.' Making me feel sorry for Graham Greene and Agatha Christie.

'Or penis,' said Celia returning with a Wendy burger and a milkshake, consumables at odds with her convictions. 'Life's not meant to be straight up and down is it?' Both of them telling me alternately, among a lot of bloodies and fuckings, that they were tired of closed narratives that they described as 'sarcophagi'. How all stories to date were mummies, preferring the ululations and undulations of ellipses, and eclipses, new stories, happy to apply their own push/pull against the arrow of narrative. Like they were bloody doing. Because the arrow, in fact the whole quiver according to Celia and Don, was more owned by Hollywood than struggling individual archers.

'But how do you put such wonderful stuff through the projector?' I asked. Don and Celia pityingly looking first to each other then to me.

'The projector?' Don said. 'Projectors are the bloody mincers of the imagination.'

'Tyranny of the frame?' I said, trying to sound helpful. Alarming Celia into saying, 'Don't they have art in Australia?' her face screwed up and worried.

'Not this quality,' I said. 'Honestly.'

'That's because they've never bloody suffered,' she said. 'Too hot down there. Bakes people's brains. Speaking of which, it's stifling in here.'

'Come on then,' Don said, rising. 'Old boy, you'll never find anything staying here. But first you need some basic research. And not before time. *Scusi* Celia,' Don said. 'Use the nail file bit if you wish.'

'I do wish, Donald, thank you,' Celia replied, chomping into her burger, this time without a tantrum, picking up a bastard file with which she began to scratch the film's emulsion. Violently, the way I once seared into the flesh of masonite and canvas.

Don and I leaving the room, going back into the hallway with the emergency light, this time dimmed.

'Now, what was it you're looking for? Oh, dear, that's right. We really will have to start with the basics.' As we went past rooms used by other film makers called Cutting Rooms where you could overhear them being nasty to each other and in the narration they used over the faces of interviewed subjects.

**5 9**   On the street, Don making me walk briskly.

'Come on, hop to it old man,' he said. 'Otherwise we'll never get started. You're so bloody slow.' Left and left again, until feeling as if we were going round in circles, I said, 'Where are we going?'

'To find what you want. I mean if you can't find it in life maybe it's in the movies,' he said. 'Where else? Or have you gone off them? Remember? We used to go to the cinema all the time. Halcyon days.'

'I remember,' I said. Don hailing a cab, instructing it to take us to Oxford Circus.

'This I guarantee you'll love. It mightn't be Visconti,' he said, referring to a time when he and I and the group were fans, 'but it just might give you that special clue,' the very thing I was looking for. He said this as we settled down in a theatre crowded with students. Waiting for the lights to dim, with me, beginning to feel dim already.

'What's it called?'

'*Anything You Bloody Like*,' he said, a title I thought sounded dull. Other than the expletive. Maybe Don meant *As You Like It*.

'Not *House of the Rising Sun*, I hope,' I said, to be smart and to bring his mind back to what I was doing in London.

'You'll see,' he said. 'You'll see.'

Then the lights went down in a quick fade, the way they must've during the Blitz. The curtain parting, the silver screen bathing itself in light. But I wasn't sure how the screen did this without a mincer. Or a butcher to operate it.

Sitting for a good few minutes, nothing happening. Before I said to Don, 'I think the film's got stage fright,' since sound and image were reluctant to make an appearance.

'Shoosh, old man, or you'll miss it,' he said, taking a deep breath. 'Drink it in. Be lateral. It might be a lead.' 'Hardly', I thought, the atmosphere in the cinema too funereal like the Brompton Oratory. A mood I didn't mind, being tired of traipsing around London. Tired of my own company. Quite happy to be with Don, someone from the past, a friend, and not overly impatient for the feature to begin, which was a long time coming.

I say this because after about ten minutes of silence and empty screen, I began to feel sleepy, the cinema overly warm from central heating and from the breathing, pulsating body warmth of a capacity audience. Sleepy because the boys in the audience weren't as pretty as the boys in my lecture halls. Nothing like the audience of that porno parlour we used to visit, the *Kotopouli*.

Falling asleep some five minutes later. Discreetly, giving it my full attention, head up and eyes closed, the way Don did when I spoke about myself. Maybe dreaming of the *Kotopouli*, its aisles and toilets. Maybe of the Hub or my first laundry. Maybe the garage where I violated my pictures. Waking up some hour and a half later, my trip to the land of nod disturbed by clapping.

'Bravo,' said Don, jumping to his feet, 'bloody brilliant,' quickly followed by the rest of the audience. It probably was *As You Like It*.

'Encore, encore,' people cried, as if we were in a Music Hall and had witnessed a good rendition of *Burlington Bertie*.

'Sorry I missed it,' I said. Which was true, I was sorry, in case I missed the clue he was talking about, also because of the enthusiasm which swept through the auditorium.

'Missed it?' Don asked, his neck craning around the room, possibly to identify friends. Or rivals.

'Fell asleep before the punch line. Did the boy get the girl, the girl the boy, or the boy the boy?' I said, thinking that like all films, ultimately its plot would be an update on the films I used to adore about swords and sandals. Automatic weapons and espionage taking the place of net and trident.

'Didn't miss anything old man,' Don said waving to someone in the distance. 'I can honestly say you have a long way to go if there wasn't a clue in that for you. Excuse me a second,' while he went to gossip. Watching him do this for some time. Catching up with him outside, where he screamed when I approached, 'There you are old man, where have you been all this time?' The way he'd done inside to half the audience. Like a smiling hound, finding toothless foxes.

'Wasn't it wondrous?' he said, 'bloody wondrous, although a bit jejune in parts,' taking me by the arm. 'Keep up, old boy. Don't look so disappointed. We still have the world of literature to go yet. That's always full of clues, although usually they go nowhere. Now move.'

**60**     Taking me again to the left, around the Tottenham Court Road corner, to a branch of Waterstone's and a book launch, that through the plate glass of the store, I could see looked a bit like a pub counter lunch. White cheese and white bread everywhere. Glasses of red wine purely for colour.

'Always room for more,' Don said, opening the door as we breezed through, just in time for everyone's favourite part, the speeches. In the fiction section, where amid a plethora of books about adultery in Hampstead, the difficulties of tenure around the world's campuses, and historical figures recently resurrected to illuminate forgotten indignities, a series of people got up on a table to thank the publisher for being brave enough to bring out this new tome.

'Without whose courage this book would have been just another casualty. Unpublished. Unfound. Like an undiscovered body at the Battle of Culloden. Assassinated by Philistines,' the speaker said, even though my history told me they lived nowhere near Scotland.

The crowd passing around copies of the book, giving the launch the semblance of some Japanese gift-giving ceremony. Maybe they were Korean Moonies. Everyone signing their names in each other's books, like a card signed by the entire office for the retirement of the tea lady.

'Don, who is it by?'

'What do you mean, old man?'

'Who wrote it?'

'Bloody hell. What sort of question's that?' Don asked. 'The readers, dear, the readers, look at them,' pointing to everyone in the room. Puzzling me as I picked up a display copy only to see that each of the pages was blank, much like an unlined diary.

'These days the reader is more important than the bloody writer.'

'There's nothing in it.' Maybe I meant both book and rumour.

'What do you mean, nothing? Text is dead, use your imagination. Whatever it is you're looking for, lovers, all this house and garden nonsense, whatever you're fucking on about, project onto that. You're the one searching. Come on. Let's go. If we linger too much they'll think we're desperate.'

But I thought in my life I'd done quite enough projecting, so I put the book down, Don telling me on the way out and as we walked through Regents Park, 'what passes as literature in this country is a middle class prison, with authors the decorators'. Saying how now there was a bloody revolution afoot, which like all revolutions began in France. Maybe that's why he kept using the word bloody. A revolution that would eradicate distinctions based on education, taste and class. And what he called the canon. Spitting on the word, 'canon', narrowly missing one of the park's ducks.

'Quack,' went the duck.

'Even that, these days,' Don said, referring to the noise, 'is a contribution.' Maybe he was kidding.

'What about the film then?'

'What about it?'

'Someone must've written it.'

'The audience, darling, the audience.'

'You mean the screen was blank?'

'Oh, dear,' Don said. 'We have eyes but can not see.' The whole thing sounding like a religious experience. Saying, 'Darling the revolution now taking place in the arts is huge. Bloody big I tell you. A turning point in intellectual history. What you see around is . . .' he meant punks, '. . . is nothing in comparison. Mere nose thumbing at the establishment. The death rattle of a corrupt order about to snuff it, as for rock bands like The Cure they're actually a curse.'

'What about The Jam then?'

'The Jam?' Don looked as if he'd tasted something rotten. 'Aptly named. They're just a bloody pit stop.' Saying something about the elliptical high road to freedom. 'As for The Sex Pistols, penile dribblers. Can you imagine any of them cracking a fat?' Making me wonder what he'd say if I told him about Skyhooks, and the neighbours' K-Tel marvels featuring Herb Albert and his trumpet. Explaining Kamahl I dismissed as too difficult.

'Know what I mean?' he said in the middle of this tirade, using England's greatest contribution to rhetoric. Which I didn't.

Saving his greatest scorn for the theatre, which he said kept refusing to embrace this revolution, this advance, making the theatre sound to me like plucky little Belgium. 'The West End's too busy with Shakespeare and pathetic reinterpretations of kings and queens portrayed as living in stultifying 1950s parlours, or in Milton on Keynes, parading about in Nazi breeches. Which is the same bloody thing really. Disgusting. Fops all of them. God I hate this country,' skimming a rock on the pond and inducing massive feathered immigration.

'*Vive la France*,' shouting his enthusiasm for the nation that provided the theories. A statement I thought any English king or queen other than Lear, even in Nazi breeches, would find treacherous.

'*Vive la France*,' he said again. Quieter. A bit depressed really. I say this because Don seemed to have calmed down. Exhausted his spleen, like a runner at the end of a marathon race who realises he should've gone in for sprinting. He looked thoughtful. Sad even. Raising a finger to his lip. Uncertain. Making me feel sorry for him. Because even though I'm explaining this accurately like everything else so far, it isn't to mock him. In many ways I admired him. Don was always way ahead of me. At least he could feel anger and fire, albeit for theories with the durability of Carnaby Street fashions. And he was trying to be helpful. Maybe he looked sad because he didn't really believe any of what he'd said. But I might be reading too much into it.

'Sometimes,' he said, a lot more serious now, 'I feel as if I'm searching for something too. Not sure what. Actually, I feel like retiring to France, because know what? When they open me up, unlike you, they'll find something specific. They'll find Calais written on my heart. Never know, maybe Athens . . . just to take up the joy of exile. Must feel a bit like that yourself old man. How long have you been away searching for whatever the hell house you mentioned? Was a house wasn't it?'

'Six months.'

'Six months is forever in some people's books.'

medea's children

'Even in an unlined diary,' I said, Don hesitating a moment, smiling, unsure if I was sending him up, or being nasty. Then staring into the lake, as if looking for a lost bracelet, his whole manner suggested this wasn't the time for it.

'Ever miss it? Get homesick yourself?' Don asked, handing me a stone. 'Or did you really have enough?'

'Miss what?'

'You know,' he said, leaving 'know' in the air, hanging. What did he mean? Youth? We still had some. Schooldays? They were finished. Lovers that had become the clouds of memory? Families or countries? A suburb. He knew what I was here for.

'Not really,' I said, thinking, like him, there wasn't any need to say more. I mean I'd already told him. Me, skimming a stone successfully across the water, avoiding a late group of smug ducks, floating by like literary critics.

'You know Australia always sounds to me so young and fresh. New blood.' He said, as if Australia were a source of nourishment for vampires. 'Young and fresh,' he repeated unhappily, like an old person waiting for an organ transplant, 'like spring lamb,' he added. As if Australia were for Sunday dinner. Maybe by lamb he meant what Britain traditionally used Australia for, to provide understudies, for their theatres of war rather than the West End. Top billing in violent and botched productions.

'I bet the men are gorgeous. All that sand and seaspray curing their beautiful hides. Yum. I don't know how you could bear to tear yourself away,' he said, turning to me, recovering his mood, the spring lamb I came from becoming bovine.

'You know old boy,' he said, 'I've been thinking, this

search for the home as you put it, might take some time. Why don't you put your stump here. You're not planning to go back are you?'

'No reason,' I said.

'Good,' he said. 'For a moment I thought you were appallingly 1960s. You know, provincial going abroad. The brain drain. Cultural desert. All that shit Germaine Dreer and Clive Inane bore us about. Let's keep walking.' Getting up from his squat position, cheerier now. I was, too, since we walked past the colonnaded terraces of Regents Park that were built by Nash, making me think of their builder followed by Edward Lear when Don said, 'Now no more nonsense, certainly don't want to hear anymore about this house. Call it something else. Don't know what though, because language my friend is dead. Nothing but a bunch of bloody street lights. Pedestrian.' Like the DON'T WALK sign we blithely disobeyed.

As we almost got crushed by what used to be called an omnibus. The sort we used to have in Newtown, a double decker.

'Come,' he said. Much his old self now. 'Tom'll die when I produce you, besides he might have hints of his own. He's like you, so filthy it's wicked,' forgetting what had dampened his spirits. Taking me again via more streets that veered to the left. Back to the warehouse, making me feel comprehensively educated. The research exhausted. Maybe even ready for exhibition.

'Honestly old man, he'll just die,' something we narrowly avoided.

**6 1**     Until we were again in a lane near Old Chestnut Road, with Don saying, 'Through here. Quicker by half.' Going through a connecting passageway to the warehouse, arriving through perspex swing doors to a room that was the size of a stadium. Except there were no nude models nor the mirrors I'd expected. Just Tom and a young man who appeared to be his assistant. Tom like Don, looking for all the world like another Michael York. Different to Don only because he was wearing overalls. Don preferring tweed and black jeans. Tom's young assistant in a lab coat, standing in the middle of the room, next to a plinth supporting the Portland Vase. The tuber roses of the worn carpet beneath the plinth strewn with pottery shards.

I knew it was the Portland Vase from its blue–black background. The white classical scenes in the foreground, like the snapshot in my pocket, reminding me of our schooldays, and what the man at the British Council said about a cameo.

Tom, still looking the same after all these years, although like Don, and I guess me, a little bit worn, in that twenty-two-year-old way, standing back for a second, his hand under his chin, briefly admiring it, before saying, 'Jason. Now!' Jason the assistant bringing down an axe. Smashing the Portland Vase into as many pieces as it had once been smashed before, by a drunken vandal. The blade almost getting caught up in his lab coat. Taking my breath away with the noise. Shards flying everywhere.

Up and down Jason jumped with the axe, bringing it down hard. Smash, smash, smash, the way I'd heard Australian farmers with sticks tend to plagues of rabbits. And again. Smash.

'Tom's got hundreds out the back,' Don said. 'Unfortunately, it's only a copy. Arts Council's budget doesn't run to originals. So they bloody claim. Bastards.' Replicas I could see from where I stood. Hundreds of vases. Not just imitations of the Portland, but vases from Sèvres and shogun Japan. As well as several full scale models of what appeared to be the Pietà of Michelangelo.

'Excellent bloody work Jason,' Tom said, moving towards his assistant, feeling the axe blade to see if it'd been blunted, still not having seen us. 'Now it'll be the devil's own work to put it back together.' Reaching over to a shelf, handing Jason a pot of glue. 'Remember,' he said. 'Always that word, remember,' I thought. 'I don't want to see any silly recognisable shapes, representations, fables or allegories,' he finished.

'What you want to see then?' Jason asked.

'Don't care,' Tom said raising his voice. 'Whatever you bloody like. But nothing recognisable. Be quick but firm.'

Tom turning round to us, 'Well look who's here.' Big grin on his face. Frightening really. Maybe looking to see if I had handles.

'How nice to see you old boy,' extending his hand, but I forgave Tom for also calling me old, because I knew twins were governed more by genes than cultural influence.

'How super you're here. Do tell all. What are you doing in bloody London?'

## medea's children

'This and that.'

'That tells me precisely nothing. Surely there's more to tell than that,' he said.

So I gave him a precis, briefer than the one I gave Don. Again I'm not sure how I put it, paraphrasing what I was looking for. Leaving out words like search and quest. Even proper names like Wayne and Newtown, talking more about finding a home where I could realise my potential. Not wanting to expose myself once again as vulnerable. A perpetual exile.

'Dear, dear,' Tom said when I finished. 'All bloody chicken and no chips. Down under does sound rough.'

But I was way ahead of him. 'Unlike Athens Tom.'

'Definitely unlike Athens old boy. Now that's a place after my own heart. But that was a long time ago. Let's not get sentimental. Come. See what we've done.' Pointing to a series of chambers near the replicas.

'I want to show you. 'Don's seen it but you haven't.' Don nodding encouragement. Taking us into another room. A smaller one. 'This one is the powder room,' pointing to the floor. On it, a ten by ten canvas with symmetrical white lines on a black background, in the manner of Bridget Riley. Except that the white lines being applied to the canvas by a group of three young men and three young women were not being applied in paint. But gun powder.

'Bloody brilliant luck. They've almost done,' Tom said, striking a match, thankfully only to light a cigarette, waving it around, as the youngest carefully poured powder on the last line from a sack. The way you do with arsenic when you want to kill rodents. In one corner of the room, a silver umbrella on a stand, the type used by professional photographers. Near it

pinpricks and bayonets

a girl with a large format camera, who said, 'Stand back kids,' the group standing back for a crew shot.

Flash.

'No one move,' she said. 'One more now.'

Flash. Flash.

'Hurry up, Bernice,' one of them said. 'Feel flat as a fallen arch.'

Tom looking on like an approving uncle, saying, 'For posterity you know.' As if I didn't know the purpose of photography.

Maybe I didn't, because suddenly after the third flash, Tom said, 'Okay. Enough.' Like a commander. And at his word, the people who'd been working on the canvas fell on it, face downwards, like glove puppets. No. More like mandarins at the feet of Kubla Khan. Sniffing the feet, I mean the powder violently, until within seconds it vanished.

'Speed,' said Tom.

'They're certainly fast.'

'I mean the powder. Bought with the money from our grant. The photos are proof it existed. Time's winged chariot. What a bloody downward spiral it all is,' he said with melancholy.

'Photo finish,' I said, thinking this witty. But Tom ignored it.

'Speed is the accelerant of art, what puts time and art in motion,' he said. Then turning to his group of workers,

'Okay greedy hogs. Off.' Then to me, 'We'll use a straw, I think it's more dignified,' producing a length of garden hose. 'Unlike these pigs and their SNOUTS,' he yelled, kicking the last straggler away. Making them scamper like dogs. One actually yelped. 'It'll clear your nasal passages. Then you can really tell me what you're here for.'

**6 2**   And we did have some speed, not from the floor where most of the powder had been exhausted but from a new satchel Tom produced, sniffing more bloody lines than Bridget Riley ever painted. More bloody strings than ever laid out by Barbara Hepworth. The acrid smell and taste hitting our lungs, throats and nostrils. Then,

everyonestartedtalkingatthesametimeaboutwhateverit wasthatcameintotheirbloodyheadlikeastreamofconsciousnessoradamthathadbrokenthatwasimpossibletostoptalking aboutourpastthefutureloversssharedloversthatdisappointed moneyinfactanythinganyonecouldbloodythinkofnoone actuallylisteningtoasinglewordbecauseitwasmuchmore importantrightthenandtheretoactuallytalkratherthanlisten thewholeeffectbeinglikereadingaparagraphinwhichthere wasnobloodypunctuationandspacingeverythingwe approvedofbeingmarkedassuperorbrilliantandeverything wedisapprovedofbeingmarkedaswicked.

'Super,' Tom said, some time later as we ran out of powder. Quite a while later.

'Brill,' Don said.

'Wicked,' I repeated.

'Know what I mean?' Don said. Although who could have known what any of us meant? Or what I wanted them to believe.

'Christ I'm tired,' Tom said.

'*Stanco*,' Don said. Not using his favoured French, but Italian.

'Me too,' I said.

'Work so bloody hard,' Tom said wearily.

'Like Trojans,' I said.

'Navvies,' he said, 'in these parts is more usual.'

'My arms feel as if they're going to drop,' Don added, wanting sympathy, reverting to English. Maybe he and Celia were aspiring to the Venus de Milo.

'Well, kids it's been marvellous,' I said. Thinking I'd had enough. Once again, they'd been useless.

'Oh, you can't go now old man,' Tom said.

'I must,' I said, which sounded sort of formal. 'Promised my landlady.' Suggesting rather cryptically that she and I had what they and I once had. The special relationship of America and Britain.

'I absolutely forbid it old boy,' Tom said, jumping to his feet with a spurt of energy.

'*Verboten*,' Don said, continuing his lingual tour of the Continent.

'Besides,' Tom said, 'we haven't figured out how to help you yet. Anyway, Jason's almost finished. You can't leave now. Hurt his feelings.'

'Finished what?'

'The assembly,' Tom said, like Henry Ford.

It was true, inside the main chamber where the plinth stood, Jason had finished the assembly. The Portland Vase was now nothing like the original. The finished product actually resembling a canvas by Jackson Pollock. Consisting of shards and pieces stuck together in a manner that was arbitrary. No recognisable shape, or representation, fable or allegory. The vase was now a mosaic of black and white. Neither conical, triangular, nor oblong. But a polygon. Itself. A collection of endlessly repeating blue–black and white colour, whose edges at times resembled the Matterhorn, and at times the plains of Egypt. Occasionally it jutted out like the oscillations of an electro-encephalogram. The whole thing like an aerial of Sydney Harbour. The stark white glue between the pieces, whiter than even what I could recall of Perkin's paste. Veins of lightning. Spoof emitted by a large and frustrated penis. Maybe all of it like memory.

'Touch it if you like,' Tom said. And I did, feeling burrs where once there was smoothness.

I'm saying this not as a put down, to use that rusted tool of irony, that the English also think has a crest on it. And absolutely not as a trite or comic send-up of deconstruction, and rather confused French theorists. That's best left to fiction, next to adulteries in Hampstead.

No. I say this because contrary to what I expected it *was* beautiful. Certainly entirely different, nothing like the original, but undeniably a thing of beauty. A thing which maybe shouldn't be worshipped, but at least cherished. Finer than the Elgin marbles, in fact anything I could remember of my own fractured life.

'A bit bloody disappointing isn't it?' Don said. Not to me but to Tom.

'Rather,' Tom said. 'I've seen Jason do better.' Like a curator at Sotheby's.

'Maybe he didn't understand your instructions,' Don said to Tom in a music hall aside.

'No, I think Jason understood bloody well,' Tom said. 'Besides it's important to avoid over articulations.' Funny

pinpricks and bayonets

how words, like smells, could conjure up a time so long ago. Me, snapping back to the present.

'And what do *you* think old man?' they both asked.

'To tell you the truth boys,' I said, 'it's a gem.' Not telling them that until I saw it, I was beginning to see them, their work, and their studios less as forges and foundries of genius, and more a bunch of old cobblers. Finding them entirely unhelpful.

'Really must fly,' I said.

'No, stay,' Tom said.

'You must,' Don said. 'I'll speak to Celia. Maybe she can bring in some food. Let's have a round table discussion about what you're looking for. Celia's good at committees.'

'Please,' I said. 'Couldn't bear it.'

'Besides,' Tom said, in the direction of the replicas, 'we're about to start on our *Pietà* of Resistance,' Jason coming back holding a ball-peen hammer.

'No I must,' I said.

'Why? Don't you like us?'

'I have to go,' I said.

'Very well. Let him go,' Don said to Tom, suddenly angry. Tom, taking the cue from Don, also angry, shrugging petulantly, resigned.

'We won't hold you captive . . .' but I cut in.

'Is it all right if you two don't call me old man? Makes me feel bloody ancient,' I said. How conceited.

'What should we call you?' they said.

'Oh,' I said absent-mindedly, 'anything you like. Isn't that what the film was called Don?' Don from his expression now certain I was having a go at them, eyebrows knitting.

'You sending us up?' he said. Furious.

'No,' I said. A lie.

'You sure?'

'Positive.'

'Hope so,' he said. 'We're only being friendly, you know. You're the one looking for some imaginary fucking pile.'

'I wasn't,' I said, 'sending anyone up,' but they were too smart for that, noticing that I'd left out any comment on the bit about the pile.

'Very well,' Don said, 'how 'bout we call you Sport then?' Much worse than what I objected to.

'Don't be so sensitive,' I said.

'You the only one allowed to be sensitive?' Don said. 'All that palaver 'bout Australia, lovers and homes. All that guff. Jesus wept.'

'Quite,' Tom said. 'Who do you think you are? Not half clever I can tell you. Jason,' Tom called out. 'The *Pietà* will have to wait. Would you be so good as to take *Sport* home. There's a good lad. Sport's had quite enough sport with us.' As if Jason were more than a bull in a china shop. In fact their servant. The whole incident upsetting me because I didn't really mean to be rude. Honest. For reasons still unclear to me, I can't say fair dinkum.

**63**   'Sport,' I said to myself, aloud in the tube, 'Sport,' on the Circle Line taking my escort, Jason and me, back to Bayswater. Admittedly sport was one of life's simple pleasures, but unlike sex, something I detested. Maybe I was talking aloud to practice keeping myself company since now I didn't have any friends left in London. Unlikely I'd ever see them again. Beginning to feel that no matter how hard I tried or where I went, an odour followed me. The sweet odour of acceptance, an exquisitely short-lived scent, inevitably replaced by stinking but more durable rejection. Particularly every time I mentioned what I was seeking.

'Talking to yourself,' Jason asked.

'Guess so,' I said. 'Don't seem very good at communicating with people. Think me crazy?'

'The opposite,' he said. 'You're the only sane one whose ever visited them.'

'Was I rude?' I asked as I moved aside so I wouldn't be crushed by a mob of German tourists.

'No, unfailingly polite,' he said. 'They wouldn't pick it up anyway. They're English.'

'And you're not?'

'Fortunately not.' Depressing me, making me think here at the end of the day when I was thoroughly exhausted

Jason was going to rave on about Scottish or Welsh devolution. Maybe about Orange and Green men, men who describe each other with these colours because they think one another Martians.

'Where are you from?' I asked.

'Not from England at any rate. From Yorkshire.' The whole thing, now we had reached Marble Arch, getting confusing.

'There's another one?'

'Same one,' Jason said. 'But most of the English down here don't care much about the North. London and Yorkshire are a bit like Rome and Calabria. Perfect strangers. Sport.'

'Leave it out,' I said, hating myself for sounding English. What was I turning into? A chameleon?

'Oops sorry,' Jason saying 'sorry', nicely, his heart, unlike Don's, containing no bitter message. The way he said it like a gentleman, made me look closer at him. Making me ashamed I'd snootily dismissed him as just a lab-coated assistant. Maybe I'd dismissed him because I'd never really had an interest in science. Maybe my view of Jason as just an employee, and my new snootiness came duty free with the booze placed in my Heathrow trolley.

But looking at him now, smiling, I saw he was extremely handsome. Perhaps Jason was one of the roses, my proprietress meant. Except not female. His complexion in parts the colour of my favourite rose called the Bourbon. His eyes, neither blue nor green, but the grey that Gainsborough and Constable used, to show the virtues the weather could offer if you chose to live in England. His hair parted in the middle the way the central line divides London, a ruddy brown of the type favoured by Titian. Giving Jason a sort of heroic look, his hair being neither straight nor curly, but wavy.

'You remind me of someone,' I said.

'Really?'

'Yeah, really.'

'Someone in the papers?'

'Hardly read them.'

'Good man,' he said.

Maybe he was a throwback to Eric the Red or sprang from a relative that had done a quite intimate grand tour of the Continent. A soft personality. His nose and lips and forehead, were sort of noble looking. His features, unlike Tom's exertions, perfectly sculpted. In fact he looked a little bit like Rupert Brooke.

'You know who you look like,' I said. 'Ru . . .'

'Yes, I know,' he said, without waiting for me to finish. 'If I had a penny every time I heard that. But I don't write poetry. Don't even like it.'

'For all you know I could've said Rupert Murdoch.'

'The dirty digger? Sod him. Anyway poetry's all a bit like England really. Depressing.' Showing me that though a little bit glum, he had a soul, and was capable of what people used to describe pretentiously as 'some finer feeling', unlike Don and Tom, who despite their chisel and theory, when it came down to it, were all hockey sticks. Quite unlike myself, people who were not looking for anything except playground praise and insults. Too insensitive and selfish to help me. Maybe I was becoming a hypocrite.

'Where would you rather be then?' I asked. 'If you don't like London.'

'India,' he said. 'South Africa, Australia, Bermuda, the Bahamas. Spain or Greece would do. You name it. Anywhere warm really.' At last, someone who was warm blooded and not just a lizard.

As we exited the tube in Bayswater, walking towards my bed and breakfast, 'Tell me,' I said.

'Tell you what, then?'

'I was going to ask . . . ,' I said, breaking off, really wanting to ask him something pornographic. Like what he looked like under his clothing. Whether he'd been snipped, or all of him was contained in his jockeys. But stopped myself, becoming very English.

'Ask whatever you like,' Jason said, 'honestly.'

I didn't. Couldn't. Instead I said, 'Why are you escorting me? You really a servant? I mean, they pay you, do they? It's only five p.m. I'll be perfectly all right. Papers say the Yorkshire Ripper is only interested in girls you know. Not boys. And he's up where you come from, not London. 'You didn't have to.' As I was about to open the door of my landlady's very proper establishment.

'I know,' he said. 'And I'm not their servant. Christ knows they don't pay. Came cause I wanted to.'

Just as she opened the door still holding a broom, saying, 'About bloody time,' as if I were her ward, then looking at Jason suspiciously.

'You thirteen?'

'No,' said Jason. 'Twenty-one actually.'

'Lucky.' How different she was to other landladies, perhaps not gay friendly. Making me think that if Jason had been the real boy from number thirteen, she would have ridden her broom straight to the real Scotland Yard. I say this because she had a suspicious look to her, the look of what Australians call, a dobber.

'A friend, Mrs . . .' I said, about Jason, trying to get by her.

'Sorry. Don't allow no visitors here.' She said. 'Visiting hours are over.'

## pinpricks and bayonets

'Is it a hospital?' Jason asked. 'Doesn't look like Saint Bartholemew's.'

'It ain't Saint Bartholemew's and it ain't no brothel either. I know you and your type,' she said to me.

'What is our type then?' Jason asked for me.

'Nancy boys,' she said. 'Just like all the other ones on *Top of the Pops* and that Elton John.' Maybe she said David Bowie.

'Why you old witch,' Jason said.

But she ignored this saying to me, 'And you, get your things and go.'

'You said I should make friends,' I said, teasing.

'Out,' she said standing at the door indicating my suitcase. While I was away she must've packed it. On top of it shamefully sitting what offended her more than my comment about the boy in number thirteen. My gay guide book, she obviously figured out it wasn't written by the slave Spartacus.

'Go on take your filth and be quick about it. Keep your money and your wicked ways to yourself.' And with that she picked up the suitcase, heavy as it was, and threw it along with the guidebook towards the street, as if it would spread another plague through London. Slamming the door, and in her haste forgetting to take her broom. After a second, reopening the door, her hand reaching out to grab it. This giving the incident a touch of comedy. Like I was in some *Carry On* movie. Maybe she was a thin version of Hattie Jacques. Jason and I obviously what she despised, a latter day *Lavender Hill Mob*.

I could see Jason also found it funny, rolling his eyes towards heaven. Picking up my bag and guide book like what he said he wasn't, a faithful servant.

'Sod her,' he said. 'Let's go.'

So this is what it's like to be evicted, I thought. A thing I'd seen my mother do so often and that I sometimes encouraged. To get rid of any one who'd offended me, who spoke to me harshly. How could I have thought even for a moment that this woman was anything like her? Could replace her?

'What you going to do now?' Jason asked.

'Don't know,' I said. 'Go back. Probably to Sydney. Had enough.' But instead of shaking my hand goodbye he kissed me. Briefly.

**6 4**   'What you on about? London's your home now. You're staying at my place.' Without even asking.

'I couldn't,' I said. 'Wouldn't want to put you out.' Falsely, like most Australians, hoping he'd insist on it.

'Load of rot.' he said. 'Ever heard of Providence?'

'Only the one on Rhode Island.' But he ignored my protests, hailing a cab neither of us could afford. And we were off.

'This'll cost a fortune. I haven't got enough pounds on me.'

'Won't,' he said. 'At any rate, no sense catching the tube, with luggage.'

'Let me pay for this,' I said, feeling bad, rooting around the lint in my pockets, knowing that being poor he probably lived with flatmates in some squat in Brixton, where visitors sleep on a ripped futon.

'No, no, no,' Jason said. 'My treat. Or as they say down under, shout. That's what they say, isn't it?'

'They do, and they do.' I said, remembering what I did on campus. But it was nearly six in the evening, and although late summer and not dark, I was tired, hardly in the mood to race and find alternatives listed in the straight guide books correctly named *Lonely* and *Rough*.

'Gents?' the cabbie said.

'Eaton Square,' said Jason.

'Eaton Square?' I said.

'You mightn't know it. It's in Belgravia if that means anything to you.'

'I sort of know it,' I said. 'Been past it.' But I didn't say anything to him about the lives I thought its inhabitants led. About graves and cemeteries. 'Sort of expensive.'

'Only if you're buying or renting,' he said.

'I needn't worry then?'

'Needn't worry. Now tell me what you're here for,' he said. 'What you go see Don and Tom about?'

'Once upon a time,' I said, being evasive, 'we had a lot in common.'

'So?'

'I sort of hoped they might give me some leads, a few pointers.'

''Bout what?'

'Where to live,' I said being really basic, 'how to recapture a time when things were perfect,' not wanting to confuse him but pushing it a bit towards the lyrical. I didn't over expand my aria though, because I was getting tired of repeating it.

Jason pausing when I finished, letting down the window of the cab as if needing fresh air. 'I think I can help you,' he said.

'How?'

'Let me judge that.'

'Very well, as you please,' I said. How condescending and grand I'd become.

As we pulled up in Eaton Square, Jason refusing the money I offered, saying I was being silly and that I could get the next one. As if there was going to be a next one.

## pinpricks and bayonets

Alighting from the black cab, amidst a group of stark grand white terraces, identical to each other but much grander than the warehouses of Old Chestnut Road. Certainly without cargo hooks and rails anywhere in evidence. So perfectly maintained they could've been the dolls houses of giants. Frighteningly bigger than Newtown's terraces. They were astounding.

'You live here?' I said. Amazed.

'If you call it living. Sometimes so stuffy I find it suffocating.'

'Don't say that,' I said, as he took my bag the last few steps to one of the grand terraces, opening either a red or a black door, I can't exactly remember. But I do remember a hallway or reception room bigger than the one in the British Museum. Full of marble busts, and paintings of men in red robes and wigs, who must've presided over earlier versions of *Divorce Court*. Separate paintings of ladies in beehives, who must've been estranged from their wig wearing husbands. As well as paintings of horses that could have been the ancestors of Rainlover, a horse I once bet on in the Melbourne Cup. Maybe Phar Lap. The interior of the house as different to my bed and breakfast terrace as a gutter to a gilded ceiling. I have to say even grander in some ways than our one in Newtown.

'You really live here?'

'When in town,' Jason said, putting down my bag in the hallway, and taking my coat from me.

'Wanted to surprise you. Won't judge me will you? There's enough of that on the walls.'

'What?'

'Judges.'

''Bout what?' I said innocently. But I knew what he

meant, figuring the old house must belong to some equally antique boyfriend of his, Jason caught up in the old sugar daddy routine of bitter relationships. Maybe he was the boyfriend of some flaccid-dicked Old Bailey Justice.

The boyfriend, whatever his name was, appearing that very instant, walking rapidly down the hall past the busts and wigs, probably ready in his polite and elderly way to greet us. Saying, 'Hello, hello, hello. I'll take that. Our Jason said you'd be coming.' Holding out his arm for my coat. As if Jason all along had meant to bring me here. As if this had been pre-arranged. As if the old bloke was a confidant of Destiny.

'Needn't worry Reynolds,' Jason said as if the old bloke were the artist Joshua Reynolds. 'If you don't mind we'd like to be alone tonight. Make a young man of yourself and go out on the town.' Jason, hanging my coat and taking off his lab coat, that he'd worn for his day's work with Don and Tom. A lab coat that was a bit like a dustcoat, the sort you'd never see in a terrace of this elegance. Only in mine.

'Very good,' Reynolds said. Not to me. But to Jason. A strange routine, the sugar daddy acting like a butler, turning away from us and marching back down the hall, past the horses and the divorcees, back to the shadows he'd made an entrance from.

'That's Reynolds,' Jason said. 'Family really,' pretending he wasn't Reynolds's lover. Or toy boy. Pretending that Reynolds didn't support him in return for a bit of 'how's your father', but that Reynolds was an heirloom. Maybe the 'family' he referred to, a group of wealthy older homosexuals sharing the house. Maybe the house was what the Fleet Street papers hoped (like me) might be in every London terrace. A brothel. A male one, which reporters, informed by shadow under-secretaries, were always on the brink of discovering. A real brothel. Not just a place of easy sex, like the one where I got my first blooding. For a moment I got excited.

'Seems nice,' I said. Meaning both the house and Reynolds. 'He treats you well?' Hoping it was one of those harmless old man/young man affairs and that Jason didn't have to wear hoods or play masters and prefects too often. About to tell him how in Australian schools, the cane was on the brink of being abolished.

'Very well,' Jason said. 'You'll love him. And I can already tell he likes you. Can smell it.' As if my odour was changing. As if he wanted to drag me into what I'd guessed this was, a sex for money partnership. As if expecting me to stay longer than the one night I intended.

'Shall we go in?'

'What about my bag?' I said.

'Leave it here for the moment,' Jason said. 'You won't need it where you're going.' The precise same thing my father said just before I left, whose strange echo I now heard in London.

Both of us walking down the hall into the gloom as if chasing Reynolds. Past the divorcees, and marble busts of women not at all like my mother. They looked at me from their pillars with an air of concern. As if here was danger. For a moment I thought they wanted to warn me. Busts that could have been the original model of tailors' busts I'd seen in a department store in Newtown called Brennan's, where the Berlei corporation advertised bras capable of lifting and separating.

Walking past male marble busts, generally of older blokes than Reynolds, which honestly despite what they were worth

I considered rubbish in comparison to the male wax busts also in Brennan's, advertising shirts by Pelaco. Utter garbage compared to my personal favourite, Chesty Bonds.

Jason and I walking past the pictures of Rainlover and Phar Lap's aunts and uncles, Jason pointing to them saying, 'Stubbs.'

'I wouldn't dream of smoking,' I said.

'No, the pictures,' he said. As if they were ashtrays. Then, 'By the way, if you're hungry, Reynolds can make us some snacks. He's good at that.' Making it clear who was boss. As clear as Bombay Gin that if you had looks, old fools would do anything.

'Doesn't mind me being here?'

'No, don't be silly.'

'Anyway I'm not hungry,' I said. Which was true, something about this terrace making me completely lose my appetite.

'I am,' he said as we entered a living room the Queen could have quite happily used without a loss of dignity, the way the French Queen Marie Antoinette used *Le Trianon*. For private contemplation.

There were pianos and harpsichords that may have been stroked by Handel, and sofas made by Chippendale rather than Namco. All in a room of green and russet marble, Victorian or Regency. Which one, I can't exactly tell because unlike the other stately homes of England I'd visited, there was no impoverished duke chatting while selling guidebooks. I told Jason he needed one, a guide that is, as well as 'Wow.'

'Yes, I know,' he said. 'But it's meant to be a home, not Covent Garden.' As if he thought guides even if they were dukes, just barrow boys in finer clothing.

'He must really like you,' I said.

'Who?'

'Reynolds.'

'Why wouldn't he like me?' he said, perplexed, convincing me I shouldn't meddle. 'I like Reynolds too,' he said. 'He might be bloody old but he's still human. Has his own needs.' Obviously despite the age gap, the relationship was more than financial and sexual, containing affection. 'Don't know what I'd do without him. If he left me, think I'd be lost. Have to fend for myself. Not a pretty sight these days in London. Nor would it be in Yorkshire or Sydney for that matter.'

But I didn't believe it. Looking at Jason, I thought there'd be any number of people like Reynolds willing to adopt him. Willing to take him in, to give him board and lodging. He'd be no more lost than I was, getting out of the maze of Hampton Court Palace. Not the type to go around in circles looking for his original suburb and terrace.

**6 5**   'I really am hungry, you know old Sport,' he said again, forgetting that last time I didn't like being called that, but this time I wasn't offended. If anything I was beginning to think being called Sport okay. Maybe because I was impressed with the house and with Jason who seemed charming. Completely at ease in these surroundings.

'Want to go out and grab a sandwich?' I said, hoping he'd say no, because I didn't want to leave the premises.

'No, that won't do.'

'The other day I found this great Greek restaurant, in Greek Street. If you believe it,' I said.

'Oh there,' he said, bored. Exhaling. 'Cypriot actually. Used to go there a lot, then I got tired of it.'

'Where then?'

'Don't want to go to Greek Street, Denmark Street or even Jermyn Street,' Jason said, lengthening the vowel of Jermyn so it also sounded like a country.

'Well I'm at your disposal,' I said. More truth than I knew. 'Whatever you wish.'

'Hoping you'd say that,' he said.

'You know the lay of the land.'

'Lay of the land?' he said, as if this meant something to him. 'Know the whole fucking globe.' Spinning one nearby. One of those globes resting on the floor in its own wood and

## pinpricks and bayonets

brass frame. An old globe not of the world but the heavens, which Cook might have used to observe the Transit of Venus.

'Must I be blunt about it?' he said, giving the globe another more violent spin, the word *blunt* reminding me of what I'd seen him do with an axe.

'It'd help,' I said.

'Damn,' he said, going over to the fireplace, and banging his fist on it. 'Damn, damn, damn.' Then pausing. Composing himself.

'You,' he said, 'are so innocent,' mentioning a state I'd long since abandoned but in fact was seeking. 'Does everything have to be spelt out?'

'Helps. I've spelt out everything, haven't I?'

'Why did I ask you here?'

'Compassion?' I said, but the joke didn't go down. He glared. I was irritating him.

'Load of rot.'

'Look, if this is a mistake and you want time to yourself,' I said, looking towards hall and exit . . . 'if I'm upsetting you . . .'

'Never need time to myself,' he said, turning round angrily. 'Never did. Can't really cope without company. Does that mean anything to you?'

To stay or go? This was getting confusing.

'Well you've got Reynolds,' I said.

'Reynolds is an old man.'

'There's the guys in the hallway,' I said trying to be light, referring to the judges and divorcees. But this didn't raise a chuckle. 'Kidding,' I said.

'Bloody paintings and statues,' he said. 'That's all they are. I need something living. Something breathing, something like me, young and ready. Know what I mean?' But I didn't. And the way he spoke was getting creepy. As if I'd gone directly from a *Carry On* film, to a Hammer movie. 'Sometimes I think I can't even get through the day, unless I have it. I feel empty. Everything's darkness.'

It certainly was getting dark outside from what I could see through the windows. The yellow sodium lights of the street were similar to the mercury vapoured fire I recalled at Ramsgate, giving the look of Eaton Square, now that it was raining and black cabs crisscrossed the other white terraces, the look of a gaslight painting by Grimshaw. Of a grey-skinned patient, not etherised, but fully awake, waiting night's incision.

'Sorry,' he said, turning towards me, his pink cheeks now red and ablaze, his eyes growing wide, almost as wide as the gargoyles.

'Sorry about what?' I was beginning to think Jason was a bit unhinged.

'Then I'm just going to have to say it,' he said.

'Then say it,' I said, not wanting any more mystery, basically thinking I shouldn't even be here. That I'd really taken the wrong direction.

Jason was now directly in front of me, inches away. Whatever was searing his soul about to make delivery.

'I want you,' he said, his face coming down on my lips then slowly down to my neck. 'Always did from the moment,' he said, 'you first walked into the studio.' Like both vampire and earnest lover, making me doubly unsure whether I was involved in a Hammer film or something by Barbara Cartland.

But the truth is, for reasons I haven't yet explained, I wanted him too. Also from the first instant. I guess I'd been pretending to myself otherwise. Trying to be sophisticated, to show that with all my experience I wouldn't be anybody's. That I'd learnt some wisdom. Circumspection. Discernment. The sort I used to exercise way back in the past when I commanded my boarders. When I decided who'd get my affection. Hoping I was now more than a slut, whose head was easily turned by flattery and pretty faces. By conductors. School teachers. Toilet pick ups. The way Jason turned my head with his hand on my chin, again saying, 'I want you.' Sealing my mouth with his lips, so in this love we wouldn't be accompanied by any protest. But the beauty of silence.

'Come on,' he said, backing off, taking me by the hand, leading me up stairs made of mahogany from Malaya, much finer than what we had for a bannister in Newtown, pink painted cedar.

With me feeling as if I couldn't resist because of what he'd planted on my neck, a perfume sweeter than pomegranates.

Up the stairs we went to the landing, opening up to another series of rooms, another hallway, bigger than the ones downstairs, where there were more busts, as well as the most monumental cliché I remembered from Australian steakhouses and roast beef taverns. A knight in dull unshiny armour. But it didn't impress me. It made me want to go up to it the way they did in comic ghost films, to open and shut its visor, knowing there'd be no skeleton in it. Just a maw of darkness.

'Tudor,' Jason said. Taking from its hand not a hammer but the spiky mace used for tenderising opponents.

'Men were very short in Tudor times,' he said, swinging the mace a little, the way you do with a bag when you're bored in the supermarket. Then he put his hand on my crutch, feeling for what was no longer softness.

'Definitely not Tudor,' he said, taking his hand away, pleased with his discovery, taking it away I thought probably because I didn't respond. Maybe not wanting to rush it.

'Tom would like it,' I said, referring not to my prick but the mace. 'With one of these, you could have a field day with his vases.'

Jason giggling at the unkindness of this, simply saying, 'You're being too hard on them. Deep down they're probably fond of you. Even though they're useless.'

'Don't you agree?' I said, not wanting to sound too much of a put-down artist.

'Oh, I think everyone sort of agrees. Really.'

'Well, why bother with them? What do you get out of it?'

'Simply put,' he said, looking at me, 'a smashing good time.' Bringing down the mace with a thud on the carpet. 'Forgive the pun.' Making me groan as he led me away. 'Anyway, let's talk about them later. Almost there,' he said, one hand still holding the spiky mace, the other taking mine, in case I got lost, or had second thoughts about what was really to me second nature.

But I stopped, reluctant to play follow the leader.

'Is it all right,' I said, 'if I hold that?' Meaning the mace.

'Too heavy for you,' he said.

'Let me see,' I said. 'Please.' And he gave it to me, although I noticed he hesitated a millisecond trying to appraise my reasons.

But Jason was right, it was heavy, because as soon as he passed it to me, I needed both hands to support it, its weight almost dragging me under.

'Fuck,' I said.

'Give it back to its rightful owner, then.' Holding out his hand for it.

**6 6**   So I did. Now that I look back on it, it was pretty stupid, but I didn't know what else I could do without ringing alarm bells, or betraying the fact that I was a little frightened. But he was much stronger. He just took it lightly and walked the few paces back to the unshiny knight, returning it to its position. Standing back and looking at the warrior made whole again, saying, 'Must've felt like a proper git in that sort of get up. Clattering around like a Foster's can. Imagine going for a fitting, what would you say, Oh, tailor, I need a bit more tin here under the arms.'

'Reynolds collects military memorabilia?'

'Polishes, this Tudor chap,' he said, 'like a knob every single day.' Indicating that their relationship wasn't perfect and that Reynolds despite his age, was perhaps quite sexually demanding.

'I collect these,' he said, opening up some cabinets behind the knight, where were stashed what I once in some way also collected. Little toy soldiers. Hundreds of them, that Jason must've bought en masse or over a lifetime, the way I once collected cars by Matchbox. How beautiful they were. Perfect. Orderly. Row after row.

'Expensive you know,' he said. 'They don't give them away,' taking one out. A Minute Man, if I'm not mistaken, turning it round and round with his hands, like a child admiring his most prized amusement. Almost as if he'd forgotten all about me, what I said about looking for a home, recapturing a suburb and a period, almost as if he'd forgotten about wanting me, and about dragging me upstairs for what I'd thought would be real entertainment.

But the soldier he fondled made me think there was something very similar about Jason and I, our interests and obsessions. Maybe this is what had silently communicated itself when I first became physically aware of him at the Bayswater tube station. Deciding not to tell him how his tin soldiers, compared to what I once held, were nothing but paltry imitations. He'd think me twisted.

'Lead,' he said. 'All of them.' Handing me the Minute Man soldier whose detail was exceptional, whose weight for its size was almost the equal of the mace I could barely carry. Okay, I exaggerate, but it was easily as heavy as a cricket ball.

'I have the whole collection,' he said. Picking up another soldier, a Redcoat or perhaps a soldier who could have fought in the Boer War. Military stuff, both his love and hobby.

'Don't know why I like them. I'm a pacifist at heart, don't believe in war. Or violence. Can't even go to violent films. But I like them,' Jason said, handing me his second example, the Redcoat, which I also turned around in my hand. Examining its detail and paint right down to the sharpness of its bayonet. Razor sharp. Drawing a bead of blood where I touched it.

'Ow.'

'Careful,' Jason said. 'Hold them carefully or you'll do yourself an injury.'

'Only a prick,' I said. 'Didn't hurt.'

'Here,' he said, taking my finger, suddenly interested. 'Let me kiss it.'

And before I could say 'no', or do anything, he took my finger and plunged it into his mouth, sucking on it as if he wanted to extract more blood from it. Deep into his mouth, a place so warm and delicious, it felt as if it wasn't just my finger that was in it, and nothing so common and obvious as my penis. It felt as if all of me, not just the tip of the digit his tongue licked and caressed had been swallowed up into a glass chamber of utter and unendurable pleasure. These days, no one would dare do such a thing, particularly gay men, living as we are in a time of fear and disease, the rituals of blood brothers forbidden, but I've already noted the year of these events, when both Jason and I were sheepish. Golden, but not innocent.

It was a sensation so delicious, not having sex if you recall since Sydney, that I didn't want him to stop, reluctantly withdrawing it though after a few seconds, the sensation being too overpowering.

'That's pretty hot.'

'Love in a cold climate,' he said, probably referring to the novel, but I was too vain to confess I hadn't read it. But he didn't mean the book, *Love in a Cold Climate*, or the sensation he'd just given me, but the soldier I still held with my other hand. Maybe scared I'd make some censorious remark, about kids playing with guns, about tin soldiers being the relics of a violent generation. 'Do you like it?' Jason asked, his anxiety rising. I looked at the soldier. How convincing he was. As if he really had lived and breathed. Had just come back from tormenting convicts. Before accidentally falling into a vat containing a magic potion like rum that shrank him.

'Do you?' Jason said, like Peter Pan, the way most collectors do, needing the endorsement of strangers, the admiration of those without collections, to feel they weren't crazy, or had wasted their life on an expensive obsession.

'Do I like it?' I said. Asking myself, unsure.

'Well do you?'

'I more than like it.' I said, looking at him, 'I love it.' Feeling sentimental with what I now held in my hand. 'Once upon a time, I had guys like this myself.'

'You still have them?' Jason asked, eagerly, a child, hoping for a private viewing.

'Nope. They lost the battle.' Then so as not to be too cryptic, 'I mean, I sold them, at least my mother did. Along with the house I keep mentioning. Thought I should be more grown up.'

'Did it work?' He asked.

'What?'

'Did it make you more grown up?'

'I thought,' I said, forgetting because of our shared interest, all about the knight, and the mace that made me uneasy, forgetting all about how Jason banged the fireplace with his fist at the first sign of frustration, 'I thought . . .' I repeated, 'that's why you brought me up here, to find out.' Forgetting even the Redcoat and the sharply honed bayonet that pricked me.

He laughed at this, and once he'd locked up the cabinet, took my hand as we went down the last hall of the house, Jason with his free hand grasping the brass handle of an enormous oak door, too heavy for its hinges. A temple-like door, three or four times as big as any door we had on even the biggest room of our Newtown terrace.

**6 7**   'We're here,' he said, allowing me to see we were in a bedroom bigger than even the drawing room. In the middle was an enormous oak four-poster bed, where must've frolicked and fucked all the kings of England. A bed big enough to contain all their hired lovers, paramours and mistresses. An oak bed resting on a green marble floor whose green was more vivid than the green you see in Dorset and Devon. In pictures on the cover of Derwent Pencils. Deeper than the dark green of leaves on Moreton Bay fig trees.

'A modest affair,' Jason said, meaning the bed, more than the room.

'If you hadn't pointed it out,' I said, 'I wouldn't have noticed.'

'Yes,' he said. 'They may have been discreet about their lives in public, but not very discreet in private. I think it looks like a boxing ring. Quite right too, because most English affairs are bloody.'

'What's the netting for?' I asked. Around it not the usual drapes and brocade you associate with four posters, but white sheets, countless yards of white muslin and mosquito netting. Netting that seemed to smother white damask sheets and Irish linen covered pillows. Big enough to prop up people with consumption. The netting was sort of odd because London, to my knowledge, unlike New Guinea, never had malaria as a problem. Sheets so thick and white it made me feel sorry for them, because if we'd come into this room to fuck, what its original occupants would've called to 'consummate passion', our spoof stains or skid marks would ruin them.

'Keeps out the wogs,' Jason said, about the netting, looking towards me. 'Bugs,' he said, when he saw I wasn't sure how to take this. 'Call bugs, wogs here. Don't they use that expression in Australia?'

'Only doctors,' I said. Not entirely truthful. 'They have lots of other expressions though,' I added. 'And when they run out they just make up new ones.'

'Must be bloody clever,' Jason said, but I wasn't sure if he was referring to me or to all of Australia, as he shut the well-oiled big oak door. Squeakless.

'Don't want to give Reynolds a heart attack,' he said, turning to me.

'No,' I said. 'We wouldn't. But at least he's got the National Health.'

'Yes,' he said. 'Then again,' coming right up to me, 'who knows how long any of us will live for?' And with that he kissed me so violently on the lips I thought I'd expire, pushing me onto the bed with one motion stronger than his boyish face and frame suggested.

Kissing me, holding my head. In rapture. His gestures rather corny. Stagy. Doing all this with the passion of a virgin. 'I want you,' he kept saying. 'I just want you.' Really unnecessary because I also wanted him, putting my hand down his shirt unbuttoning him, exposing part of his chest. Young and boyish. Hairless like Wayne's, but different. As if it hadn't yet reached full maturity. Unbuckling his belt, he doing the same with me, going down on him, not even waiting for his trousers to come off, discovering he had a prick the length of a ruler, strangely whiter than a Georgian column. Thick as the rolled scroll of the Magna Carta. With a perfect pink tip that I licked and knew any moment could unleash enough spoof to put out any future fires of London. The eye of his penis, large and dark. Unknowable. Much like what was contained in the unshiny knight's visor. Jason pulling my head up and kissing me again with that mouth of his which had all the warmth and lust of Bermuda. For what seemed an eternity, until I went back down on him, not to his penis but his balls. Big pendulous balls perfectly spherical, they too almost hairless with just a light down of blond and ginger. Taking one, then the other into my mouth. Balls the size and beauty of which I lolled around my tongue, caressing them with both hands, as his eyes went back in his head with pleasure. Feeling orbs the Queen wouldn't have been embarrassed to hold during her coronation. Kissing his lips.

'I want you,' Jason said again, both of us on the bed naked, he on top of me as his floppy Titian hair (the only thing floppy about him) fell across my face like a veil made of silks, hiding out the world. The whiteness of the sheets, the greyness of his eyes. Their flint sending out sparks neither he nor I could extinguish. Blocking out the sight of the green marble in the room, and anything I'd feared. As well as whatever reason I'd come here for.

Pinning me down, strong with those boys arms, which to have looked at him you'd never credit. Able to see though how beautiful he was. Not just in his face but in body. Like a statue made by Remington. Like all the young men, English playwrights went to gaol for or willingly let

## medea's children

themselves be compromised by. Stomach flat as a bedpan. Thick blue veins in his arms that suggested at some point muscles tormented by labour. Legs unceasing. Perfect limbs created solely for his body.

'I want you,' he said again. Why did he keep saying that? He already had me. It encouraged me to say, the thing that I shouldn't have said, the thing that so many people had said to me and that so far I'd avoided. The thing you should never ever say. Certainly not close to ejaculation, taking his mouth again into mine. 'I love you,' I said. And he pulled back and smiled at this as if this was just the starting point, the very thing he wished for. Confession. Using not Brylcreem or KY gel, but spittle from his hands that he rubbed together to lubricate me. A spittle that from anyone else would've been disgusting, but from him was like dew shining in the lamplight. Glistening in the phosphorescence made available by the evening outside the window. Using it to enter me, not like Wayne did, fast. But slowly and consistently. Imperceptibly. Until his entire length was in, and I felt for the first time in a long time, complete, a state from which I didn't want movement.

'Stay in,' I said. 'Don't move. Not yet.' Not yet wanting the ins and outs of penetration and withdrawal which I knew would give both me and him delirium. Wanting to savour this moment in eternity.

But Jason did start to move slowly as if he feared giving me pain which wasn't the reason I implored him.

'No, wait.' I said, my arms around his masculine but boyish shoulders, 'wait.' As if expecting the revelation of some mystery.

After a minute of this unendurable bliss, when he again began to move and I again said, 'Stay.' Jason spoke.

## pinpricks and bayonets

'Leave it out,' as if he could no longer risk containment, maybe even complaining.

'No,' I said. 'Leave it in,' which made him giggle not with laughter but with the shared understanding that he and I were meant for each other. In perpetuity. Achieving what it took Australia one hundred bickering years to achieve. Not sexual congress. But homosexual Federation.

'Now,' I said, giving him the signal like a starting gun as he begun to thrust into me, slowly at first and not too deeply, his thrusts getting slightly deeper as if promising me there were more inches to discover.

As Jason blew. And blew. Sealing my mouth while he did this. As if there might be spies next door listening. Maybe Guy Burgess. As I simultaneously came in canals and rivulets all over his chest and stomach, Jason finally lowering himself on me, gluing us together. In a new sort of vase that could never be the subject of destruction. Me, tracing my hand through his hair, grateful, kissing his eyes, feeling they were my eyes, which I'd be happy now and in the future to have as my vision. My witness to all emotion. Jason kissing my cheek, his tongue tracing it, both kiss and tongue hotter and more exquisitely felt than the bayonet that had pricked me. Sharper than betrayal. Until exhausted in a sweat of our own making we paused to draw breath, falling into a brief sleep that was complete and unapproachable. Ecstasy. Now, how easy it was to forget what had brought me here, the names of faces and places that sent me. That house. That suburb. Faces made of flesh that was beautiful. Places of stone and brick that were ugly. A woman sent away for meddling. At times it seemed what had brought me here was as diaphanous as the muslin, as empty as the squares in the netting.

Waking up some minutes later our hearts still racing, and doing the whole thing again. Him again fucking me, saying, no he didn't want me to fuck him that night, even though he usually preferred this, being by and large passive. Saying he wanted to save this pleasure and his 'little piece of England' for a more idyllic occasion. Me, content to rim him, so small and firm was he, his smell unlike so many English arses, inoffensive. His having a sweet scent to it. Delicious. Rose leafing, what the landlady must've meant by English Roses.

I don't know how long we were in this position, fucking and laughing and sucking and fucking and caressing each other completely uninterrupted by the pedestrian events going on in the outside world. In Eaton Square. Farther down in the Houses of Parliament. Reynolds certainly didn't interrupt us, probably knowing his young charge needed young flesh. Maybe knowing that paying for him didn't, and never would mean, ownership.

Maybe the whole thing only lasted one night. That night. Till midnight. Maybe it went on the next day. And the day after that. And the evening after that. I can't really say, because it felt as if it went on for a year. Maybe two years, maybe two hundred because from that night Jason and I became what I'd never had. More than admirers. Lovers. Although he never actually said to me, 'I love you', as I did, just the more pithy and more pleading, 'I want you'. And, 'please don't leave me', which he never tired of uttering.

**6 8**   And more spectacular than our commitment, he told me what stupidly I hadn't realised, what should have been obvious in the first place. That the house didn't belong to Reynolds at all. That I was correct the first time. That Reynolds *was* the butler, that the house actually belonged to him because he was the son of an Earl.

'You're kidding.' Of a county that for reasons of privacy I promised never to reveal. Saying he was a Viscount, which I thought sounded like a cigarette or an aeroplane. With me saying, 'Get away,' and Jason saying, 'It's true, sod it, believe me, why would I lie?' Showing me a crest like the Queen's, but smaller, that he said belonged to his 'family'. A family that was less busy than the Queen's, because under their crest which featured wheat, and a fox and a hound (which to be honest, looked like the sort of thing you see displayed outside boozy country taverns) the need for appointments wasn't mentioned.

'There, I've told you now,' he said, 'but promise not to tell Don and Tom. I'll die if you tell them,' explaining that it wasn't fashionable in artistic circles to be part of the aristocracy. That he'd be mocked for not having working class origins. That's why he always said he came from Yorkshire. 'Please,' again from him, me promising his secret was safe, saying, 'I'd rather die than tell them. Honest.' Jason looking at me suspicious. 'I won't tell,' I said.

'No,' I thought 'Not even the man at the British Council.'

He and I were happy those next few days, a head cold I felt coming on almost gone, just touches of it lingering, an occasional flush of temperature. Once or twice vomiting. Maybe this flush coming and going because of our fevered passion. And I'm proud to tell you, there didn't really seem much point in continuing my search, because as far as I was concerned it was over. Content with Jason showing me around the house. Its history and passages easily pre-dating anything by Dickens. Even Miss Havisham. So superior to what we had in Newtown, what mother and I operated.

He and I returning to the bed as often as possible. A bed from which I wanted nothing, so perfect were we, wanting less than nothing, just us and our bodies. And every time he fucked me, just seeing his beauty there on top of me, feeling his manly cock attached to that boyish body, the tip of his penis inside me, which by the way wasn't snipped, was the Spirit of Ecstasy.

Until Jason said, 'Why don't we go abroad?'

'Overseas? Can't really afford it. I'm almost out of money.'

'That's ridiculous. Money's a commodity like everything else. I'll get it from the old man.'

Me stupidly saying (the only thing I really regret now) that I respected him too much and, more hypocritically, 'I don't want to be a gigolo. I want us to be equals.' Which was only partially truthful.

'Very well, but let's be first amongst equals at the end of summer. Allow me, this once.'

'I don't know about this.'
'Sod being poor. It'll be brilliant.'
'I think it's wicked.'
'Trust me.' Which I did, the way a long time ago, I once trusted someone who was his social inferior.

**6 9**   So Jason took me to places I never dreamed I'd ever be able to afford to visit. Warm places he liked, the ones he'd mentioned on our tube journey. Like Bermuda, where I'm embarrassed to say we wore those ridiculous shorts. Getting drunk on the portico of a hotel on sickly sweet pina colada. Or was it curaçao? While Jason paid a house call on the Governor, a friend of the family, just to keep them happy.

Going to Spain which he said was rather dry and dusty, me saying, 'mate, you don't know the meaning of dusty', not the first time I'd ever used the word *mate* in my life, but the first time in ages, a word once so foreign on my lips not just because of my ethnicity but that other sexual foreignness, homosexuality. Remembering how when I started shouting it, no one was listening. Only phantoms.

In Granada, looking at the fountains and the gardens of the Alhambra, which for all their publicity I didn't think the equal of our Moreton Bay-filled parks. Nor our Botanic Gardens. Too internal, introspective.

Going on to Gibraltar where Jason said, 'I can't see what all the fuss is about, it's just a piece of old pumice.' Where there were apes and monkeys as well as lower species Jason called 'tourists'. Throwing nuts at them, the way I once threw a paddle pop stick at a house full of Aborigines.

## pinpricks and bayonets

Going on to, of all places, Calcutta. He'd been there before. The city of dreadful night, which to his credit, Jason didn't find depressing or filthy, impressing me with the way he was able to relate to even the most common beggar. Making me think maybe he'd be happy to live with me in a place like Newtown. If we needed to find it. Which we didn't. Showing me Calcutta mansions swallowed by vines, and humidity, vultures and weaver birds that blocked the sky with screeches, the way black cabs bleat and block London. Showing me roads so filthy, it was as if the torn bitumen implored the sky, to unleash the mother of all monsoons to wash them.

And to Delhi, where Jason said one of his ancestors took part in the Delhi Durbar. Me asking, 'What's the Delhi Durbar?' Jason explaining it was the Indian Court, or a convocation of all the Maharajas called together by Curzon, 'a bit like a concert in Wembley Stadium, but not as interesting'.

Going to Benares, where we floated down the Ganges, looking at the Gats, the steps where people did their laundry and did obeisance in the biggest laundry tub and bathroom of them all, immersing themselves repeatedly, getting rid of less sins than I'd committed. People who knew, unlike westerners, that it is not from dust we came or to dust that we will return, but the waters. Jason saying that morning, as a body floated by wrapped tightly in the bright silk sari of Benares which I have to confess, now that I'd seen it, was finer than body shirts and track pants, 'Do you believe in Karma?'

'Sometimes.'

'Before I met you, the thought of dying didn't horrify me at all, I would've been glad of it. Would've welcomed it like a lover, where as now, sod it . . .' looking at me, giving me a brief kiss that repelled the boatman, controlling the rudder. 'I couldn't think of anything worse, than either being dead or losing you.' Tipping over the boat in the process, he and I having to be dragged back in by the disapproving boatman, narrowly missing an early date with the new lamps for old shop called reincarnation.

Going to Udaipur, where Jason again said, 'Sod it.' His favourite word. Then, 'Let's splash out!' Not meaning a dip in the lake which to tell the truth was at low tide and covered with algae, but to stay at the Lake Palace Hotel, that white castle on the lake that floats around as if it were just a shimmer, the abode of my mother's father, the sun when resting. A palace hotel that seemed to me basically a giant version of the white sheet and linen bed of Jason's, back at his Eaton terrace, where we sucked and fucked with much more inventiveness than has ever been carved into the walls of Hindu temples.

Once, being naughty, having a threesome with the bellhop, who caught us at it when he brought in the hard boiled eggs that Jason very wisely said was the only thing he ever ate in India. The bellboy holding the tray, not shocked when he opened the door, but delighted, saying as he shut it behind him, 'Would you like some fucking sirs? With me?'

Which couldn't have been put more concisely. Enjoying us, and we him, immensely. Giving him a big tip, which I said was only right, but which Jason said wasn't, as it might encourage him into prostitution.

Jason saying, 'Damn this heat and humidity. It's getting to me now. Let's go to Darjeeling, we can take the toy railway up the mountain, it goes through the clouds, a bit like going to Heaven.' A toy railway often out of service but fortunately just repaired. Jason showing me slopes of green that unbearably shone like the eyes of a man I'd once admired.

'My family had estates here, actually one of my uncles was one of the original tea planters. Personally I loathe the stuff and have never been able to understand what the English see in it anyway. Dead leaves. That's all tea is. Dead leaves that have had the life boiled out of them,' he said, on the terrace of the Windermere Hotel where we sat drinking tea's replacement, appalling coffee, with our backs turned on the sight of the second highest mountain in the world, Mount Kanchenjunga. How small and dwarfed it and the rest of the Himalayas were, compared to the lofty peaks we'd reached. Of sex and happiness. Jason and I were unable to get through the day without fucking at least four or five times. At night in the bar of the Windermere, a rather chintzy faded Victorian parlour that was supposed to have the redolence of the Raj about it but in fact had all the redolence of a second class train carriage, not listening to the Jam or the Cure, but to snatches from an antique record player with a megaphone on it of Elgar's Cello concerto.

'Sod it. I also like classical. Don't know what everyone gets so het up about talking about bands.'

'Well what about the Jam?' I said, expecting something similar to Don's tirades.

'Love them,' he said, 'Sex Pistols too. They're a necessary antidote. I think England's big enough to accommodate a lot of points of view even though everyone keeps saying it's too small and full already.' Saying how unlike me, he actually admired Don and Tom. 'I know you think they're laughingly experimental, but where would we be without them? Back in the National Portrait Gallery with those cigar chomping duffers.'

'A bit like your place,' I said.

'Leave it out,' he said. 'I've got plans for that. I was talking about the National Portrait Gallery. It'd actually have a future if they got rid of all those miserable busts and pictures, and put in pornography. So that each generation can see what the most beautiful boy of the time looked like naked. If dicks change through the eras. At least it'd serve the real purpose of art, titillation. Then there'd be queues all round Trafalgar lining up for admission.'

'They'd hang you in pride of place.'

'Sod off. You having a bit of a lend are you?'

'No, I'd never lend you to anyone.' Scared of losing him the way I once lost someone. And a location.

'But I suppose the Greeks did that first. All their art's basically pornography. That's why it's lasted. People salivate at the chops for the sight of it. That's what I plan to do anyway, get rid of all that junk at home when the old man carks it.' Exciting me a little, at the thought that somewhere, somehow, someone was planning a massive peephole. But I kept this private.

'Couldn't put it better myself,' I said.

'You're more Greek aren't you than Australian? Maybe that's why I'm attracted to you. Your body. Your face. Everything about you.' Then with inspiration, 'Say, it's only October. Why don't we go there? To Greece I mean. I think it'd be super. Been there before?'

'Yes, but I sort of look on it now as a foreign country. Not really sure I'd enjoy going back. Last time I left in a bit of a rush.'

'Misunderstanding?' he asked, trying to prise information. But I surprised myself with how reluctant I was to offer it.

'No,' I said. 'No misunderstanding. I think we understood each other perfectly.' Not wishing to name the party involved, whom I blamed for holding up so much of my happiness, who I hadn't really thought a lot about. Leaving it blank, leaving her blank, as if truly referring to a lost and forgotten country. Cursing myself for all the time I wasted because it was clear I should've come years ago, to where I belonged, London, where my search took flight, and finally ended.

**70**   So we went to Athens which Jason said he adored but which I no longer did, finding it not draped in incense and perfume but smog leaching away at buildings the way unresolved tensions leach away personality and memory. Hearing no conches or gongs, seeing no festooned parades. Seeing this time only what my brother had prosaically described as heavy traffic. Going to Mykonos which neither of us really liked that much, being as it always was, full of French and German queens whom Jason said were 'the worst', leaving 'worst,' hanging in the air, absurdly intransitive. Leaving out my story about the coup and being there years earlier. Judging any story about military jets and evacuation too boring, too serious, lacking in variety.

Going on to Corfu which he said that ever since he read Gerald Durrell's *My Family and Other Animals* had always been his favourite island.

'Although the way Durrell talked about sodding insects,' Jason said, 'he might as well have been talking about the Royal family really.' Telling me at the Achilleon Palace where I admired the mural of Achilles dragging Hector through the dust that resembled not the fields of Troy but the Simpson desert, stories about the Royal family he'd heard from his father that he said I should never repeat. 'What really

pinpricks and bayonets

goes on below decks of Britannia makes what we do look perfectly modest.' And how Princess Margaret was the finest of the lot, using a word to describe her I can't bring myself to mention. Telling me his father once dragged him to some garden party, and he actually met Prince Phillip who wasn't really as bad as he seemed even though he had said some terrible things about unemployment.

'That shows a great deal of self-hatred,' Jason said, 'because as far as I can tell the sod's never done a stitch.'

He was like that, Jason. The moment you thought you had his measure, or that he was betraying some Tory sympathy, he'd turn it around and make you think the opposite. But Jason finally decided that he was getting tired of travelling, and he thought that maybe he and I should repair back to England.

Which we did, via France, where we had some truly appalling meals that cost more than the North Sea oil wells. Perfidious. Where Jason said, 'Want to see the Palace of Versailles?'

'No, I think I've had my fill of parks, hotels and palaces.'
'Well America is out of the question. Hate that place. Provence then, or Brittany?

'I'd like to see Passchendaele, the Somme.' The fields of emptiness. Where he and I went one wind-swept morning overlooking stony fields that probably still had bombs planted in them. Bombs and graves, and undiscovered bodies. More bodies than were ever laid to waste at the Battle of Culloden. Unlived and unpublished.

'A lot of Australians, died here,' I said.

'Yes, I know, but most were volunteers. Silly enough to march off to God-forsaken wars every time Britain whistled,' he said, as the wind did exactly that, whistling about our ears. Making me think for the first time that Jason, though accurate, could be a little bit hard-hearted.

Looking across the now part verdant downs and stony battlefield of the Somme, thinking that here in these foreign fields there is no small part that can be described as either Australia or England. Just France, another country happy to swallow victims.

Feeling though rather comfortable in a macabre sort of way, on the hill where we stood, probably because for the first time in a long time, other than with the occasional backpacker we came across, I guess I was with the largest collection of Australians outside the country. Its real and permanent emigrants. People (I mean the lads) I once fancifully thought I could have saved, or accommodated.

**71**     Returning to our bed in our Eaton terrace, Jason again saying to Reynolds, 'We won't need you tonight Reynolds.' As if he were Dirk Bogarde and me James Fox in a forgotten movie from the 1960s called *The Servant*. Lolling around on the bed, drawing the netting around it not so much because of a fear of wogs or bugs but because we liked our own private white gauze heaven. Fucking and sucking some more. The glass chamber of happiness.

Me, falling off into a dream sleep, feeling as if I had a head cold. Maybe that in the rivers of the Ganges I'd caught some disturbing middle ear infection, getting up and going to vomit a couple of times because it made me feel nauseous. And better after I finished. Frankly in a way tired of this monied and empty existence where the only things we could think of for entertainment was either sex with each other or travel, because he had money. Also, because the next day, when Jason took me to some party where there were others of his class, I got introduced around not as his lover but as his 'friend'.

'From down under.' Where I thought people asked patronising questions about my origins, making me feel like Bennelong at the Covent Garden Opera.

Saying to Jason later, 'Why did you call me "your friend" to that silly woman?'

'Which silly woman?' he said. 'There were lots of them.'

'You know who I mean. You ashamed of me?' Taking off my bow tie.

'That's what you are. Aren't you?'

'I would've thought after all this time you wouldn't be ashamed to call me your lover.'

'Lover isn't a word I'd use, old boy.' Almost as if we'd gone back to the beginning. To the first time I met him when he was with Don and Tom.

'Companion is more like it,' he said, as if he were some elderly spinster I helped with her circulation. And constitution. But I felt too ill and nauseous with the middle ear infection to argue about it.

'You're being too sensitive. Come to bed.'

Which we did, where I again pricked myself with the bayonet of the toy soldier, and Jason coincidentally with my fountain pen, that was in my back trouser pocket. Maybe we pricked ourselves to feel we were living. My pen piercing him the way his toy soldier pierced me for blood. Giving us another delirium where there were no arguments. Falling into probably the deepest sleep I have ever had the way the Brits used to with laudanum. Thinking of schooldays, Moreton Bay fig trees, monstrous paintings by Turner and, strangely, of industrial workers toiling in muscular throngs in Macdonaldtown. People Jason would never have met in a lifetime. Maybe in my dream they were copies. Hearing in the background the sound I most feared. A motorcade. Sirens. As if someone had really blown up the Parliament.

Waking up one morning, I don't know which morning, but months and months later not in Eaton Square, with a young peer beside me, but in an Earl's Court bedsit where we'd always lived. Waking up on a torn futon. Jason's white body, next to me. Now more wedgwood blue. Black and grey. My arms and his arms, full of marks the size of beads used to mark the rosary.

Waking up neither rich nor as travellers, but to reality. To what I'd become. To what we really were. Broke. Full of bullshit. Pathetic junkies, living not the life of Riley, nor a monied melody but off forms called UB 40.

'One, two three, clear,' someone said. And it was. The closest we'd been on trips, what we could see in the travel agent, the bucket shop across the road, outside our cracked bathroom window. Okay, maybe once or twice we went to France, by ferry, looking for new dealers.

'One, two, three, clear.' The medical mantra applied with discs on those floating out of existence.

I just made that up, to make me happy. Knowing that my search for this infernal house, because of the drugs, had been stymied. Maybe even levelled.

book five **the man in charge of half hours**

**72** So I left England, to begin my search again, knowing I'd never find what I wanted there. Leaving Jason to his special poison of self-delusion and opiates taken in increasing doses. Jason using drugs as an escape from class rather than the way mother used them, as a chemical religion.

Leaving because far too much had happened between us, as well as too little. Anyway I figured Jason would survive quite well, and with his charm, find someone else to replace me. Perhaps from the Common Market.

Approaching my new home, Manhattan, on an airport bus plunging into the Newark tunnel, I fell asleep, losing the first opportunity to see where I should've headed to all along, the Empire City.

'Time to get off the bus buddy,' the driver said. 'End of the line for you.' Which was sort of true. Well, it would've been if I'd stayed any longer in London in that culture of dependence. Not that I was stupid enough to think New York was without temptation. I knew junk didn't just come in the form of powders and capsules, but also memory.

'Where am I?' I asked, waking up.

'In an underground coach station below 42nd Street. Up there's Times Square.' The driver pointed to the escalator,

## medea's children

not realising as far as I was concerned, Times Square was actually in me.

'Word of *advice*,' he said, emphasising the first syllable. 'Don't let them fuck you around. Watch *who* you meet. And *how* you meet. You'll thank *me* for it.'

I wasn't exactly sure what he meant. Looking around the station, I kind of liked the beggars crumpled in corners. They reminded me of drunks and the homeless who used to adorn Newtown's doorways. A bunch of Paul Reveres who'd failed to cross the last few inches life demanded as their mission. And they seemed to recognise me, putting out their hand in greeting. Maybe just for money.

'Buddy, can you spare a dime?' they said, almost like gas heaters.

'Sorry,' I replied. 'I don't have much local currency.' Which was true of every country I'd been in, and doubly true here, since I'd barely been in *old* New York, as Kylie and her song called it, for more than an hour. Actually I didn't understand why it was called old. Because right from that first moment I thought New York modern, a place where a more contemporary Wayne might be living. In today's terms, a yuppie.

But I dismissed that idea because I wasn't here to chase after him or terraces, or any sort of phantoms. No, I'd promised myself that in New York I definitely wouldn't traipse around looking at brownstones. London had already taught me imitations were silly.

Actually, London, well, Jason and the fantasies he spun, made me decide it was much easier to write about a world and recreate what you're looking for on paper, guessing that was the closest I'd ever come to it. Thanking the gods for this moment of perception.

## the man in charge of half hours

I mean it was obvious. If a place doesn't exist, recreate it. All I had to do was rediscover the style I wrote in as a kid which so impressed me, and it would come tumbling out. Brick by brick. Column by column, balcony by balcony. The house, the Greeks, the sex, a cruel and unforgiving mother (wherever she was), as well as the friends who disappointed me, who couldn't help me. I just had to recall some of the simplicity and directness I had when I was a poet better known than T. S. Eliot.

And I was more than happy with this decision. A decision I didn't see as defeat, but sophisticated and realistic. Yes, that's what I would do, writing for therapy. Self-purification. Ink like ghee, feeding the flames, consuming the limbs and body of experience. Ink my Reckit's Blue, immersing and bleaching the past's ghosts and characters – hopefully drowning them.

Although I must say, I didn't realise New York was so hot in summer. I found the heat discouraging. I mean the city was hot enough to melt the wings of both Daedalus and Icarus. I say this because the drought I experienced in London seemed to have floated across the Atlantic. Maybe it was directly imported from Sydney. So hot, the local newspaper carried a story about Park Avenue matrons having to water the bushes on the traffic strip with Perrier. So the New York greenery wouldn't wither in this cloudless 'accident' of hot wind like the hopes of reservation Native Americans. A blowtorch-type heat that in a proud, but brief moment, I thought emanated from my fingers. Probably because in my shirt pocket the fountain pen I described as a needle was leaking.

'Fuck this weather,' I thought. 'This summer keeps following me.' Thinking, 'Doesn't any place have winter any more?' All this, years before global warming.

Not being able to afford the air-conditioning of fancy places I moved to a downtown YMCA, booking in to the ninth floor, facing the Chelsea Hotel (whose history Kylie had closely studied), absolutely convinced this was the place to start my opus. That here I was finally going to recreate the Newtown I wanted. A floor the Y's hotel clerk said I'd find more comfortable than all previous eight floors combined.

'Hope so,' I said, 'because I've sure had some doozies.'

'The ninth floor is for our *special* people,' he said.

'I've just come from England.'

'Well you must be special too,' but the way he said it made me sound disabled. A ninth floor, the clerk was correct about – it was 'special' and quite run down.

But its seediness, its shared concrete bathrooms, torn carpets and yellow walls, reminded me, sexily, of my own once precious accommodation. The search for which had sent me spinning across continents. So I thought, 'Great, this is really going to be inspirational.'

It also made me wonder for the last time in a long time how Jason was, and if he missed me. Because to be honest this floor wasn't much different from the dump we'd been sharing. Certainly better than that silly landlady's house in London.

**7 3**  What made this ninth floor truly different however, was the fact it was occupied mainly by long stayers, the strangest of people, many of whom said they were magicians, dancers and painters. All of whom had been living there for years waiting for employment. I say strange, because I thought employment in America, as in Australia, was pretty easy to gain.

A thirty-year-old guy called Mike, was the first to speak to me, saying when he saw me in my room sitting at a small desk with a fountain pen that had yet to scratch paper, 'What ya doing?'

'Trying to write.'

'About what?' he asked. 'You ain't said.'

Popping some peanuts in his mouth whose smell, Kylie told me Sylvia Plath employed to describe New York, just before she stuck her head in a gas oven. The crew-cut, tight jeans, white T-shirt and wire-frame glasses Mike wore, sort of gave him the look of a marine. Boy he was handsome, leaning against the doorway with his arms folded, chewing nuts – as if teasing me. Why was I always meeting clichés?

'Just stuff,' I replied.

'What exactly?'

'About a long search.'

'For?'

'A haunting house.'

'A haunted house? Ghost story?'

'*Haunting* house,' I emphasised.

'You're pulling my dick.'

'No, but maybe everybody else's.'

'Personal stuff?'

I nodded yes.

'Fancy pen you got there buddy. Hope you use it. If there's anything I can do to help, or if you want to go out . . .'

'Thanks, but fancy stories need time,' I said, trying to hide what I was doing, which so far was nothing. My perfect world and suburb, despite my decision to write about them, even on paper, strangely elusive, as distant and as far away as their geography. Maybe even the Andromeda galaxy. I must say I was not really sure why I couldn't begin, but I wasn't overly worried, being mainly concerned with why I couldn't write simply any more, like T.S. Eliot or Judith Wright.

'I kinda tried writing once,' he said, 'but it didn't work out.'

'Why's that?' I asked, more interested in his body than his writing.

'Was about a small-time love affair with this guy I met . . .'

'Back home?'

'No, military academy. We were just a couple of farm kids horsing around. Hick stuff.'

'Really?' I said. This was getting sexy.

'Yeah, they caught us fucking like hill-billies, didn't exactly throw us out but let's say it was a career-limiting move. Thought I could write it out of my system. But I tell ya, I blew it. Golly,' he said, like Gomer Pyle. 'Blew it in more ways than one. Still remember him though. Tow-haired kid. Freckles and stuff.'

'Didn't work?'

'Nope. Too much heaving and pumping. Came out like pornography.' The way he emphasised porn, made pornography sound like a subject.

'Maybe you should've tried to tell some other story around it,' I said, getting editorial which was a bit rich. I mean, I hadn't actually done any writing myself recently other than the letter to my family.

'What kinda story?'

'About where you're from. What it was like to grow up.'

'Hell, that's obvious, isn't it? Right here, the land of the brave. Where you think I'm from, Paris?'

'No, I mean you could've strung all that personal stuff together by giving it a theme.'

'Like in a theme park?'

'No, no, a theme . . .' I said. This was getting difficult. I was glad we weren't getting on to metaphors. '. . . A theme like acceptance . . . stuff like that. What it's like being accepted.' I was sounding like a counsellor.

'Hell, that's dumb,' he said. 'The academy *had* accepted us. That's where it goddamn happened.'

Something told me Mike was no intellectual giant.

'And what do you do now?' I asked.

'Not muchly. Live on welfare for the time being. Gave up on being a writer and that's for sure. Ain't that smart. Chew the cud with new recruits to the ninth floor. Cruise down the village. That's my ship these days. Where you from anyway?'

'Straya,' I said, the way people do now. 'Straya via Greece. Because I'm Greek. Spent a bit of time in London.'

'Helluva swoop.'

'Epic,' I said. 'Australians travel all the time this way, sort of in their blood.'

'Uncle Sam has a lot of bases in England, Greece. Down under too.'

'Yeah,' I said, 'but no one knows what they're for.' But I really didn't want to talk politics. I didn't think he was up to it.

'Been to the one in Okinawa, Guam . . . The name's Beef anyway,' he said, straightening up, holding out his hand. And I was certain his name was Mike.

'Hello Beef,' I said.

'Not Beef,' he said. 'That's for cattle. Biff. It's my nickname. Hate any one calling me Mike.'

'Sorry. Biff,' I said. Which sounded clumsy. Why were we having so many problems with pronunciation?

'Guess I'd better go back to my room huh? Give you time to write about the haunted house.' I was irritated he hadn't been listening.

'I guess.'

'Sing out when you dry up.'

'Meaning what?'

'As a buddy I'd like to go out with ya. So sing out,' he said, 'if you get bored.'

But I wasn't bored at all. In fact his little story stirred something in me. Maybe something between my legs.

'So, I'm singing,' I said.

''Bout what?' Biff said, adjusting his glasses.

'You said if I dry up to sing out, so I'm singing.'

'Hell, great, let's go on the town. Might give you some clues what to write.' Biff not knowing that in some ways I was actually getting heartily sick of towns and tearing around for clues. I think I just wanted to be with him. Probably because being American, he sort of reminded me of Mark, my old high school friend. Anyway, I figured an ex-marine might have a lateral big gun approach to the problem.

'That'd be fun,' I said. Which it would be, compared to sitting at my desk. I think I was developing a crush on him.

'Neat,' he said, like an American teenager, even though he was at least thirty. 'I'll pick you up at four.'

And he did, saying on the way out, 'I'm from Texas, the lone star state,' which explained why he was so muscular, maybe even his nickname. He sure looked as if he had a dick like a bull beneath his jeans. Telling me when I prodded him that the military academy was West Point. Or was it the naval school in Annapolis? Anyway, I liked the fact that he and I had sort of shared a similar experience, at least partly. And the way he began sniffing the air, the moment we hit the pavement was as if we were on the deck of the USS *Missouri*.

'Breathe that, kid. Ah, New York how I love ya.' Like he were Al Jolson. Then, 'Let's find us some fruits in this here big apple. Put some lead in your pencil.' By fruit meaning what Australians call people like him and I, poofters, or in Greek, *poustides*.

'Sure thing,' I said, thinking that Biff might be right, that this tour through a land where there were no terraces, might give me clues about how to begin writing. Hints. Grist for my mill, which to be honest I didn't know how to operate.

Biff was asking, 'Seen the river yet?'

Me saying, 'Seen plenty of rivers.'

'Nuh uh, not like the Hudson.'

So he took me to the Hudson and the Battery where we sat on park benches and chatted, me looking at the ground for these hints, or maybe just at the cigarette butts I extinguished. I think he liked looking at ships now he was no longer serving.

'Sure is great here. The carrier anyway. Look at the mother-fucking bitch. Ain't she beautiful,' he said, pointing to the USS *Independence*, currently in town. But whether it was beautiful or not was something I could neither confirm nor deny. In fact to me it was pretty ugly. 'Now if that don't beat all and give you ideas.'

'Might,' I said, just to be agreeable. I think he really meant the sailors working on it, stripped to the waist, a bit like Biff actually – gorgeous.

'Come on,' he said. 'It's getting dark, let's find us some bars.' Biff taking me to look for trails as he put it (maybe just sending me up) in legendary bars now as shut as the lives of their most frequent patrons. Bars and tunnels known as The Mineshaft, The Anvil, The Spike. Their names conveying a hard-edged, synthetic, industrial masculinity rather than the authentic one I had known in childhood's soft folds and edges, the one I still hadn't started to put on paper. Places disappointingly similar to the fucking corrals of Sydney.

'Hope you ain't wearing perfume,' Biff said. 'The bouncers don't like it. Perfume and aftershave are sort of considered *unmascoolean*.'

'No,' I said. 'Just the stench of memory.' Which was true, breezing past the doorman. Biff laughing at this, although I'm not sure he understood me.

After midnight, Biff and I taking more trails down to

the wharves near the meat market, where ships weren't pulling in, but young men eager to show off and exercise their carcass on the hooks of passion. In the hundreds of parked meat trucks they climbed into nightly. So that their bodies in stationary vehicles could be transported to a different realm of the senses. I could see them lifting the rear canvas hoods of the trucks. Climbing in by the dozen as if escaping a war. Maybe like me, needing to find something, somewhere. A point of entry, or evacuation.

'Oo, wee,' he said. As we climbed into one of them just to have a look at the activity. 'Love this. More gear shifts in here than a Detroit factory.' Until someone shushed him. Biff answering, 'Shush yourself. Jerk.' Which he was. I mean, he was jerking.

When Biff and I were exhausted, going back to the Y, to sit in the lobby, watching early morning TV, where one station as a courtesy to me, maybe for encouragement, actually broadcast old episodes of *The Roller Game*. Although I must say the lesbians didn't seem as violent as they used to. And I sort of got bored with the game's circularity.

Biff said, 'Guess I'd better hit the sack.' Disappointing me because he meant by himself. I'd sort of hoped he wanted company. 'Hope there was enough of a scent out there for ya on the wagon trail.'

'Plenty,' I said, 'I can smell them from here,' meaning none.

Me, spending the next morning looking for more hints by myself, checking out apartment blocks, leering at them as if they were sexy even though I'd promised myself I wouldn't. Strolling, a bit like that old man in Como, escorting the less visible corgi of my discontent. That rubbed its nose and bit, and shat. Maybe I was just irritable my time in England had been wasted, I mean if I'd come here earlier when I was fresh, it would've been easier to write about that world, to conjure it the way I conjured and projected men on my wardrobe in Newtown. In both technicolour and Panavision. The way I also did once with a coup and a revolution.

Spending the rest of the morning thinking about Biff and the night before, rather than writing. In my singlet, leaning out of the window like the old men in Edwina Street's houses. Looking at neons that may have beguiled the hustler in the film my brother mentioned, *Midnight Cowboy*, about a gigolo who dies dreaming of Miami.

Doing the same thing the next day and the day after that. Copies of *The New York Times*, forming ever bigger pyramids in my room, in case some item, some little thread I'd missed, required examination and could offer further clues as to how to recreate the story of that house and suburb. Ironically knowing I could only find it again with what *The New York Times* was full of, the stuff I had yet to write: fantasy.

Occasionally looking for that new perfect opening and paragraph that would lead to my special world of the damned in the beer froth of my Budweisers, at Julius's – New York's oldest gay bar. A bar that was once a speakeasy, five decades ago, when people were forbidden to be under the influence. Why was it so difficult?

I ran into Biff sitting on a bar stool. 'How's my little boon companion. How goes it for ya buddy? Made a start?'

'Almost,' I said, 'but the start's the hardest.'

'What's your hurry anyway?' he said. 'You've got the rest of your life ahead of you.' Not realising that like his, mine was all behind me.

## the man in charge of half hours

Excavating, I mean, going with Biff again to look in the Mineshaft and other places of groping, unilluminated sex, places so dark you could really use a white stick. But there were no clues there about anything. Even if there were, how could you see them in a place darker than the University tunnel? And as soon as we got there, in no time at all in some room or corridor, Biff would vanish, like that phantom Wayne. But that didn't worry me too much because what he and I had, despite my interest in him, was just friendship. Anyway, I'd already had my fill of stuff like that in Sydney at the Barracks, the Signal, and the Ox, not to mention London, where I met and touched so many of the steers of heaven. And the sharp-toothed steed of hell.

Biff eventually rematerialising, taking me to other fuck bars that weren't much different, only bigger, with a bigger reputation to live up to in a city as immodest as men about their size. Biff never showing the slightest interest in me, just being *palsy*. Or as he would say, *budsy*. Liking him as much as I'd once liked Mark, certainly more than Jason or Archie. Probably because Biff was less complicated. Straight up and down.

Looking for clues with him in pizza joints, where attendants pummelled and stretched dough like love handles on boys grown old, where he always said, 'extra anchovies and extra cheese'. The way he said it, sexy. In Greek coffee shops, with booths and checked tablecloths, bigger than the milk bars I remembered. In Queens and Astoria where he said, 'A lot of Greeks here, the place is crawling with them,' as if they were the enemy, but all I saw were Americans.

'Do they make you feel more comfortable or something?'

'No, I wouldn't say that,' I said. Which has always been true.

'Maybe you want to hear their language. It's different isn't it?'

'Actually,' I said, 'my Greek's not so hot, sort of kitchen Greek.'

'Stuff you learn round the fireplace? Like Abe Lincoln?' he chuckled.

'Sort of,' I said. But what he said about hearing was interesting. I was thinking maybe I should spend more time listening rather than looking, since looking wasn't working out that well.

So I tried listening for hints and suggestions. Listening to the noises under grates, over subway stations I wanted to hear hiss as loud as the Eveleigh Street goods yards. Listening in case it was in the rumble of trains taking people to Queens and Jamaica, suburbs neither royal nor tropical. Not even set on rivers, like the Georges, or the Thames in London.

Resorting to drinking, which was easier, in a bar called the Barbary Coast, different to our coast and beaches. Biff and I going to some of the other bars and clubs I hadn't tried yet, attendance at which the media all over the world said was essential. Places like Studio 54, popular because it kept people out rather than in, but like most celebrities, Biff and I knew it was past its prime. Choosing more current places such as The Saint, where we flattered ourselves (like the two thousand other people there) we were the centre of attention. This self-promotion and highly targeted public relations, courtesy of amphetamines, taken for this very purpose. On some drugs I still had a partial dependence.

But Biff unfortunately kept saying the same thing at the end of every night.

'Guess I'd better hit the sack.' Retiring alone, which was

## the man in charge of half hours

annoying. 'Hope that was helpful fer ya.' Which it wasn't. Making me angry at myself for lusting after him, for hoping he was getting attached to me the way I was getting attached to him, for not being content with friendship. In fact I began to feel he was wasting my time.

So I started to look for clues by myself, going to the greatest temple the world has ever seen. Bigger and more important than the one at Ephesus, Bloomingdale's, to stare at underwear, and towels. A place where credit card indulgences get inscribed on carbon, rather than parchment, wanting to buy grey shirts, shorts and white Y-front underwear even though I knew they were just modern copies. Taking my time, chatting to assistants, cautious, studying items with all the attention you'd devote to your wedding dress. The shop assistants saying, 'You buying or dreaming?' When they saw me lost in a trance.

'Hoping,' I answered.

Looking for clues how to start in Hell's Kitchen, rather proper and prim compared to what I'd seen in Newtown. And Harlem, where happiness for blacks over several generations had been at best, like cabs asked to take you there, uncertain.

Just once, sentimentally visiting for old time's sake at least for its name, the theatre called the Apollo, a sort of giant version of the Roumeli, a Circus Maximus, probably built for the performance of an early version of the Shangri-Las. For black female soloists singing about their personal destruction. About strange fruit hanging from sycamore trees. Maybe gargoyles. But once was enough, even this wasn't sufficient to propel my writing. My world was still hidden from me.

Going to the Paradise Garage, to look for a way to

begin. But it was neither paradise nor a garage, although better than the one in Como. A disco barn for unstoreable Puerto Rican emotions. A place like Pierro's on Mykonos where patrons gyrated hips not in fear, but like Iroquois choppers. Where a guy said to me, 'You like salsa?'

'Yeah, I like salsa,' I said, meaning sex. But first we did the dance of the brolgas.

Admiring, by day, apartment blocks such as the Ansonia, which had art nouveau finials and beaux arts features. An apartment block I briefly considered in the same light as our Newtown terrace because it was built in the same period. But it wasn't as beautiful. Ceasing these comparisons because I wasn't *doing* terraces *no more* anyway, as Americans say.

When I needed food, poisoning myself at Zabar's, the world's largest delicatessen, where floor after floor was devoted to the dried and cured skins and genitals of every creature in existence. Creatures already desiccated, that could be splayed and baked in Upper East Side and West Side dining-rooms, in flats big enough to contain padded giraffes. And zebras.

'Is this fish really from Madagascar?' I asked.

'No, a trout farm in Kansas.'

'Do you have lamingtons?'

'No, but we have pheasants.' Having truly terrible problems with pronunciation.

Remembering, on a trip taken on a Staten Island ferry, the film Kylie so loved, about rain, parades and a *Funny Girl*, shrieking wildly for all the world to hear her. It was even raining.

Going to the Broadway theatres alone because Biff didn't like them, going in case there was a clue in a play along the Great White Way to see pearls, retrieved from the precious shell of the great tradition. I think Thornton Wilder's *The Matchmaker* was having another incarnation. Or was it *Our Town*? More honestly looking for clues in burlesques, in the hustler bars of 42nd Street, visited purely out of curiosity. Three dimensional living I could sift through my fingers.

Looking for suggestions in Times Square, where I believed all the epochs and eras of the world, Medieval, Modern, and Hellenistic, met, like me, in one great colliding intersection, the biggest billboard there at the time featuring Brooke Shields whose Calvin Klein jeans concealed her own young tunnel of existence.

**74**   *Nope*, as they say in the states, there *ain't* no two ways about it. I just had to sit down on my *ass* and do it. And I did. Saying to Biff I didn't want to go out for the next couple of weeks, if that was okay by him.

'Sure, whatever you say, kid.' I mean he didn't want to fuck me anyway. So I sat down and began. Not worrying about any goddamn clues. Just writing whatever came into my head, my writing becoming more powerful, page after page reeling off the pen, hour after hour, day after day.

Biff saying when he saw me at it on his way to the bathroom (I always kept my door open) things like, 'You're gonna wear that pen out if you don't watch it. Guess you got talent.'

'Hope so. No offence.' Referring to his own effort.

'No, no offence taken,' he said. 'Need to be pole-axed these days to get offended. I ain't that touchy. If you get my drift.' I didn't really, but I didn't say anything more because I wanted to get on with it. And I did. But if I'd had a particularly good day, though, I would take a minute or two to kid around, I mean, I still liked him. And while I was writing, I noticed Biff sort of took a protective custody approach over me.

'Anyone here on this floor gives you trouble, while you're writing, lemme know,' he said, as if he and I through our friendship were now in some defence pact. Not that Biff needed defending. But there wasn't anyone on the floor who was threatening, so I wasn't sure what he meant. Maybe he was getting a little attached to me. No, that was just wishful thinking.

I think maybe, like most Americans, he just liked me because I hailed from somewhere really obscure, Australia, Greece, finally London, the way Americans like all foreigners. Which they do. Actually, I figured out it was probably because I was the youngest person on the floor. But I also liked to think it was because, I kept what I was writing secret, to give me more of an air of mystery. Telling him no more about it than he'd told me about his sexy but disappointingly interrupted military experience. Once when I took a break, actually asking him further about it, only to get, 'There you go again, trying to upset me,' A deflection.

'Okay,' I said. 'Have it your way.' Deciding not to reveal too much either, my story too valuable for airing, while it was taking final form in fiction.

I really did like him though, because unlike Jason, Don and Tom, he was funny. Maybe because he also said he came from a background a bit like mine, that he alternately called white trash or dirt poor.

'Better get on with it coz success is important — the two greatest things in this whole damn world are fame and money. Moolah. That's what saves you from the ashcan.' Useful advice I suppose. Anyway, I liked the crassness of that. At least what Biff worshipped was popular and specific.

But I have to say, even though my recreation of that world I no longer sought physically was now moving ahead like a champion at Flemington, I had to keep asking myself what was I really trying to achieve with it? The simple recreation of a world? The sorting out of memory? A first lover? Of mother? Of a house? The paraclete of unhappiness. I hadn't even come to them.

Strangely despite all the clues I'd hunted down, I was avoiding my life in Newtown. Avoiding bits about mother. Certainly anything to do with Wayne or University. Athens – forget it, that might as well have been ancient history.

None of them were there on the page. Not Wayne, Jason, Mark, or their finery. When I could've (if I'd wanted) described them like the Greek statues I so admired. Wayne as the most beautiful, a statue of Praxiteles. Mother and my family happier than peasants. Newtown and the house as the gates of paradise, but more pearly. As well as the real Australia which Wayne once described to me.

Cursing myself for not having freely borrowed from his speeches about deserts, cattle and bushfires; for not throwing in some sexual story about a jackaroo, just to hold attention. Cursing myself doubly because I hadn't done any of that. Australia did not seem on my pages, much more than a backdrop for westerns. The pictures Wayne detested.

All because I had wrongly decided that it was best to write this tale not with my own personality, which still remained hidden like so many things, but like Zane Grey and Ben Hecht, in the house style of important magazines. The style of American writers who unlike me could describe with thrift – excesses. Such as what I'd experienced in England. I had to confess my attempt at writing about this world was stilted. Maybe I'd been exposed to too many influences, even though now it was clear to me. I should've looked into the myths of my own soul. Should've been local to be global.

## the man in charge of half hours

I should've been vain with my pen. Should've had me, whoever I was, as the protagonist. Occasional references to childhood, both its architecture and activities, pornographic. Any ideas about my absent mother, if not blown up, at least inflated.

Maybe even inflated to the size of that other lady waving her arm for help and drowning in the distance, the Statue of Liberty. Standing on her own island, an island much smaller than Australia, glowering at anyone who wasn't foreign. Who had her back turned to me as if disgusted. The more I looked at her the more I worried about why I was so attracted to objects of stone and lead. Objects for whose hardness and coldness, ever since childhood, my attraction was more than an obsession. A fetish.

I remember visiting her one windswept day, the statue that is, I don't know why. Staring from the base at her folded skirt heavier than any wedding dress. Looking up at her pea green envy, which faced me and Europe, where she'd been welded and hammered. Thinking she was probably smaller than that vanished wonder of the ancient world, the gold statue of Athena.

Climbing up the stairs of her entrails and gizzards. Up to the crown, to that tiny chamber of echoes and bleary sockets, smaller than my room at the Y. Climbing back down the steep stairs, which reminded me of other stairs that led me away from that other ghastly creature of stone, who recommended I should come here, before (like so many old fashioned Australians) I chose a detour to London. Finally reaching the earth, and discharging my imagination's electricity.

## medea's children

And looking at it all put down on that swollen pile of paper and suppressed in ink that wasn't Reckitt's Blue but sentimental soap powder, I knew how untruthful it was. In fact, it was a lot of rubbish. Now knowing exactly what to do with it.

Throwing the entire lot out. Along with that complete fantasy of politics, *The New York Times*. Cheering up, because at least at self-recrimination I'd become excellent.

Knowing I'd failed miserably, until finally one afternoon I found the clue that told me how to recreate this world, in a gallery called the Met that was better than the Tate. I found it while staring in the mirror, I mean at a painting by Magritte, of me and Wayne, appropriately called *The Lovers*. A painting showing the peephole of Magritte's own life, blown up out of all proportion on canvas. The stockings over the faces of his subjects, the world's finest depiction of what I once called *inhalation*. Enough to kick-start my masterpiece.

Deciding the intellectual way didn't suit me. No more of this crawling around cities like Inspector Clueseau. The picture making it obvious that I needed to get back to my own unique experience, my old style of charity. Knowing that if I couldn't find this house, this world, or at least create it on paper, then with my body I could at least give it form. And substance.

Anyway with Biff I had to face it, I'd developed a crush on him. A crush that was crushing.

**75**   'Sir, may I ask who this Westpoint uniform is for?' the attendant at Bloomingdale's asked. Smarmy. Maybe this happened at some military outfitter's.

'It's for my brother,' I said.

'And how big's he?' the attendant asked. 'Shall I guess? About your size?'

'Correct,' I said.

'Ain't been wrong before,' he said, as if he knew my type, or what I was up to.

'He's coming up to graduation,' I added.

'Truly?' he said.

'Truly,' I said. 'You bet.'

I must say it was difficult selecting this uniform, not being well acquainted with the American military system of education. Settling on the one he showed me that had a white cap, gloves and white trousers with a stripe. Remembering how I'd worn white in my best production, a veil and gloves, which if they hadn't been poisoned, would've been perfect.

Taking the uniform home, finding the white slacks fit my legs, and my buns (I could now say buns). Finding the tie and the white shirt of superior quality to ours. The cap, becoming. Snapping on its shorter wrist-length gloves.

Waiting in my room at the Y until it was almost dark.

## medea's children

Waiting for the confusing hour near twilight. My favourite time. Making sure no one saw me go down the corridor to Biff's room, where I knocked three times because three is the number of ritual.

No answer.

'Mike,' I said. 'Psst. It's me. I can help you. You can help me.' But nothing.

'Psst, Biff,' I said, remembering he didn't like being called Mike. But again nothing. Making me turn the handle to enter, where I saw Biff with the top button of his jeans undone, lying barefoot on the bed and staring at the ceiling like a patient rejected by the American medical system. Or the navy. Just staring at the ceiling, the way I once stared at the gold balls of our perpetual clock.

'Want company?' I asked. 'I've completely dried up.'

No answer. It was as if he had neither seen nor noticed anyone enter let alone a cadet capable of giving happiness.

Going over and sitting by his bed, taking his hand and stroking it, I said, 'Hey, cheer up. You look kind of down.' Putting my hand down his jeans, then his T-shirt, which was stained from last night's solitary cavorting. Stroking him, caressing him, trying to make him feel desired. Getting up from my position, taking off my West Point cap and throwing it across the room like a stripper. Loosening my tie and my top button. Taking off my white socks, and shoes. Unzipping my white band leader's type trousers in case he wanted to play with my erection, for I was determined that I would grow stiff for him if he wanted, as I had done so many times for so many people to ease their depression. Maybe even mine. Taking off the gloves like a surgeon. Peeling back the skin of memory.

'I really think you need company,' I said. 'We all do.'

## the man in charge of half hours

Putting my hand farther down his jeans and taking out his penis and balls, seeing how big it was and how floppy. Stroking it with both hands to get a reaction. All of which Biff ignored. Pretending I wasn't even there.

'Relax, Biff. We can be friends. Think about nothing. You said to sing out if I wanted help.' Pulling on him some more. Biff turning away from me, turning to the wall like a child admonished by his parents. As if he didn't want to know me. Me not letting go of him, knowing this would alleviate loneliness. Mine anyway.

'Pretend we're at school,' at the academy, I said. 'And I'm the special friend and that I haven't been anywhere.' Going down on him, sucking cock till against his will it achieved erection, not much bigger than when it was floppy but respectable. Making me think I'd been deceived when I thought it was the size of a bull's. Why wouldn't he talk to me?

'Relax,' I said, pulling on his prick some more. 'Everything will be okay in the morning. Just as it was. And always will be.' Just then, Biff giving a small yelp, coming over my hand, emitting a reluctant lotion.

'Better now?' I said. 'It's better this way for me.' Kissing him lightly on the cheek. Just hearing his hard breathing and seeing his eyes closed behind his glasses. Perspiration due to the New York heat was trapped on the scalp of his crewcut.

But when he regained his breath he suddenly turned and looked at me in horror. Saying what I hadn't expected. Propping himself up on the pillow, peering through his glasses at me as if I were a ghost from Arlington.

'Get out of here,' he said. 'Get out of here. Who the hell asked you to suck my dick? Cock sucking fag.' So much self-hatred. Maybe Biff was what America had always been, an isolationist. Unlike me, probably happy with his own company. 'Who the hell do you think you are? And take your crappy uniform with ya. Freak. Pervert.'

I didn't know what to say. All I could do was leave. Grabbing bits and pieces of the uniform and fleeing. In the corridor, hiding my face with the cap in a vaudeville gesture of humiliation, embarrassed by the compliment. Hearing him yell in the background not to me but to some unseen force, 'Officer take these two fags to the brig.'

**7 6**    As the weeks went by, noticing I no longer wrote, my gold-tipped fountain pen ran dry through lack of use, so I didn't bother to even hock it throwing it out. Dark outside. Late autumn. It really might as well have been Como. Or Jason's bedsit in Earl's Court.

My traveller's clock said six. What I could see of it. Above newspapers surrounding me, in which no clue featured as to how to begin again. The news – that a space shuttle had crashed. Time for dinner in any of the hundreds of minced meat establishments near the Y hamburger joints that were usually named after women, like ships. *Wendy's*, *Jilly's*, *Sally's* as if the softness of a woman's name could add some delicacy to lukewarm slop and thin chips served to soak up the masculinity of blood.

Time to at least seek out more bars. In this I was practised. Becoming a late night regular. Suspected by the hustlers who thought I too did it for money.

Time I spent in late night coffee shops where Vietnam vets, or maybe other marines who wore flak jackets, spoke loudly to themselves, eating blue donuts you now only see in *The Simpsons*.

'Twenty dollars is too much for a cigarette.' Or is that a line from some forgotten GI Joe movie seen in the lobby on TV? Realising I would have to begin my search again.

## medea's children

At one point writing a letter to Mark, my old schoolfriend, who I looked up in the phone book. He was living in Malibu. He sent a postcard back, saying, 'Hey you, good to hear from ya.' But that it wasn't a good idea to visit. The job he had as a pool attendant kept him too busy.

Not bothering to answer knocks at my door. Which I now kept closed. If anything maybe I was a little scared. In case Biff was angry. Being strong, he looked like the sort who could take vengeance at my presumption.

Cashing the uniform in at Bloomingdale's for what I nearly always wear these days, black leather. Leaving the ninth floor of the Y, and New York, still haunted by the memory of a whole house. Maybe by what Biff said about a ghost story. Deciding it was time to start paying attention to my own Gods, which for reasons of courtesy during my stay in America I'd deliberately kept in abeyance, to give my story, the thing I've never had in life: veracity.

Deciding to go back to Australia, to grace the world if not the suburb I'd come from with my holy presence. Thinking maybe I'd treated my life too much as a joke. A travelling circus. From now on I would be like all Australians, butch and serious. Besides it was still too hot in New York and I could do with a storm. Thinking if I couldn't find my world in narrative or by imitating experience, then it had to be in poetry, which is shorter. Convinced what I was looking for did not lie in comedy, but in what the Greeks have always been good at, tragedy.

**77**   *Land of the rainbow gold* I thought, ignoring the movie, staring out of the plane's porthole at the horizon where clouds spilt a rainbow, like petrol in rain-soaked streets, fracturing it into colours. Perhaps reminded of these lines of poetry by what was served on Qantas: a rainbow slab of Neapolitan ice cream.

*With flood, fire and famine, she pays us back three-fold.*

Where had I heard these lines before? I'd never uttered them. I thought I only knew the first stanza of that poem. Noticing for the first time Dorothea Mackellar considered Australia a spiteful woman.

Casting my mind back to what Biff had said, 'Pervert', when he flattered me. As well as to what Jason had said, 'Don't go, please'. And to something about needing me, rather than loving me. A line once upon a time I'd certainly uttered.

I also thought, why do they say all Australian stories are nothing but *exile and return?* Aren't all stories, *separation, initiation, return?* Even if only from the Great Sandy Desert? Or Perth, or Brisbane, where young men drown in pools barely a foot deep. They're just images from books that now seem to me so quaint. And cowardly. Skating on surfaces. Books and films that are basically Dad and Dave soap operas, where my sex, my face, my race and place just feature as ancillary characters. To swell a scene. Thinking this, just as my fork went into vanilla, a favoured flavour, except in sex. Then chocolate, the deep forbidden zone, before blooding itself on strawberry, the hue of resurrection, what foolish priests believe in.

To while away the hours, beginning to sing the way mother used to. Quietly. But not her tunes, nor the Moody Blues, the Cure or Peter Allen. Actually, a song that could've applied to Biff if he'd been more willing, and to Jason who last time I looked, wasn't supporting me, but a narceine habit.

'Say goodbye,' I sang, 'my old true lovers,' very softly, making it plural, remembering an old song surprisingly Australian. And because I didn't actually want to see Biff broken by memory any more than I wanted to see Jason dead. Wanting them, like me, to do more than live in poverty, to have a design for living.

'Would you like something else?' a handsome steward said, interrupting my aria of melancholy.

'Actually I do,' I said. 'But not right now,' while I looked at his trousers and the bulge in them that made me want to say, 'Maybe some nuts, big luscious nuts.' I mean, I'd met enough of them. Deciding not to be provocative, waving him off, almost my old self again. Impertinent.

'Don't be like that with me, girl,' the steward said, recognising a fellow faggot. 'It's Jimmie you're talking to.' And it was.

'Jimetha?' I said.

'Paleese! Not so loud,' he said. 'I'm so embarrassed. You're the only one who knows I used to call myself that. Oh, God, the things we do in our youth coming back to haunt me on a 747. And in economy, ugh.'

the man in charge of half hours

'The things,' I said, remembering what he and I did at Ramsgate and at Waterfall. 'Gave up on business, huh?'

'Years ago, doll. We all have to make a living. Even you.' Something I hadn't considered. 'Anyway, good to see you or as we say in this business, you're very welcome.'

'Good to see you too,' I said. Which it was. I just hoped he wasn't feeding the Captain, Mandrax.

'Give us a call sometime,' Jimmie said. 'I mean, when we land. If you've still got my number.' His eyes still a beautiful Harpic blue. Winking, walking off. Seeing him sort of cheered me up.

But it was cold on that plane, something I wasn't used to. So cold, no amount of CSIRO non-combustible wool blankets Jimmie gave out could keep me warm. Maybe I had a problem with my circulation. Not just because I was freezing but also because it seemed to me all I'd done over the last few years was rotate around the globe, around the cities, printed on the perfume bottles of Jimmie's trolley. Visiting a seedy New York, a run down London, a stinking Paris and the Athens of my imagination. Looking for a house, a bit of nous could have told you wouldn't be there.

On arrival getting sprayed by Jimmie with a can for purposes of hygiene, mental disinfectant so I'd leave behind whatever troubled me. The spray forcing weaker passengers to do their own inhalations through handkerchiefs.

But at least I'd returned, as they say. The way I always promised. Returned to a place that gave me my first experiences of heaven and then so much hell. To begin my search again. Returning not heroically as a television critic nor like the woman who once studied Shakespeare's comedies then sexuality as if there were a difference, the Australians Don hated, Clive James and Germaine Greer.

Not even like Barry Humphries, the nice drag queen. But as a veteran of my own bloody wars. Wars that were neither American, Greek nor English. Just occasionally comic.

A veteran who still had all his limbs but whose heart was like the heart of all poems and popular lyrics, a Portland Vase in pieces. Still not knowing where on earth my Newtown would be, let alone Wayne or my terrace. Needing to get on with it.

Deciding though, not to go home and visit my family yet. Or what was left of them. In fact not even telling them I was back, because I thought the unalloyed joy they would get out of seeing me might require preparation.

Deciding to take 'digs', as the English call them, rooms that might as well have been trenches, by going to Kings Cross where the drug dealers said to me, 'Want to get on? Want to get on?'

Where I said, 'No, I want to get off.' Deciding to avoid Kings Cross since I didn't want to get tangled up in the Opium Wars I'd survived that the locals were still fighting. Choosing Surry Hills, because it was dark and cheap. Finding a shared flat close to Oxford Street through the newspapers, in my favourite section, the *To Share* column, even though the ad I chose to respond to was a little too blunt and unpoetic for my liking.

The girl who placed the ad opened the door after I knocked, saying, 'You easy going and broad minded?'

'Course.'

'But you look as if you've been in battle,' which was accurate. Then when I told her where I'd been, 'How fabulous.' A serious error.

Using the room as a base so I could begin my usual after

midnight inquiries. What wowsers call, 'cruising'. What Biff and I did in New York before our little falling out over the appropriateness of intimacy and dress codes, and what I did with Jason in London. God, I could take this all the way back to Athens, to white sticks and fevered passions.

Actually, by now, cruising was a courtesy extended to every city I lived in. Ahead of retracing my steps through the local clues I had ignored to find the way to what kids and only kids call the magic kingdom.

But I was broke and needed what Jimmie had: a job. I mean all this searching and rooting around was expensive. Now I thought it was probably best done with a career. Figuring I needed a vocation, a job that was sexy and much more obscene than peeping. So I went into television.

**78**   As my vehicle for this search, I mean my victim, I picked our finest channel, the ABC at Gore Hill, a place not so different to those warehouses in Hackney. Going to see my first prospective employer, a man with grey hair risen in the ranks because of what I was told was genius, which was a bit difficult to detect because he was disguised as the Head of Production. Maybe he was Don's distant older cousin.

'I am the Man in Charge of Half Hours,' he said. Unnecessary because it was on his door. Or did it say, ABC Documentaries? Those living and breathing records of the dead and dying. That cover issues like flood, fire and famine.

'Down the hall,' he said, 'is the Girl in Charge of Seconds. Here, we won't have any talk about the scoundrels who run *Sixty Minutes*. We don't want reports like that. Do you understand?'

'Yes, one hundred per cent,' I said, because just like him, I was good with numbers, though maybe not telephone numbers.

'If you're lucky, one day you might work in Features,' the Man in Charge of Half Hours said. A department most people were in awe of, because occasionally it assembled melanges and blancmanges of ninety minutes. But I'm not sure if that was to be a reward or a penance.

## the man in charge of half hours

'Do you understand? You seem a bit distracted,' the Man in Charge of Half Hours said, leaning back in his chair, balancing on it the way we did at school. His hands were behind his neck, supporting it in case some underling wanted to break it.

'Perfectly,' I said.

'But remember,' the custodian of Australia's most expensive time machine said, balancing backwards and forwards, moving like a perpetual clock, 'always remember,' as if I was forgetful, when all he controlled were fleeting moments, 'here we don't want any funny business.'

'What do you mean by funny business, sir?'

'I'll let you figure that out. This thing you mention about your need to search, as part of your mission statement. I don't fully understand. Might be best to take it out of your c.v. Almost cost you the job.'

'But it's important to me. What about Burke and Wills?'

'Burke and Wills never found anything, they perished in the desert.'

'What about Blaxland, Wentworth and . . .'

'Try Henry Lawson,' he said, 'he's much simpler.'

'Hume and . . .'

'Hovell,' he finished. 'Look we can carry on like this for quite some time pretending we're explorers. What I'd like to make clear is that we're a serious network. We need things that are current. When we first spoke you said you were leaving comedy behind you. That you're better at emotion.'

Apparently humour, despite so many internal absurdities at the ABC and the country that paid for it, was forbidden.

'The ABC has a charter. Try to fill it,' he said, as if the station were an airline like Virgin.

A station with a presbyterian and concerned approach to broadcasting. The only titillation offered, purely in terms of salary. Which was amazingly high, compared to that which was earned by people who wielded jackhammers. Too high for using watercolours they call film, and video, pencils driven by electronics.

Maybe this didn't happen at the ABC but a place called Film Australia, which to me still sounds like an order. Maybe at the Special Broadcasting Service, 'special', because it was about people like me, its transmitter capable of bypassing reception. Or maybe, just maybe, this happened at one of the commercial networks, run by fat men and slim men and their well-groomed ponies. People who play polo. I forget.

All I know is that the reporters I worked with there weren't interested in searching for anything, Worse, they sent me on assignments that were nowhere near Newtown or its neighbours. Interstate. To intimidate people who'd failed a course in ethics.

'Tell me,' I said, to a minister who looked uncomfortable, 'when did you first realise that Government funds were missing?'

The minister saying, 'Round the time you showed up, after my trip to the Caymans.' Stuff like that.

But it wasn't so bad really. And I too got trips, if not to Newtown at least to the Pacific, the supposed warmest sphere of Australia's influence, even though you can't hold it or suck it.

And to the Outback, that large Australian yard, which is so much easier to film and write about than the cities and boxes most of us live in. So much easier to find because of its vastness. Chasing after what so many writers say are,

# the man in charge of half hours

'figures in a landscape', as if people like me and the house I came from are situated on the moon.

Some of the television life, though, I enjoyed. For instance, between interviews, cutting out paper dolls for stimulation. The only substantive thing from my youth I could think of other than masturbating.

Occasionally talking to nice women from the religious department, who said that as a result of the demystification brought about by Vatican Two, life had lost its meaning. Because the pale horse with the golden saddle and silver stirrups had bolted. As if Rome was Old Regret in need of new stockmen. Making me think of Kylie, and what she kissed around her throat, the last time we saw each other: the locket. And it *was* Kylie. God I was glad to see her.

'Kylie,' I said. 'Of all people. What are you doing here working in the religious department?'

'Yes,' she said. 'It's me, older, more experienced but no wiser. For all my talk I haven't been anywhere. Life for me has lost its mystery.' Making me think her Melbourne elm trees had suffered die back.

Kylie starting to sing, but not Streisand. Not even Peggy Lee or Sinatra.

'Amazing Grace, how sweet the sound . . . Come on,' she said. 'Don't be like that. Sing like we used to.'

But I couldn't. Just couldn't.

'Don't get me wrong,' she said. 'I have no complaints. I love it here. They all have such exquisite manners.'

Gore Hill, named because it had impaled so many who tried to change it. Or had them broken on the Catherine wheel of the middle class spun by the middle aged who were pretending to be generation X'ers. Whatever that is.

Flayed with the cat o' nine tails called cutbacks. Screening endless retreads of *Fawlty Towers* and *To the Manor Born*. Programs I actually liked, but for all the wrong reasons. Presbyterians and sentimental Catholics who defy my Gods. Never really broadcasting to Newtown or Como or people from Athens, but to all Australia's north shores. Concerts and ballets for Sunday roast Anglicans. People who never had to search for any house, because unlike the despised, they always had it.

The other reporters said my reports were getting too complicated.

'Hurry up. Give it to us in a sentence. Give it to us in a sentence.' As if sentences were bullets. Loathing words as much as Don and the Frenchmen. Narrative considered something ugly, merely functional. Like a toilet door at Wynyard. Letting some people in. Others out.

And, 'Think in pictures mate, think in pictures,' as if the rest of us only think in hieroglyphics. The most sentimental of them saying it wasn't his fault, in the old days it was different, lamenting the loss of language.

'It was different then,' he sobbed. 'What would you know? You were in short pants. They had respect for us, the way they had respect for judges. Now the only ones who don't slam the phone down when I ask for interviews are victims from the western suburbs. Fat ladies in track pants.' Breaking down utterly. I gave him my handkerchief.

Maybe all the reporters thought they were musketeers. Maybe me, D'Artagnan. At least cavalier in our approach to Australia's problems. While I thought about my house, filing reports on how the public sector was expensive and expansive. On how the private sector was shrinking and sullen. Maybe the other way round. Reports about problems that usually had to do with misplaced spells that could open the door of caves where the jewels called the Terms of Trade occasionally went hiding. Terms of Trade? More like Rough Trade, the people who always governed.

All I know is that during this period while I put my search on hold, because I needed money, that several eras were over. Certainly the one true believers in the sacred suburb of Balmain said took place by the Pushkar Lake of Burley Griffin. An artificial lake where White Papers and Green Papers, suggesting equality got scattered like marigolds. The period, predating the man who said life should never be hard, who got made a cardinal. Everyone calling him eminence.

It happened when they put in power one of the sharpies or the bodgies. No, actually a silver-haired old man I remembered from my childhood. One of the old men who used to lean out of windows in singlets listening to horse races. A man who at least paid lip service to their syndicates. I mean unions.

Okay, maybe I didn't like this job, but I did graduate to textas. Actually film that was sixteen millimetre. Even if it wasn't Don's oils of seventy millimetre that he strangled. I guess as I said, holding on, because I needed money to continue my search and explorations.

But strangely, I didn't use any of the money to go directly to Newtown. I mean you just can't buy that sort of road map no matter how much you save up or as they say these days, *network*. Besides it would've been corrupt. Worse I might have been exposed in someone else's documentary.

No, I thought I'd better ease myself into it. By first picking over the other places I was familiar with.

'Go on,' I said to myself. 'Use a camera to wend your way through the tricky streets till you find it.'

So I did. Going with a camera to visit the Oxford Street I'd known, past the Piazza San Marco and Liverpool Street's Grand Canal, as Kylie used to call them. But there was hardly a soul there. No men with shoestring ties, in chaps and akubras. No sign of rope or lassoes used for restraint. No boys sitting on corral fences chewing straws. No strains of the loud barn dance music called disco and its crescendo of 'yeehas'. No one even saying, 'Howdy, stranger.' Not even a 'G'day.'

In fact nothing to film there. Just a street of tumbleweeds. Probably because the massive shoot out called AIDS was still in progress, infections like snipers picking off what was left of resistance. Casualties higher than what Lincoln caused when he tried to get rid of the Confederates.

Tumbleweeds blowing down Oxford Street. Whistling a mournful howl. Tumbleweeds shaped like discarded wanted posters. Hundreds of them blowing in the wind. Okay, maybe I'm talking about obituaries sandwiched between ads for undertakers. Dry Gulch's great survivors. Ads in the gay newspapers.

'Anybody here?' I called out. No answer.

Me walking up and down Oxford Street's silence with a cigar in my mouth and a camera like a gun by my side. Feeling a little bit like Clint Eastwood, the Man With No Name, the unshaven man out of the spaghetti westerns. Listening to the crows in the sky. For vultures. Maybe army helicopters.

Looking at other unshaven men behind swing door

saloons splayed out on tables, as hot and flat as their *cervezas*. Sweating. Listening hard to the buzzing of flies, the silence, in case around the corner was the killer I could shoot, the unidentified bandit called a virus.

I guess it made me too scared to even think of progressing to Newtown, too scared to even think of what had become of it let alone our house, when all about me in the inner city all I could see was devastation.

Doing a report on the carnage, feeling it was my duty. The least I could do. A 'stand up', as they're called, as in stand-up comedy, but I was serious. Deciding to be original by not doing it on Oxford Street. Once and for all, dropping references to westerns, the pictures Wayne hated. Instead using images from pictures he and I liked.

Going and standing instead on the cliffs of Bondi with a microphone while they filmed me. For a national audience. Me, saying to the microphone and the world, while pointing to the windswept heights, almost feeling like the man who once mocked me.

'Here, as you can see, down by the mighty cliffs of Bondi facing the Pacific, are some of the finest minds, and some of the finest bodies of my generation. Thousands of men standing on cliffs all around the harbour stretching to North Head and South Head, Coogee, Clovelly, even Malabar where I'm pointing to, over there in the distance. As far west as the upper reaches of the Parramatta River. They've got their various uniforms on, tunics and plumes. The signature of their Legions. Here and there some are wearing Ned Kelly masks hoping that by being ashamed of their faces they can go on living. What their leader, a certain Mr Cicero, calls closets. We were hoping to cross to Mr Cicero for comment but he has declined to be interviewed.' Probably because I didn't ask him. Anyway I'd heard the University had fired him for refusing to charge for meetings.

I continued, 'All these men are waiting, staring starkly not just at the waves below them but what all Australians are good at staring at. The middle distance.'

Brett, the sound recordist I was using saying, 'Oh, brother. I'm running out of tape.'

Craig, the cameraman saying, 'Where are you getting this shit from? Give it up or give it a bit of oomf, because we're losing the light.'

'Brett, Craig, – will you two stop that,' I said to them. The cheek. 'From the past, where do you think? Besides I was just getting into it. Roll camera.' Annoyed, but continuing, remembering how devoted they were to games when we were studying, appealing to their better nature, but this time more like a football commentator to keep them interested.

'And there it goes, the signal like a handkerchief dropped by Frank Thring playing Nero, the signal that says it's time to push them over. One in every ten. The first to topple is random.'

Anyway that's how I reported it. Really I did. Reporting on how bodies were collected from the rocks with tractors and spades. Maybe combine harvesters. Reporting from where I stood above the cliffs at Bondi and from Watson's Bay near the beaconless lighthouse. Telling of decimation. The fall of a briefly sexual empire. Gay men tumbling, uncomplaining, believing that like the apartments they used to live in silence was more decorous. Others falling screaming. A noise so hideous it could have rivalled the worst sound on earth, the screams heard when aeroplanes are compressed into tiny black boxes.

## the man in charge of half hours

I finished with this coda: 'Some are old men, but most young. Some die in each other's arms. Dashed against diseased rocks not of their making. Some choosing the imperial exit, opening veins in their legs. Sort of finding virtue in beating the gun by being first to stand in front of it.'

Maybe I was thinking of the ultimate sword and sandal films, *The Fall of the Roman Empire*.

Most of these scenes for what they're worth, didn't really take place on cliffs. To be accurate, they occurred at the hospital belonging to Saint Vincent. My inspiration for this, and everything I said to Brett and Craig drawn from childhood. Maybe University. Where I learnt how to appease them and make them like me.

**7 9**   'Do come in.' The Man in Charge of Half Hours said wanting to see me to discuss what warders in Long Bay call probation. 'Make yourself relaxed and comfortable.' Which was ominous. Not just for me but everyone. 'I remember,' the Man in Charge of Half Hours said, while rubbing his glasses with a kleenex. 'I remember when I was your age,' he said pausing as his picture of youth grew dimmer, and short-sighted. The signal, weakening. 'Full of high hopes. There were things I wanted to find as well. I too had great expectations, towering ambitions.' Bringing back to my mind what I reported on the cliff tops. 'But I too had to compromise.' He said. 'Do you understand? For the sake of all of us. Don't be so fuzzy. Or witty. Try to think of us as mates. Mates happy to make the ultimate sacrifice when required.' Selfless. 'Tell me what was the greatest television influence on you in your youth?'

'That's easy,' I said. '*Homicide*.'

'*Homicide*?' he chuckled.

'Well it might've been *Matlock*.' I didn't dare mention *The Roller Game*. I was too smart for that.

'I used to be in *Homicide*,' he said. 'How the past comes back to embarrass us.'

'It does?'

'Must be things in your past you're embarrassed about.'

## the man in charge of half hours

'No.'

'I used to play a detective, used to wear this hat and trenchcoat chasing...'

'I know what you're going to say...'

'Crooks. Crooks is what they were called then.' The Man in Charge of Half Hours said, now sort of reminding me a little bit of that editor at *The Herald*.

'Anyway, your reports,' he said, 'well we don't want any of that. We're a much more sophisticated market and culture now. Global.'

'I know,' I said.

'Irony,' he said, 'is a very delicate tool. Very English. Americans are no good at it.'

'I experienced it.' I said.

'But I'm not sure it's very Greek either,' he said. 'Tragedy is more your people's line. I don't know if you've studied the great tradition or not, actually we have a series on it we've just bought from the Beeb...'

'Can we wind this up?' I said. 'I've got things to do.'

Then, from him, the cadenza. 'We certainly can. I'm afraid your talents are a little too wide for us. What you're searching for is not really here.'

'No,' I said. 'Hope not.'

'Maybe you should put it back in your c.v.'

So I did. Accepting my new position on the dole, created especially for me and the other half a million winners of the Australian economic boom in progress, which I'd also reported on. Maybe I was waiting much like the magicians, painters and dancers, I met on the ninth floor, for some unusual far off employment. Maybe like Biff, for popularity.

**80**     All right. I admit I'm being a bit harsh. But it went something like that. Anyway I was glad he fired me, because now it was time for me to stick down all the clues and hints and trails I followed, the way I used to in my school projects. The final assembly.

And for that, I needed time. Time to sink the tone and myself into what I had been avoiding and had come from, the gloom which lies at the heart of every terrace, the only thing I've never liked about them.

Promising, no, swearing there'd be no more skating on surfaces, and lakes – sticking to the shallows. Needing to seriously find that house that had caused me so much grief and pleasure. From where I'd been torn like a postage stamp and sent abroad in case I found an album.

Wisely deciding this time round not to trust the street directory, all those maps deliberately written to confuse me. Nor the deceiving passages and *communiqués* of real estate agents. Ghosts and phantoms. Also because as the cameraman said, I did have to hurry because I was losing the light.

Going to visit the one man who would know, called Dad, going back to Como by the banks of the Georges River, knowing this was dangerous. Avoiding its banks. Just going up the main street that now had crazy paving. Where

I saw the same old man who first spoke to me, now without his corgi, still chatting away to cars, street lights and garages.

'What happened to your dog mister?' I asked.

'Oh,' he said. 'It's you. Oh, he just got up and left one not so very fine day. Much obliged to you for asking. Haven't seen him have you?'

'No,' I said. 'I wish.'

'I wish, too,' he said. 'Neither have these blokes.' Pointing to the garages. 'But I don't think he's dead. Just cranky or sleeping.'

Going down the street with the jacarandas stiff and dry this April because it was only in November that they wept. Past the paperbarks, whose soft split skin could be used for novels and newsprint. Into the flat with the dots and whorls in the carpet.

Opening the door, hearing only the TV, fortunately not the ABC but another channel which said, 'Ladies and gentlemen in the left-hand corner we have the jerk and in the right . . .'

Going farther in where I saw my brother watching what I thought I'd already been through: *World Championship Wrestling*. But it didn't feature Mario Milano, Killer Kowalski, or my favourite, Larry O'Day. Just some fat guy in a mask. Combatants in short supply, probably because in Australia now there weren't that many new European immigrants.

'Hey, you wouldn't believe it,' my brother said, as if I'd never been away, 'they've got this on cable, except it's no longer free.'

'Who's winning?' I asked.

'Doesn't matter. Does it?'

'Suppose not. Where's Dad?'

## medea's children

'Dad,' he said, 'in a word . . . ,' just as a combatant got dropped on the mat, '. . . is dead. Died about a year ago.' And then, after pausing like the referee for effect, 'Don't say you weren't told, coz you never sent a letter.'

'Did too,' I said, possibly because of the situation being childish.

'Yeah, deliberately without a return address.' He said, as if he, like me, could read thoughts. 'Anyway, he left you that.' Pointing to a shoebox on the mantelpiece, above the fake log fireplace and near the perpetual clock.

'That's it?' I said. 'I mean, that's all?'

'He said that's all you need.' Actually, my brother said, 'all you deserve.'

A shoebox whose paper I unwrapped liked bandages. In it just a photo of all of us standing for the last time in front of our old house. On the back, its number and address. And my Katoomba cable car pen.

'What's the pen for?'

'I told you,' he said. 'Must've lost the fancy one we gave you, so Dad figured you might need this to pen your address.'

I guess they were angry.

'Bye,' I said, while a combatant got up from the floor.

My brother turning to me, saying, 'For the time being let's just say hello.'

I didn't dare ask any more than that. About any other people who once lived in this flat. Not wanting to spoil the moment.

On the train looking at the picture, in which the house seemed so unreal. Getting off at Central. Finally knowing exactly where to go. At least with what. I mean with this picture and the precise address I was sure to find it.

## the man in charge of half hours

Deciding to take what I once adored, not a train but the thing I rode with the man I loved, a bleating diesel-belching bus. The 422, the 423, the 426. There were so many it surprised me.

Getting off first at the University whose gates were still intact. Maybe rebuilt stronger to repel future advances. The whole campus restructured to look like the offices of accountants.

There were no scary phalanxes of gargoyles there or griffins, nor the tumbrels that once rolled down espousing revolution. Only motorbikes and convertibles so that students could do victory laps when their paper chase finished. Laps around the speedway of ambition. The dark tunnel connecting the two parts of the campus was now illuminated for safety. Apparently there'd been rapes in its precinct.

But up high, on the stone battlements, I could still see one gargoyle, the one that had first looked at me, salaciously and then threateningly before finally speaking. Now it was truly unmoved, much like I commanded it. A harmless goblin, waiting for masons paid by the funds of Old Boys to restore it.

Going back up the stairs of that Gothic main quadrangle building, past the dark red and blue leadlight, sliding once again down the mansard roof to where it lay. Small and pathetic. A tiny stone dummy whose porousness I patted.

'Still here my friend,' I said. Not being able to think of anything else to say. Feeling like an idiot for talking to statues. Even that time I spoke to the obelisk. 'Still here.' I said. Possibly describing the atmosphere.

But the gargoyle must have been too embarrassed to

answer me. Its nose and mouth not pouring blood but sweating a little bit of moisture from the humidity, as if it too was suffering from a virus.

Quitting the University to walk up King Street, now relabelled City Road in Sydney's honour, maybe more regally, the Highway of Princes. Holding tightly onto the photo in case I lost it. Gliding past what used to be the Master Builders' Association, the headquarters of men and boys I liked, called brickies.

Shuffling past warehouses now converted to bedsits, similar to the one I had in London. And shops featuring aromas and oils capable of reviving the inhabitants.

'Try this one,' a girl said, 'lavender. It's essential.' Which it wasn't.

Going past gift stores selling not wrought iron for balconies but candelabras and candles to light a new age darkness. And there I was.

Finally I'd arrived in Newtown. Finally after all these years and turmoil. This constant series of disappointments. But I just couldn't believe it. I just couldn't believe how much it had changed. There were even gay bars here, in the toilet pubs once devoted to Wayne's worship. In the old pubs my father liked going to, putting on a jacket for those outings. If I'd known, it would've saved me a lot of trouble. And lots of coffee shops everywhere, hundreds of them, using satanic machines to press the life and steam out of beans, making not Greek or Turkish brews, but black blood drunk for sustenance. Ristrettos and mochas.

The cinema called The Hub that was the centre of the universe was still there though. But it now looked like an ugly old bicycle spoke stuck into Newtown's sophisticated engines. Its billboard trumpeting films that had neither swords nor sandals. Porn films like at the Kotopouli, where everyone's tunics had been lifted.

But some things were still familiar, like the spherical balls attached to the shop awnings for lamplight, and the other balls of the Money Lent shop, the pawn shop featuring Breville dryers, unwanted pancake makers, Casio watches with flat batteries, rather than the simpler things of life, then. Like non-graphite tennis rackets. And reel to reel tape recorders. I certainly couldn't see barbers selling Brylcreem or California Poppy.

The shoppers were strange, hurried, younger than what I recalled, pierced more by metal than emotion. Rings and pins in belly buttons. Not many Greeks or Yugoslavs. Certainly no Italians. I guess most of them continued their journey on the bus, shunning this Newtown. No, tricked or deceived into going to the suburbs. Maybe the old one I knew and loved now only existed in Cabramatta. I felt humiliated having to ask for directions.

'Mate, do you know,' I asked a man clad like me in black leather thick enough to repel arrows and feeling fake because the word mate never suited me, 'where Edwina Street is? This house?' Taking out Dad's picture of it.

'What's in it for me?' he replied. I don't think he was being rude. Just mouthing the national motto. To be honest, he said, 'Excuse me?' So I repeated the question.

'Everyone knows where that is. It's famous. Follow your nose, a hundred metres as the crow flies. Can't miss it.' He wouldn't have been any older than twenty, definitely not born in the age of yards.

And he was right. It was only a hundred metres up the road. I'd walked right past it, not noticing its name had changed. I had walked past it so many times in my life, missing it because I was either blind or hurrying. Maybe just insensitive.

*Edwardia Street*, a plaque said, mystifying me. Why was the name now masculine? There wasn't any one there who could tell me. At the commemorative bubbler standing at Edwardia Street's entrance, another plaque stated this *was* its original name, uncovered along with yet another mention of Dickens, not by enthusiastic amateurs from the historical society but by professors who had bought into Newtown as a place fitting for their study.

It's very hard to describe the emotion I felt looking down the entire length of the street as I stood next to the bubbler. It was almost as if it wasn't there, as if I'd stepped into a dream only psychoanalysts could resolve. Maybe architects.

The street sort of shimmered in the afternoon light, the haze over the terraces made up of the years that had vanished. An ink thrown up by sea creatures who don't want to be discovered. Not like the Camelot miasmal haze I saw floating around when I stared at it from the University battlements. But a defensive haze. A coy haze, shy about giving me an invitation. The street looking like the terraces in Eaton Square, the Ansonia and the warehouses in Hackney all combined. I just hoped it didn't have their pretensions.

Me, hesitating to go down it until I felt the Moreton Bay and Port Jackson figs had spotted me, felt them whispering to each other that I was here, swaying backwards and forwards in a welcoming wind.

'Hello, boys,' I wanted to say. 'Hello my old friends.' And it was as if they could hear me. Almost as if they were swooning with delight, their grey branches waving this way and that. Beckoning. Asking. Pleading for me not to stand at the bubbler like a stranger, but to come down. Making me feel they weren't sentries any longer blocking my path, nor advisers telling me to run quickly, but big, beautiful trees grown to their full height. Grown to what took them more than a century to achieve. To blossom. Several generations.

So, slowly and cautiously I walked down towards them as if treading over landmines, wanting to say, 'I don't know if I really can stay.' But this was false politeness, to be blunt, cowardice. I knew that and it agitated them. Their grey branches and dark green leaves as well as the vines they'd grown as tap roots, like hair uncut as a sign of mourning, were shaking. As if they wanted to gather these branches, their skirts, and come up to where I was to greet me.

'I didn't think you'd remember me,' I wanted to say, but they just seemed to laugh, spitting figs over the park and the pavement, unable to control themselves, or their exhilaration.

Walking the last few steps up to the spot where they were thickly planted, I looked up at them, wanting their vines to stroke my hair, my face and body. To wipe away tears that had come for no reason.

'I'm glad I'm back too,' I wanted to say. But it was like they were all chatting and talking at once, so it was difficult to give any answer to their questions, to get in the wind-blown commotion any sense of meaning. Until exhausted, perhaps frightened because another stranger began walking down the street, the trees stopped moving, regaining composure, not wanting to show that they were also capable of memory. Of feeling. Or that to me they gave preference. But I was so glad to see them. Thrilled. Even though, to be honest, they were of secondary importance.

Then, after the stranger had gone past and it was safe for all of us, I thought of asking, 'Is it still here?' About the house they once gave shade to. And warning. But I realised that this question would be too direct, that it would plunge them into silence.

'Is it?' I wanted to ask, not the tallest of them – the bully, but all of them, hoping just one would speak up, just one would do what I was always good at – speaking out of turn. Impertinence.

'You can tell me,' I wanted to say. 'I'm not expecting miracles.' A lie, because in a way I was. But only silence returned what I thought was a reasonable enquiry and all of them seemed to bend their heads ashamed of the shadows that they cast. One or two dropping single and solitary figs, not sweet figs to feed birds and vampires but salty figs to feed the brown leaf carpet.

I knew I wouldn't get an answer, that it was impossible for them to tell someone they'd liked news of disappointment. Me, forgiving them, wanting to say, 'It's okay. Really it is, I'll find it myself. I have a photo, look.'

Whereupon as if at a signal from each other, perhaps after their peaks consulted a conference of the birds, they separated like green velvet theatre curtains. Their boughs and branches creating a space for me, a heart-shaped opening, like a chocolate heart, revealing all the terraces of Edwardia Street still standing, like what they always were. Monuments. The trees separating and bowing as if laying down what Sir Walter Raleigh did for Elizabeth the First, a cloak across the mud of change that is both fertiliser and dirty.

Me, stepping through this opening, this vista to the first house, recognising it as the house of the Russian man, but changed. Finding it like the University, sadly reconstructed. The filled-in balcony of cheap louvred glass and fibro I adored had been torn away, to show what I knew all these terraces had before immigrants like us arrived, wrought arabesques. What the Russian man and our then President had feared. Iron curtains. Me, wanting to see whether there was still the peach tree out the back that he dreamed about when exposed to frosts and blizzards, dreading that it too might be chopped down, or replaced by a gazebo.

Going up to the second house, the black house at which I once threw my paddle pop stick when I first practised persecution, a stick neatly returned like a boomerang. But this house looked really neat and prim. Nothing like what I remembered. All its railings were painted white. White people with white teeth peering through white lace curtains. I guessed, probably correctly, that it was now owned by dentists. A bougainvillea in the balcony for effect. Maybe as a red badge of courage.

Until I was at the third house. The house I'd been seeking, that strangely I'd spent my life looking for and had paradoxically avoided. Number sixty-nine Edwardia Street. The number was correct, just like on the back of Dad's photo. But the house was completely different to how I remembered it. It wasn't in green and pink and azure, the colours of the Mediterranean, but also in vivid white. Its Corinthian columns more bone coloured. Obviously its new owners treating it like a clean slate on which to write their signature.

THE EDWARDIA, a brass plaque said, *A MAXWELL BOUTIQUE HOTEL FOR THE DISCERNING TRAVELLER*. Underneath, *Part of the great tradition of fine accommodation*. And in really big letters, *EVERYBODY WELCOME*. The ad which, not only me, but everyone should've written.

Where I rang the bell, a button set into the wall, the knocker that we used being now encased in a strange perspex box, the sort you see at the Powerhouse, once much better called the Museum of Applied Arts and Sciences. Actually the knocker was a video camera. Maybe the house was owned by the Man in Charge of Half Hours. Or someone on an equivalent salary.

But there was no need to press the bell, because a voice instantly came through, saying, 'Welcome to the Edwardia, reception is down the hall, please push.' And I did, entering the long Victorian hallway, now painted in russet colours. And carmine. Gilt mirrors holding back the walls. Its tiles no longer echoing as they once did, hidden by a carpet runner with a pattern of fleur-de-lys. A runner obviously ashamed of the boarding school echo of the tiles beneath. Maybe it wanted to stifle them. The tiles visible under this woollen landslide, barely breathing, peeping from the edges like earthquake victims.

At the end of the hallway, not the kitchen I remembered beneath the stairs, but a desk where a girl sat in front of a sign stating her name was *Information*. Next to her a little unopened packet of Wrigley's Spearmint Gum. Really sticky stuff.

'Is there anything we can help you with, sir?' she said. Why was she calling me that? I mean I wasn't as old as the Man in Charge of Half Hours. She was pretty though. Sort of innocent. Completely different to the girl I once saw in here blowing gum with Mr Maxwell. Grown up. Nothing at all like what I thought she was, what my scripture teachers threatened us with, the Handmaiden of

Nebuchadnezzar, the Whore of Babylon. Different to my landlady in England. Also quite different to the woman who once cooked here. Actually she looked eager, as if she enjoyed her job. Maybe like me she really liked giving service.

'Mind if I look around?' I said. 'Even if I don't stay?'

'Course you can, sir', she said. 'Picked the right time. It's out of season. Most of our rooms are empty.' Exactly the same words that once devastated me.

'Summer,' she said, 'we're normally as full as an old boot. This is a key to one of our better rooms, the others are being made up. Or open. Mind the stairs. I'll be happy to answer questions when you're done. Here, we're all family. And oh, the rate card,' handing it to me. 'For your information.'

Then from inside where the dining room had been, someone called out, 'Rebecca . . .' while making an entrance. He was older than I remembered. Thin, more grey than blond. 'I mean Miss Maxwell,' he said becoming formal when he saw me. His eyes burning through me as if trying to recognise a forgotten enemy. To tell you the truth, he didn't say Rebecca, I only say that to make it sound like a Daphne du Maurier story, a bit creepy.

'Patricia, see if the bakery's willing to give us any more croissants. At breakfast we ran out. Japs and Yanks don't seem to eat eggs any more.' Obviously the house now lacked festering cakes. Moussakas and lamingtons. He kept staring at me, waiting for me to speak. Wanting me to give him my name, rank and number.

'G'day,' he said. Extending his hand. 'I'm Mr Maxwell, Patricia . . . is taking care of you?'

'Fine,' I said.

'Good,' he said, looking suspicious. 'Then I'll leave you in her capable hands.' Returning inside to the dining room, which I could see was decked out with lots of small linen-covered tables. Probably not for breakfasts but for spiritualists to hold seances. The fluorescent lights that I remembered, the circular ones with the anodised cap, were all ripped out and replaced with little twinkling halogen lights that looked stolen from a starship like the *Enterprise*. Controlled by dimmer switches, rather than the brown bakelite switches we had, whose single flick divided, like a taxidermist's scalpel, day from night.

'My brother, Jeff,' she said, smiling at his back. 'Runs a very tight ship.' As if this Maxwell were the captain of some new sort of *Galileo*. Then, being charming, 'Feel free to have the run of the house, I mean hotel.' Noticing I needed encouragement, permission.

So I went upstairs, holding onto the cedar bannister whose beautiful glossy pink paint had been stripped. Onto the first landing, opening up door after door of rooms, that had all the exquisite smooth lino we'd installed ripped out. Replaced with hideous wooden floors, shiny parquet best split for coffins. Completely unfit for the habitation of the Greek boys I once admired.

On the second floor where we had a communal early Kooka was a strange looking palm tree, to remind whoever it was that now stayed here, of their homes in the tropics.

From a small window behind the palm, above where the Kooka once stood, I could see the backyard. But not any of the hydrangeas we'd planted. Predicably both the concrete concourse and the hydrangeas had been ripped up. The backyard was now hideous, like a common garden.

And I was really disgusted to see a stone lion's mouth attached to the garden wall, like a gargoyle. Pretending to vomit water to keep the garden green, thinking it'd be much better if it just poured acid over this scrub, because this scrub could never replace what we'd laid down: cement icing.

On the desk in one of the rooms a leather-bound diary was stuffed full of stationery. A blurb tooled into the leather said that all the hotel's plants were natives. Salt sown in the fields of Carthage. Maybe there to absolutely guarantee I'd never return. My elimination.

Then I went to the top floor, to the room with the biggest balcony, the room by whose door I'd stood and faced mockery. The room I'd always wanted. Going in not with a veil, but with sunglasses which I took off. Where I could see a bed made up not with white Reckitt's Blue-bleached sheets and pillows. But blood-coloured linens that looked as if they'd been baked and set in the clay oven of the noonday sun. Crimson pillows and silk bolsters awaiting arrivals. Certainly not young men, since Australia no longer had a big immigration policy, but middle class odalisques and their middle aged consorts.

The fake burr laminex walnut wardrobe we had, against which I'd projected so many naked boys in Technicolor and Panavision, had been replaced with real and hideous mahogany. Ghastly dressers of authentic rosewood. And side tables of teak, the wood that's the brown fingers of the jungle.

Running my own finger over them, I noticed that it got covered with oil, not Californian Poppy nor the Brylcreem I once used so brilliantly, but 'Beeswax,' as the can said, a tin can I found on top of the wardrobe. It made me remember how our own laminex wardrobes never needed maintenance.

I was even more disappointed to find that the bedside didn't have any photographs of the pink Gobi desert, or snapshots of the Outback, the Wayne I knew and loved called home. Just clammy colour brochures of islands called Hayman and Lizard, and a stupid place called Cairns, where people with floorboards on their feet were dragged across the water by speedboat-shaped chariots.

Finally, I went into the bathroom I knew so well, where I'd been decontaminated of poison. But I found even this changed, tiled in feminine floral patterns. There wasn't any shower here, or exhaust fans but an ugly vat. An enamelled Victorian bathtub with claw feet, ready to drag down its victims. The vanity's drawers were empty of hand-held shaving mirrors. Styptic pencils. Brushes made of pubes. Now lined with green felt and an array of eau de Cologne bottles, the sort I saw being flogged on duty free trolleys.

Then I went up to the French windows at the front that had replaced what we'd put in, the sliding door of aluminium. Stepping on to the balcony gripping the rail pared back to the original iron, looking at my trees in the street, trees that I suppose were now communal property and tended by a council.

And after pausing for a moment to regain my breath, I blew in their direction, not mustard gas but tear gas. Maybe just smoke from a cigarette, – which wasn't necessary, because the trees knew what was going on and were already crying.

I wanted to say, 'I'm sorry boys. Really sorry. If I'd

known . . . I'd never have gone away.' Wanting to say, 'I tried to come back, I . . .' but they were embarrassed and turned their backs. Neither wanting to see me or the modern obscenity the house had become. This travesty called magazine good taste.

So I went back into the room, and threw myself onto the bed, not to fuck or masturbate, but to lament what it had come to and what I'd become. A spinster. No, a bachelor. Sterile. Unwed, as newspapers used to say in the 1960s. Not it was obvious that despite all the places I'd been to I was still without a home. Not even having found a personal metaphor for my life, just what all Australians are truly obsessed with, real estate. Dead bricks.

I don't know how long I was in this position. Maybe five minutes. Maybe ten. Probably long enough for Patricia to feel justified if she wanted to charge me the tariff. Getting up off the hard bed, which felt hard like a rack fit only to straighten spines. Going down the stairs but this time feeling weak, having to hold the bannister like I was old and infirm.

'You okay?' Patricia said, worried at seeing how slowly I descended.

'Fine,' I said.

'Do you want a glass of water?'

'No, I'm fine,' I said. 'Trust me.'

'Was it satisfactory then, sir?' she asked as she started to shuffle brochures, pawing a reservations book that looked like the Book of Kells. And when I didn't answer again, 'Was it satisfactory then?' Boy, she was innocent. But I was at least glad she wasn't chewing gum.

'It was very satisfactory. *Then*,' I said, giving 'then' extra emphasis. And when she looked puzzled as if I were sending her up, I added, 'Perfect, in fact.' But about the present, it was abomination I really meant.

'As a guest you'll be happy here, sir,' she said, repeating 'sir', as if I'd been knighted. 'That's if you decide to stay.' Giving me the option. 'But I'd better say right from the outset, despite our sign we discourage children. Because of noise and privacy. And you must have a valid passport.'

'I used to live here,' I said.

'Really?' she said. Incredulous.

'Yeah, really. When I was a child.'

'Sorry about that, I thought you were foreign. I mean your appearance and everything. Jeff,' she called out. 'Jeff.' Maybe Jeff wasn't her brother. Or part of the Maxwell clan. But security.

'Must've been a long time ago,' Patricia said, uneasy, hoping Jeff would arrive.

'It was.'

'Because when we got it, you should've seen it,' she said, dropping her guard and becoming friendly, trying to be charming. 'Gruesome. There was lino everywhere and the laundry downstairs was like something out of *Doctor Who*. Had a huge old copper tub the sort you see in comic books used by cannibals. It used to be owned by . . .' and she stopped.

'I know,' I said.

'You do?'

'Yeah,' I said. 'By wogs.'

'I didn't say that,' she said, hurt. Offended. Modern. It's amazing how easy it is to get people upset. All it takes is a syllable. Then, 'Jeff!' Louder this time.

'I didn't mean anything by it,' She added.

'No,' I said. 'No one ever did.'

'Patricia,' he screamed from inside. 'Keep your voice down. I'm on the phone to London.' The way they used to in drawing room comedies.

'I was going to say by Dickens,' she said, exaggerating, returning her blue eyes to me.

'Really?'

'Yes, Charles Dickens. Know the story of *Great Expectations*? Kids study it at school,' she added so she wouldn't sound pretentious. Very Australian.

'Great expectations,' I said, 'usually have small beginnings.' I could be so cruel. 'Anyway, Dickens actually lived in England, but I guess if that's what everyone wants to believe, it's okay by me. All part of the great tradition.'

And I left, hating myself for still being such a smartarse. Going to the park, ignoring the trees since now they also ignored me. Wanting to say to them, or did they want to say it to me, 'What did you expect? Mandalay? Brideshead? Belle Reve? It's only a fucking house. Only a goddamn fucking house.'

Which is true, that's what it always was, and always will be. To the dull and the insipid.

**81**     Disgusted, I caught a bus back to the city, past streets named after dead English prime ministers, George, Castlereagh, Pitt, looking at the holes in the ground of the city's once great Gothic and rococo cinemas that tried to rival the Hub and my laundry. I felt it was quite right they'd been razed because of their arrogance and vanity. Now they were part of a cinema complex. The bus going past the Queen Victoria building, and its fat statue and slim plate glass shops.

To that most mysterious of all places, Circular Quay. Remembering that to the right of me were the Botanic Gardens and particular flowers more powerful than anaesthetic. Going in and cutting one as a keepsake. The flower with the ridiculous name which at this moment I can't mention.

After I'd done this, deciding to do the bravest thing of all, to actually catch a green and yellow ferry that floated and bobbed, on waters still sea green. Ferries that once teased me. Avoiding any glance towards the murderous heights. The eastern suburbs, the cliffs. I'd seen enough carnage there.

Fortunately my sop for Cerberus, a red and white day pass, was unnecessary because the ferry no longer floated on the Styx, but the Hellespont. The ferry, actually a hovercraft, bigger than a trireme.

Getting off at Tyre, the small peninsular city. To be honest, Manly, a suburb whose name is still attractive. There I caught another bus, that went past Gaugemela near Ninevah and Arbela. In dull present day language, Harbord, Queenscliff and Newport. Doubling back when I realised I was on the wrong track, to Wollstonecraft.

Where did I think I was going? Susa? I thought I'd already been to what's called overseas. To all the places you can't get to either overland, by train, bus, or subterranean paths. Neither with friends, planes, tricks or jobs.

'Hello mum,' I said to the figure occupying the bed. I had to say something even though the male nurse said not to say too much.

'How you been?' My grammar was slipping.

But she didn't answer back. Maybe she didn't recognise me. Maybe her illness over the years was Alzheimer's disease, contracted after bathing in the river. She was lying on one of those old Florence Nightingale beds made of iron that could've been pinched from terrace balconies. The hospital itself contrary to what I imagined was pleasant. cypress trees, more French windows. Pines. A lot of the furnishings were exotic. Lots of other bodies in the room similarly exposed to the Dreamtime. The room dark though, rejecting light as a suitor.

'You're not to upset her,' the male nurse had said. As if I ever did.

'We don't know if she can hear.' Maybe she was finally deaf. Looking at her in her nightgown in that bed on her side, I thought she looked crippled by a shell. Longish shadows in the corners leading to the hospital portico reminded me of a country club where we danced. The sun, low slung because at long last Sydney's winter had come. Possibly there'd be rain. The air fresh and crisp. At least I no longer felt condemned to live in lands where it was always autumn or late summer.

'She's been coming along nicely,' the male nurse had said, as if talking about renovations.

'Although,' he said, 'the treatments are taking longer than expected to work.'

'Really?' I said. Or did I say 'No joke?'

I can't remember the name of the hospital, I think the gate had some sort of sign saying Betty Ford. Or was it Rachel Ford? The cheaper local version. Maybe it wasn't a mental hospital, anyway most of them are now closed, maybe it was a place for the battle fatigued.

Can't really say why I'd never been to visit her. Who said this place was so very far? Unbridgeable. That you can only get to it via London and New York. Unfathomable until you're ready to learn. Learn what? From who? What can you learn from those with the animation of a store dummy? A bust at Brennan's.

'Been a long time,' I repeated. Maybe more telling myself, what I didn't want to hear. Settling down next to her the way father used to, on what appeared to be a Namco chair. They way he'd still do had he been living.

'Do you remember?' I said purely for old time's sake, 'our games. Mucking around? What didn't suit you? Or us?'

For the hell of it.

To see if I'd get a response. I don't know how long she'd been in this hospital. A couple of days. Months. More like years. What is it about these places that doctors and shrinks think can provide a cure? Enforced dreams? Pills? As if I could talk. I'd had enough of that. As if she could.

Her hair was all grey now. Matted and long. Here, Medicare didn't cover hairdressers. Skin the colour of what Americans call sidewalks and we, footpaths. Lost in her own world of recriminations. In the whorls and dots of axminster carpets and printed towels.

I did bring some chocolates for this visit, Black Cat I think. Or Black Magic, the milk bar's cheapest brand. A box that unfortunately didn't contain strychnine or any other poison she was familiar with.

Placing the box on the sheets as an offering, as well as a bunch of carnations. Flowers that reminded me of a brand of tinned milk. Putting them in a vase by the bed, filled with water that this unheated room would find difficult to evaporate. But more importantly I placed the small dried twig of the out of season flower I plucked for sentimental reasons, from the Botanic Gardens near Circular Quay. My keepsake. My sprig. A flower as purple as a ribbon on a military cross. Both white and gun carriage black.

Its scent stronger than the carnations. Stronger I suppose because it was half-dried. Drowning out and smothering the hospital scents of urine and chlorine. A flower more brutal than incense. If they distilled it, I was sure it'd make a truly useful medicine.

By contrast, outside the French windows near the portico, where people in commode chairs accommodated oblivion, I could see an odourless yard, full of the same Australian natives as our Newtown house now had. Feeling with my fingers both the sheets and the flower, taking the cellophane off the chocolate box. Having one. A soft-centred cherry. Praline. Not chocolate.

'Do you remember?' I asked again. 'That house, and

how much you hated it. How you said if we didn't sell it, you'd have it burned?' Did she say that? I can't remember.

So much you can say to people who can't answer back. Particularly in another language. 'Throwing us to the winds, first north, then back to the south? What did you think we were? Kites? Remember the wars you caused and that I caused? Your silly battles with relatives. Feuds. Minor victories you said wouldn't be followed by major defeats. Remember? And after all you put us through. This.'

'Remember,' I said, like an order. My face now huge in front of hers. Not like a Greek. More like a Turk. Maybe the Kansas City Bomber. The most feared combatant of *The Roller Game*. Leering. No longer son but fiend. Maybe the dragon she'd been. Monstering her the way she monstered me. Glad no one could see.

'Well remember now,' I said. 'Because I'm back.'

To silence. Only a moan in the distance from some other soul-crippled fool. Possibly someone foolishly thinking a nurse would stop his thirst.

'What have you got to say for yourself?'

No response. Encouraging me, making me continue. Getting more polite now. Anger subsiding in my throat.

'In your own words,' I said, more controlled, using skills I'd learnt at the ABC. Very much the reporter. The late-night talk show host. 'Can you tell us what has been the point of all that weeping and screaming. Ever asked yourself that? The point of all those tears? Look around at where you are. And why you came here in the first place. What you wanted to achieve. In your own words.' I said again. 'You can even speak Greek. Apparently it's fashionable. What did you want from me? From us?'

How large my face was in hers, my breath from alcohol

and cigarettes, mercury vapoured fire, my eyes like torches held aloft by the Klan. No longer snuffed or dimmed. Lips quivering like cowards holding guns.

'Wake up and look at how pathetic you've become.'

'Keep your voice down,' the male nurse said, appearing at the door. Impossible I thought. If people don't speak your language it's always best to shout. Hanging my head, waiting for him to leave. Continuing. Whispering. Or did I hiss?

'You're the one who said we're just pieces from comets. Falling from stars. At least you should've. You could say things like that without people falling about, because you believed. And while we're here, take your time. No rush. I really would like to hear what was it exactly you wanted from me?'

But she didn't avail herself of this opportunity, me her studio audience. So I continued, both as an audience and as a relentless talk show host.

'Power? Control? Exactly who did you think you were?' Then being more colloquial, Australian and current, using the great Australian catch cry. 'Who do you think you are?'

Really going for it.

'Well I can tell you what you are.

'A mad old hag. Know that? Everyone says it. Where are your gods now? Nowhere. That's where. They never did exist. Even if they had, why did you think they'd speak to you? To us? Then more compassionately, loud enough to wake the dead.

'Haven't you spent enough years eating tears? No? Go on, you can tell me. Where are now your Gods?' But only silence followed. So to prompt her a bit, to fill in the blanks, I said, 'In the other beds? Is that what I hear you say? Back in Greece? Do they need a map? Must do. Because they've certainly forgotten you.' Picking up and throwing the purple, white and black flower in her face.

'Better go now,' the male nurse said, hearing the noise. 'Half hour's up.'

'Haven't finished,' I said.

'You're finished all right.'

'Fuck off,' I said. 'I'll go when I'm ready.'

My voice louder than both the subway and the underground. What could he do? Ring a bell? The alarm? Nothing. That's what he could do.

'You deaf or something?' I said. 'Cat got your tongue? Don't you speak English? Fuck off.' How well I'd learnt.

Making him walk backwards out the room. A minute of silence purely for respect. Then a real alarm. Maybe a fire drill. An alarm like her voice.

Saying, 'I remember.' Astonishing how alarms can break spells.

'I remember,' she said.

'Nurse,' I wanted to scream in that room. 'Nurse.' Wanting a witness.

Her nightgown more a silk sheathed evening gown. Maybe from one of the places I'd been, like Benares.

'I remember it all,' she said. At last, what reporters call, 'an exciting development'. A big break, if not a scoop. At last she was going to tell me the truth.

But all she started to say were unusable libellous and defamatory things. About how when she first arrived in Australia, she had to beg accommodation door to door. Sleeping on benches in parks. Disappointing me since these were the same sentimental old chestnuts of hardship and gloom I'd heard all through my adolescent and young adult life. Distracting me with tangents about how she was orphaned in the war, mentioning the six younger siblings she had to bring up. Telling me trivial things like how her father died during the Occupation. The Occupation, the part of the war, Greeks refer to like a factory job. Getting side-tracked with stories about murders in the village. Saying defamatory things about young Greek men who believed it was better the Left should win over the Right. About young Greek men who said the Germans would only leave if they first defeated the Left. Hideous but useless stories. Of floods. Fires. Famines. Libelling strangers and soldiers I loved, saying this had consumed her life. Using loaded words like 'incest' to describe affectionate brothers, events in unused parlours, cellars and barns.

Lying. Saying that they'd all been stronger than her. And how at the height of all this, just as her father was buried, her mother much like her went nuts. Wandering around fields, talking to rocks. And how she, the eldest, was compelled to leave for Athens, the town of bony streets, leaving behind more than the farm house, stone crops and merds. Saying to siblings left hostage, one day she'd return.

Saying in Athens she met men who said they'd help her emigrate, men who could provide documents to prove she wasn't a spy. Ludicrously saying the only reason they bought the Newtown house was because no one wanted it, insulting it by calling it cheap. And how the Australian men she at first let the rooms to made advances she repelled. Telling me pseudo-heroic stories about stowaways she hid in the laundry, who'd escaped from Greek cargo ships. Young men who preferred death to being sent back. Finding many leaning backwards in a chair hard against the bathroom door. Pennies used for the inhalation of unlit gas.

Saying she was the one who had to write to their relatives back home. Enclosing news of their success. Wallets, lockets and engagement rings. The full round trip.

Saying all this happened before I was born, during the fifties and the sixties, during what I say was a Golden Age, when the house at times resembled a morgue. And how she'd hoped to forget all this including chairs against doors when the house got rid of gas.

Lying. Saying how the house had never been sold, because it had never been owned. Fabricating stories about how it was surrendered for an unpaid mortgage. Leftovers paying our schools. Saying the most deceitful and unprintable thing of all, that no young men ever touched me. Nor was I interested in them. That was just me in the backyard playing and feeding the stray cats. Worse that there was no Wayne. Wayne just didn't exist. 'No Way In', with her terrible accent. And no Way Out. I simply never felt anywhere that I fitted in. Neither then, nor now, only briefly as a child, always hating here, blaming her, in place of me.

'No,' I said. 'Stop it. What's it to you? Stop it.' As she accused me of just sexualising the past. Invention and filth. Of twisting metaphors and myths. Maybe of living out the second generation's, if not an old Australian, curse. Saying tears may have been her meat, but for me spoof has been my ink. The only substance in adult life I found honest. And direct.

Why was she bothering to tell me these things? What purpose did it serve? Then her final words, 'You have another mother now. Maybe even then. As I once did, to whom I couldn't return. Maybe it was she who betrayed you.' And as some thunder cracked, '*Aliti.*' Smiling, dropping my hand. Letting me know it was more blessing than curse.

The alarm growing stronger. Her lips and body unlike mine, weaker and unmoved.

'Off you go, sport,' the male nurse said. 'She can't hear you now.' Moving a sheet over her face so she wouldn't catch chill. Reinforcements next to him. Doctors. Nurses. Maybe defamation lawyers. Just as her voice, and the bells, ceased.

Why did she tell me all this? Perhaps it was another trick of hers, a spell. To confuse me. Probably because she was ashamed of giving me birth. Didn't matter really. Never did.

Because against all these lies I knew where to get evidence. Leaving that place of death and its bodies to bury themselves. Seeing what the sign on the gate really said, not Rachel, but Chelmsford, a hospital, much like the country, that practised deep sleep.

Catching the same series of buses and ferries, numbered like incantations and psalms, back.

Not to Newtown to take one last look because now it, and the house wasn't worth a glance, but Macdonaldtown. The seat of power, where the Iron Age was born, in the shunting yards and goods yards that forged us. Hot pokers hammered against rocks.

**8 2**  Walking to Macdonaldtown, hoping that, too, hadn't been similarly altered. But when I got there I couldn't believe how tame this place also was. Its iron wheels of industry, the balls of its glory were cut. Discarded. New trains silently gliding on noiseless welded tracks. No sense of their once exquisite racket. XPT trains, silver bullets with fixed buffet seats, flashing past rather than lurching, to legendary places like Goulburn and Tamworth, which *then* might as well have been Samarkand.

Worse, in the middle of the goods yards of Eveleigh, that used to terminate at the funeral stop of Regent Street, the biggest warehouse of the lot was now cleared of saws and lathes and used for the Performing Arts. For training young men and women how to be buskers, rather than conductors on a bus.

And the final indignity, nearby the IXL jam factory that had so sweetly inspired a generation, minced. An ordinary three-floor block of flats, in place of this former brown brick cathedral and its magnificent unstained beer glass.

The ACI factory much farther away I didn't even bother visiting, knowing its windows would also be shattered and smashed. Maybe what was left of the glass pounded and ground. Making me think that at last this place, this land, this city had become, with my assistance and experience, if not a brothel, then at least what it was meant for, a prison no longer needing bars. Where only one inmate waited to be slain or released.

And I knew exactly where he was.

He wasn't in the desert, the city, nor up in the hills or any of the valleys I'd been. But in my favourite house. In the biggest and most wonderful of our palaces. Bigger than Hampton Court and Fontainebleau. Bigger than the Opera House that looks like chalky fingers scratching against a blackboard. Not catching a bus this time which I didn't need, but walking through the night-cloaked city streets that seemed to divide, pushing me faster and further on. Going past Grace Bros at the end of City Road where now, in the dark, the entire world rotated on the bayonet spires of the department store's roof, holding up crystal balls. Past Victoria Park and Lake Northam, its sycophantic swamp. Past Saint Barnabas', whose weekly billboard still announced the Apocalypse.

Up Broadway, where there were no theatres like in New York. Not even the grey *Herald* I once knew, its roller-coaster print runs having moved. Passing the site of the People's Palace, that old immigrants' slum. Until I was near the Piazza San Marco and the Grand Canal. Arriving not in Oxford Street where I'd been too often, but my favourite place in the whole Milky Way, the City of Sydney's Hyde Park.

Walking through its starlit gauntlet of camphor trees, so different to figs, where it looked as if there were eyes plucked from whores sparkling above me in the trees lit by electric globes.

Until I was at the Archibald fountain featuring gorgeous naked men and bulls. Apollo and my peers. Perfect bodies sprouting water and froth. Wetting my hands and face in this midnight fountain, just to make it extra cool, and continuing through Hyde Park, looking at the black hills of the city filled with fluorescent snipers. Neons saying, *Surrender. Surrender now.* Mountains named Aetna, Pacific Power. Centrepoint.

Until, when I grew hot despite the water I'd splashed to cool me down, I lay down by the most beautiful lake of all. *Reflection.* What foolish architects and civic leaders had called it. A square lake in Hyde Park shaped like an Olympic swimming pool, barely a foot deep. Nothing like Mark's pool in Malibu. A pool dissolving like a Radox bath all those who never had the chance for acceptance, or what I prefer to call it, sex. And love.

Plunging my hands (or was it my fist?) into the water. Slowly. Softly. Feeling all its folds, water holding my hand the way it had once been gripped in youth, the glove of soul fitting happiness. Plunging again and again, until I felt grow beneath my trousers, underwear and belt. An erection. Touching it. Stroking it. Leaving it alone. Knowing it throbbed for a purpose.

Looking at my face in the moonlit pool, I was wise enough not to allow myself to get entranced. Hardly difficult because all I could see in the reflection was someone who looked old and crazed. Taking my hand out of the water, drying off my fingers with my lips, noticing the water was sweet as honey, sweeter than spoof. Getting up off my knees. Turning around to see what I'd wanted to see. The house at last.

The ANZAC Memorial. No, the temple greater than any in the Valley of the Kings, the Splendour of Splendours, the Temple of Hatshepsut.

## the man in charge of half hours

Going up its steps like an Aztec. To a place greater than any Cleopatra's needle and its bastard child the obelisk. Opening the doors of the Memorial, entering not a temple, beehive or a ziggurat but the Palace of the Damned.

And inside as I looked around the Hall of Memory I could see it was huger than anything I'd ever seen. Dwarfing all toilets I'd been into, as well as the Sagrada Familia, Saint Peter's and Saint Paul's. As well as bedsits, warehouses and the ninth floor. Inside its Circular Quay, many terraces and mansions. The interior made of substances I loved, cement, maybe marble. A marble whose middle had been hollowed out by taxidermists and other fake preservers of the flesh, where below, I could see three chambermaids happily making up a bed.

Getting closer to the circular perimeter made of alabaster type finials, Greek columns and stone flowers called fleur-de-lys, I could see the most perfect body in the world, a young man they said was made of bronze. But I knew he was carved from air. Naked. Supported by draped maids, holding him aloft on a sword and shield where he was untroubled, probably at rest. Maybe those Caryatids, were his brides.

By the wall was an eternal flame handy to light his cigarettes. A flame lit by yellow windows featuring sharp etched spires, in shapes like the Chrysler building and Battersea Powerhouse. Maybe Grace Bros' bayonets. How beautiful he looked. More beautiful than anything by Magritte, Turner or Mapplethorpe.

Where I pronounced the most fearful of all spells and poems. Basically voodoo. I said:

'By the light of Gaza, Beersheba and Damascus. By the darkness of Ypres and the Somme.' Mentioning places I'd

## medea's children

been to where my feet were warmed. Reading these names straight off the walls where they'd been carved.

But nothing came my way, not even a nod, as a begrudging acknowledgment. More beautiful than ever he lay perfected, forcing me to bring the big guns out now. 'The Otranto Barrage,' I said just as thunder cracked. Then, 'Wayne . . . ,' I said, knowing it was the young Wayne I once knew and loved.

'Wayne,' I said again. But nothing. Just more dry thunder and lightning that couldn't threaten us, because we'd dug in. We were safe in the place I wanted to be. Making me go the whole hog, *over the top* as they used to say, as I looked down at his perfect face and chest. At his long prick more beautiful than the Barrier Reef. I said:

'By what we had and suffered, both the Landing and the Evacuation, what so many will suffer still, get up.'

Using all the powers my mother had given me, all the recipes and spells I was permitted to use now I was son and heir. Causing enormous peels of thunder. Timpani. White and blue veins, the blood of Gods pulsing through the yellow windows, ripping the city from side to side. Monstrous anger of the guns. Where outside against the windows, through the temple doors and the lake, a cyclone bigger than Tracy shook. Wind. Thunder. Hail. Rain, strong enough to knock down Chinook helicopters and safe Qantas planes.

But I wasn't scared doing any of this because I knew the cannon and the shells wouldn't touch us since I controlled the storm, as well as the eye. Going downstairs to where he was, probably because I wanted to get closer, to stroke his body, his stomach and what must be full after all these years of inaction, his balls. To do what he always hated, to

## the man in charge of half hours

run fingers through his hair. Maybe to kiss his lips. Maybe to stroke perfect legs that were bent over the shield like a boy fishing at a dock. To be honest, impertinent even. To fuck. I mean hadn't we done it before with such brilliance?

I knew it was useless to read the spells carved into walls like hateful public toilet written chants that now tell certain races to get out. So I looked up at the domed ceiling for inspiration, where twinkled pieces of gold filigree of what I was and other people were. Fragments. Like him, *Sacrifice*. Little pieces of stars. Abandoning arrogance and mystery. Deciding not to mention again lost towns and hopes.

'Wayne,' I said. Saying what teachers used to say to us in school assembly. In the playground. After standing at attention. Getting a little bit more regimental. And stern.

'As you were!'

But when this too didn't work, 'At ease!' I shouted.

Then it occurred to me that the only thing that would work, with which I'd have a slight chance, was if I went back to where I belonged, the place I'd come from.

A time of innocence. A time less angry. So I grabbed a chair because he was too high for me, climbing onto it, whispering in his ear so that neither parents nor the enemy could hear, dropping all pretence to spells, myths, poems, false canticles, and voodoo saying as I once did, 'Psst, Wayne. Old mate.' Pausing. Like an eleven-year-old kid embarrassed. 'It's me.' His emerald eyes the colour of Magnetic Island's coast at last opening, shining like hurricane lamps. 'I said you still live. Don't make a liar out of me.'

His prick finally moving, stirring. Inflamed by what I'd said and what he could see.

'Yeah, rightio,' he said. 'But give me a minute. I'm a bit stiff.' As if waking from a dream. Then seeing me, like an artist at his ladder staring at his monument, he said, 'You'd better climb up,' reaching over, about to lift me high off the chair. Stopping, remembering. 'But get that wet gear off first otherwise you'll catch your death.'

And I did. Jumping down, throwing off jeans and socks and T-shirts, all the grey vests that had poisoned me. Wedding dresses and uniform codes. Maybe just complexes. Casting them not in the Eternal Flame but the wreath marked *Best We Forget*. Standing naked. Getting back on the chair, feeling as if once again, I was really eleven. Realising I couldn't get in. Or up.

'I need a hand.' I said. 'I'm too short.'

'For Chrissakes,' he said, rolling his eyes. 'Come on.' His prick now pointing to the East. 'There isn't much time. Get in otherwise they'll pick you off. You'll drown.'

'I can't,' I said. 'I can't. Too much has happened. And I'm just too small.'

'Okay,' he said. 'Hold on. Ready, steady, go.' And he did pull, trying to lift me with jackeroo veined arms, to his boat. The safety of sword and shield.

'I can't,' I said. 'I can't.'

'Come on, mate. Now,' he yelled. 'You want to be a victim all your fucking life? Because that ain't how I remember you. Push yourself. Don't wait for them. Because trust me, they will never wait for you.'

'I can't,' I said. Slipping from his hand, the storm outside now lashing at the doors, gale winds blasting them apart. Sheets of rain charging in like water cannon, maybe the killers of the Light Brigade here to pick off fallen prey.

'Jump mate,' he said.

And I did, right at the point he lifted me with one great

swoop. To where he was. Where he didn't have to use Brylcream or spit, probably because both were out of fashion. Wayne entering me slowly, a process I had wanted as much as flames. Fucking me, he said, for old time's sake. Me, then fucking him, which was new for me, but he said, not that new for him. Since the army had made a man out of him. Which was warm and nice. The bronze of his mouth becoming flesh.

Me, glad age hadn't wearied his prick, nor its rigidity the years condemned. Wayne not looking any older than I looked. Much as he had enlisted. As he did in our house. Near twenty. Maybe twenty-one. Where I placed lips on nipples. How young they still were, like his prick, stiff and fresh. Where he sucked me and I sucked him. Doing this and plenty of corny gay porn stuff, usually written just to turn people on. In a position that has a number, but whose digits I forget. Feeling muscles in his shoulders with my palms, his young man's waist and back, the firmness of strong legs. Unfortunately the hair on them singed not by wax but by the heat when they had him cast in bronze.

I don't know how long we were at it. Minutes. An hour. A good half-hour anyway. An excellent half hour in fact. Now I was in Charge of the Days, the Years and the Hours. Yesterday, Today and Tomorrow. No longer needing a white stick to find anything. Until Wayne asked, 'You ready?'

'Yeah,' I said, 'I'm ready.'

Now ready to go over the top.

'Well then let's blow,' he said. Blowing in my mouth at the same time I blew in his. He with the force of the Murray Darling Basin, and me the Nile. Sucking each other down. Figures on an Attic, maybe even a Portland Vase. Swallowing hard not contempt or Perkin's paste, the stuff

I once used to stick things down in picture books, but what that viscous stuff really was, or could be. Love. Until exhausted and in a fever, Wayne said, 'Better call the storm off now. I think it's enough.'

He was right. It was enough. I'd forgotten I'd left it on like a bathroom light.

'Sorry,' I said, to him. And the world outside. Me, Master of the Storms. Of all my winters and more importantly my summers. Of lost hopes and despair I carved from air. Of the way I began and I guess, will end. I won't say of the Timeless Land because that doesn't belong to anyone, but everybody. Only that would be obscene and blasphemous. 'Okay,' I said. 'But only for you.' As we kissed feeling fully inflated balls. Grape shot we could fire at will.

When suddenly through the door burst a cop.

Well, maybe not a cop, but the man who once mocked me. Maybe it was just one of the radio evangelists, the talk-back radio hosts, the vendors of hate. Anyway someone equally hideous.

'Hello world,' he said. As if he owned it. The way I heard his awful voice on the transistor when I ran from the obelisk. When I thought him and his type were masters of the courts and justice.

'Hello,' I said. To be polite.

'Well, what do we have here? A national disgrace.'

I couldn't believe my bad luck. What was he doing here spoiling my life, destroying one delirious Cracker Night?

'Okay mate,' he said. Using what he thought was my rank. Shining a torch. 'What do you think you're doing? Get your gear on. Can't you read son? Cat got your tongue? This is a sacred site.' Me, at least grateful he spared me the *'let silent contemplation be your offering'* bit. Taking out of his

## the man in charge of half hours

holster with his free hand what he used for intellect, a microphone, as a .22 gun. Not much.

'And you, digger,' he said pointing to Wayne. Who amazingly didn't really seem to care. Lying back on the shield, one hand supporting his head, as if holidaying on the beach. As if this guy were a sandfly he could crush.

'Bloke like you ought to be ashamed of himself. Wait till the listeners get a hold of this. I mean police. Although beats me what they'll call you in court. You ain't really got a name.' Laughing.

'And you son,' he said. 'What's your name? Or are you nobody like him?'

'Here,' Wayne whispered, taking from behind him the sword where for so many years he'd rested his head, as calmly as if it were sunblock.

'Use this.' Handing it to me. 'Go on mate,' he said. 'It's people like him or us. They don't understand anyway.'

'You deaf? Cat got your tongue?' the radio evangelist said. Not seeing me take the sword, me deciding for the first time to go against what I always thought I was. A pacifist.

'My name mate?' I said, stalling for time.

'Yeah, what is it? Listeners want to know.'

'Is this . . .'

Throwing the sword with all the force of Thor's hammer straight into his heart. Seeing him fall backwards onto the floor. Unfortunately, still living, barely stunned. Forcing me to go down away from Wayne, who said, 'Give us a cooee if you need help.'

'No,' I said. 'I need to do this alone.'

Climbing down and going up to twist the sword like a trident into his heart. Seeing him writhing in his death throes up and down, like a cable car. His heart stuck to the bayonet I'd finally found. What I only now could properly use. My Katoomba pen. So much more powerful than the jackhammer father used to dread.

'Go on, tell 'em now,' Wayne said, 'haven't got all night. It'll be light soon,' when I stood back to show him my handiwork.

'My name . . . ,' I said, well actually I wrote, like so many other childhood fables, fantasies, allegories and suffocated truths on the kitchen table of my family, clearing away the past's crumbs. Casting my mind back to how and where I began, thinking in terms of words of one syllable as charades and parades end.

'My name . . .' I said, feeling quite shaken, because no one really ever bothered to ask, 'my name . . .' I said, while mum, dad and my brother watched and craned an ear to something, someone, speaking not on radio but on TV. More Medusa, than Medea, a woman with red flames in her hair, short red snakes, scaring boys and girls of a different generation. When I'm finished I will deal with her in one flamin' second.

'Is me.' Maybe with different shards and paste, you.